Gustave Flaubert

The Ambiguity of Imagination

Giuseppe Cafiero
Translated by Peter Christie

Clink
Street

London | New York

Published by Clink Street Publishing 2017

ISBN:
978-1911525387 - paperback
978-1-911110-45-3 - ebook

Everything one invents is true, Gustave Flaubert.

Round about the corpse of Monsieur Gustave Flaubert there are machinations and human documents from which one could create a fine novel, Frères de Goncourt.

The jackals of posthumous literature continue their sad work of gathering the remains of dead lions in order to live on them, Barbey d'Aurevilly.

The life and the death of Flaubert were ambiguous in merits and intentions, Anonymous

Every history that wishes to interrelate the death and life of Monsieur Flaubert gets entangled in improbable fictions, G. C. Manliar.

After Madame Bovary Flaubert should have written livelier works, and Salammbô is unreadable: it is the worst sort of Classicism, Charles-Augustin de Sainte-Beuve.

Solitude and work will make Flaubert go out of his mind, Suzanne Langier.

Flaubert had the economic security which allowed him to free himself from many things, while I am constrained, in order to live, to write also unworthy things, Emile Zola.

It is horrible that a man like Gustave Flaubert could frequent a courtesan like Marie-Anne Detourbay, known as Jeanne de Tourbey, Princess Mathilde Bonaparte.

Flaubert is cynical with men and sentimental with women, Alphonse Daudet.

If one takes away from Gustave Flaubert the ox, the laborious and plodding animal within him, the constructor of books with the rhythm of a word per hour, one is faced with a very ordinary man of little originality, Edmond de Goncourt.

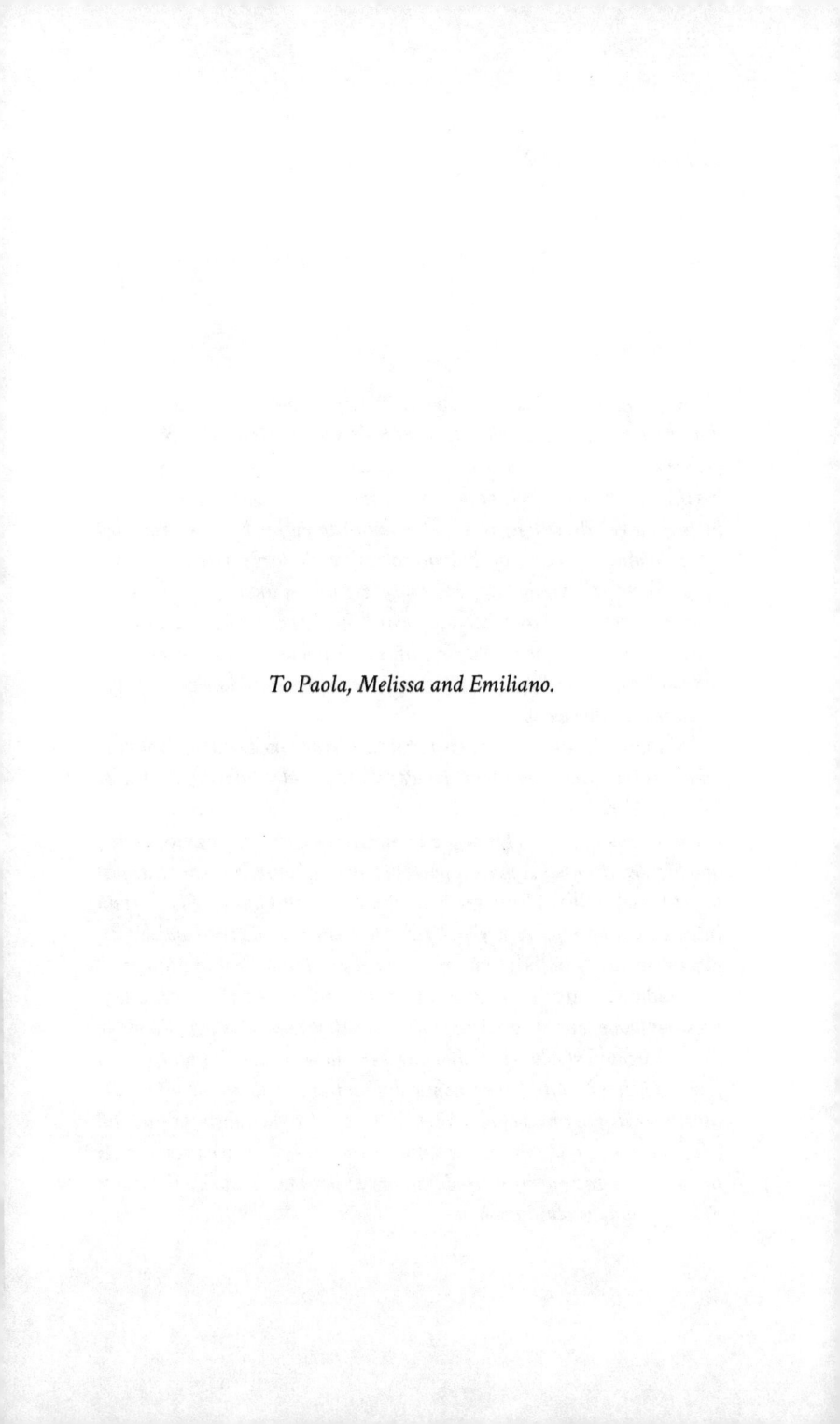

To Paola, Melissa and Emiliano.

Characters:

Monsieur Gustave Flaubert: *Writer from Rouen, author of novels, stories and theatrical texts of little success. Apoplectic, neurotic, shameless consumer of food, drink and cheap sex. He spent a large part of his life hidden away in his country house at Croisset on the Seine, where he wore a red dressing-gown and a skull-cap on his head, surrounded by billowing curtains of Indian cotton, with large flowers, which ornamented the windows of his study. He wrote, among other things, a novel, called* Madame Bovary, *which made the Imperial Advocate, Monsieur Ernest Pinard, Public Minister, famous for daring to set in motion legal proceedings for obscenity, due to presumed unworthy pages contained in this work.*

Madame Louise Colet: *Poet of little literary merit but of profound amorous impulses, given that she was sentimentally linked with Victor Cousin, Alfred de Musset, Alphonse Karr, Christien Polonais, Franc Polonais, Franz Noller, Deputy Bancel, Octave Lacroix, Auguste Vetter, and Flaubert himself. A muse capable of burning houses and churches just to get herself talked about, she had with Monsieur Gustave Flaubert an intense relationship, stormy and given to reciprocal distrust, which took place principally in the rooms of the Hôtel du Grand-Cerf in Mantes.*

Madame Caroline (Lilline) Commanville, née Hamard: *Lazy, presumptuous and capricious niece of Monsieur Gustave Flaubert. She lived comfortably, first allowing her uncle to sacrifice money and fame to help her with her economic difficulties caused by the profligate investments of her husband, so that, at the death of her uncle, taking full advantage of it and with irresponsible carelessness, she was responsible for incorrect and harmful republications of her uncle's works, the rights of which had devolved upon her.*

Baron Maxime Du Camp: *Writer, memorialist and thoroughgoing narcissist, he spent most of his life in the attempt to be accepted as the trustworthy confidant of Monsieur Flaubert; in truth, he was an unfailing detractor and loved to gossip about Flaubert with loaded insinuations and incurable ill-will.*

Monsieur François Denys Bartholomée Bouvard: *formerly copy-clerk with the firm of Descambos Bros.,* & Monsieur Juste Romain Cyrille Pécuchet: *formerly copy-clerk with the Ministry of the Navy. Protagonists of adventurous tales and impracticable manners of life in a village of Calvados named Chavignolles. They were also passionate advocates of research and investigations on human knowledge, so that they engaged – in the chapters of a novel which never arrived at the word 'End' – in a thousand trades, arts and adventures, all catastrophically impracticable but which offered them the opportunity to acquire the faculty of collecting, annotating and transcribing the stolid stupidity of humanity.*

Harel Bey: *An Arab who spent his existence in the drawing-room of the brothers Jules and Edmond de Goncourt, authors of a celebrated Journal, where he was born, amidst various revelries on the evening of 29 March 1862, from the fervid imagination of Monsieur Gustave Flaubert. It is precisely in this Journal where it is possible to find, even today, traces of his eventual life.*

Khédive of Cairo: *An official whose task was to deal with the unusual and inane questions of travellers and tourists visiting Egypt. He had a decisive role in confounding, with meaningless words and false actions, the wordy pretensions of Madame Louise Colet, intent on knowing, in the most minute particulars, the events and hardships of Monsieur Flaubert's journey in Egypt.*

And also:

Félicité: *The domestic servant of Madame Aubain; she was a very pious woman, silent and lovingly linked to the family who gave her hospitality. She spent her entire life living in the garret of her employer's house, having as her sole companion and source of affection a parrot called Loulou.*

The unknown traveller on the train from Deauville to Paris: *An uxoricide? Certainly a man who had spent his time, hours, days and weeks, amidst tribunals and hippodromes, transcribing acts and noting on cards the names and numbers of disdainful, capricious, losing horses.*

Father Tabarant: *Prelate of the church of Saint-Sauveur au Petit-Andely, who believed himself to have correct information about what had happened to Gustave Flaubert on a night in January 1844 at Pont-l'Évêque.*

Madame la Chanteuse: *Singer who spent her life reciting and singing the legend of Saint Julian in the Restaurant Bonvalet in boulevard du Temple in Paris, waiting for a writer to grant her a role in some novel.*

Mademoiselle Julie, called la Tata: *Domestic servant in the Flaubert family, who spent her entire life with them. And to Gustave she loved to say: It is we who revive the memories of past times.*

Monsieur Leon Grappin: *A small, unpleasant and obsequious man; nevertheless a bookseller at Sens where he owned a well-stocked bookshop. He was also a passionate collector of licentious books.*

The man from Mantes: *An individual who loved to rub his hands with assiduity and zeal, and with assiduity and zeal smiled with subtle malice. He was small, thinning at the temples, dressed in black clothes shiny with wear and parsimony.*

The gendarme of Yonville-l'Abbaye: *A tall, thin figure with a black moustache and sideburns – à la Dumas fils which seemed artificial – of a bronze complexion and a familiar look.*

Monsieur Lèger: *Gravedigger of Croisset with a passion for daguerreotypes. He made, perhaps for Gustave, a number of photographs: perhaps indecent ones, perhaps useful to compare physiognomies of places and persons.*

Aboard a ghizeh
November 1869

Cher ami, cher Maxime[1]: my confidante and most courteous knight.

For twenty years that devotee of love has battered and soiled with his coarse hands the pedestal of seduction, concealed in an unknown temple, beautiful and rare as a temple of Ancient Greece, uncontaminated and hidden for centuries. What can one expect from a man afflicted with a tyrannical and possessive mother, with her emotional blackmail, and with an obscure nervous malady which made him megalomaniac and presumptuous?

I remember well the letter in which, with impertinence and arrogance, he blamed me because I was jealous of the heedless love that he nourished for his mother. An incontestable truth: I was immoderately resentful in the face of that impudent genetrix. And he? He delivered sarcastic judgments. He was annoyed and bored by my wearisome loving solicitude. He also made pronouncements with scorn and arrogance. He warned me that it was really not his business to prevent me from nourishing resentment and rancour towards the person who had brought him into the world. He held forth in this way with arrogance and meanness. And he also observed that it was his mother, Madame Anne Bustine Caroline Flaubert, *née* Fleuriot, who was more important to him than anything else in the world. Yes, indeed, his mother, who sighed with amorous pleasure when she saw him return home, who sighed with amorous suffering when she saw him leave, who sighed with amorous yearnings every time she heard him speak. A river of sighs, indeed. His mother, preoccupied

---

1   Maxime du Camp (1822–1894).

1

as she was with obsessive funereal hallucinations, obligated him, with concealed malice and amidst fantasies of ill-health and artificial fainting-fits, to pass unwholesome and tedious moments close to her, to hold her hands, to kiss her forehead. Madame Flaubert thus acted out a drama of ceremonious lamentations and reproofs, using only her own silent and lethal presence, which was like an indiscreet convulsion, a purulent and occult burn.

Thus Gustave was pedantically indifferent and presumptuously haughty in relation to my own feelings, so agitated by an immoderate and uncontrollable love in regard to him. He soon forgot what he wrote to me with a lover's intensity – that, worn out and disconsolate because of the distance between us, he thought continuously of my face, of my shoulders, of my white neck, of my smile, of my passionate voice, violent and at the same time *as sweet as a cry of love*[2]. He was slothful and distrustful, since he took to wounding me, almost to injuring me with his ferocious sarcasm, putting forward pretexts, as it seemed to him in fact of little value to have to throw himself at my feet to talk himself hoarse declaring his love like a boorish child with false and deceptive words. "*They say that love is heaven,*" he wrote to me in December 1847, and added jokingly – "*But the heavens are often cloudy without taking into account the fury of storms*[3]." It's true that I had become fatter, that I no longer had an enviable figure, though even then I was still very elegant and well-formed. I had breasts, shoulders and arms of great beauty. My neck harmonised perfectly with my face ... My legs were perfect, slender at the ankles, and ended in *very beautiful feet, which were extremely slender in contrast to my figure*[4].

What more could a man desire?

Instead Gustave became increasingly impulsive, disloyal, full of animosity. He shamefully lamented when my menstrual period didn't arrive on time, almost as if he was afraid of compromising himself with a possible pregnancy of mine, since paternity was for

---

2   Gustave Flaubert, Letters.
3   Gustave Flaubert, Letters.
4   Mementos of Louise Colet.

him an obscene thing, horribly obscene, a thing which resolved itself always in a squalid, disgraceful experience. He reproved me bitterly for my exuberant requests for affection, for my longing desires for a requited love, for my impassioned reproaches in regard to him, because I had persuaded myself that he compensated his own sexual exuberance with orgiastic and masturbatory intellectual games. Because, in fact, he wrote to me in March 1847: *"Your ideas of morality, of homeland, of devotion, your tastes in literature: all these were antithetical to my ideas, to my tastes, to my emotionality, as I am aroused only by pure line, clear contour, beautiful colour. In contrast, I encountered in you always and only a confused tone, a sentimentality capable of attenuating everything, of rendering it sentimental in a mediocre way, also and above all your spirit".*

And you, Max, to console such conjectures of mine, revealed to me many times that Gustave, between the age of twenty and twenty-four years, had made a show of his own sexual abstinence, because, he asserted – honouring incoherent aphorisms and very personal statements – that a man models himself on certain vanities, on a particular pride deprived of instinct, on secret theories that facilitate the ostentation of one's complacent diversity. Do you remember Max, do you remember these disquieting revelations of yours?

Gustave then drew forth, in disparate and unwholesome circumstances, ironic blows and biting words, attesting to me that the supposed acts of wildness ascribed to him were in fact performed only at his writing-table. He was forced to wear himself out, between writing and note-taking, for long hours and to dissipate, with scrupulous pedantry and endemic neurasthenia, reams of paper simply to spell out and order with obsessive precision sentence after sentence, word after word, syllable after syllable for the sole and unique pleasure of appeasing his own senses and morbidly satisfying his own sensuality, with the singular concern of drawing up a page which might have appropriate concepts and pleasing and appropriate writing.

What can you expect from a man overwhelmed by an instinctive and immoderate frenzy in the need to frequent brothels, above all on the night of St. Sylvester so as to inaugurate in this way, in commercial love-affairs, the year that was to follow, or to swiftly and brusquely submit to a lascivious, dissolute and shameless love for an Oriental prostitute? Remember, Max, do you remember? I have in mind stories that you had the effrontery to tell me, haphazardly filling pages of frivolous correspondence when you returned from the Orient with our man, or that you had the smugness to set out in detail for me when, finding ourselves by chance in some boudoir speaking about him, you had the boldness to profane my chaste pride in telling tales about the ardent and impudent conquest of women of easy habits when you accompanied him, loitering about in distant lands, roving fecklessly and impudently through Egypt.

Monsieur Flaubert, Gustave I mean, wounded me with those infamous acts of concupiscence. He besmirched our love not only with the libertinage of his body but still more, and what is worse, with the libertinage of his soul and with the lowness and squalor of his vanity. He outraged my pride, my honesty and my honour without remorse. I was and am an upright woman, respectful towards those close to me and obsequious in love for one near to me. Never haughty, frivolous or defamatory towards noble hearts and spirits, I have indeed courted, with admirable and noble modesty, the intellect of others. I had to learn and consecrate myself to the cleverness of lofty intelligences at the time in which I took to frequenting the *Bonne Compagnie, journal de fashions, toilettes, ameublement, théâtre, livres nouveaux, romans poésies, causeries*, which was located at 20 rue Bergere in Paris, a few steps away from the Conservatory of Music, and frequented by Victor Hugo, by Charles-Marie Leconte de Lisle, by Théophile Gautier, by Pierre-Jean Béranger, by Alfred de Vigny and by other subtle and extremely acute minds.

Gustave, instead, preferred Egypt, abruptly and without warning, in order to travel to turbid places, to Esneh, the city of *almées* and *ghawazis*, of dancers and prostitutes. As a result, indeed with melancholy, I was obliged to make a voyage to Esneh to assure myself of replies, to recompense a wounded pride, to escape exacerbated anxieties, to rummage in the introverted negligence of a man named Gustave. Gustave had in the meantime begun to blurt out on all sides that it was inevitable that we separate, that he was the absolute master of his sentiments, that at present neither I nor any other woman had the soul or body to conquer him and to bind him to us, that in Egypt he had had the opportunity to encounter an *almée* – Koutchouk-Hanem – and that it had been extraordinary, singular and unforgettable to spend a night with her, with Koutchouk-Hanem, the *almée*.

Perhaps Esneh and Koutchouk-Hanem conserved desired answers, or at least justifications, or even plausible reasons for a promise rent twenty years ago when the sky of Egypt loosened, in the dead calm, the triangular sails of ships, the litanies of sailors who accompanied the changing of routes, the herons and the storks that rose up in flight from the banks of the river crowded with their flocks, the nights that were languidly warm and welcoming like the soft bellies of the Egyptian women, and the sycamores whose shadows protected villages stifled by heat. And the women who danced with the lightness of sinuous bodies, their fascinating gazes lost in dissolute thoughts, amidst inadmissible desires of carnal loves.

Egypt, hieratic and monumental, deprived of shade, yet rich in taut and splendid light and enveloped in colours which became changeable and dazzling in a luminous dimension, which in truth we neglect. Then, indeed just then, the softened keels of the cangias – concave, flexible, carved by expert hands according to long-lost rules – opened to the winds, with the splashing of waves, the boisterous uproar of the river birds, the barking of dogs arriving from distant embankments and sandbanks, the shouts of the dragomen when the paths of two boats crossed and they began to exchange greetings and conversation from a distance.

The heat deepened the wrinkles on faces burnt by the sun, increased a sort of contemplative laziness, sharpened the rancid stench of the sweat of armpits, revealed the shameless dancing of the transvestites who delighted in moving sinuously while wearing commodious breeches and short blouses embroidered so that one could glimpse the navel, the uncovered, shaved and indecent genitalia of the courtesans. It showed caravanserai skilfully quartered, camels lazily traversing the bazaar, tinkling bells of men who spent their time sucking the aromatic tobacco from hookahs, and fields of sugar cane, and the ritual whirling dances of the dervishes amidst fierce banging on the tambourine, and the market of slaves – one could acquire one for a few *para* – and syphilis, and cholera, and death enthroned amidst the carcasses of camels, asses, horses.

The cities, from Benisouf to Minieh, from Beni Hassan to Assyout, from Thebes to Dendara, from Karnak to Esneh, were drowsing in a languid lassitude, under the alert watch of the new lords, while the great river flowed placidly, winding amidst lands buried in sand, though they had been conquered in stretches along the banks by waves of vegetation: palms or reeds consumed by the wind. The seasons changed in the convulsion of events, and the friezes of colour took on mysterious foreign accents. The waters of the river symbolized marriages between the city of the living and the city of the dead in the slow change from light to darkness, from darkness to light. Then suddenly, in a horizon lit by the first light of day, the colours baptized the surroundings. Thus came a thousand sensations and alternations of the mind. The dazzling light brought to view things never seen or imagined: pink-tinged mountains, turtle-doves nesting in the branches, storks and cranes, and boats which, silently furrowing the waters, carried slaves to the market.

Each town had been baptized as a daughter of the great river. Some, enclosed within white walls and erected like a fortress rooted in a river delta open to the sea, exhibited bazaars laden with pottery glazed in red and black, embossed silver, percussion instruments, coops crammed with chickens, weapons chiselled by skilled hands, *chibuk* from inlaid fireplaces, *habar* with beautiful embroidery, *tarbuk* adorned in red. Then, in the abandonment of memories that had never wholly vanished, there were sanctuaries, obelisks, necropolises, tombs of caliphs, minarets as vestiges swallowed up in cities, there beyond every periphery, where the women wore blue costumes adorned with the glittering gold of bracelets, necklaces, amulets.

El-Bahar, the Nile, had allowed itself to be conquered in all its immensity without opposing excessive resistance to the Ottomans. It had given itself up to a stronger foreign people and had consumed its maternal lap in the sacrifice of subjection – and without any desire for deliverance now that the Mameluk sovereigns had begun to exercise the local powers. The feverish fires of the river banks were the only memories kept by the men of the river, the great river, and they gathered together in prayer, in the calm of a silence imposed by memory.

Today, deafening sounds run together in an agitation of names pronounced frenetically, barely distinguishable names in dissonant, unknown, obscure tongues. The Nile in any case had conceded itself to the infinite melancholy of antique and vanishing remnants, to shoddy gestures and signs, to ambiguous sacrifices in the midst of populous banks, among low houses in grey stone, oppressed by pale minarets in white limestone there at the crossings of salt water and fresh water canals, in quarries smothered by the heat where sand is dug up for seventy cents per cubic metre due to the shrewdness of Monsieur Ferdinand Marie de Lesseps[5] who has at his disposition, dependency and orders millions of francs, thirty thousand men, thousands and thousands of animals and a part of the Compagnie Universal de Canal Maritime de Suez, capital 200,000,000 francs, for a period of ninety-nine years. Each Share of five hundred francs to the Bearer gives the right: 1st, to the ownership of 1/400,000 of the company assets; 2nd, to an interest of 5% on the sum spent, payable by the semester on 1 January and 1 July of each year; 3rd, to an annual dividend payable on the 1 July.

Monsieur Ferdinand Marie de Lesseps, having reached the right bank of the great river – it was in 1859 – allowed the harmonious waters to flow behind him and began to scrutinize the narrow strip of sand which stretched from the Mediterranean

---

5   Ferdinand Marie, Vicomte de Lesseps, planned and oversaw the construction of the Suez Canal.

to the Red Sea for about 100 kilometres, cut here and there by the lakes Amari, Timsah, Ballah and Mensaleh and meeting in an angle the spur of the El-Guisr rocks.

A succinct narration, in which I believed with enchantment and ingenuity, my dear Max. And then to mention events, to reveal that there were about twenty thousand *fallah* or Egyptian peasants conscripted to the work. Is it possible, Max? Only shovels and picks to fill up wicker baskets with sand and rocks, so that camels and asses could drag them away to deliver the rubble to distant places.

Finally, to bring to an end such an imposing labour of hydraulic engineering, the rash Suez Canal to be clear, there were dredging machines and elevators operated by diligent European labourers. Superior orders, it was whispered and they whisper to me in telling of the events. Is it the truth, Max? Is it possible that the Sublime Port – *Bab o Qapi*, Arabic or Turkish as the language of Istanbul might be – forbade Monsieur Ferdinand-Marie de Lesseps from using the *fallah* for the difficult labour of excavation? Does that seem credible to you, Max? Does it seem reasonable to subject to hard labour, in the blinding heat of the desert, men of our race solely for arrogant and senseless revenge or for the unmotivated senselessness of miserable Oriental customs?

Meanwhile Isma'il Pasha, Khédive of Egypt, benefited from this majestic work, committed as he was, and by his own will and determination, to the rite of a Masonic Lodge offered to him by Monsieur Ferdinand Marie de Lesseps. Thus Isma'il Pasha became, and quickly, an astute charlatan and clever huckster, but also a reckless profiteer since he began to speculate on cane sugar to compete with the Confederate States of America which were in the midst of losing their slaves in a deadly civil war. Max, you met Isma'il Pasha did you not? You met him when you frequented those places in the company of that character Gustave Flaubert?

With noteworthy attention, Isma'il Pasha, Monsieur Ferdinand Marie de Lesseps and the entrepreneurs of the Suez Canal Company requested my presence in the land of Egypt to celebrate the Grand Opening of the Suez Canal on 17 November.

There were sixty ships of various tonnages to witness the event. And royal yachts. And flags and pennants. And roaring cannons. And unfurled sails. And the puffing of smokestacks. And tents spread out on the river banks. And fields of sugarcane to frame it all. And cotton plantations. And teams of buffalos. And saddled donkeys. And camels in processions. And shouting dervishes. And costumed dances of the *almées*. And eyes painted with *kohl*. And the strident sounds of the *tarabuk*. And litanies of rebecs. And rhythms of cymbals. And horses at the gallop. And court carriages. And the Khédive's *conak*. Janissaries, Mamelukes, uniformed cawas, sheiks in zimarras. The crowned heads of half of Europe. Majestic candelabras, faint lights, liveried servants, Sheffield silver, Limoges porcelain, Baccarat crystal, Bruges tapestries. A sumptuous menu, with a *Grand Souper* set up for that exceptional event, around the succulent and fabulous dish *Poisson a la Réunion des Deux Mers*, created especially for the occasion.

All splendid, Max, believe me: splendid!

Royal ships then carried us guests along the ancient paths of Upper Egypt, allowing us to steal a slice of pure sky, uncontaminated because of that wind which, from North to South, in November, sweeps the sky and lightly ripples the waters which, in their earth-tinted colours, are fragrant of fertile magnanimity. Herons and storks immobile on the banks seemed to become inebriated by the sinuous waves of the waters. The palms seemed black as ink in a fire-red sky while the women on the banks were wrapped in intense blue fabrics.

Then a song, slow, melancholy, persuasive. The song of an *almée* to the rhythm of a small drum while a *milayah* covered part of her face: *"I sing for you drunk with your beauty / with my hands on the harp I celebrate / the beauty of your face / I sing for you drunk with your beauty / for you all beings are dancing / Imploring they gather in front of you / I sing for you, drunk with your beauty / the young shoots turn to you / and become as beautiful as lilies".*

Aboard a *ghizeh*, marked by the memory of new and old seductions, I slowly lost the lament of this song and suddenly saw a town, ships of the Compagnie Azizié, dark waters, nocturnal, glittering with the reflections of the lights of the port. I saw Bulak disappear on the horizon: a vivid periphery piled up on the right bank of the river, suffocated by factories, workshops, warehouses and a port teeming with lowered sails, men burdened with the weight of the loads they bore, excited voices, various jargons, Arabs amidst the reckless rituals of the *courbach* and the magnanimity of the *batchis*. Now distant from the Citadel, the pyramids of Abusir and Dahshur, while a shrill voice recalled the moving words pronounced by Monsieur Ferdinand Marie de Lesseps at the inauguration of the Canal, of قانة السويس or Qanat al-Suways on 16 November 1860: *"Oh God, let your divine breath descend upon these waters! That you pass and repass from Occident to Orient, from Orient to Occident! Oh God! Make use of this pathway to draw men closer to each other!"*

Glancing now at the waters of the river, I read signs of the passage of very tender nostalgias, of vanished sweetness. The treacherous waters cradle desires in a soothing and persuasive rise and fall, defacing truth amidst hollow sounds of sides of boats struck by waves, by winds, by a light composed of milky, languid, reflected glimmerings. The horizon stands out vividly among purple reflections as the sun plays hide and seek with the striking profiles of the pyramids. Lethargy subjugates the comfortable harmonies of the mind.

Thus melancholy mingles with recollections, recollections with melancholy. Reality becomes an indecipherable, ambiguous game, subject to perceptions lost and acquired, acquired and lost in an indolent, neglected, slothful cadence. Recollections finally scarred truths, yielded to desires, to untoward psychological wounds, ambiguously deceived by lucid thoughts. Shadows, the shadows of the mind have taken meaning in objects, in faces, in places signalling dangers and expectations – perhaps desired and sought.

For a moment, I recognized next to me Gustave's face, his penetrating eyes, his massive, dark, offensive body. Almost *"a wild bison of the deserts of America / Vigorous and proud in his athletic force / Jumped on my breast, spread out his black hair, / And without ever tiring me instilled life into me[6]"*. It seemed that I was once again in Mantes, in the Hôtel du Grand-Cerf, when I made him dizzy with my love, when it was the moment for sighs and desires, when something mysterious and sweet united us, and thus he wrote to me in a time long past *"I am enfeebled, befuddled as after a long orgy. I am bored. I have an unprecedented emptiness in my heart ... Your love has made me sad ... I should like never to have known you ... and yet at the same time when I think of you I feel myself inundated with a great sweetness[7]"*.

I also recognized Gustave's mouth. A mouth marked by a sarcastic smile, a mouth intent on kissing another mouth, a horrible mouth marked by heavy make-up: the mouth of a courtesan, of an *almée*, of Koutchouk-Hanem certainly, who knew how to sing *songs without meaning and incomprehensible*[8] for Gustave, but also knew how to offer her splendid body, perfumed with sweet terebinth, to the inauspicious desire of Gustave, who consummated this mercenary love on a filthy bed of palm-canes.

I imagined then alliances among women to decipher the secrets of a man, his ordinary love, his sexual manias, the erotic frenzies which had overcome and offended my purity, my virginal ingenuity, my passive submission when, in the Orient, and in your company, my dear Max, you devoted yourselves to the most bestial sort of sodomy, frequenting baths and young nude masseurs.

My native land, Provence, dazzling with light, left me heir to the pride of humility, the power of being attentive, wise, allured only by simplicity of form and mind. Provence, a land that has never generated unworthy men, capable even of assassinating the youth of fragile women.

Thus I was overwhelmed by punitive ambiguity, by bitter reproofs, by emotional dismissals, by friendships corrupted by the egoism of others. It was so with Gustave, but also with Victor Cousin, with Alfred de Musset, with Alphonse Karr, with Champfleury or rather Jules François Felix Fleury-Husson. It

---

6   From a poem by Louise Colet.

7   Gustave Flaubert, *Letters.*

8   Gustave Flaubert, *Letters.*

was so with my husband Hippolyte Colet, and with many others who entrapped me with various deceptions and with deception abandoned me without reason or cause.

My life, to look at it closely, seems fragmented, as in a kaleidoscope. Yet my childhood and my youth, spent in the Val d'Arc – overlooked and protected by Sainte-Victoire, the mountain that culminates in the Pic des Mouches and was cursed by the Teutons and the Ambrones, joined by a Castellum, by the Aquae Sextiae, the thermal springs – my childhood and my youth were nobly enhanced, by virtue and wisdom, by my city, by Aix, liberated by a Court of Auditors, by a Court of Donatives.

From Aix I inherited ancient wisdom, ancient prudence, ancient shrewdness, which accompanied me on the road of life, without permitting a single departure from the healthy morality of an ethos, from each divine messenger who, like a magical Ariel, might appear in the guise of a mortal being.

Verse became a signal. And I, Louise, *piscôum doumeiselle poulida comme une fade*[9], I, at eighteen years of age, beautiful and desired and marked by the concupiscent looks of men, took to the difficult labour of composing four beautiful verses on love, profane love, though tender and devoted. I learned Latin with a firm and decisive obstinacy to be able to read the great poets of antiquity in their own tongue, to draw near to them, to share with them the joy and pain of composing verses.

I never engaged in sentimental outrages towards anyone, still less towards a boy, a youth. The vicissitude of the suicide of a lover – an event that occurred when I was a young girl and the boy was afflicted with a notable ugliness – was a lying piece of gossip and an ignoble slander. If there was indeed a violent death, it was caused by the unhappiness of a soul because *beauty alone is beautiful, love alone is great*[10]. In Aix, a small city, it was permissible and necessary to frequent only faithful, devoted and honest friends. It was often my custom, in order to forget the melancholy of vulgar chatter, to converse with myself, reciting blank verse

---

9   Provenzal dialect: *a small woman pure as a fairy.*
10   Louise Colet, *Notes de voyage.*

or hendecasyllables, so as to wander freely on Parnassus, thus eluding bothersome visits.

Née Révoil, from an ancient parliamentary family, from a father, Antoine, director of the post office, associated with an earldom on the side of my mother, Henriette Le Blanc, I was free to engage in study or in joyous acts of cultural ardour. I read and acquired learning while others devoted themselves to the turbulences of youth.

I gave charitable help to the needy, unfortunate and rejected, offering them pieces of stale bread stolen from my noble table. I lived at that time in the castle of Servannes, at Mouriès, with aunts of noble lineage, severe, of aristocratic principles. I took part in the fable of the most touching generosity, I offended the uglinesses of the world, discovering myself to be an enchantress raised for poetry.

I was beautiful, charming and envied. The great linden trees of the avenues accompanied my passing and the organza of my dress fluttered in the midst of the worn, ordinary, banal clothing of the peasants. Like a celestial apparition, *et vera incessu patuit dea*[11], people admired me and I, thanks to Aix, home of the Mistral, embellished myself with a sentimental education that precluded my becoming a *fantaisiste cruel*[12], a haughty person.

It was then that Hippolyte Colet irrupted into my life, bewitching me with his music while his loose-knit, suffering figure, oppressed by fatigue, gave itself up to the execution of sonatas, arias, variations. Then came Paris, when Hippolyte was appointed professor of composition at the Conservatoire. It was 1835.

The shadows of Parisian evenings were reassuring even in the leaden colours of autumn, in the first chills, in the rains, in the mud of the streets and in the bewilderment at the opaque splendour of bridges and a river hosting barges. I felt nostalgia for the intense colours of Provence, for the odours of the orange trees and myrtle and, desiring bay and not myrtle, I soothed myself with a dream long-nourished, delicate and scandalous.

---

11   In her gait a true goddess is revealed. Virgil, *Eineide* I, 405.
12   Cruel fantasist.

Juliette was the long-sought light. Madame Juliette Recamier was a wise friend. She opened the doors of her literary salon to me, and the Abbaye-aux-Bois, at 16 rue de Sevres, became my habitual retreat to recite verses, to listen to poetry. Chateaubriand was more than a father to me, he was the consoling angel. The *God of an ideal world, the living lyre, the divine messenger, the immaterial being*[13], surrounded by a myriad of cherubim, of guardians of the sacredness of art, of immortality, of life. And so too were Alfred de Vigny, Leconte de Lisle, James Prandier. Later came the consoling friendships of Victor Hugo, Alfred de Musset, Barbey d'Aurevilley, Pierre-Jean de Berange, Armand de Portmartin.

The salon of Madame Recamier and the Abbaye-Aux-Bois also echoed with opportune notes, with cadenced musical schemes, with symphonic articulations representing prodigious designs of musical writing and magical interpretations.

But no particular mastery accompanied Hippolyte, neither his own inventions nor his loving, infectious anthologies. Hippolyte had only a mediocre musicality to offer. He didn't aspire to better himself, to embrace a new kind of polychromy when he performed for money; he didn't try to dress himself up with a charm more seductive than mere banality, as was appropriate to him.

But I had already fallen into the trap laid by Hippolyte. Perhaps I had been conquered by the romantic fascination which an uncommon artist inspires, one little inclined to the usual social life because he was a humble professor at the conservatory, because he was a composer of little value. Hippolyte was inclined to elude the painful fatigue of applying himself, of the hard labour of creativity, of strong-willed instrumental investigations. His *Panharmonie musicale* had only a modest reception – and it couldn't have been otherwise.

Hippolyte consumed himself, meanwhile, in vigorous and shameful drinking bouts, in the satisfaction of ordinary, mediocre, plebeian tastes, while I accorded myself the companionship of an accomplished guide, of a wise Virgil. Victor Cousin was a

---

13   Louise Colet, *Lettres*.

dear friend to me in my suffering as a wife, in the bitter labour of writing poetry, in the arrogance and jealousy of uncivil intellectuals, in the lack of affection from my husband.

I worked with application, with method, with intelligent ability. I inspired the compassionate interest of critics, admirers, readers. I became the Muse of the new France, without however betraying my duties as a woman, as a student of life, of position and a valued frequenter of salons.

I overcame ill-natured gossip and devious people who intrigued amidst the mutterings of grumblers. I wrote, I published, I gathered praise while, with an outstanding mastery of behaviour and courage, there grew ever stronger in me the determination to reach objectives that continually became more coveted, more fulfilling, more secure. His Royal Majesty the Duke of Orleans wanted to honour my person, and for the highest poetic merit awarded me a platinum medal – with a commercial value of well over a thousand *scudi*. Victor Cousin, in that circumstance, did not exert any influence of any kind or any authority or prestige – nor could he given his rank and prestige. Evil tongues were, promptly and with reason, proved wrong, even though they continued to insinuate that my adored daughter Henriette was his also.

Victor was, I confirm this vigorously, a dear, affectionate and good friend. He corrected errors of application, of writing, of human and social approaches. He helped me to attend salons. He spurred me to moderate my obligingness, to conceal my good nature which led me to overvalue friendship. He urged me to trust in my innate provincial intuition – which led me to be unyielding towards adulation, vanity, baseness.

I was not in fact *la piqûre de Cousin*[14], as Alphonse Karr went around saying. Karr with whom I had, in fact, salutary relations. Then proud of my liberty of judgment, I was the Charlotte Corday of literature, and my *La Jeunesse de Mirabeau* was a brilliant example of intellectual coherence, while the perfidious and calumnious accusations of plagiarism could take on body and spirit only in

---

14   Cousin's mosquito.

petty, shabby, conniving minds, not at all those gifted with good taste. Never have I been the maid-of-all-work of French poetry, but rather the manipulator of verses cadenced with Latin rhymes, with a unique instinct, with the teachings of skilled and correct masters.

To follow a path, without searching for shortcuts!

I always strenuously defended my dignity and never, I repeat never, gave way to arrogant flattery, nor to obscenely wretched proposals. I was the sister of the muses, sister of the graces, and not the industrious bee that comes and goes, always plundering and looting. Monsieur Cave, director of the Beaux-Arts, knows this very well. Unfair, Monsieur Cave! He will certainly remember my name. Unfair, Monsieur Cave!

The circumstance by which a pension was granted me was a dishonest farce, artfully contrived by one who wanted to discredit me, to treat a defenceless woman with ferocity, to injure a sincere and valued friend of a philosopher like Victor Cousin. He gossiped with much worthless rubbish, and the malevolent aphorisms and the slanderous judgments of Monsieur Paul Ginisty, a third-rate journalist and writer, were wisely ignored. Unfair, Monsieur Ginisty!

The truth did not hold correct judgments and accounts outstanding! It was my nobility of soul which made me reject the first offer of an annuity from Monsieur Cave – beyond the meagreness of the proposed amount, which could well have provoked irritation and poisonous fits of anger. I did not give way to treacherous proposals. And I had good reason not to do so.

The dignity of the poet must always be safeguarded *ante omnes*. And Monsieur Cave's offer humiliated my artistic respectability, because it was unnatural, apart from uncommon in suggesting a need to redeem with such a miserable annuity the illicit privations and immoral suffering involved in dedicating oneself body and soul to art.

Monsieur Cave repented, however, and in time. Indeed, Victor explained to him, with the intellectual tenacity that distinguishes him and with the reasoning of a subtle philosophical and ethical nature, the reasons behind my instinctive refusal. Monsieur Cave made amendments and invited me, with frank and convincing words and with a vigorous supply of concrete examples, not to wrong the Institut des Beaux-Arts, which would be proud to number me among its protégées. Well done, Monsieur Cave! Really, well done!

Thus dignity was restored to my intellectual honourability since, with a conspicuous increase of income, certain wounds that had been inflicted were healed, certainties were offered to my future as a poetess and the vileness of earning money in order to live could be avoided.

Now I esteem, and more than ever, the Institut des Beaux-Arts. Monsieur Cave esteems, and more than ever, my work as a writer and my reputation.

Hippolyte, meanwhile, busied himself with his existence amongst infantile caprices, lulled himself with indolence, in the equivocal game of being a *maudit*[15], in the subterfuge of coarse and cowardly lies, he busied himself between *fée verte* with its seductive emerald colour and the rustling skirts of prostitutes. Hippolyte took to frequenting the salons, but his carelessness of dress, his negligence of bearing, his neglect of washing himself rendered him unpopular, undesirable, sometimes detested. It would have been sufficient to look after his person more attentively and not to execrate water, in a peremptory manner, as a cruel ablution.

Hippolyte was also corrupted by an absurd professional jealousy in relation to me. As a narrow-minded, petty man, idle, little inclined to recognize the worth of others, he wished to impose restrictions on my status as a successful writer, a woman loved for her sagacity, for her verve, for her amiability in surrounding herself with personalities and personages who were both likeable and famous.

Hippolyte finally descended into absurdity, engaging in vile intrigues and deplorable behaviours when he became aware that he was considered merely the husband of a famous poetess. He also lapsed into the fraudulence of blackmail and embezzlement,

---

15   Accursed.

obliging his students at the conservatory to lavish on him conspicuous sums of money in order to obtain promotions.

Victor Cousin was, in contrast and with the true nobility of a gentleman, a man of dignity, of worth, consecrated to study, to philosophical research, to academic teaching. An authoritative spirit, a revered intellectual, a distinguished master, an excellent teacher. But his ideas, his labour, his republicanism constrained him to sacrifices and mortifications, so that with the changing times Victor had neither the shrewdness nor the cunning nor the prudence to adapt himself to history, which moved forward imposing a new path, one which enjoined a new order of things.

Victor believed firmly – and foolishly, within the conceptual utopia of the philosopher – in historicism. He believed in its eclecticism. He believed in Immanuel Kant of Konigsberg and Gottfried Wilhelm Leibniz of Leipzig. He believed in his *Du Vrai, du Bien, du Beau*, but he held any recompense in the form of money or privilege offered to him to be indecorous and shameful. Eighteen fifty-one and the Second Empire were, for him, rash symptoms of history. Thus, as an aged professor, he was forced to beg for economic tranquillity and decorous teaching. And he kept busy, in order to forget affronts and acts of disrespect, in lugubrious and unmannerly soliloquies of philosophical architecture.

Hippolyte and Victor, even though they ignored each other and frequented each other rarely, had much in common. If they had seen something of each other and had known each other better, they would have come to an understanding. They were brothers in simple-mindedness, inconclusiveness, modesty. They fought shy of important friendships and any social influences whatever, they imposed futile values which enriched nevertheless by the prestige of a notable frequenting and by the conversation of the literary salons.

Hippolyte followed one road, Victor another, leaving me alone to confront tough adversaries, individuals thirsty for fatuous glory and for prestige purchased at low price, all in all scoundrels without scruples.

Hippolyte drowned himself in discouragement and illness. Victor lost himself in solitude.

Infirmity was for Hippolyte a pretext for authenticating moral blackmail, for imposing his emotional despotism, for adeptly wasting time among uncontrolled outbursts of anger and silent accusatory sulking. He had no words of gratitude for whomever helped him charitably, for whomever offered him help without claiming anything in return, for whomever advised him without giving weight to open and bleeding moral wounds.

Hippolyte slowly fell into a woeful, cruel, inhuman indolence. Day after day, his body appeared more bent, his gait more hesitating and insecure, his movements more encumbered and slow, incapacitated by shooting pains, by uncontrolled trembling, by a cough which lacerated his lungs. To die because he wanted to die. And Hippolyte played skilfully with the many wounds of his body and his soul. Desperation, all in all!

I gave myself up to helping him. I underwent abuse and vexation when I welcomed him once more into my house, offered him comfort and supported him in irresponsible manias, in pretentious and insensate solicitations. I helped him in his agony even though henceforth I had no tie that constrained me to involve myself closely with his infirmity, his body given over to corruption, his mind clouded by confusion. The separation of many years had given us different life choices. For me, this had been very healthful. Hippolyte died on 21 April 1851.

Victor also slowly became a stranger to me: an old man, stubborn and irresponsible, basking in the past splendour of *maître à penser*, an old republican intellectual. Out of false self-love and misguided modesty, he broke off all links with the external world. He broke off our affectionate relations to redefine a friendship based only on reciprocal esteem.

He put forward puerile excuses, accused me of arrogance that profaned his virtues, blamed me for a language unsuitable for a woman and a poetess, for slang expressions, for incorrect, unseemly, scandalous phonemes. Infantile accusations in insisting on rights for *glances more tender now that nothing remains*[16].

---

16   Louise Colet, *Notes de voyage.*

I found myself once more alone, with my daughter Henriette. A new father, in the interim – Gustave, in fact! Yes, Monsieur Gustave Flaubert: your dear friend, Max – eager for unsuspected attentions, seemed to want to raise her attentively. It seemed that he wanted to adopt her, with exceptional affection and eager and loving attention.

He deceived me, equivocated in a trivial way, committed painful errors, put forward perceptions which were divergent, well-concealed, indolent. A further wound lacerated my sentiments. An indelible scar marred relations which had been solid, secure, sincere. A rejection finally outraged my dignity as a woman, created a brazen violation, a dishonourable rape of time and affection.

Mantes, *la Medunta, la Jolie* shone forth meanwhile like the citadel of love, of inviolable sentiments, of secure tenderness, intimate, enveloping, there on the right bank of the Seine, with the fountain of place de l'Hôtel de Ville, the tower of St. Maclou, the church of Notre-Dame, the place de la République and the Hôtel du Grand-Cerf. Mantes was the custodian of our intimacy when *we still loved each other, on and on, when we had enjoyed sublime pleasures ... and Gustave was proud of what he had been saying, and that is that I had never before enjoyed such happiness*[17].

Mantes, that lovely hotel in Mantes, a white inn which had as its sign a roebuck painted on a banner, became the painful open wound of verses written in the joy of the moment, in the ardour of turbulent and excited senses: *Two tongues in the same mouth / mingled with seductive licking / our united bodies seemed to want to shatter the bed / below our ardent outbursts / ... / oh, bed, if you could speak!*

I let myself be bewitched by a man without scruples, without love because *the grotesque aspect of love prevented him from abandoning himself, as he thought of the strange face that he must have in those moments*[18]. And that man, in love with himself, persevered for years in making fun of me, in dragging me into ridicule, in

17   Gustave Flaubert, *Lettres*.
18   Gustave Flaubert, *Lettres*.

abandoning me and taking me up again, in running off to the Orient with you, his friend, my dear Maxime.

I had self-respect, and that preserved me from becoming a woman offended by a shameful and dishonest rejection, without resistance. I had the wisdom to render honour to myself, more than he would have done. I had the good taste to cede to that individual only a part of myself, I reserved the privilege to reject and the wisdom to renounce frenetic, illicit, licentious, immoral sensualities.

When my senses led me to sublime ecstasy, I abandoned myself, with propriety and intimate virtue, to narrating my melancholies to myself. Not a single gesture, not an action, not an overture which was contemptible towards that man. I conceded my love – it's true, I dreamed of a love, I shared a love in order to recover that human warmth that Hippolyte and Victor had mislaid, amidst meanness and personal advantage. I asked very little of Gustave, only tenderness and understanding. I was overwhelmed by emotional bullying and by the indecent irascibility of the character of a misanthrope.

I allowed myself to be compliant to his will. I went so far as to let myself be bent to the will of others, renouncing my own rights. I confided my intentions and purposes to convince Gustave to listen to me, to sustain me, to comfort me. It wasn't easy for me to throw away my life as a poetess, as a Parisian, as an intellectual. However, I was ready for anything. I made no mystery of my intentions, of my desires.

I opened my heart to him, confessing to him that I would have liked to live – in the circumstances of the moment, in the uncertainties of life, in the inability to be understood – Yes! I would have liked to *live in some village (near Rouen) to work, to raise my daughter, to be at his disposition – because this would have been my happiness if he loved me*[19].

Monsieur Gustave Flaubert was sceptical, he had compassion only for himself, for his adored mother. I was

---

19   Louise Colet, *Lettres.*

ready for sacrifices and privations in order to remain near him, to look after him, to support any trouble of his. He dismissed me clumsily, as one would dismiss a domestic without justification, without motive, without a reason which might be acceptable. He showed me the door as he would have done with an Oriental courtesan.

Croisset buzzed in a summer night. It was June 1851. I had arrived unexpectedly at Gustave's house to heal deep wounds, to try to understand his intentions, to beg him – if it were necessary – to heed my cry of pain, my suffering as a woman and as a mother, my desire to satisfy the legitimate wish to live beside him.

I didn't try to force time and destiny. I didn't try to violate any familiar intimacy. I didn't want to make him pity me. I didn't have, above all – never, never, believe me Max! – the pretension of making myself accepted in his house, as his woman.

The lies of this man are shameless, false, irritating. He accused me of hidden manoeuvres; with impunity he persuaded friends and acquaintances of his interpretation of the facts to the point of arguing, with the falsity typical of him, that I wanted – yes! – that I wanted to constrain him to present me to his mother and to introduce me into his house in order to obtain the position that he believed I expected in his life.

Gustave refused to receive me that evening, at Croisset. Our missives – carried out in a dialogue which was strained, tense, at times cruel – seemed to exhaust themselves in commonplace and vulgar replies, through the perorations of servants appointed to safeguard his privacy. Gustave first of all deliberately ignored my clarificatory note, then shamelessly disappeared when, taking risks and chances, I tried to inform him of my legitimate reasons. Then, thoughtlessly and inconsiderately, he allowed himself to be surprised alone in an angle of the park. And there were the lindens, the calm shadows of the twilight, the intense perfume of a summer evening beguiled by the rippling of the river.

Vis-à-vis then, I begged him for explanations that might help me to understand his senseless behaviour. I set forth arguments, I demanded justifications for his secrecy, his counterfeit reluctance, his incivility. He scrutinized me, at the same time avoiding my glance. He pronounced few words – timorous, embarrassed: *Madame*, he declaimed, with awkwardness, *I will see you at your hotel at 8 o'clock.* A Gustave without wits, spellbound by dishonest scruples. A Gustave who was reckoning up memories gone astray in ambiguous sensuality, in stories experienced on the far banks of a sacred river, beyond the Nile, beyond cities, dragomen, sailors, *almées* of every race and kind, beyond temples contaminated by sand, where a singing *melot* evoked the signs of time, his pilgrimage to Mecca.

Nostalgia and recollections defined also by the penetrating odours of noisy brothels, by the scents of lightly touched bodies sprinkled with unguents, perfumed oils and balsams, by nocturnal languors, by the frenetic rhythms of drumbeats, by excited senses dazzled by a golden sun.

Gustave wished to preserve the memory only of his fleeting love. His heart had a place only for Koutchouk-Hanem, the *almée* who had offered him her majestic body, her bed, an entire night there, at Esneh. Had Gustave really known the body of that woman?

Mantes had been forgotten by then.

Adieu, Mantes, *adieu* Hôtel du Grand-Cerf, *adieu* 29 July 1848. There remained Croisset, its obsessive presence, its perfidious guests, with its lacerating dailiness, with its lugubrious imprisonment. Madame Anne-Justine-Caroline Flaubert, *née* Fleuriot, kept watch over the destiny of her son, of her Gustave.

Gustave's memory became, with time, the memory of Madame Flaubert: *the dear old lady, the poor much-beloved one, the poor adored one, the poor, very dear, old lady.* Madame appointed herself the guardian of every sentiment, so that Croisset would be the sanctuary of acquiescence, of silence, of the immutability of feelings.

And even of Love! Amidst embraces, caresses and kisses between the everlasting child Gustave and his mother. This in the summers, in the warm afternoons in the shadows of the lindens, Madame sat on a bench and spoke of things, of persons, of her memories, and thus cancelled all present time, enveloped in melancholy a reality which was vanishing forever.

And Gustave, *always like a little child*, played the part of a loving son, full of attention, of affection. He ran to *his dear-dear-dear mamma* to tell her about his life, his loves, his secrets, his fantasies. Conversations that were solitary, confessional, ambiguous, so that tenderness took the upper hand amidst embraces and kisses exchanged a thousand times, a thousand times received and given.

Croisset inviolable and unviolated. Gustave and his mother celebrated their rituals without importunate interferences, without extraneous meddling, without irritating intrusions. Croisset was not and is not Mantes, it was not and is not a room in the Hôtel du Grand-Cerf, it is not a bed perfumed with bodies fulfilling themselves *with all the delights of the flesh* without pretending, in the desire of an overwhelming passion.

Croisset was not and certainly is not the spacious hall where, enveloped in the scent of resin and honey, on a purple rug with golden fringes, an *almée* would have danced, ennobling her lascivious and provocative body. Croisset was and is the delirium of agony, far from the desert where Gustave had dragged his soul, had captured the assassin of his youth in his horrible barbarity.

Meanwhile the *ghizeh* cuts through the waters, barely wrinkled with tepid puffs of wind, besieged by the cries of birds, and Esneh draws nearer. The noble kite rises up in flight. Perhaps also the cormorant, the duck, the teal, the flamingo, the peacock. Now, at dawn, the ravenous howling of the jackal breaks out menacingly in the ruins of the temples, and the date-palms make a hissing sound, caressed by the first heat of the day which stripes the sky with azure, which brushes with ochre the tranquil waters of the Nile. A woman weeps, and Sirius, the star of Isis, covers me with its veil of spouse, of mother, of lover, awaiting a truth which could be discovered at Esneh, from Koutchouk-Hanem perhaps.

Farewell, farewell my dear friend.

With unchanging gratitude,

Louise Colet

24 June 1870

Madame Colet,

We have acted according to your wishes, and as rapidly as possible. Delays and unforeseen events are not due to negligence on our part, nor to specific intentions. For the rest, His Highness Isma'il Pasha and your illustrious fellow-countryman, the Viscount Ferdinand Marie de Lesseps, have supported your application with resolution and determination, and we could not be indifferent in the face of such commanding exhortations. Thus we have been able to move forward with all our energy, with all our investigative resources, with all our knowledge. The question that you have put before us has become the principal motivation for our operations and it has brought matters to a conclusion in the best possible manner, indeed the only possible manner.

In truth, we were initially surprised by your unusual request, then, compromised by contingencies and happenings of which we gradually became aware, we became participants, in the first person and in a suggestive manner, in the circumstances you told us about and of which we made ourselves aware. Thus, we spared neither energy nor minutes, so that once and for all the truth on these matters could be recognized and seen as valid questions which had, on various occasions and in a manifest manner, involved and disturbed you.

We must confess to you, in all frankness and good faith, that while we were proceeding with the investigation we often asked ourselves with a pinch of Oriental malice why you, Madame Louise Colet – illustrious Poetess of France, a woman born a daughter of Apollo, a woman with the appearance of Venus, a woman who had the daring to write the splendid composition *Le Monument de Molière*, a woman singled out at least four times for the poetry prize awarded by the French Academy – manifested such careful diligence and solicitude regarding what traces could be discovered of a certain man and a certain woman who, by good luck or sheer chance, had encountered each other in our country about twenty years ago. A meeting which had been the preamble to an overwhelming night of love marked by a passionate exaltation of the senses: *as to the fucks: all of the best quality, the third assault was brutal, the last the most sentimental (exchanging) infinite affections so that (we embraced each other) with sadness and love*[20]. Hence, your desire to know the destiny of such individuals, their next movement, their present residence, is eccentric and extravagant. But we are attentive to your suggestive request and to your unusual desire.

And so we have retraced itineraries, interrogated persons, visited places, inspected maps and notebooks so that we might be able to furnish you with the information you seek, above all on what happened on the night between 6 and 7 March 1850 in a modest mud house, there amidst the scents of sandalwood, a humble bazaar for merchandise, a café, a mosque, dovecotes. I am speaking of the small city of Esneh in Upper Egypt, flanked by an embankment and set apart from the negligence of a jumble of shacks and wild and domesticated rams, by luxuriant palm-groves and by the remains of a temple, its twenty-four columns lending it an aura of charm.

We investigated then, and with noteworthy scrupulousness, the past of those figures about whom you have requested stories and accounts of their relations and histories, that is of that man and woman. We sought to have at our disposal elements that would be useful, enabling you, Madame, to decipher in all their possible veracity both the remote and recent past of these people, enabling you to understand the existence that they have led, their present occupations and entanglements, above and beyond everything else that might be instrumental to gratify any appreciable indiscretion.

It appeared to us supremely opportune and convenient to dig up facts and events which have involved these two individuals, also because you, illustrious poetess, have refrained from making mention – we do not know if by deliberate discretion or from actual forgetfulness – of any possible relations you have had and shared with them. If, indeed, there ever were such rapports, such as relations, mutual influence, connections of any kind.

---

20   Gustave Flaubert, *Letters*.

In your invitation to us to undertake these investigations you, Madame, have in any case, albeit with wise sagacity and virginal blushes, given support to the suspicion that the man is not completely foreign to you or, at least – so we have believed ourselves to understand – he has had with you occasional rapports or perhaps chance meetings. It thus seemed probable to suppose that you had experienced displeasing annoyances, perhaps even moral attacks, perhaps even harassing and aggressive molestations – even considerably before that fateful year, 1850.

In regard to the woman, we have had from you, Madame Colet, only inadequate and approximate indications and traces. It is true that we were dealing with a person of dubious morality, and she confirmed it to us with words of contempt and infamy, words that her station makes it permissible to render publicly. A person willing to welcome adventurers of every class and country sailing along the Nile, who perhaps was by profession a dancer, perhaps a courtesan, perhaps – it cannot be excluded – a *khaonal*, a transvestite engaged in prostitution.

We know nothing else of her. We have however the sense that Madame is nurturing an extreme interest in what we might discover when we have acquired more knowledge about this woman. Your stubborn curiosity appears to us to hide a dignified injury, now almost pushed to one side, but with which you were inflicted right from the start by her.

Now to the investigation true and proper.

It was difficult to go back in time, to revisit streets that have changed, that is to travel through times and places swept away by new epochs and altered courses. Nevertheless, our attempts obtained reasonable success to the point that, at the moment, we can offer you such useful documentation and arguments as will permit you to be able to sift through this information, and if you wish, to utilize it in the way you believe most suitable, even having recourse to judicial authorities if injury or deception was carried out in relation to yourself.

We carried out our investigations first of all on the man, since we had certain information on the date of his disembarkation in

Egypt, information which you yourself had furnished us with, including an abundance of details. He was not alone: he was indeed accompanied by Baron Maxime du Camp, invited here by the Secretary General of Commerce for investigations and a survey of our territory, that is to gather during his journey – accompanied by two notebooks of instructions from the ministry, a diplomatic passport and a photographic apparatus. So Monsieur du Camp embarked bearing with him, apart from the equipment of the journey, also 9 kg of hyposulphate of soda, virgin wax, photographic scissors, distilled water, positive printing paper, negative paper, filter paper and a box of chemical products.

Monsieur Maxime Du Camp arrived in our land escorted by his domestic servant Louis Sasseti, Corsican by birth and an expert dragoman, a true and faithful person on whom he could well count in every circumstance and matter of urgency, since in fact Monsieur Du Camp could certainly not have relied on the help of that man for whom you requested information. Monsieur Du Camp left Marseilles on the morning of 4 November 1849 on board the *Nil*, a 250-horsepower steamer, and arrived at Alexandria on 15 November after a disagreeable crossing due to the seasickness which afflicted both passengers and crew because of the unbearable persistence of blustery winds and high waves, with whirlpools and a strong undertow. Everything was governed, as a point of honour, by *the contempt of the first class towards the second, of the second towards the third, the third towards the fourth, and by the rivalry between the administrative personnel and that of the ship: precedence at table, artificial affability, licentious words, allusive gestures. It was all, indeed, very diverting and educational*[21].

Monsieur Du Camp is a person of the highest reputation and of esteemed consideration, so it is not unclear why he was accompanied by that individual about whom you have solicited information and notes. Later, from information obtained at first hand, we were informed that he, in a very altruistic and generous gesture, took on the honour of including in his own expedition that man who, at

---

21   Gustave Flaubert, *Letters*.

the time of which we are speaking – it is now known with certainty and a wealth of details – suffered from a grave, preoccupying and broken state of health. He was connected to the expedition in the role of representative of the Ministry of Agriculture, and he too obtained from this advantages and diplomatic backing.

Above all, therefore, he was an invalid: perhaps epileptic, but mentally weaker still. We are not able to reveal his name to you. The French authorities have enjoined silence. We can however reveal the initials of his name: G.F., and G.F. is a man of affluence and a man of letters, at least according to information received by our trustworthy and prudent informers. Your police force and competent officials have scornfully refused any – even partial – collaboration. The reasons are unknown to us. We are inclined to believe it is because of the usual pressures issuing from Paris, exceptional constrictions, unwholesome intrigues.

However, so as to avoid misunderstandings, it is opportune to attest with clarity and honesty that our G.F. is also, at least so it is reputed and judged, an author who is highly esteemed. At the same time, it is his recognized peculiarity to have stubbornly rummaged through the obscenity of society, in particular into the usages and customs of the life of the French provinces, publishing a vulgar little book, one which is very dangerous and full of perils for morality and good taste. But we will report this to you further on, with disconcerting particulars which are nonetheless very central to the matter.

A few remarks first of all on our man. G.F. is a mysterious, lugubrious and sibylline sort of person. He lives precariously, not practising any profession, between Paris and Croisset, near Rouen. He has frequented, with suspicious secrecy and careless negligence, an inn in the little city of Mantes, halfway between Paris and Rouen, along the railroad. The circumstances are unreliable and unusual. But let us proceed in order.

G.F. stayed in Paris for four or five months of the year, from 1858 to 1869, at 42 boulevard du Temple. On the third floor, and, according to the archives of the land registry of the Seine, the rental value of the property is 1000 francs, the land registry value

375 francs. The apartment comprises: an antechamber, two rooms with fireplaces with windows on the boulevard, a dining-room, another room with a fireplace, a kitchen, these last three rooms being lit by an internal court. The study, *pleasantly lit by a window that opens onto the boulevard,* (includes) *a clock which represents a Brahma in gilded wood, a large round table with a manuscript under the window, a bronze plate with Persian arabesques, and, above an ample leather divan, a copy of the Psyche of Naples*[22].

In July 1869, our G.F. moved to 4 rue Murillo, between rue de Courcelles and avenue Ruysdael: still in Paris. He lodged on the fourth floor of the main building with a view onto the park. Of this apartment, constructed in 1868 – rental value 1100 francs, land registry value 412 francs – we have obtained neither the floor plan nor anything else that could give us the details or, at least, define it better in its internal subdivisions.

However, there is a curious, morbid and intriguing condition of the life of G.F. in Paris. On the second floor of 42 boulevard du Temple there lived at the same time as our man – now about forty years old – also his mother.

Pitiful circumstances, according to many. She imposed on her son a thousand unimaginable tyrannies and repeated endlessly that she needed to have him beside her; that she had a heart continually tortured by each absence of her son; that she wanted her boy weak like a child who suffered from scolding; that she passed entire days torturing her brain about the misfortunes and accidents which might befall her adored son; that she ran around breathlessly to fulfil his every desire and request; that her anxiety was steadily more acute with the wild fear that her son might be struck unexpectedly by a violent nervous crisis. The life, all in all, of a good woman with an acute sense of family and the need to be surrounded by her dear ones but who was only appeased in the silence of agonizing migraines with the help of laudanum.

At Croisset, G.F. lived – and still lives when he is not staying in Paris – in a vast country house surrounded by an avenue of

---

22   Frères de Goncourt, *Journal*.

lindens, overlooking the ample curve of the Seine, which reaches Rouen within a distance of barely 2 kilometres. The rooms of the house, even though numerous, are large. A long corridor divides them. On the ground floor there is a vast study – made luminous by five windows that open onto the garden – where G.F. passes most of his time.

The seasons, the river, the trees, the wind often disavow this corner of Normandy caressed by pregnant odours, toned-down colours. Croisset and Rouen, Rouen and Croisset, embraced by the Forêt de Roumare, by the Forêt de Rouvray, extend along the river amidst narrow, overlapping streets, hardened by dust when the summer heat or the winter frost crystallizes the silence, immobilizes the horizon, and *les canards viennent tous de Rouen*[23].

At Croisset, the story of our G.F. intersects, with bizarreness and anxiety, with that of Antoine-François Prévost, who had stayed, and for some time, in the same habitation as a guest of the Benedictines of Saint-Ouen – even if it was a hundred years earlier.

Were there links between the two? Nothing is known for certain, or verifiably. It is possible and not improbable that our G.F. had inherited letters written by the Abbé Prévost, or had received accounts or discovered secrets of the ecclesiastic, who, let us remember, led a life that was very tormented, devious, and involved in obscure manoeuvres which constrained him to unforeseen flights, sudden returns, hasty moves, and changes of his conditions and places of residence without explicit notice.

Abbé Prévost stayed at Croisset – among other reasons – to write down his thoughts and annotate his writings. It was here that *Les Mémoires et les Aventures d'un Homme de Qualité - tomo VII, Histoire du Chevalier Des Grieux et Manon Lescaut* were created.

Dreams, troubled visions, counterfeited realities? *To penetrate into the heart which seems impenetrable ... and the secret paths, preferred by nature, give access to those capable of discovering them,* the *Mémoires* recite. In a dark night, on the road from Deauville to Rouen, on the outskirts of Pont-l'Évêque, our G.F. fell, bewildered and

---

23   All the tall stories come from Rouen.

unconscious, swept away and overwhelmed by a flaming torrent, amidst inscrutable dreams, disturbed visions and counterfeited realities. It was January 1844.

G.F.'s swoon was excruciating, it paralyzed feelings and desires. Why would one ever try to kill oneself aboard a calèche driving home? G.F. was swept away by the bewilderment of an unexpected loss of senses, of a lacerating solitude, of an uncontrollable raving in a Normandy evening, in the blinding flash of a distant sign, in the deafening sound of another calèche which rendered spaces tormenting, which overwhelmed him in the cold and fears of an indefinable disquiet, between agitated horses and the silence of the sky – in the face of a glance frozen with fear and of a nocturnal sky torn by flashes of lightning. Then, odours. Pregnant, suffocating, homicidal. The acrid reek of dung, the overwhelming stench of human urine, and gusts of wind laden with the smell of damp earth.

Our informants have gathered fragmentary information on the circumstances which determined this event. An arcane and enigmatic concatenation of events fell ruinously, so it seems, on the emotional fragility of G.F., who was certainly afflicted from infancy onwards by nervous debility, deep personal suffering, disconcerting manias.

G.F. accepted at this point – it hasn't been given to us to know whether by his own will or by the coercions of the hospital – a therapeutic methodology very much in vogue in your country, with curative interventions involving assiduous, stressful and debilitating blood-lettings, following the prescriptions of the illustrious clinician Monsieur le Professeur François-Joseph-Victor Broussais.

Our G.F. did not draw tangible benefits from such medical treatment. As documented by our investigators, a certain Doctor Alfred Hardy and another Doctor Fortin repeat even today that G.F. is only *une vieille femme histerique, une grosse fille histerique*[24]. Why *femme*? Why *fille*? We do not know.

---

24 A hysterical old woman, a fat hysterical girl.

Then, distinguished Muse, there is Mantes and the mysterious Hôtel du Grand-Cerf which, between 1846 and 1848, between 1851 and 1855, our G.F. frequented with assiduity, with maniacal regularity, with obsessive punctuality – punctuality in days and in hours. At the Grand-Cerf, even though the testimonies are sometimes vague and time has spoiled the records, it is certain that G.F. met a woman, it is thought *une putain remarquable*[25].

We have been able to obtain only scarce information about the woman. Her name is unknown, as is her nationality and profession. We are however persuaded that it is a question of a lady no longer young, who wore, it would seem, striking clothes – questionable, I would say reprehensible. Regarding this, testimonies agree – in particular, feminine ones. We have thus obtained a general portrait, or better, a seemingly truthful description of her habitual bad taste in dress.

One evening, for example, the woman rigged herself up for the meeting *in black taffeta. With the entire petticoat covered by a black lace tunic, with the corset generously cut low ... In the pleats of the skirt and on the corset ran two rows of little buttons of the same material. On her head she wore a hat of white lace and horizontal bands of blue French taffeta, ornamented with spring roses ... Then some jewellery ... a bracelet with amber stones, another of cameos. A portrait on ivory, surrounded by aquamarines, was the pin which fastened the corset*[26].

Abruptly, without apparent motive and without leaving traces, the woman disappeared – this was in March 1855. From then on she is nowhere to be found. We believe her to have taken refuge in Croisset – where in 1851 she had tried to make herself welcome and to live with G. F. as his wife. Nothing. We were afraid of some extreme action on the part of our G.F. Perhaps a homicide. Our hardworking detectives investigated in this direction. In vain. It nevertheless appears strange that no one should have announced the disappearance of such a woman. It is evident that it is a question of a poor derelict, alone, unknown, whom necessity had induced to practise ignoble licentiousness.

---

25 A remarkable whore.
26 Louise Colet, *Modes parisiennes*.

And was that woman – a lady of love for money – the inspiration for the scandalous little book written by our G.F., a book soaked with vulgar coarseness, shameful details of intimacy, the scurrility of a voyeur? Some deny such a connection. In their opinion the inspirer of that libel was a certain Madame Delphine Couturier Delamare of Ry, a woman of honourable habits, whom we have not succeeded in any manner to contact. She too has disappeared, it seems.

Is Emma Bovary our *putain remarquable*, or the honourable Delphine Delamare? An obscene little book by our G.F. narrates in fact the life of a certain Madame Emma Bovary. A title, *Madame Bovary*, which has scarce acceptance, but clarification comes instead from the subtitle: *A Tale of Provincial Life*, i.e. usages and customs significant in their ethical precariousness. It is precisely because of such a prurient and untruthful piece of writing that G.F. was subjected to judiciary proceedings.

Before the court, the accused, our accused G.F., showed himself to be arrogant, irreverent, impudent, while at the same time knowledgeable, erudite and adept in the use of words; and those of the Imperial Advocate, Monsieur Ernest Pinard, Public Minister, were pronounced resonantly in favour of condemnation. Arrogant, beyond what is permissible, our G.F., with that sort of tacit impunity which he is reputed to owe to whatever little piece of writing; he never showed signs of second thoughts, repentance, contrition.

But we come now to the contents of the piece of writing, that is to the imputation raised as the safeguard and defence of morality of those who think and behave wisely.

Madame Bovary, the novel by that G.F., was meant to recount and comment on excessive feelings, perhaps on social contrasts, perhaps on moral precariousness. Those were the intentions, perhaps. Our man G.F. *did not in truth follow this or that philosophical system. He painted only genre scenes ... in which the figure of Emma Bovary illumined other figures*[27]. An intrigue of desolating

---

27   Trial of Gustave Flaubert. Statement by the Public Prosecutor.

events, of the squalor of a childhood (Emma's childhood) in harsh circumstances, in villainous scheming, in repeated sensual deceptions, full of intrigues.

Madame Bovary was transformed into *Emma Bovary and her lovers* and, with goading and treachery, we experience in the onrush of pages written with harsh delight a succession of perverse loves, of cruel erotic games, of indecent winks of the eye. No regard at all for the etiquette of good intentions. What woman, oh sublime Muse! Oh illustrious Madame Colet! could possibly count in her life such an elevated number of lovers, of overwhelming passions?

We know well, divine Muse, that our words will make you indignant. Knowing the elegance and purity of your soul, we should not have had to tell you about such scabrous details, but only recount briefly the writings of G.F. *tout court*. To understand the behaviour of this person, to explore his contorted and corrupt soul, it has been necessary, however, to expose and go into details, even if with a certain brutality and through his writings, his instinctive vulgarity, his scarce intellectual flexibility – already cruelly undermined by the nervous disorders of his youth, by an irregular life, by uncontrollable sexual impulses. The frequenting of the *putain* of Mantes is a remarkable example of this.

To explain to you appropriately the unhealthy and vulgar lapses of our G.F., we shall transcribe for you a few passages extracted from *Madame Bovary*, taken from the summary of the Public Prosecutor: *Emma's eyes turned ... to something extraordinary. He* (the Duke de Laverdière) *had lived at court and slept in the bed of queens ... every evening* (Charles Bovary) *... found a well-dressed woman* (Emma), *charming with an odour of freshness, though no one could say whence the perfume came, or if it were not her skin that made odorous her chemise ... Domestic mediocrity drove her* (Emma) *to lewd fancies, marriage tendernesses to adulterous desires ... And she cursed herself for not having loved Léon. She thirsted for his lips ... They* (Emma and Rodolphe) *looked at one another. A supreme desire made their dry lips tremble, and softly, without an effort, their fingers intertwined ... The cloth of her* (Emma's) *habit caught against the velvet* *of his* (Rodolphe's) *coat. She threw back her white neck, swelling with a sigh, and faltering, in tears, with a long shudder and hiding her face, she gave herself up to him.*

Is this art, Madame Colet? In the judgment of most people it is a matter only of the writing of a man who is psychologically unstable, certainly afflicted with grave disturbances, manias, with a morbid sensuality. *Art without rules is not art*, Monsieur Ernest Pinard, Public Prosecutor, has affirmed. Proceeding with his words we add: *We must impose on art a single rule: to obey public decency is not to enslave art but rather to honour it.*

We do not know, Madame, the verdict of the Tribunal[28] because our investigators have not provided any details or clarification about it. We must in any case maintain, and with good reason that, beyond the verdict itself, our G.F. will be judged and excoriated as a clear social and moral peril. Indeed, his French amours, his frequentations of brothels, his Egyptian adventures and misadventures provide us with ample and exhaustive confirmation.

Our informers then report on a beach and a phantasm. Eighteen thirty-eight and the beach of Trouville, the Hôtel Bellevue, the square of the Casino, the Avant Port for a juvenile passion of G.F. A love that was unrequited, indeed derided at times, but never forgotten. The shadow of that phantasm accompanies our G.F. even today. It appears and disappears, solicits letters, writes missives to keep alive the frenzy of a sentiment – perhaps platonic, perhaps secretly consummated, perhaps exhausted in a rape perpetrated by a woman named Élise.

The information regarding Élise is uncertain, often contradictory, as Élise herself is a contradictory, ambiguous woman, though reliable in propriety and temperament. Our investigations, Madame, were often hindered by impediments and obstacles which seemed to want to conceal facts and people essential for knowledge of the reality of those events.

The woman Élise conquered – this is certain according to a variety of gossip and chatter – the heart of our G.F. when he was

---

28   The Tribunal acquitted Flaubert of the accusation of having outraged public and religious morality, and good manners – Sentence published in the Gazette of the Tribunal: 9 February 1857.

scarcely fourteen years old, while Élise was a mature woman: she had already reached the age of twenty-six. Élise enchanted him and seduced him, leaving him overwhelmed with unrestrainable impulses, disturbed feelings, uncertainty about love.

About four years later – information attested to by several sources – G.F. obtained the full appeasing of the senses with another woman: a young and lovely wife who lived in Marseilles, a certain Eulalie. An overwhelming passion, without subterfuges, flesh drawn to flesh in the violence of nights spent in furious amorous assaults, degrading sexual rapports.

The youth of our G.F. was marked, as you can well see Madame, by unhealthy habits, perilous encounters, delirious desires, amorous precocities. He emerged from them confused, excited, illogical, and yearned for the whole of his life for amorous excesses, so that he took to frequenting brothels and finally kept company, for months and years, with the whore from Mantes.

Oh Divine Poetess, can love fall so low to the point of involving a fragile and ill young man in dissolute experiences? Today this boy has become a perfidious man, abandoned to the fury of the senses, to a deleterious lasciviousness, to an immoral and pornographic sort of writing. This man then yielded, simply to appease unwholesome wishes and desires, to the temptation of a journey in the Orient to experience perturbing exoticism, dissolute impulses, carnal passions.

Madame, our G.F. travelled in fact through the territories marked out by our great river only to appease erotic fantasies, to experience degrading promiscuity, to satisfy an ill-concealed and abject sensuality. In this regard we have collected sure testimonies, all in agreement, explicit.

Certain scenarios in Egypt satisfied the expectations of our G.F. They revealed, in fact, degrading and vilifying spectacles to one accustomed to frequenting the lower depths of the city, and to reaching, aboard a *dagabieh*, villages and towns along the banks of the Upper Nile, hidden to the eyes of the honest and of the gods.

An infernal itinerary, then. Our G.F. was compromised by immoral squalors, repudiated by intelligence. Recklessly he harmed himself just to obtain shameful pleasures. He practised sodomy and *possessio pubis*, he engaged in fellatio with both men and women.

The brutality of our account, Madame, will have filled you with horror. But you asked us for truth – truth without holding anything back, even scabrous details, little suited to the virginal ears of a poetess. We have respected your desires and, deferentially, we now ask your forgiveness for the crudeness of our words, and for the grim circumstances and events of which you, Madame, asked us to give an account.

Once he had arrived in Egypt, our G.F. busied himself in frequenting brothels, baths and streets of ill repute. Even today he is well remembered – in Cairo for example, when, starved for sex, he ran to the poorest houses to sully women dressed in *clothes which were blue or yellow, white, red – ample clothes which swayed in the warm wind*, to engage in filthy acts, to *enjoy solid flesh and stupendous derrières*[29].

At that time we were not keeping a watch on him or paying any attention to him, apart from anything else because he was the travelling companion of that gentleman Monsieur Maxime Du Camp. Then a few of his observations attracted attention. On our women: *the tits of the Egyptian woman are very pointed. Not at all exciting*; on our musicians: *persons of a strange fascination, feminine in their movements, with their eyes made up with antimony*; on the masseurs of the baths: *with their left hand they carry out their work, with the right they masturbate the member of the client*.[27] He is still well remembered. Not by chance!

But here we are, Madame Colet, on the voyage which brought G.F. to Esneh. Here we are, Madame, at the woman of Esneh, at the *almée* of Esneh – about whom you asked for detailed information. Here we are, Madame, at the famous night of March 1850.

On the woman we have reliable information. It is necessary, however, to take a step backwards to understand better her story, since the woman in question was an *almée*, a famous *almée*. A brief annotation first on the court of Muhammad Ali, in the year 1833.

---

29   Gustave Flaubert, *Lettres.*

The *almées* – the dancer caste, daughters of the Barmakids, who allured men with the amiability and charm of their dancing, and who diffused a joyous animation with their exuberant presence, with their fascination, with their seductive clothing – yes Madame, the *almées*, like the *ghawazi*, were removed from the city because they stirred up the emotions of the soldiers of the French garrison.

The laws of Muhammad Ali imposed exile or habitation in the seraglios, in noble palaces or in hideaways unknown to the authorities. Then came Abbas Pasha and things changed. First of all, he became completely infatuated by the smooth buttocks of Saphia – the most beautiful of the *almées*, the undisputed *émiz-el-nezl* – the leader, with ebony complexion and a noble aquiline nose, supreme mistress of the arts of gallantry and of dance. Abbas Pasha later repudiated her, overcome by his own tender affection for boys, with the desire to defend a healthy and orgiastic pederasty, with his own excitement in going on the hunt for curly-headed and very beautiful boys in the streets of Cairo.

The dancers, the gallant companions, the pleasing prostitutes – *almées* and *ghawazi* that they might be! – were, for this reason, peremptorily confined to Upper Egypt – principally to Esneh. Deprived of sustenance, *almées* and *ghawazi* practised, if only to survive, the arts of love: some with the taste acquired in the years and habits of palaces, seraglios, noble concubinage; others in the slovenliness of a habitual profession, though now carried out in old hovels and dumps, along the banks of the river, in narrow streets blazing in the midday sun, scarcely illuminated by torches at night.

However, this had nothing in common with the squalid meretriciousness of our *putain remarquable* of Mantes. That is obvious, Madame!

The *almées* and *ghawazi* know the secrets of love, the fascination of seduction, the sensuality of a gesture, of a look. A gentle legend pervades them: the pleasure of showing and hiding themselves, yielding or refusing while the perfumes and the curves of their body reveal the harmony of forms concealed by gauzes, by flowing hair, by feigned reluctance. In the end, the genitals open gently to coitus.

It is poetry, Madame, true poetry, that our *putain* scandalously profaned in the alcove of a hotel room, conceding herself without grace, chattering of purity and sacrifice, morality and contempt of feelings, while G.F. enjoyed her vice-ridden graces in the most contemptible manner. The most reliable witnesses have passed on these particulars to us. Let us return to the story of the travels of this character G.F. in our country. G.F. engaged in dissoluteness, betrayed the rites of hospitality, held the women and men of Egypt in contempt. Indeed, he frequented precisely the places where pleasure was offered most cheaply: women in the grip of sexual aberrations, boys brought up with the sexual market in mind, young men trained in sodomy.

The unbridled immorality of G.F. became an obsession for *the quick motion of a muscle, for a veil resting on the hips, for a pelvis, for a woman who lies down to let herself be kissed on the stomach, the derrière, the lower back.*[21]

Thus G.F. planned escapades in a country where the women *are nude ... and covered only with rings.*[21] He fantasized Nubian girls who let themselves be *kissed, who had necklaces of gold pieces which descended as far as their thighs,* and had coloured beads on their black bellies. He fantasized erotic dreams, and lost all reason.

But here we are at Esneh. Here we are in the citadel of Upper Egypt to which you seem to attach particular importance in this reconstruction of facts and events. It was difficult to gain information on that particular visit of G.F.: to Esneh, on his stay there, on the night for which you are seeking information and details. It is true that we had irrefutable dates. We were thus able to revisit, with the help of the registers and books of the local *Mondir*, the arrivals and departures of men who disembarked from cangias, *dahabieh* or *bari*.

We know – an essential matter – that at the court of that woman – Saphia in Cairo, but Koutchouk-Hanem or *petite princesse* at Esneh – at her court there lived a young and very beautiful Ethiopian slave, Zeinab, who would have been able to furnish us with clarifications on the facts, events and meetings of that year, 1850.

The young and extremely beautiful Zeinab is no longer either young or very beautiful. A painful and cruel existence has withered her limbs and marked her face. She lives in the slums of Esneh, along the banks of the river amidst square towers, low houses and markets seething with merchants and money-changers, in a nauseating stink of sex, heavy with the smells of sweat and sperm.

Of the dwelling-place of Koutchouk-Hanem, the *petite princesse*, the Saphia of former times, we have instead only vague and contradictory indications. Certain people affirm that she is – now for some time – at Carthage, where the moon *was spreading her light at once upon the mountain-circled gulf and upon the lake of Tunis, where flamingos formed long rose-coloured lines amid the banks of sand, while further on beneath the catacombs the great salt lagoon shimmered like a piece of silver*[30]. Her name seems to be Salammbô. Others affirm that she is in France, at Sens, in the Yonne, where she lives under the name of Zoraide Turc, courtesan and instructress in *Éducation Sentimentale* to a certain Frédéric Moreau. Names doubtlessly inexact and untrustworthy, since no traces have been discovered at Carthage, nor by our investigators at Sens, in the Yonne.

Let us return to Zeinab. She has provided us with details, particulars, confidences. She remembers perfectly that March of 1850. She remembers the visit of our G.F., who they called Abou Shenab – the father with whiskers. She remembers that night, between 6 and 7 March.

Abou Shenab arrived at the dwelling of Koutchouk-Hanem accompanied by another man, who was extremely thin, and a dragoman called Joseph, in the early hours of the afternoon of 6 March. Abou Shenab was handsome, Zeinab affirmed, *of a heroic beauty ... He had a somewhat pinkish complexion and fine hair. He was of an imposing stature and build. Enormous eyes, lively, mobile ... of sea-green*[31]. He was dressed in Nubian style, with a long white cotton shirt ornamented with tassels. He wore a red fez on his head, which was shaved except for *a tuft of hair on the back of his head so that Muhammad could seize him on the day of judgment*[32].

---

30   Gustave Flaubert, *Salammbô*.
31   Maxime Du Camp, *Souvenir littéraires*.
32   Gustave Flaubert, *Lettres*.

This man, bizarrely dressed in Oriental style, was billing and cooing, uneasy, excited, and tried in every possible way to obtain the favours of the *almée* of *almées* – of Koutchouk-Hanem, the *petite princesse*, who was a grand and splendid creature, whiter than an Arab, with solid flesh, abundant breasts, anointed with a pink essence, with the flavour of sugared resin.

Zeinab remembered the warm light that enveloped Koutchouk-Hanem when she appeared in the court where Abou Shenab and his friends were waiting. She had barely come from the bath, and wore wide white pantaloons striped with pink; on her feet she wore yellow slippers, on her superb body a gauze veil. Her eyes were marked with *kohl* while gold coins tinkled amongst the tresses of her hair and golden bracelets adorned her wrists.

They drank in the ample salon. They drank *raki*, a beverage made of rice, fermented in chalice-like glasses. They spoke softly, softly engaged in amorous skirmishes. Then, to the strident sound of the rebecs, to the cadenced rhythms of drums, the *almée* of the *almées*, the *petite princesse*, Koutchouk-Hanem, began to dance, yielding her body to studied rhythms, to refined sensuality, to troubling eroticism.

She rose up lightly on one foot, then on the other, with adroit, gracious movements. Everyone remained *astonished by the mobility of her limbs ... The glances, the gestures, the winks expressed something indefinable, fascinating, exciting ... The undulating veils revealed bare arms, a very beautiful body, finely-shaped legs, an inviting sexuality. Her braided hair fluttered on her shoulders, on her face, between her tightly-closed hands, on her shaved thighs, amidst the scents of roses*[33].

Koutchouk-Hanem danced again. She danced with a tambourine resting now on one knee, now on the other. Her torso curved, her head bent. She played with infinite grace, Koutchouk-Hanem, beating her fingers lightly on the skin of the drum while the sun's rays caressed her, played with the polychromy of her clothes, created sensual shadows on the hollow of her pudendum, gilded the sweat of a vibrant, tense, lewd body – which excited, which was excited.

---

33   Anne-Jean-Marie-René Savary, *Memoires.*

Then evening arrived, recounted Zeinab, continuing her story. The wicks of the oil-fuelled candelabra blazed, fastened to the wall. Yellowish shadows swallowed up the room, then bodies, faces and movements assumed different aspects, more seductive, more excited, more intimate. They drank, and drank, *raki*. Then they danced with furious passion to the point that they were exhausted, overwhelmed with tensions, tiredness, alcohol. Then Koutchouk-Hanem said that it was time to go to bed.

Zeinab's account ends here, Madame. There is no further description of the night, neither indiscretions nor suppositions. Zeinab retired to her room. She saw Abou Shenab only fifty days later when he reappeared with a cangia at Esneh, and rendered homage to the *petite princesse*, to Koutchouk-Hanem.

This much, Madame Colet, we have verified since and – this is to be believed – nothing else of relevance occurred. Our inquiries ended at Esneh, as you requested and ordered us. In conclusion of our assignment, we cannot fail to ask you, Madame, for the high honour of considering us your humble and devoted admirers, some remark from you, a word, a hendecasyllable which would satisfy our devotion to you. Hence we await verses in which you will have the courtesy of celebrating the illustrious Isma'il Pasha, Viscount de Lesseps, the Canal, the city of Cairo, the Nile, Egypt

Allah Kerin, Allah Akbar, God is merciful, God is great.

Office of the Khédive

Governorship of Kasr-el-Nil Province

Croisset, the Pavilion.

From the forced confines of sedentariness

My dear Max, my friend Du Camp,

The Muse – our divine Muse, Louise Colet – is out of control. She is free and poisonous as always. After visiting Egypt, she is giving free expression to her eccentricities, and dangerously. She has been and still is conducting an investigation into me, into us. She is seeking piquant details about our lives, she is searching out the virgins we raped with the ancient art of Bedouin gallantry when the Barmakids were supreme procurers and pimps.

To put it in a nutshell she investigated without restraint or modesty. She unleashed a pack of voracious dogs with the very worst kind of sense of smell, even on the trail of the sublime Koutchouk-Hanem, debasing our feelings and passions when, for example, we remained enchanted, in Upper Egypt, in admiring the resplendent yellow gradually extinguishing itself in the West in a single pure and dazzlingly white light, or when Esneh made haste to hide the houses of the *almées*, sheltering them behind the portico of an ancient temple.

The folly of the Muse, of our Muse, is unpredictable, between disgraceful senility and long-meditated vengeance. I foresaw for some time her senseless revenge, for about twenty years as she scourged herself, proclaiming herself a holy virgin while at the same time giving herself like a vulgar whore. In what way can we stop this Erinys? Your good offices, your advice, your suggestions would be welcome to me.

I place myself in your hands, Max. I am not asking you to investigate, to sniff the air like a bloodhound, but I ask you to intercede with friends, acquaintances, protectors, so that the Muse might mitigate her mania for making up verses or drawing up prose accounts with the intention of divulging damaging information on her birth, her forebears (whom she believes to be illustrious), on her lovers (among whom were some who were celebrated and of a certain usefulness), but above all on me.

If I ask around, among friends and enemies, both ours and hers, they are terrorized merely by the sound of her name. If only we can close ranks, we can banish her. In Egypt, at least, Isma'il Pasha and the Court of Miracles of Viscount de Lesseps are fascinated by our Muse. Don't ask me why! She obtained noteworthy personal success at the inauguration of the Suez Canal. She went off in a *ghizeh* to retrace the places to which we had ventured in our younger years. She searched for Koutchouk-Hanem, perhaps to make her a prisoner, to lock her up eventually in her house in rue de Sevres, to learn from her the art of seduction, of being a courtesan, of erotic dances.

In the meantime, she left menacing messages, recruiting very dubious characters with the main intention of robbing us of our memories. *Mon cher* Max, I am living in the well-founded fear that this ancient monster of blonde beauty, of vanity, of presumptuous immorality is holding salons about us. If, according to the witty gossip of Barbey d'Aurevilly, the Muse and her friends have chosen to conduct this type of salon life, they will find themselves with a fistful of flies, because they know nothing except how to linger over idle chatter, devoted to the pleasure of revenge, whose artifice exalts them and gives them erotic gratification.

You ask me often, *mon cher* Baron, why the illustrious city of Aix-en-Provence, which gave birth to Madame, exiled her, sending her off to Paris armed with a permit enabling her to freely carry out forays into Rouen, Mantes, Croisset. Is there no pretext, prohibition or other possibility that might keep this Muse far from these places, she who has sworn to profane them, to shake them out of their provincial torpor and throw them into the existential chaos of lewdness to which she is so suited?

Nonetheless the Poetess is maliciously guilty of a very grave fault, *mon cher ami*. Only with great difficulty could she extract herself from an accusatory trial instituted against her with judicious discernment and moral conviction. As an Aixoise, that is as a native of Aix, and thus a descendant of a race so iniquitous and bloody, she has in her genes the grave sin and inextinguishable responsibility connected with the obscure affair of the Ursulines in 1602, regarding above all the condemnation and capital execution of Louis Gaufridy, priest and exorcist, who underwent, prior to his death, torture and savage villainy, even though he had demonstrated, *to all appearance, deep repentance – which was not believed, just as it was not believed that he had told the entire truth*[34].

The Muse, if only as a descendant of this barbarous lineage, ought to purify herself, otherwise she could be accused of witchcraft, since, and spontaneously, she declares herself to be a thaumaturge, a woman of occult powers, and she goes around spreading gossip about my obscure malady and her therapeutic intervention.

---

34   Acts of the trial of Louis Gaufridy – Bibliothèque d'Aix.

You know the truth well, *cher ami*. If my old illness sometimes is allayed in silence, I owe it to a regular, temperate life, but also to the very wholesome journey we took together in the Orient. But all the same, anguish remains anguish. Thus the violence that burns my eyes. Thus the pallor that freezes the sweat of unexpected fainting fits, spells of confusion. Thus the desperation of the senses, at times subjected to false perceptions. Thus the catalepsies that become a refuge, peace and silence in the midst of torment.

The Muse was instead a pernicious companion. Her road was strewn with famous corpses. Metaphorically or not. Your epigraph about her – and which outraged me, it is true! – aptly traces the profile of the Muse, renders her justice, offers her little in the way of escape. Thus her invocations as a betrayed and abandoned woman are empty.

Here lies the one who compromised Victor Cousin, who ridiculed Alfred de Musset, who held Gustave Flaubert in contempt, who tried to assassinate Alphonse Karr[35]. And the others, *mon cher* Baron? You will remember the long list of names which the Muse has available to dig up treacherous terrains, to instigate sentimental blackmail, to enrich those writings of hers, based on events occurring in the delirium of the senses.

I don't know whether her other bed-companions, of the bed of Madame the Poetess, have gone through the same vexations, if they too were subjected to obsessive tantrums, to bothersome investigations, to annoying and senseless pressures. Meanwhile I am discovering, in the iniquitous investigations of Madame, vices and stratagems that I never believed part of human nature, which seemed to be exclusively literary or born from the imagination. Do you believe that the Muse belongs to the human race, despite turning out a literature seasoned by a strange and sterile fantasy?

I implore you, *mon cher ami*, reassure me. I sometimes have the sensation of dreaming with eyes open, of detecting behind me the black silhouette of our Poetess, who is trying, with malign

---

35   Maxime Du Camp, *Souvenirs littéraires*.

impudence, to drag me into the bedroom of some inn of the lowest order so that she, in jodhpurs and with a riding-whip, can read me her celebrated dithyramb *A ma mère* or the poem dedicated to Alfred de Vigny, *L'Acropole d'Athène.*

What worse nightmares can there possibly be? *Soit, soit*, as you usually say. Think of those poor Egyptians at the mercy of the Muse. I have not been indoctrinated in their way of thinking but, knowing well their cunning, they will have made *bonne mine à mauvais jeu*[36]. They will have benevolently welcomed the Muse, they will have listened to her delirious words, they will have promised *monts et merveilles*[37], and in the end they will have cajoled her with some pleasantry of little count.

What else can one offer to requests and reasons that refer to events that happened twenty years earlier? What else can one put forward to hoodwink and deceive a Muse accustomed to making use of a thousand wily tricks to get herself taken seriously, and to corrupt with the graces of a virginal lady? Armand de Portmartin, the *vieux critique*, saw it well: the Muse, this Muse of ours, with her contorted mentality, perfidious to the point of creating an uproar, would be capable of burning down ten houses and a church only to get herself talked about.

Undeniable is the obstinacy of the Muse in dragging up the past, in putting herself forward today as the prison-keeper of my existence, enquiring and eavesdropping, with scurrilous malice, at the keyhole of my memories. In Egypt, at the inauguration of that blessed canal, within the glory of the *great collective labours which are perhaps the ultimate form of the outlines and preparations of monstrous conflicts of which we have no idea*[38], she searched, Madame the Poetess, a place which might do her justice and which I had frequented and later abandoned.

The Muse has never been a tranquil woman, respectful of the feelings and lives of others. She is invasive, possessive, indiscreet to the point of tedium. She has consumed, with her

---

36 The best of a bad situation.

37 Heaven and earth.

38 Gustave Flaubert, *Lettres.*

blonde grace and languishing simpering, an entire generation of intellectuals, she has engulfed some of the most brilliant minds of our epoch. Still not content, and now mature in age, she has taken to investigating and enquiring into the past to provoke new troubles, to be tediously importunate, to make herself definitively hated.

Our Muse, *mon cher* Max, has never known or wanted to accept the shadow of anonymity, to which she seemed inevitably condemned, in which it was permissible and legitimate to foresee that she would have finished up after having stirred up so much dust, after having long played the role of the beautiful statuette. Worse as a writer, worse as a woman. She tried to become a George Sand and has ended up a caryatid who has put into print poisonous little books and verses.

This blonde Muse, *tall, strong, rather masculine, whose amorous adventures, in other times, would have created a great stir*[39], has remained an immodest libertine as you well know! She has always concealed herself behind victimization, behind factitious virtue, behind her disconsolate acts of contrition. A whore with few equals, and like few others rich in sensual virtuosities which make you lose your reason when she gives herself to you with zeal, with the vulgarity and presumption of ravishing your member.

She certainly possessed no hidden virtues and yet, a few months after her arrival in Paris, had gained a discreet fame which was rapidly transformed into impudent acts of intemperance. Was *L'Artiste* a review or a brothel? Dear Max, as you well know, the Muse had *de gros affaires dans les mains et tira les choses en longeur con Monsieur Ricourt e con Louis Boulanger*[40]. With Victor Cousin she comported herself diversely. It was the manna she was waiting for and the Muse ate it until sated.

Why ever did she go to Egypt to unearth traces and matters which we had thoughtlessly left unguarded and ill-concealed? Ought we have brought her with us on our travels, so that she

---

39   The best of a bad situation.
40   Major affairs in her hands and and prolonged relations with Monsieur Ricourt and with Louis Boulanger.

could have learned to make love like the whores of the Orient? Do you remember Max, do you remember Keneh? Do you remember that large woman called Osnah Taouileh who fucked me only because I had beautiful eyes? She was a great sow of a woman with a great big arse. What a good time we had, how we enjoyed ourselves, she was really wild!

And our Poetess? She would be filled with horror at the sight of so much voluptuous pleasure, of so much amatory skill. Certainly she would not have felt envious because of inexperience, because as to experience Madame was second to none. In the years in which she was my mistress and Hippolyte's wife, the Muse was fucked by Victor Cousin, by that Christien Polonais, by that other Franc Polonais, by Franz Noller, by the deputy Bancel, by Octave Lacroix, by Auguste Vetter. A web of relationships and ties difficult to imagine. Nevertheless, she swore that she loved only me, that I was her unique, great love.

If Madame had come with us, if she had visited with us the brothels of Cairo, the Turkish baths, the lurid dwellings of the *ghawazi*, the welcoming houses of the *almées*, she would have been scandalized, because she loved to be scandalized when the talk was of sex, even though she didn't disdain to behave like a whore, to lie down holding tightly between her thighs a rose that she had been given, or to attend to her man in her hospitable arms to become *a warm sweetness which melts and inebriates*[41].

The divine Muse knows how to vindicate herself in the eyes of the world, lavishing with full hands the elegance of her own squalid soul, pure but also inspired with elegiac and sentimental virtuousness. *Tout semblait rayonner du bonnheur de nos âmes / la nature et le ciel confondaient leur splendeur*[42], she wrote, believing what she said. An insolent dishonesty? She was obscurely overcome with remorse, with the thirst for redemption, with the temptation of appearing virginal even after having copulated in each and every kind of circumstance and occasion!

---

41 Gustave Flaubert, *Lettres*.

42 Everything seemed to irradiate our spirit with fortune / nature and heaven mingled their luminous beauty.

Mantes has now turned into a squalid little city, because the Muse has rendered it squalid. I loved Mantes very much, but today the sight of it fills me with disgust. Did you know, *mon cher* Max, the Hôtel du Grand-Cerf? It is a welcoming refuge where one can fuck in complete tranquillity without having to frequent the brothels of Paris – at least, for me. However, in the brothels you find more vivacity, lightheartedness, sincerity. Mantes was for me a lugubrious bawdy-house with fixed hours, with the Muse to poison one with her fears, her perplexity, her fits of remorse, with her unappeasable desire to be a whore and an angel at the same time.

I managed to dig myself out of other wretched sentimental hotchpotches, happy enough to pay a heavy price. With Élise, for example. Even though I loved Élise. I loved her *immoderately ... without being requited. I loved her profoundly, silently ... because each of us has in his heart a royal room, which I have walled up but not destroyed*[43]. I have conserved intact the memory of Élise since, without hope. I watched her *bathing at Trouville, along the beach of my passions, and the gentle and calm waves wrapped up her flanks and covered that panting breath with foam ... There was in me something intimate and sweet which drowned in ecstasy, in most beautiful thoughts*[44].

The Muse has never aroused such profound feelings in me. However, I loved her, and she loved me. But Élise, Élise had *stupendous hips, hips that were truly womanly, which curved out above two slender thighs ... while the sweat which pearled her skin seemed to give her an aura of freshness*[45]. Élise perhaps loved me quite differently.

The Muse loved me, hated me, tyrannized me, *mon cher* Max. She experimented with emotional revenge, words laden with contempt, menacing innuendos, insolent allusions, falsehoods, and even the dolorous plaint of a ravished virgin. I was, according to her, a calamitous roughneck because I belonged to the world of pleasure-seekers, of smokers, of cursers, while Madame, beautiful and virginal, aspired to a certain veneration as an austere and God-fearing Muse.

---

43   Gustave Flaubert, *Lettres*.
44   Gustave Flaubert, *Mémoires d'un fou*.
45   Gustave Flaubert, *Novembre*.

You well know, *mon cher* Baron, that the Muse is irascible, vindictive and harsh if one doesn't offer her the respect that she demands. Ours was not an easy love: each time we encountered each other there arose *a discussion, a quarrel, a sulk, a wounding word*[46]. It was what it was, but for what recondite motive did the poetess go off to Egypt in search of gossip? She is pondering the possibility of writing, I am sure of this, some worthless book full of our Oriental escapades and of her wild state of mind.

She has never understood love, even though she ate it up by the handful. Poor Cousin succeeded in escaping from her clutches when by then he was discredited as few others have been for having, among other things, begged that the Poetess receive a life-membership and prize from the Académie Francaise. He had his own benefits they say: perhaps it's true, but liberty is worth much more than a fuck, even if it's with a poetess laureate like our Muse! To paraphrase Michelet, I agree with what you have repeated to me many times: *there's nothing but to try the impossible.* We ourselves tried it in exploring the pleasures of the flesh in the Orient, even if at times with displeasing setbacks. Remember Beirut, *cher* Max? That time you couldn't sample the amatory skills of the Lebanese women because *your cock was painful from the effects of an ulcer that you had picked up in Alexandria*[47]. Do you remember Max, do you remember?

Cher Baron, now you can no longer fail to assume your responsibilities. I know perfectly well that you will smile at this, shake your head, thinking of me *as a poor boy locked up in his solitary life*[48]. But you, *Bedouin with a slender, curved foot and hair as frizzy as that of a Negro*[48], you are as compromised as I am. What were you doing in June 1851?

If in that year, in that month, my relations with the Muse were ending as they had to end; it was because I, the most helpless lunatic, who went *from Rouen to Croisset to Paris, dreaming of spaces, deserts, biblical river*[48], I could not act differently. You, Max, you

---

46   Gustave Flaubert, *Lettres.*
47   Gustave Flaubert, *Notes de voyage.*
48   Maxime Du Camp, *Souvenirs littéraires.*

didn't dare take up my defence and consigned me to the mercy of the beautiful Poetess.

The Muse then asked for your comfort, your advice, your intercession, she solicited you as a scatter-brained panderer. You, avoiding the elegant phrases *cleverly constructed, harmonious, resounding ... those which can be included in any discourse without changing its meaning*[49], you wished to be very amiable and judicious, and you advised the Muse, betraying me shamelessly, to follow her instincts, to hurry to Croisset to convey news to me which might interest me ... and to convey obsequious respects to my mother.

Lunacy had taken possession of you, that's clear. Fortune had it that I, as always, kept my sangfroid and, locking doors and windows, prepared myself to put up a strenuous and courageous resistance. It wasn't easy to stand up to a woman beside herself with humiliation and anger, ready to strew ashes on her head, to dance nude in my garden, to bribe the servants, to get fucked without reining in her lasciviousness in the least, to cry out to the four winds that she was the most distinguished of whores if only ... if only to be welcomed in my house, by me and my mother, like a new *petite princesse*[50].

Madame the Muse was raging, sullen, indomitable as always. I was right about her violence, showing myself haughty, contemptuous, indomitable as always, and urging her to meditate on her immoderate behaviour as a *maîtresse*, as a brothel-keeper, as an old provincial whore, exhorting her also to get the better of her past, with her activity as a woman of the world, illustrious poetess and young widow.

I finally had some sway with our Muse, celebrating reminiscences and memories which moved her, made her more aware, silent, sensitive, controlled. I evoked with a perfidious hotchpotch of words – I admit it – the liturgical figure of Hippolyte, of a husband, of her husband.

There is no doubt, *cher ami*, that the Poetess was not thinking of her widowhood and that the death of Hippolyte had been for

---

49   Gustave Flaubert, *Notes de voyage*.
50   Little princess

her a disagreeable incident that had prevented her from having amorous encounters and from frequenting salons. At the same time, the image of a deceased husband seduced her because of that singular and charismatic fascination it suggested, for the poetic charm it evoked.

The Muse fell into a swoon. She let herself be led by the hand through evocative memories, then expressed encomiums and regrets for past times, displayed a careless commotion for the departure of her noble consort.

I believe, *cher* Max, that you never had the opportunity of making the acquaintance of Hippolyte Colet. However, I'm sure that, as a refined cultivator of bourgeois ease, you would never have been able to accept the plebeian vulgarity of Hippolyte who, as I well remember, gave his unfaithful spouse tit for tat amidst licentious scurrility, uncommon boorishness, obscene verbal flourishes.

Triviality was the virtue proclaimed by our Muse, who will have had the opportunity, in her journey in the Orient, to enrich and colour her own glossary with vulgarities learnt from sailors and whores of all races and kinds. She will certainly have noted in some memoirs, as is her habit, the expressive scurrility of the women in the brothels with whom often, in horror, she liked to identify herself.

Do you believe that this would be sufficient to justify a journey of Madame in Egypt? I am looking for reasons plausible for us, unknown for her. I turn respectfully to you so that you can enlighten me with your sagacity and your wisdom as an old scoundrel. True it is, *mon cher ami*, that protagonism has always guided our Muse. I wasn't suspecting however a voyeuristic frenzy with alienating forays amidst celebrations, literature and brothels. Indeed, it seems to me pathetic to look for traces of our past after twenty years, to initiate investigations about us, to solicit research on Koutchouk-Hanem.

Do you remember, Max, the *almée* of the *almées*? Do you remember, *mon ami*, when she welcomed us into her house at Esneh, on that hot afternoon? We were sweating with excitement, and you couldn't manage to rein in your cock. You burst out, with a grave and serious tone, that you would like to enjoy yourself a little with her. She satisfied you, and shortly afterwards satisfied me as well, almost as if it were a toll necessary for entertaining foreign guests. We paid dearly for that bed, pregnant with the scent of resin.

Even today those memories are indelible. I cherish them in the secret depths of my soul, well knowing that in any moment they are capable of restoring to me a part of my life consumed in the frenzy of youthful furore. Why then would a Muse now have to cheapen these sentiments, making them coarse and shoddy?

I allow myself to be overwhelmed with melancholy and worry, my old friend. These recollections lead me into treacherous regions, seeking memories that may be roads to travel over again when one wants a bit of warmth, even at the risk of ineptly evoking misdeeds, even smiling with scarcely veiled sadness. Life already lived unrolls before my eyes in a sequence of extremely precious images, and I don't wish to hide from you, *mon ami*, that I feel defrauded of a part of myself, knowing the stubborn obstinacy of our Muse in investigating and wallowing about in the mud.

Today Croisset represents, in the sweetness of its colours, in its familiar sounds, in its lights and shadows, it represents, *mon cher ami*, its own omnivorous presence in the years gone by, in documents written without haste, in readings stretched out to savour the silence. Memories then become the instinctive game of confusion, of a solitary and strenuous bond between oneself and imagination. Figures are marked with the imprints of ancient perfumes intermingling among themselves, recomposing themselves in images filtered by nostalgia, involving you, allowing you to become aware of extraneous and hostile presences.

It seems then that the Muse wishes to debase our most secret intimacy, to lay bare expressed desires and furtive caprices, to display, in public squares and decent salons, our journeys into memory and into the alleyways of one or other kasbah. I should like, dear Max, putting reserve aside, that you strew sharpened knives in the path of Madame, so that painful lacerations might force her to come to her senses. I am convinced instead that you will do your utmost to negotiate an armistice, to promulgate this undeclared state of war.

You know how to use, as few others, the arms of mediation. You must however take into account the possibility that the Muse might discover, and this would certainly not benefit your reputation, what happened at Muglah, when your sexual intemperance prompted you to require masturbatory practices from a thirteen-year-old girl. I don't wish to alarm you, *mon ami*. Besides, Oriental girls are women already in the age of puberty. Among us, in our conformist Western world, this information would draw upon you the barbs of the right-thinkers and the ostracism of certain envious intellectuals.

Thus cancel Muglah from the Muse's notes. Convince her to restrain herself, to not base all her chances of revenge on pornographic books in which the adventures and scandalous behaviour of two obscenely immoral intellectuals are narrated. Not that I am afraid of licentious stories about my life, I am dismayed only in relation to the insult to memory, and Koutchouk-Hanem forms part of my memories.

I know that the Muse is implacably raging. So she has always been. She will take no pity on you, *precise traveller, fussy pedant who made daguerreotypes, made casts of the inscriptions, collected information; for you who were imposing and monumental when you smoked the hookah and recited the rosary; for you who just having disembarked ... was already excited by a Negress drawing water from a fountain*[51]. The Muse will have no pity for me who blushes for maternal charms, who kisses my mother every evening, who has a profound affection for my most affectionate mother, and who went to Egypt, Palestine, Asia Minor to fuck girls of every type, beauty and race, to the point of contracting *la pissechaude*[52]. The Muse will have no pity on either of us because we both engaged in filthy misadventures in the Orient.

There is little more that we can do, *mon cher ami*. Perhaps to rouse pity in Madame by illicit means, regaling her with tales of

---

51   Gustave Flaubert, *Lettres*
52   Gonorrhea.

anguish, setting out for her the errors of the past as mortal sins, for which today we are expiating the guilt.

I have various arrows in my bow. The important thing is to know how to use them in the appropriate way and with accuracy to put a definitive brake on the insolent investigations of Madame. I could write to her at length, for example, reminding her of my illness. Do you believe, *mon ami*, that I would obtain some results?

I was – I would write to her – extremely unhappy during my youth and you, Madame, know it. My faults, both of today and of yesterday, are the logical consequence of that strange state of confusion which assailed me in January 1844. At that point I lost my senses and my reason. I was no longer myself, to the point that I found myself transformed into a perverse satyr who assailed women, men and young boys, only to possess them. A regrettable phase of the malady, Madame, difficult to cure, impossible to control. Before then, Madame, I was only a timid and foolish sentimentalist.

You, Max, could indoctrinate her appropriately with convincing words, with your *savoir faire*. You could tell her about that beautiful Chilean girl. Do you remember that adventure of mine, Max? You must relate to the Muse this amorous event of mine filling it with touching notes, with sublime accents, with harrowing feelings. No sex, clearly, no fucking, no obscenity, fiery kisses or lewd desires. Recount to her the story of my heart shattered by love at the moments when, in that far away year, 1840, at Marseilles, I caught a glimpse of the supremely beautiful Eulalie, singing in a patio filled with exotic flowers, circled by a jet of water. It was, confess to the Muse, a youthful infatuation, the palpitations of an innocent heart, a sweet sigh of Platonic love.

Madame the Muse has been a woman of *longue orgie*[53], in view of which it was impossible not to ascribe to her certain bestial desires, carnivorous and lacerating instincts, while at the same time her blonde curls waved over her naked white shoulders. Often however – but I must beg your discretion on the matter – instinct and tactile sensations were transformed in me into a

---

53   Prolonged orgy.

mass of gloomy sensations, intertwining with disassociations of the mind and olfactory sensations, so that her naked body made me think of her skeleton, of the stripping-off of her flesh, of death. At such times the phantasms of the past appeared before me, the indelible visions of a childhood spent close to a room where autopsies were performed, in Rouen, at the Hospice de l'Humanité, where *mon père*[54], Achille-Cléophas, was head doctor, as you know well.

I submit myself to your good heart, to your tact, *mon cher ami*. You are very capable of finding a thousand solutions, you who know how to navigate in tempestuous seas, you who succeed in coping with the stolid perfidiousness of Madame la Muse, you are the elected one, *coram populo*[55], the saviour of our soiled souls and of our misdeeds. Neutralize Madame in the manners and times which you find most opportune and wise. My own feelings suggest homicide, a brutal assassination. A sentiment not at all absurd or senseless, true?

If you wish to effectively give relief to a wounded humanity, the one, let it be understood, which is hated by the Muse, write a perfidious little book about her, you are capable of it. If you dare to spread about that I am not suited to compose verses, *that I have never succeeded in understanding metre and rhyme ... that to Alexandrine verses I give a cadence of 11 to 13 feet and never of 12, that I am tone-deaf to the point that I have never succeeded in humming an air or a lullaby*[56], you will certainly know, with cunning gossip, how to fool Madame. A capacity for invention, perfidiousness, cursing, insulting and negative prose are gifts that belong to you, *mon cher* Baron. Will you have the courage to use them against Madame?

You genuflect like a servant knight, kneel down, prostrate yourself to the skirt-swish of learned ladies, of maidens endowed with prizes by the Académie. To other women, on the other hand, you offer your scurrilous language, obscene words, piffling

---

54 My father.
55 By popular consent.
56 Maxime Du Camp, *Souvenirs littéraires*.

advances, licentious groping. Your future will be tinged with darkness if you dare to betray me or accuse me of inventing circumstances and situations. It is true, *cher* Baron, that I have never heard or seen you go too far, in words or in gestures, *avec Mesdames* or Ladies, whereas I have surprised and admired you in your indecent and coarse performances with women of low standing, of a foul stench, of indisputable shamelessness, of indecent pandering. You have offered, *mon ami*, very unedifying spectacles to whomever thought you a man of good standing.

Undoubtedly the Muse will discover your vices, dragging up our Oriental explorations, our Parisian life. You will in no sense benefit from the investigations which Madame has conducted or will conduct into me, because, on reflection, she will learn also of your *affaires. Mon cher ami*, I want you on my side, even if fear-stricken, even if you're afraid of the worst. Our tranquillity is in play, our desire to live life to the full without any interference. The Muse, now of mature age, has no other objectives in her life but to *déranger nos affaires*[57], like a worldly Mary Magdalene intent on denouncing obscenities and intemperate and excessive behaviour.

I should like to remind you that a certain melancholy forms part of my nature. I don't wish, *cher ami*, to provoke banal intrusions into this sentimental melancholy, which I hide and protect jealously. The Muse is no part of it: I informed her of it right from the beginning of our relationship, and with such clear emphases that denials of any sort were not to be feared. *When I first knew you, I said to her, I was ready to love you. I loved you. After I possessed you, I did not foresee the weariness that men imagine is inevitable. I was attracted to you with my whole heart ... and together we completed an impervious journey, an ugly path*[58], only to end up with nothing, with arid feelings, without inspiration or impulses.

Instead, the *almée*, the courtesan of Esneh, the *petite princesse*, Koutchouk-Hanem, marked me deeply. I remember every moment of our night of love. I remember the sky filled with stars, the tremulous lights of the oil lamps, the scent of resin, her

---

57   Meddle in our affairs and mess them up.
58   Gustave Flaubert, *Lettres*.

majestic body, her look, her lips, her warm and welcoming sex, the silence of love-making. In twenty years the recollections and the sensations I experienced have never weakened, vanished or changed. I relive even today the sensual rapture of her flexible movements, of the warm colours of her clothes. Why should one renounce one's own joy?

Cher ami, I don't know if the years have marked us. The detritus of memory appears today as signs of small indecipherable scars. Confidences like secrets, rarefied curiosities of time. The events of long ago seem now like stains, violated by successions of days, hours, minutes. What happened and what is happening. It is inevitable. The Muse is part of the detritus of time, of the dystonias of an open weave frayed by the precariousness of feelings.

Instead, Koutchouk-Hanem appears to me *as the light that envelops things, that penetrates like an atom into the depth*[59] of my most recondite feelings.

Adieu, mon cher ami. Adieu mon baron. Adieu, mon Max[60]. How lovely it would be today to regain and revisit the past, *to mount our horses, weapons in our belt, in the shade of some carob tree and watching a caravan of camels passing in the distance ... and the flight of a stork in the sky*[61]. And to run, Max, to run, *cher ami*, as far as Esneh, to the court of the supremely gentle and sweet *petite princesse*, crowned by the broad blue arch of the evening when the last rays of the sun explore the waters of the Nile. The silence, *mon ami*, makes the soul swoon, inebriates the spirit with the impalpability of perfumes, of spices, of wax, of rose-scented unguents.

Esneh, reconquered by the ancient pagan spirits, gives itself generously to memory, tempers itself slowly to the presence of new affections, of new silences, of new colours, sensations, fragrances, which surround me. Today Croisset embraces me, suffocating me in misty shadows, in chiaroscuro, in an earth sodden with rain, amidst chestnuts and yew trees, and a meandering of the Seine echoes the sound of one's breathing.

---

59 Gustave Flaubert, *Lettres*
60 Farewell my dear friend. Farewell my baron. Farewell my Max.
61 Gustave Flaubert, *Lettres*

Meanwhile, an aged mother travels along a road marked by the years, by pains, by profound feelings, by migraines, by funereal visions, by farewells, by my murderous love, and does nothing but brood on the accidents and incidents that could befall me, and to warn me, with obsessive petulance, not to misspend money even if there might be somewhere an entirely honest woman.

For you, *mon cher ami*, nothing remains but the road of redemption, of temperance, of eternal salvation. Choose the weapon, the moment, the manner most consonant with your dignity. It is opportune for the good of the Muse, for her recognized fame, for her imperishable glory in the future that you eliminate her rapidly, perhaps in a room of the Hôtel du Grand-Cerf in Mantes, or on the tomb of her defunct husband, Hippolyte Colet.

Adieu peuvre cher vieux. Mille tendresses. Je t'embrasse et j'ai une rude envie de te voir car j'ai beson de dire des choses incompréhensibles[62] and to have confirmation of your glorious misdeed.

A toi,

Gustave

---

[62] Gustave Flaubert, *Lettres*. Farewell, my poor old fellow. A thousand tender thoughts. I embrace you and I have a very strong desire to see you because I have the need to tell you incomprehensible things.

The Letter
Paris, 19 April 1885

Monsieur Bouvard,

I have things to tell you. Indications. Or better, addresses and words. I impose on them an urgent need. I will not seek to convince you: it would be useless. I will oblige you instead, with subtle shrewdness and veiled extortion, to accord me obedience. In these presumptuous orders and in these pretentious suggestions of mine, uncertainty and risk appear to be ineluctable presuppositions for docile obedience which, at the same time, I insist on and prescribe.

It is urgent and pressing, in substance and without scruples, that you do what I clearly and unequivocally ask, since you have to understand that they are dispositions which do not presuppose or imply denials or remonstrations. I urge you to prepare yourself, with humble benevolence and firm deference, to satisfy my demands, *juvante vel non juvante,* as my spiritual father, the Reverend Didon, *Ordini Sanctii Dominici Adscriptus et Meae Conscientiae Moderator*[63], suggests to me. Even if Latin – as this reverend father often reminds me – by which I have been conquered, I confess it without remorse or embarrassment, by a profound and absolute mystical love, indeed Latin which is a language congenial to man, spoils writing because one has need of it only to read the inscriptions on public fountains. This is a circumstance which it is sometimes necessary to distrust (and gladly), in that it often hides something profoundly and insolently

---

63   Of the Order of Saint Dominic and Guide of my Conscience.

improper, as is underlined by my illustrious uncle, Monsieur Gustave Flaubert, in his *Dictionary of Received Ideas*.

In truth, in the story which I am about to relate to you, in such surprising, indeed convulsive, events, my reasoning might appear only a hazardous and risky sort of testimony, an ill-founded conviction, and thus precarious, perhaps even incongruous and confused. You, in any case, acquitting the job I am entrusting to you and dissolving doubts as to the accuracy of the chronicles and events which I will narrate to you, will have to suggest and propose verifications, proofs and unarguable propositions, so that the uncertainty of the events themselves do not generate perplexity, illusions, hypocrisies, disloyalties and foolishness: in which case ambiguity might dominate, without equivocal events that merit, or rather might merit, absolute and unequivocal conviction.

I ask you, *in primis* (the Reverend Father Didon *docet et in amore inducit*) to consider (if you have not already had the opportunity to do so), with an attentive and courageous reading, the manuscript which accompanies this letter. You can ignore, if you like, the bearer of this missive, who is a person disfigured in his bearing and countenance, now that only the shadows of a stupefied blindness seem to guide him, although indeed without any excessive suffering or complaint on his part.

Never – and I console you in this – let yourself become involved emotionally by his petulant presence, which is adept in transforming itself often into disagreeable insolence and distasteful suffering, or by the sad occurrences which assail him, a product above all of a fervid imagination, or by his unending and tedious laments, worthy of his Levantine origin, or by his eloquent winks, accompanied by gestures and actions tried out and re-rehearsed with a presumably seductive effect, or by his maleficent and harmful fantasy, which convinced and influenced my uncle – at least so I interpret the matter having read about unseemly situations and having heard the testimonies of Uncle Gustave, to renounce him, repudiate him, abandon him in the negligence of solitude, leave him to himself without ensuring that he was, as was Uncle's initial intention (true or false as it may have been), the probable hero and protagonist of a novel on the Orient, of a book dedicated to excess, dense with memories accumulated in travels and memories of travels, packed with vagueness and restlessness, with frenzy and yearnings, of maniacal dreams and voluptuous fantasies, a book with the title *Harel Bey*.

This book which was to be a sort of journey, and whose aim was to become lost in the magical Orient, amidst scenes of ill-omened squalor and of uncivil lowness and dirty tricks, amongst slavish natives and European colonists from amongst other places Cairo, Mount Farchout, the banks of the Nile, Aswan, Girgeh, Alexandria, Jerusalem, Damascus, Rhodes, Constantinople, Smyrna, Syria, and so on and so forth, amongst cities and places that seem set forth by an eccentric and sensual imagination. And again, amongst granite obelisks, sweltering gardens, harems, the seductive bodies of women, severed heads, repugnant stenches of blood, nauseating odours of sperm, and hearts as arid as those of prostitutes, and senses drawn tight as violin strings, and ancient dances, and the intriguing moon matched with the minarets, and lanterns perfumed with resin, and the sound of the tarabuk, and palm trees and orange-trees, and mosques subjected to the play of jets of water, and the smoke of oily tobacco, and men dressed as women, and bodies of mellow fluidity, and the green sycamores oppressed by Veronese green plants, and palms full of sugary dates, and camels mounted by proud men, and the seductive eyes of the prostitutes, and the soft banks of a river, and the watermelons open to the aroma of the sun, and the bazaars loud with singsong voices, and caravanserai squeezed between courtyards and porticos, and the tombs of the caliphs, and the minarets, and the white veils of the cangias, and the sunsets striped by shrill colours, and the rapacious flights of shrieking gulls. The Orient, in fact! The plausible Orient of Uncle Gustave. A possible Orient that might have as protagonist the bearer of this present letter: Harel Bey.

This did not occur through wise consideration and instinctive artfulness. That Orient was only a testament to daydreams and longings. Uncle Gustave set forth projects and ideas which then became linked to other projects and ideas, while he remained stretched out, in Turkish style, on the divan in the salon of Edmond and Jules Goncourt at 41 boulevard du Temple. It was an ample salon with on the walls the best drawings from the precious collection of the Goncourts, *a tapestry ... that covered the ceiling ... ten ample armchairs and a huge divan, a writing-desk and a wardrobe: made of priceless Marie-Antoinette marqueterie ... in the corners two vases of Sevres porcelain ... in the centre a great bronze bowl ... finally, illuminated by a mirror without side-pieces but which revealed a wall of climbing plants, a chimney-piece composed of a statuette and two vases of Clodion terracotta*[64].

And in this salon, after dinner on a Sunday evening in March, after the days of the Carnival of 1862, Uncle Gustave spoke of his project, of his desire to write a story which would have as its protagonist a certain Bedouin who would respond to the name Harel Bey and who today has presented himself to you as the bearer of this letter.

In truth, this individual, or character if you prefer, has become, from this unfortunate moment and declaration of intentions, *et in secula seculorum*, a sort of phantasm, an indeterminate entity, a larval presence, hardly reassuring, troubling, and at times malign. This is how he should be considered. At the very most, to be as fair to him as possible, consider him a messenger with a determined will to survive, as a sycophant of intellectual salons, as an infamous divulger of lost or unknown manuscripts. It was he, in fact, who brought back to light – so at least he has the impudence to proclaim with diligent presumption – the manuscript which you now possess, and which I had brought to you by the very means of our man (*nuntius codicium et scriptum*, suggests that good man, Father Didon).

A manuscript, which I point out for your own conscience and to make you realize its merit, which is the occasion of my principal concern in the discussion of my letter to you, and on which I urge a boundless attentiveness and the most precise guarantees

---

64   Edmond Goncourt, *An Artist's House.*

of diligence and good will. In truth, nothing but complete dedication, which must be unconditional, as unconditional as my need to obtain sacrificial obedience.

I return to the moment: as I am writing to you from a study which opens upon a luminous landscape of the Cote d'Azur, there are zealous and quiet footsteps which draw near to me, which take pains to remain silent, to disturb me with their weighty presence. I am no longer able to enjoy intimacy and reserve. Turning my gaze behind me I am aware of a dark face, burnt-out eyes, with an untrustworthy gaze that spies upon me. The Bedouin seems to want to keep watch on me from close at hand, and with arrogance and insolence. I am constrained to submit – and this seems to me relentlessly inconsiderate – to distasteful examinations and close investigations, tactile and olfactory. I become aware of our ambassador as he molests me with his olfaction, sniffing the air while drawing closer and closer to my body, with a scurrilous sneer and nosing about obscenely even at intimate regions, with pretexts and wiliness, while an obsequious *salaam* enables his head to draw rashly close to my pubis. Thus, he literally sniffs me with repellent immodesty, and then begins to laugh sarcastically and to utter some rigmarole, babbling about the manuscript which he entrusted to me, accompanying it with untrustworthy words and deceptive circumlocutions.

I am sure that he is nourishing personal intrigues and ambiguous interests, which I, unfortunately, am not in a position to describe, nor do I have the capacity or the means to intuit what they may be, as his way of carrying on, bawling out stories stuffed with episodes and events, seems sometimes to be putting forward trustworthy fantasies, sometimes fantastic truths.

Without attaching undue importance to the words and gestures of our man, to his obsequious presence, to his proceeding silently with his investigation, to his disconcerting sniffing of the air, and, indecently, of my body, I have frequently asked him his name, his true name and not that with which he presented himself, boasting arrogantly of a solid and old friendship with my much-loved uncle, with Uncle Gustave.

He told me then, as he repeats today, that his name is Harel Bey, like the title of that story about the Orient that my uncle perhaps thought to write. The Bedouin also asked me, sneering sarcastically with sly and cunning glee, if this name aroused recollections in me, memories, images of the period, of a period passed: I don't know, truthfully, whether he meant exclusively in a piece of writing.

I know, however, with certainty, that he liked to create deceptions, and shamelessly. I well understood that he wished to involve me in illegal affairs, certainly very advantageous for him. Indeed, he well avoided explaining to me his intrigues and dramas, or whatever else he was cooking up in some labyrinthine scheme or other. I am convinced that he deliberately kept silent about his intentions and plans on matters which could be used to identify him – at least, so I suppose. Indeed, he spoke, albeit while claiming an equivocal filial friendship, of Uncle Gustave in a resentful manner. Despite recognizing that he owed my uncle a great deal, and while in the rambling talk and exaltation of a bizarre character he flourished words like *arbitrary existence and literary invention*, he never expressed a single word that might shed some light on his past, on the years of the relationship and friendship with my uncle, or on a very ambiguous series of adventures and circumstances, never properly clarified. No names, facts, events, meetings or witticisms.

Indeed, I have often asked myself, and above all in these last years, which characters in Uncle Gustave's books were in truth credible personages, and which ones unreliable, since at his death something extremely ambiguous happened, as always occurs at the death of a writer. That is, the manifestation of that odd and abstruse mixture of roles and presences for which it is probable that certain personages, profiting from the disappearance of my uncle and of the lack of vigilance on my part as the only heir, exited from the pages written by my uncle while others, not at all contemplated in the writings already issued or only imagined by my uncle, introduced themselves deceitfully into his books. And so today it is possible to encounter, in this or that story by my uncle Gustave, protagonists or secondary figures who have nothing to do with the original composition or with the primary idea that my uncle gave or wished to give to this or that story.

I have, in fact, had the opportunity to learn the truth, and indeed also to evaluate thoroughly hereditary rights and not fall into gross errors, that is those that can be prosecuted by law, establishing claims on the dramas whose characters are in fact creatures born from the fervid imagination of Uncle Gustave.

Let us linger once again on our Bedouin. I have the honour of informing you that he has deliberately withheld the truth about the manuscript, even as to its discovery. He spoke of a sumptuous house in rue St. Georges, a little beyond rue de la Victoire. Certainly the house of the brothers Goncourt, of those evil-tongued infidels who accused my uncle of being a violently litigious provincial exhibitionist. A passionate neurasthenic, since, according to them, Uncle Gustave liked to exhibit himself in gasconade, in telling dishonest, blusterous tales.

To support this claim they told me what happened on 12 January 1860, when, in the splendid room of the Goncourt house where the dining-table was adorned very elegantly to welcome people of high lineage, Uncle Gustave began to brag, affirming that if one wanted to make love with women it was sufficient to sleep at night on the side of the body where the heart is.

Then he reminded me of what happened on 2 December 1862, when Uncle Gustave, in reply to ferocious and vulgar criticism by Charles Augustin de Sainte-Beuve which referred to one of his works, burst out abruptly, violently affirming that Sainte-Beuve was nothing but a modest valet, capable only of slithering, with indecorous humility, at the feet of Prince Napoleon.

He reminded me then of what happened on 14 February 1863, on the occasion of another of those inimitable and superb suppers at the house of the Goncourts, when Uncle Gustave began to ramble on about Victor Hugo, declaring that if he was indebted to him in the matter of verse and knowledge of painting, nevertheless it was necessary, for love of truth, to recognize that Hugo concealed, to the nth degree and with levity, a great deal of coarseness in his writings.

And on and on: he began to remind me what happened on 1 November 1864 when, on the occasion of a festive evening among intellectual friends, Uncle Gustave affirmed peremptorily that between the ages of twenty and twenty-five he had imposed upon himself complete sexual abstinence, to demonstrate that he wasn't only an instinctive man ready to live, speak and think in a manner completely apart from what was natural, but that he was above all a man of will dedicated to an obedience which kept his vanity under wraps.

All this our Bedouin narrated to me now that he had been, for a long time and, he said with subtle malice, immemorially, an invisible guest in the house of the Goncourt brothers, in that house of 18th century taste, full of dust, books, worthless furniture, amidst furnishings, paintings and various knick-knacks. Amongst the various testimonials and notebooks, forgotten above all by Monsieur Maxime du Camp, lazy and untrustworthy – so claims the Bedouin – there re-emerged, by pure chance and casually, the manuscript in question.

Might it be true? Does one need to put faith in appearances and guises? Perhaps, or better, seemingly, since Monsieur Du Camp is the person destined to receive (if the manuscript is authentic, obviously!) letters and warnings in the first and third part of this same manuscript. And Monsieur Maxime Du Camp is a man of honour – in so far as it is possible to gather from the gossip of the literati. Most interesting, in my view, are the first part of the manuscript, where one can read the injurious and disgraceful perorations of a certain woman named Louise Colet – a woman, according to what I seem to be able to gather, who flowered at the age of thirty-five and was very finely fleshed so that she tried to pass for a great beauty, ruffling up her long hair with blonde curls like *une garçonne* – and the third part where it is possible instead to read the breathless and scornful confabulation of Uncle Gustave, who tried to justify gestures and actions which had been engaged in light-heartedly.

Monsieur Du Camp was in the habit of being, I remember well, a trustworthy and devoted confidant of my uncle, and from the time of the excursions in the Orient and in neighbouring zones. Only afterwards he became, with bad grace and ungrateful presumption, his unshakable contradictor of loves, of writings and of women to such a point that, at the death of my uncle, he considered it extravagant to send me even so much as a line of condolence, or flowers or a few remembrances. Indeed, when Monsieur Du Camp was elected to the Académie Francaise, my uncle repeated to me the maxim "*honours dishonour, titles degrade, positions demean*". In any case, it is fair to observe that, in relation to the rediscovery of the manuscript, Monsieur Du Camp was merely an occasional visitor to the home of the Goncourt brothers. And not at all an assiduous visitor like my uncle, who passed entire evenings in eating amply and well in the Goncourts' dining-room: *with the walls and ceiling covered with tapestry, crammed with drawings on blue backgrounds, among which we have hung Moreau's stupendous* Revue du Roi, *resplendent and enlivened by the evanescent glow of a Bohemian crystal chandelier*[65]. Around the table were Edmond and Jules de Goncourt, Uncle Gustave, Paul de Saint-Victor, Aurélien Scholl, Charles-Edmond Chojecki, Madame Julie Charles-Edmond and Madame Charlotte-Marie de Plunkett Doche, called Eugenie, with a *red net on her lightly powdered hair*. And so on and so on, passing time in uncontrolled chatter and in exhibitions of vainglory. As on that evening of 12 January 1860 in which Uncle Gustave, once dinner had ended and he remained alone in the company of the Goncourt brothers, with his eyes popping out of their sockets, *his face impassioned, his arms raised to the sky like a powerful Antheus, began to recite, with all the force he had in his throat and in his chest, fragments of* Montesquieu's Dialogue between Sulla and Eucrates, and which the same Montesquieu had read at the Club de l'Entresol in 1722, if I am not mistaken. Or also when that Friday, 1 September 1876, he began to recount that, and it was at the Goncourt house, *during the two preceding months he had remained closed in his room writing "*Un Coeur simple*" and had thus worked for fifteen hours every day ... a grind interrupted only by an evening swim in the Seine*[66].

---

65 Frères de Goncourt, *Journal*.
66 Frères de Goncourt, *Journal*.

More convincing, therefore, are the opinion and observations according to which the manuscript had been forgotten in the Goncourt house by Uncle Gustave, assiduous frequenter of that house, and not by Monsieur Du Camp.

The fussing about and the possible fraudulence of the Bedouin do not allow one to arrive at the truth, since so many ambiguous truths or even manifest lies are, for him, only ordinary precepts for confounding beliefs, ideas and written evidence.

Some timely mention now of the babbling of our *nuntius codicium et scriptorium* (does Father Didon concede too much honour to him, pampering him and apostrophizing him with such illustrious terms? Yet it is always pleasing to listen to Father Didon declaiming Latin with wisdom and competence) regarding the substance of the manuscript. Our Bedouin swears that he obtained the entire manuscript but he had copied for him in braille, by his trusted compositor, only a few pages and in a manner so as to be able to confront his own iniquitous blindness, and that, having read the excerpt and being persuaded that it involved an unpublished and unknown piece of writing, he silenced his translator in a cruel manner, thus liberating him from any obligation of absolute confidentiality.

He then saw to it that I would have the entire manuscript, insofar as I am the only heir of my uncle Gustave and because he assumed that I was interested in verifying its statements, and perhaps to draw from it speculative, affective and concrete interests. Thus I can offer you only marginal comfort in the paraphrases of our man, whose ambiguities are a constant, daily matter. Thus I give you only partial sensations, inane comments, constant mutterings, ill-digested considerations.

I do not know the treacherous traps set skilfully by the Bedouin, or his reasonings, or the chicaneries of his petulant pertinacity ensuring that the manuscript would reach me promptly, and that the facts and happenings would become public, rather become widely known in a villainous and malignant manner. It depends now on you to scrutinize and investigate its pages, and then to offer yourself, with concern and without fear or hesitation, to my needs.

Monsieur, I am turning to you, and only to you, in the certainty that your friend and companion, Monsieur Pécuchet, that is Monsieur Juste Roman Cyrille Pécuchet, is ill, as usually and by ill chance befalls him. Is he, in fact? Does he continue to be the faithful disciple of François Vincent Raspail and of his *Manual of Health* in which he demonstrates that all ills and maladies in their entirety originate in the bodily infestations of worms, which are capable of ruining the teeth, which eat into the lungs, swell up the liver, consume the intestines, and that the unique and universal remedy against them is camphor? Or has he become the faithful disciple of Armand-Jacques de Chastenet de Puységur and of his cure with magnetism, which is very easy to adopt, since it is sufficient to make use and take advantage of an old tree, or a young fruit tree, or even a bamboo-shoot, or a simple peduncle of a shrub as long as it is opportunely impregnated by magnetic fluid? Or perhaps he has become the faithful disciple of Monsieur Montacabère and of his guide for the magnetizer, which functions because it makes use of a common magnet as a unique and universal energy to recover from illnesses, insofar as only a magnet is able to uproot such maladies from bodies weakened by illness by the pure force of attraction? Does he treat himself now with such instruments and methods, since it is to be supposed that any possible healing of his can occur exclusively by a fortunate coincidence of miraculous circumstances and that, at the moment, he lies suffering from imaginary and imagined illnesses without arriving at any remedy even after such study, learning and speculation?

Thus, persuaded of the precarious and unsatisfactory conditions of health of your companion Monsieur Juste Roman Cyrille Pécuchet, I make so bold as to explain only to you certain requirements and necessities, and to invite you to lend yourself to my urgencies without perplexity or embarrassment.

Using your own judgment, you can confide the contents of this letter to your friend without scruples. At your own discretion you could also keep silent about our epistolary encounter, or recount untrue happenings, diverse causes, distorted truths. This will be and would be a useless incivility, because the Bedouin, who is already your guest at the moment in which you are reading this missive of mine, will be an impudent chatterer, and your friend Pécuchet, if present, will be informed of the letter and of our intrigues by means of very exclusive, artificial, fictional, perhaps even false words and signals. The truth, in essence, is an aleatory and suggestive certainty.

I wish to inform you, for your own profit, that I have chosen you as my only interlocutor – now that your companion Pécuchet is too much involved in his own speculative affairs – because you, Monsieur François Denys Bartholomée Bouvard, among the persons linked to my uncle through affection and consideration, possess a subtle and fervid knowledge, flexibility of understanding, of investigation, of shrewdness. Qualities and merits that you owe, and I believe you well understand this (as, if you did not understand, it would be useful to concentrate on the facts and events which have determined your invention), to the fervid imagination and wise steadfastness of my uncle Gustave, to the languid affection which he feels toward you and your friend, since he has made you the protagonists of a novel of his, so unusual and at the same time so rich in fervent fantasy. An affection that I hope you will return so that, because of it, you will have the wisdom and the concrete conscience to celebrate and venerate my uncle.

I ask you then, because of such affection and solicitous devotion, to investigate the facts and persons mentioned in the manuscript that I have sent you and that I hope you have already read or have at least had a partial and fundamental vision. Assure yourself that the narrated events, or a portion of them, really took place or were experienced, and that there are verifications or testimonial proof of them – even if partial, partisan or contentious. This is a necessary premise for every future undertaking of mine, in consigning, for example, such evidence to a public reading by means of publications in the press, or perhaps in granting them to the care of trusted friends, or of notable writers, so that finally I might have a suitable recompense. This last is a necessity which is, I assure you, because of the times and financial conditions in which I live, compelling and urgent.

I am turning to you in particular, Monsieur Bouvard, because I recognize that at the moment, in addition to his interests in remedies against illnesses, your colleague and friend, Monsieur Juste Roman Cyrille Pécuchet, with whom you have experienced and still experience all sorts of adventures, is also occupied with other laborious commitments. I have even heard of his stubborn desire to elaborate and transcribe a *De Moribus et Descipinis Hominum Orationem* – which Father Didon thinks is an excellent idea as long as your friend gives pre-eminence specifically to the *Oratio Eccelsia* and not to the *Oratio Civica*. I refer opinions to you without entering into the merits, form, capacity or attitudes in question.

It is true that your companion is glorified – *vox populi*, Father Didon aptly suggests – by such noble abilities, just as he is recognized (the fault or merit of my uncle?) as possessing tedious scruples, as well as continual doubts in executing and proposing, even as to choices which might succeed simply in avoiding courses which might possibly be considered rash. Must I then judge him to be a man troublesomely irritating and presumptuous? If this were the case, and I wish that it were, he would be the best possible companion of tedious impertinences, for which he would make an excellent prison-warden, with his worries and his fussing, for the Bedouin, curbing him with timely banalities, lending an ear, with obvious boredom, to the fantastical adventures that our Arab will have the rashness to recount, with original fictions and lies and a troublesome logorrhoea.

It would give a salutary boost to us, to you and to me. It would be necessary, in fact, to appease my ambassador at least for the time in which he will be a guest in your house, so that he will have his spirit pacified when you investigate, in his company, the dramas and volumes in my uncle's life and also pursue the loved and hated traces of a certain Madame Louise Colet who, with a certain official of the Khédive of Cairo, has been a presumptuous writer and injurious defamer, as you will have or will have had the pleasure of discovering when you look through the second part of the manuscript that I have sent to you.

As an investigator and biographer, you will have to be guarantor of the unpleasant depressions of spirit and of the improvident and grave infirmities of my uncle. You must not trust the tempting rigmaroles of the Bedouin who presents himself as an intriguing preacher, full of devious and uncertain meanings and suggestions, such that it is difficult and arduous to understand him and distinguish truth from fiction in his accounts. Are they strange and singular events and behaviours? It's possible if they have had the opportunity to irrupt frequently, in words and actions, in life as in novels. I am aware of this because I was instructed at the treacherous and glorious court of my uncle's writing. Thus I learned how to lead my life, since my mother was dead, following the dictates and judgments of an uncle. There was for him no privileged choice whatever between reality and fiction. There were only marginal dissonances. Of greater interest – for him, certainly – was an existence devoted to a writing-table, with wisdom and awareness, indeed in that very room which you well know through having had the honour of having your life and your experiences created there.

So many memories, then! Forget them? I have before my eyes images which run on resolutely, which invite me to lament, which constrain me to bewail. Yes … the very study where Uncle Gustave closed himself up so that, in solitude, he could take pleasure in his own things: books shelved in oak bookcases, the bust of Hippocrates to remind him of his father Achille-Cléophas, the etching by Jacques Callot representing *The Tentation de Sant'Antoine*, the bust of my mother Caroline sculpted by Pradier, the knick-knacks collected in the course of travels in the Orient and finally that ample Turkish-style divan, piled with cushions, with its beautiful white bearskin.

In this workroom of calligraphic tasks and studies, with its five windows facing a florid and vigorous magnolia, a river landscape, evergreen trees, flowers in clusters of colours, boats that furrow the Seine, an elevated walkway, and a hillside park, my uncle-shaped complex, devastating and obscure plots, constructing and scattering existences like a wise old demiurge. It was his custom to busy himself with a deeply pondered and reflective writing – phrases, words, verbs placed with pride on the paper. Commas in precisely the right place, and similarly with semicolons, periods and also exclamation points, question marks ... and without sentimentality towards those who did not love the rigour of writing. Out of such signs and arrogant stylistic precision were created stories of noble and seemly illusions.

Uncle Gustave gave great weight to his feelings, his loves, his hostilities, his passions, and cherished them with extraordinary tenderness and lacerating devotion. And so much for that character Madame Louise Colet, for example, who, in the manuscript that I sent to you, makes use of vileness and infamy in relation to Uncle Gustave! A devious and disloyal woman in my opinion, bursting with jealousy, which, not infrequently, was able to undermine the devotion of my uncle towards myself. And this Madame was a treacherous pilgrim and unpunished traitor in districts and avenues by means of a dense correspondence, mementos, embittered passions.

Without the poisonous and excessive inclinations of this woman, would my uncle have espoused the amiability and ease of laziness and sloth, consuming his time in sedentary habits? Or did the tranquil and execrable preferences of my uncle induce this woman to lynch him with words and actions without any recourse to pity?

I am saying all this through intellectual conscience and honesty, and so as not then to be unmasked by your shrewd investigations.

I always loved my uncle, and I began to love him even more when I plundered his writings and committed myself to them without prejudice or superstitions, even though at times without fully understanding the significance of such literary efforts. However, in sailing through such singular and suggestive passages, I was surprised to discover, with avidity and immodesty, images defined by pen and ink that created events and sentiments with a rare and extraordinary ability.

My uncle was for me an upright teacher, a mother and a father too, perhaps also a husband – certainly more conscientious and responsible than the one who befell me in fate and love, who insisted on distancing me from the places of my childhood, carrying me with him to Neuville, near Dieppe, to experience a banal and muddled marriage, also determined by a dowry system then in use and common practice in Normandy. Ernest Commanville, my husband, was at first a commercial dealer attentive to his earnings, then a clumsy scoundrel who mixed himself up in crooked affairs. He took to speculating in a rascally manner, getting bogged down in risky financial affairs, in doing accounting without knowing how to count. Uncle Gustave gave him his help and understanding with a justifiable altruism and remained caught up in the silence of mendacity when the price of timber, the commodity in which my husband Ernest dealt, *diminished as had never happened before. What had been worth 100 francs had fallen to 60, and when bankruptcy was threatened, he naturally took over the debts* (of Ernest). *Thus all his capital went up in smoke*[67].

I learnt then to look well beyond appearances and discovered that the fantasy of reality can be more indiscrete and disconsolate than the reality of fantasy. And so I allowed myself to be swept away, by need, by unsatisfying affections, into passionate love affairs: for the handsome Baron Lezoy, for Doctor Franklin Grout, not to mention an adolescent infatuation for Professor Johanny Maisiat.

I now feel obliged to offer you suitable and fitting references for the task that I require. You must, with wisdom and judgment, investigate, as I have said to you, personages and writings, and then certify to me, with marked reliability, the authenticity of the manuscript that I have remitted for your reading. I must know, I must be able to know if I can expect from that text, in the very near future on account of my pressing needs and precarious economic situation, valuable and substantial deserts as the only heir to the rights accrued by my uncle, Gustave Flaubert.

---

67   Frères de Goncourt, *Journal.*

Thus it is fundamental that you have careful interest and proper knowledge to inquire into facts and passions, before and after fatal quarrels and improper wrangles might lead to diverse claims: on the part of eventual heirs of Madame Louise Colet, I mean. Reflect also upon these possibilities – with caution certainly and according to conscience. Always safeguard, however, the name and interests of my uncle.

At the same time, it is permissible, and even in accord with scruples, to refer to you certain truths that can be found in the missives that my uncle wrote. Madame Colet was betrayed in an uncivil manner by my uncle, who confessed openly that he no longer was of an age to love as the lady would have liked, that he didn't want to give up that part of his feelings that belonged only to himself, that he believed that love was something completely independent even of the person who inspired it.

It behoves you nevertheless to try to know fully the circumstances and actions of Madame, leaving to one side all the amorous banalities that I have referred to you. Madame has indisputably conserved many specific secrets concerning my uncle, his writings, his thoughts. Madame will have deciphered feelings and ambitions. Looked into weaknesses and loves. Evaluated emotions, words, silences, mistakes. Frequented, to the point of delirium, unforeseen squabbles, the critical conscience of my uncle, such as he often found himself confiding to his lovers in carriages, on moors, in improvised and uncomfortable alcoves, in the salon of Madame Récamier – who was then being transformed into Madame Bovary, protagonist of a book by Uncle Gustave – as you well know, destined to suicide, to being a victim, perhaps of a suicide of convenience. The designs of my uncle seem ferociously cruel. Are they so indeed?

Madame Bovary could, it's true, dissolve enigmas and offer us certainties. However, it is necessary, I repeat, to act with care. Certainly you will, in inspecting documents and events that will lead you to investigate also Madame Bovary, have to venture skilfully into the writings of my uncle to take possession of truths, understand ploys, clarify muddled intrigues. It is necessary that you know how to pose questions and interrogations, even disquieting ones, and to define proofs and confirmations.

The investigation must aid you in the best possible way in coming to conclusions, and, in the end, to be able to report with certainty whether the facts set out in the manuscript respond to the truth or not. If they were really drawn up by the compilers of the account, just as you now will have or have already had the means to examine.

Harel Bey is beside me and is smiling maliciously. It seems that he is intuiting what I am writing.

I am comforted in my requests to you by the assertions, declarations and attentions that many people, among friends and publishers, have dedicated to your relationship with Uncle Gustave. You, Monsieur Bouvard, together with your friend and companion Monsieur Pécuchet, are debtors in perpetuity towards my uncle if it is true, as they say, with proven testimony, that both of you owe to him your condition of being, your social and economic condition, your human and scientific knowledge, your intellectual activity, your liberation as simple, banal, busy city copyists, one with the firm Frères Descambos, Alsatian fabrics, 92 rue de Hautefeuille, the other at the Ministère de la Marine, 2 rue Royal. Even though, and this is evident from the documents left by my illustrious uncle, you ought to have had a very diverse and very obscure destiny, perhaps similar to that of Harel Bey, given that my uncle, at the time of the creation of your persons, saddened by melancholy thoughts, very troubled and moody, was subject to iniquitous temptations and aberrant seductions. Thus he had the well-founded fear that, if chance or destiny had overwhelmed him, his aspirations as a writer would have been irremediably scuppered in the silences of unforeseen melancholies. And if that had happened as it seemed about to happen?

You would have remained, my dear Bouvard, a pure and intangible intention, the hero of an inchoate novel, and you would have spent, my dear friend, your entire existence among Alsatian fabrics, clothed in canvas, a shirt all puffed out in front, waistcoat left unfastened, collar without a tie. And there, with your great bulk, pulling out on the counter a metre measure of cloth, pieces and laces following the peremptory orders of rude buyers who would have made fun of you for your nervous clumsiness in bustling about with your rubicund physique. And in the summer, certainly, you would have come down to the Bastille every Sunday, wrapped up, bulky and bulging more than ever in the heat, to walk up and down the boulevard Bourbon lost in idleness and banal thoughts, solely to pass the time as it had to be passed. No noise would have bothered you if not that of your own footsteps frittered away in wearing out hot paving-stones among narrow streets in the grip of the boiling heat, slate roofs, the milky glimmer of the facades and from a distance, at a stone's throw, the Canal Saint-Martin squeezed between two locks.

Instead, you and your friend Pécuchet have been graced with the decision of my uncle who wanted to follow his own route and bring to completion a work which was alive in his intentions and which has granted you and your friend the possibility of being how in fact you are, and of having a debt of eternal gratitude towards my uncle Gustave.

Moreover, you, if an iniquitous death had not overcome my uncle Gustave, would have acquired still further lustre and prestige since my uncle's projects and plans accorded you further space in the second volume of the work in which you figured. Uncle Gustave in fact had planned to concede you an additional existence as hard-working copyists, taking up again your former employment, that is as scribblers totally dedicated to a punctilious and diligent labour which consisted in wanting to transcribe everything that would have come your way. Transcribe, transcribe, transcribe, to fill up an entire volume of narrative. Transcribe, without lingering or rest, nothing but dull-witted idiocies. Transcribe, transcribe, transcribe pages and pages like two *cloportes*. You would be transcribing perhaps a punctilious documentation on stupidity, perhaps also a sort of dictionary of commonplaces, or else a catalogue of *idées chics*. Transcribe, transcribe, transcribe in a satisfying new existence beyond that which you had as protagonists in the first volume.

I ask you, Monsieur, for the sake of everything that has happened and for that which has not occurred but could in fact happen, I ask you, Monsieur Bouvard, indeed with strict devotion and inclement injunctions, to take an immediate interest in the affair in question, since you have, because of secret initiatory sequences, relations of kinship and acquaintance with all the actors, places and events of the story narrated in the manuscript which I have sent you, with the books and characters created by my uncle, with the sentiments and passions of Uncle Gustave, in addition to possessing a lively propensity to gossip, to the habit of asking and investigating, to that type of ingenuousness which is a necessary and expeditious mania in every kind of shady enquiry and inquisitive sort of dealing and in knowing how to busy yourself in the midst of that which pretends to be fictitious and that which is truly false.

Thus, I put my faith in you, Monsieur.

Before closing these lines of mine, I have the honour to suggest to you, and in some way to insist to you, with verbal injunctions, and indeed with intuition and bad faith, to grant refuge to this Bedouin who will be found, in the moment in which you read these lines, in your house as the devious bearer of this letter and of the manuscript.

Manipulate him by arousing *amour propre*, his verbose eclecticism, so full of malice and imposture. Try if possible to discover the causes and reasons of his appearance on the scene, amidst the memories, characters and books of Uncle Gustave.

Therefore, watch Harel Bey carefully, do not allow him to have liberty and sovereignty. I fear, with certainty, that he might engage in iniquities, create complicated intrigues, stir up revenge – even more so if he is an interested party.

He is an enigmatic man, who knows how to cleverly conceal reasons and purposes of his strange presence among us, of this wandering as a nomad and prophet, of his behaviour as an escapee from custody: from a manuscript? from a remembrance? from an intention or from an invention?

What is certain, at least according to my impressions, is the ambiguity of his presenting himself at my house to offer me a manuscript as a gift, almost as if he wanted to deceive me with stories and consciences sculpted from history.

So, Monsieur Bouvard, be wisely brutal in your investigations, in the way you conduct your research, in your manner of excavating secrets and digging into intimacies. If you so desire you can, it is understood, *ex occasione vero non stare*[68], *opportune ex mendacio aestimare*[69].

I hope we shall speak again soon. Your investigations and observations may be of valuable and futile utility.

Satis existimatione[70]

  Madame Caroline Commanville, née Hamard,

  niece of Gustave Flaubert, writer

P.S. I am afraid that this Bedouin, bearer of the present letter, might also be an assassin, and that because of vexations suffered he might want to kill people dear to Uncle Gustave, perhaps also characters created by him.

  C. C.

---

68   On the occasion do not keep to the truth.
69   Judge opportunely with mendacity.
70   With sufficient respect.

The Investigation

On the road to Trouville,
3 June.
My dear friend, dear Pécuchet,
Here we are Bouvard and Pécuchet! Here in the guise of Monsieur
Bouvard and Monsieur Pécuchet. Here we are mixed up in a
chain of events which has neither beginning nor end for us
born without being able to know the epilogue of the adventure
which Monsieur Gustave Flaubert invented for us. It's true that
we were born, born under the sign of stupidity since our father
Gustave desired us in flesh and blood as protagonists of a story
in which he intended to demonstrate the stupidity of the human
race – of which he was ineluctably fascinated, thanks to his keen
immorality, the impossibility of putting it at the service of reason
and intellect, and to his overweening, arrogant and peremptory
nature.

I often ask myself why Gustave took to deceiving himself, as
even from boyhood he was quite prone to give birth to characters
like ourselves, who were surrounded by and submerged in the
insipid, senseless ideas that were current and the frivolous
notions that were fashionable. Remember, Pécuchet, remember
how many times I reminded you of that letter that Gustave wrote
to his friend Ernest Chevalier on 1 January 1831. The letter said
"If you want to associate yourself with me in writing, fine!... and since

there is a lady who comes to Father and always tells us stupid things I'll write about them". Thus infamous nonsense, since our father Gustave took it into his head to bring glory to us in one of his books meant to be a true and proper encyclopaedia of modern stupidity. We, however, and with certainty once created, wanted and still want to give sense to the simple attempt to embrace, by means of our investigations, analyses and discoveries, the whole of human knowledge and to try to distance the human race from stupidity and insipidity. Have we succeeded?

From the beginning, our father Gustave nurtured the high-flying aim and the tenacity to closely observe stupidity, to analyse it and study it in its most striking aspects, to assess it in its most ambiguous manifestations, to mock it as sharply as possible and in its most deplorable pretexts, since nothing at all could ever withstand his imperturbable onslaughts. And thus he took to associating this purpose, with complacent sarcasm and humorous mockery, with two poor and unknown copyists like ourselves, with two fools like us created just for the purpose, two dimwits, two poor little slobs, defenceless but devious, as he wrote to Monsieur Jules Duplan on 2 April 1863.

So here we are then, my dear friend, under the guises of Monsieur Bouvard and Monsieur Pécuchet, possible investigators in an equivocal plot: stupefying in its own insipid incongruity for, as characters only half-formed because never fully defined, we are obliged to fulfil a debt, to follow treacherous paths through novels already written and complete or not, bristling with extraordinary deceits and obscure machinations, entirely due to envy of a certain reasonableness we possess and the contentious susceptibility of other characters – those too the offspring of Gustave and of his writings, but in fact half-formed, just as we are.

However, it's true, my dear friend, that if we had wished we would have been able to reject such signs and attributes of certain aspects of our appearance and take no interest in such solicitations and injunctions, in order to take on a more accurate investigation: in so much as ours is a fictitious appearance, for which the certainties of our belonging to reality are very scarce, if one excludes those conceded to us by the comforting warmth of pages knowingly marked and ruminated by time and by our father Gustave.

So here we are, once again right at square one, to consider our destiny, defaced and wounded by an uncertain future. And since Gustave abandoned us in an adventure not represented fully, there weighs upon us, daily and with reason, the desire and the will to look for those duties and characteristics which are suitable to our expectations, once the mission entrusted to us by Madame Caroline Commanville, nee Hamard, niece of Monsieur Gustave Flaubert, has been accomplished. Even if only to continue to live, once and for all and in the best possible way, in the silence of the Normandy countryside, which awaits us now in Chavignolles, and to begin once again there our daily customs and rituals, perhaps also in order to continue to satisfy readers, editors and copyright holders. And in this way earn our daily bread, if only in a fictionalized reality.

Do you remember how we arrived at Chavignolles? It was Gustave who chose the place, as he wrote to his niece Caroline on 24 June 1874: *"I shall make Bouvard and Pécuchet live between the valley of the Orne and that of the Auge, on a dull plateau, between Caen and Falais"*: at Chavignolles, to be exact, in a smallholding of 38 hectares, in a house with a large kitchen which communicates with a small sitting-room, also an antechamber and a drawing-room on the ground floor. On the first floor, four rooms which will give onto a corridor which opens onto a courtyard. Adjoining the house, a carriage-house, the cellars, the woodshed and the bake-house. A house painted white with ochre friezes in relief, surrounded by a road with yellow hornbeams, with their beautiful elongated foliage, the oval leaves pointed at the tips with serrated margins, which in autumn, before becoming detached from the branches, take on a vivid yellow colour – almost orange. The entire property cost us – do you recall Pécuchet – 143,000 francs. Since then, from the time we took possession of the farmhouse at Chavignolles, many things have changed, and today we have a lot to regret about our past, on the marks that have been left upon us by our passage through time. Remember our garden Pécuchet? We planned horrible things, my dear friend. We constructed a garden with themes that were obscene: an Etruscan tomb to represent melancholy, next to an artificial Rialto Bridge which was meant to represent Romanticism, plus a pagoda which was a symbol of refined exoticism, then rocks and trees uprooted as a manifestation of inane catastrophe. And then to complete our extravagant museum, there was a medley of all sorts of incongruous bits and pieces: from a gallows-beam to a bird-bath, from a basin to a halberd, and on and on without rest or pause to give ourselves reasons for possessing such miscellanies, such heterogeneous assortments and rubbish of every conceivable kind.

In the end, we succeeded, dipping into Voltairean determinism with passion and resolution, to develop a faculty worthy of malicious compassion: to recognize our past stupidity and that of the human race, and thus to confirm our own will not to want it and not to have to accept it. Were we returning to reason? I believe that we were only maintaining some sort of dignity while waiting for Gustave to bestow the next development upon our lives. But nothing happened. And nothing will happen from now on. And so we have to make the best of what there is and start to put into practice, with good will and favourable auspices, this new art that Madame Caroline is inviting us to partake in.

So then, let's strive in the best possible way to carry forward our investigative mission, as Madame Caroline invites us to do: the impertinent sender of an uncommon manuscript and of a Bedouin bearer of this same manuscript on which we have been asked to investigate. Of course it's true that Madame pressures us to carry out rather reprehensible acts and behaviours, and turns us into participants in personal affairs, since she has had the impudence and determination to grant us the right to read and examine a piece of writing of dubious origin and controversial veracity.

Truthfully, I don't know, my dear friend, how to consider the peremptory requests of Madame Commanville. Or better: not so much the requests as Madame herself. I have the suspicion that that stupidity which Gustave wished to mock had irremediably taken him over and almost seduced him, since he had to engage continuously and affectionately with Madame the niece. Madame Caroline, to interpret her behaviour in respect to this manuscript, has remained, with all due scruples and in all conscience, in a state of futile arrogance, lacking, I believe, a certain creative intelligence. Moreover, she appears to have fallen into a kind of stupidity which is current and fairly common: the very same stupidity which Gustave perceived as the current folly of society. Is this an unmerciful and iniquitous judgment, my dear Pécuchet? Stupidity, if we listen to our father Gustave and share his assertion, is very common among that bourgeoisie scarred by an obtuse and blameworthy haughtiness, by a lazy and out-of-date sense of well-being, by a bewildering intellectual inheritance: not at all deserved.

Madame Caroline Commanville, née Hamard, the irresponsible niece of Monsieur Gustave Flaubert, enjoins us to respect codes and conducts now that we owe her our new existential roles, now that we owe her for unprecedented responsibilities which she has commissioned and entrusted to us. The pathways of life, in such difficult situations and times, are indeed risky; there are in truth injunctions which we can and must adhere to in our own fashion, to our own benefit, at our own discretion.

I must confess to you, my friend, I have, right from the beginning, mistrusted Madame Caroline, the manuscript she sent to us, and its Bedouin bearer: a Bedouin, that Harel Bey, who, albeit in the unnatural uneasiness of a disability as severely afflicting as blindness, has been prompt and disrespectful in lording over our house to the point of impertinence, even impropriety, quite arbitrarily. Above all with you, my kind friend, who are so accommodating in charity, ingenuousness and laziness.

To tell the truth I believe that I have acted for the best in conveying to you my peremptory resolution in violating with impunity the memories of Madame, in planning this journey of impropriety, of fiction, of ceremonies and of litanies in the company of this Bedouin who, at the same time that he presents himself to us with ambassadorial credentials, seems in fact to be a person born from the remote silence of a crazy imagination, from

87

the outlandish ideas of a writer – or better yet, from the silliness of a piece of writing full of holes, incomplete, by a mendacious scribbler, and whom Madame has asked us to leave to her precious care.

I must honestly confess to you that the Arab has fascinated me, with his multi-coloured clothes, with his odour of a man from the lower Nile, with the blindness of Argus or of a mendacious guardian, with his tales emerging from the depths of apparently fictional memories, punctuated here and there with imprecise notes which reveal the hand of some mad narrator who, nearing the end of his days, believed himself capable of liberating from the restrictive yoke of a page or a paragraph characters whom he has delineated only in haste, in blurred and approximate images.

However, for certain aspects and emotional transports, I became convinced that the Bedouin was in fact a decent man, a wretched individual burdened by physical suffering. Do you remember, my friend? We believed him to be, in fact, a possible companion and acceptable servant: this we said to each other. Never did we express or notice signs of contrariness in those first days in which he was our guest. Never were there occasions for doubts as to his frankness. Together we explored paths of common friendship. Then we lamented unforeseen desertions. Then our ideas changed as we began to see something senseless and impudent in this individual.

We lamented a lost father, a niece rediscovered but childishly superficial – above all, we asked ourselves why Gustave had left the Bedouin sightless. Such an indefensible forgetfulness in tracing his profile and giving him a soul! Was Gustave then an unremitting tyrant? Useless questions perhaps for useless replies, without any doubt. Certainly Gustave was ambiguously sadistic in his literary inventions and in his apodictic speech. Certainties characterized him in the originality of fictitious, almost illogical, reasonings. Do you remember, my dear Pécuchet, do you remember?

It was January 1864 when Gustave took to prattling about women, as was his custom, there in the Goncourt brothers' court. He began to blather on about how beauty wasn't erotic, that beautiful women aren't made for bedding but only to inspire artists. He jabbered on that love is an unknown and impenetrable passion, and that the consequence of a banal carnal excitement is never a source of fascination attractive for one who, having to fuck a whore of inauspicious beauty, preferred to make use of women as stratagems. He thus preferred to substitute, both in his imagination and in his thought, one who enchants him by her beauty. There was nothing else to expect then from the disconcerting encounters with whores, since for Gustave sexual intercourse was not in fact necessary for health, in so far as it is a pure and simple derivation from a fantasy which permits one to enjoy a fictitious orgasm.

According to his continuous and tedious ramblings, a man did not have the need to ejaculate but, solely and sternly, the need to find an outlet for his nervous burdens in order to function well and to provide correct stimulations both to the spirit and to projects.

So, my friend, let us remember that our Bedouin was born from the pen of an individual like Gustave. Do you understand what I mean? From an individual who was fascinated and bewitched by Donatien Alphonse François, Comte de Sade. From an individual fascinated by the perverse turpitudes of that Count – an individual who would be happy and satisfied, as the Goncourt brothers relate, if he had found a latrine-cleaner who ate shit. An individual fascinated by de Sade above all because he represented the true perverse spirit of the Inquisition, of torture as an end in itself, of a Church symbolized by Psalm 73, *Exuerge Domine et Judica Causam Tuam*[71] – and because he regarded the ordinary nature of things with horror. Do you understand, my friend, the true nature of our father Gustave? What can we then wish for and expect from a Bedouin born from Gustave's perverse fantasy?

The Oriental began – and it was only to be expected – to bewitch us right from the start, harking back to his ancestors. Because of this I dare to believe that in this business, so skilfully supported by appearances and fictions, our man had understood, long before we did ourselves, how necessary it was to travel through streets marked by illusion and simulation just because his

---

71   Arise, O God, judge thy own cause.

mission was stamped and characterized by deception, perhaps like his soul-destroying affliction of blindness.

Why put oneself out for no reason? And even with deceptive games, well imagining that we would soon find him out, isolate him and pillory him?

He has lived, and still lives, in deception. Because his existence is tied to deception. Nothing is more consonant to his nature as the desire to inhabit a fiction which, in paradoxical circumstances and times, could become a paradoxical reality, or at least to inhabit a reality which, in extravagant occasions and measures, could transform once again into fiction. A crime, or several crimes, carried out in literary surroundings or in literary fantasies, and among similar and adventurous novelistic timewasters, would be convenient opportunities to alter circumstances and events.

I seem then to have understood in the intentions of the Bedouin such auspicious eventualities, when our man invoked a hereditary justice, never obtained in his view.

He has lived, and lives, with excessive fastidiousness and painful torment, the dissatisfaction of being an incomplete character, and he has manifested his embarrassment with ill-concealed awkwardness. He even gave us to understand that he would have obtained specific advantages if certain of the characters in Gustave's books had lost their personalities and substance, thus being denied, as already successful or at least known protagonists and actors, to works, to readers, to copyrights – in the specific circumstance to Madame Caroline Commanville, née Hamard, the irresponsible niece of Monsieur Gustave Flaubert.

He confided all this to us one evening in front of a bottle of water adulterated with Vichy powders in the gentle dusk of our garden. The powders, I must admit publicly, were a brew of your devising, dear friend. Do you remember? I understood then that, if unlucky occurrences had intervened unexpectedly, our guest would have been a character and hero rediscovered for the needs of a new piece of writing and the new protagonists would have had to be taken from other possible stories by Gustave and offered to the lovers of novelistic reading, as well as to the second-hand shelves in certain little bookshops to be found along the banks of the Seine or in some deluxe brothels. For example, at the Farcy, frequented by the entire coterie surrounding Monsieur Flaubert. Yes, at the Farcy, or at Elisà's where it's possible to choose from *at least ten women, wearing multi-coloured clothes – blue, red, white, yellow – spread out, sunk into the divan with the mawkishness of cows – in an inane licentiousness* (between) *pleasure and the excesses of a chic, cultured, even intelligent youth*[72].

And then, confronted with such disconcerting circumstances, I was anxious about you, my friend, because of your laziness and negligence when it comes to knowing how to be aware, vigilant and a guardian of your own ethical and intellectual security. And so, because of this, I enjoined you to be observant and careful. I imposed upon you, with friendly severity, the strong necessity that the Bedouin be my assistant in the journey I had to undertake among the plots and stories sketched by Gustave, and with the sole aim of obtaining exhaustive replies to the imperious and necessary requests of Madame Caroline.

And thus the manuscript sent to us by Madame once again became the protagonist – the characters that appeared in it, the deceptive truths and the risky lies. Turmoils and slanders perhaps, or perhaps not. Gossip certainly, in the midst of intimacies declared in the delirium of piques and vindictive manias by each of the correspondents. And so, accordingly, there is nothing for it but to protect my back. Thus I am very inclined to exercise a certain prudence and not play around with useless and dangerous rashness. I should also like, and it is no small matter, to be the resolute caretaker of this Bedouin who dogs my every step, who is continually sniffing at me, who philosophizes and puzzles over me, with hazardous hypotheses and indecent temerity, who prefigures projects so obscure and arcane as to often render him intriguing, terrible and dangerous.

And so I nourish ambiguous feelings towards this man who has erupted without warning or notice into Chavignolles, into

---

72   Frères de Goncourt, *Journal*.

our town, anxious to destroy friendships and regards for which we had particular affection, to investigate our respectability as characters and sons of Gustave, also our integrity and moral rectitude now that we seem to be autonomously living in a novel, and our devotion to Gustave and his descendants. I recall that he recounted improbable happenings to do with him, and even that he had arrived from Paris and confirmed to us that a certain Hurel, superintendent of our neighbour, Count de Faverges, is a habitual frequenter of low dives and inns, scampering about between Chavignolles and Paris in a hackney carriage rented at 40 francs per day, with another 20 francs for the driver. Was Madame Caroline settling the accounts?

The Bedouin stayed for a few days, once he had reached our area, at the Hôtel de la Croix d'Or, along the main road of Chavignolles, amongst houses shaded by very tall deciduous trees. With zeal and solicitude, he inquired about us without remorse or reluctance. He acquired news and information, but also encountered a quiet apprehension and a frenetic silence which bothered him and rendered him malevolent towards the customs and surroundings of our village.

He felt aversion towards the countryside because it was tedious and melancholy. His spirit was wounded by the insistent and capricious rains and by the narrow streets filled with gossip, with muffled voices, with chatter that was rancorous, indiscreet and dangerous because of his blindness. However, he obtained what he wanted to obtain, since Madame Caroline had chosen him as bearer of pledges and injunctions. By shameless gossip he acquired very intimate information about us. He benefited by means of a crooked and scoundrelly art, scraping together information about our feelings and thus shamelessly involving us in obscure and stirring matters, certainly borrowed from some note of Gustave's.

When Harel Bey arrived at our house, it was 15 May and in the afternoon. He clutched in his hands, I remember clearly, a stick by which he brusquely and fearlessly felt his way and a leather haversack with silver filigree embroidery and bordered with fringes. This bag contained the letter and the manuscript.

Harel Bey took some care in informing us that that text was put together with academic and editorial discipline, corrected with punctiliousness and judiciousness, albeit with scorn and irritation (he quoted the words of Madame Caroline, he confessed to us with hilarity and malice) since the three presumed authors of the manuscript had intended to affirm hypotheses and support fictitious realities or correct imaginings which opposed or contrasted each other, deformed probable truths, restated habits and expedients in implacable diatribes.

The Bedouin related all this, showing indifference in the face of our perplexity and just and indulgent ingenuity. He nurtured personal interests, so much is certain, which prompted him to show indifference and indolence. It seemed to me then that the man had no features, indeed a face. Only lineaments formed by a careless and uncivil nature. Thus he had irregular lips, certainly ambiguous in their expression. An erect carriage, an ethereal body, wrapped up in a caftan which descended almost to his feet, with the reds and blues of its fringes punctuated by rhombi knotted together and also fastened to wide, gilded vertical strips.

An ambiguous and obscure figure, even if only a messenger of titles and directives. Also an attentive and involved witness: thus he explained to us. His sense of smell and touch were excellent confidants, he hastened to suggest to us. Moreover, he was devoted to benefits of announcements, assessments and interrogations which you and I, kind friend, asked ourselves concerning his unexpected arrival, his insolent manner, his role as bearer of secret things, of a letter, of a packet of ungenerous writings and stories.

Neither of us, do you remember Pécuchet?, had ever encountered this man of missions, nor had we heard of the unpublished manuscript which has now been delivered to us, nor of the existence of a letter by Madame Caroline, this lady whom we now remembered above all as the melancholy, troubled and unfortunate niece of Gustave. Nothing of what occurred was of comfort or comprehension to us. To that there was to be added, given the troubling and indelicate presence of Harel Bey, many artifices and very few certainties since these seemed to espouse doubts so that truths seemed to us false and authentic, reliable and fallacious at the same time since compressed in the calligraphic ambiguity of a manuscript. And thus we wondered if also the messenger was true or false. If the manuscript was true or false. If Madame Caroline's letter was true or false. If the whole intrigue was true or false – devised perhaps by Madame Caroline.

Harel Bey was willing to console our doubts with the duplicity of his arrogant Levantine aspect. But he was also careful and clever in trying to dissipate questions and uncertainties, while at the same time taking advantage of and trusting himself to our predisposition to love and devotion, for which we were deferential to his affected daydreaming, to his ceremonious psalmodizing, to his very adept leading of us into vile temptations through his wise and perfidious adulation.

I am speaking now particularly of our love for Gustave. Of our devotion to Madame Caroline. Also because of certain firm desires, and indeed because we were in a position – as was he – to offer availability and sense to an invitation, to act out well the parts which had been assigned to us, to investigate in depth Gustave's writings, to know if and when that Madame Louise of the manuscript had gone about recklessly recounting vile episodes and improbable stories about Gustave.

Madame Caroline went so far as to have the impudence to push our curiosity beyond any limit. She led us into temptations with cruel malignity and ugly malice, begging for supporting opinions; we supposed that, even if only by chance or accident, Madame Louise had had the boldness to write an apocryphal work, that is the manuscript of which we are speaking, and as much as anything to do herself justice as far as Gustave was concerned, Gustave who had offended her or indeed had abandoned her with impunity. We hypothesized instinctively, having scarcely exchanged the merest mention of this, that it was likely, and quite possible, perhaps probable, that this bit of writing was concocted and written down by him, our Bedouin, hoodwinking everyone and looking after his own interests.

Intuiting our intentions, Harel Bey then described himself as the impudent comforter of Madame Caroline: of that small and fragile woman, he maintained, of her sorrows, of her amorous crises, of her weakness and exhaustion. Never did he refer to his own enigmatic subterfuges, to his own ambiguous appearance, to his own reasons for life and existence, which seemed very obscure – perhaps also to Madame Caroline.

Harel Bey spoke at length about himself as a tireless and diligent messenger of the will of others, as he was ready to subject himself, without embarrassment or anxiety, to the fatigues of a journey into lower Normandy to track down our dwelling-place (had he never at that point read the book by Gustave in which we are protagonists?), to meet us, and to offer me, the agreed-upon recipient, pieces of news and injunctions.

It was then, and for the first time, that we could attentively scrutinize the letter that had been entrusted to us. With curiosity and care we began to examine the manuscript. We discovered that it was not in fact easy to express a suitable literary and human appraisal or to give assurance of sincere presuppositions or deliberate equivocations. Often the judgment and token of human adversities hide extraordinary vendettas. Even devious harassments. Also mental derangements. We are constrained then to accept upsets, apprehensions, vexations, excitements, banalities, deceptive appearances, envies and unmotivated rages.

Thus Madame Caroline Commanville, née Hamard, niece of Gustave Flaubert, appeared to us, and with all too much evidence, very weak in health, judging by what we read in her letter and by what we knew through the murmurs of imprudent and impertinent friendships. And the Bedouin also added words that further increased our discomfort. We believed – rightly so? – that Madame was prone to reckless ménages and to bilious indignation, all amidst compilations and corrections of manuscripts and letters: if we accept that these are indeed in her own hand.

Furthermore, the letter testified to contradictory observations. Let us attempt to move back in time. We discovered affections and feelings lost in the adventure of existence, in the jousting between subtle impostures and writings both genuine and apocryphal, given that creation could only be an act of acknowledged paternity for Monsieur Gustave Flaubert.

Madame Caroline could be considered in a certain sense our own niece, now that Gustave was dead.

The letter, written in black ink in clear handwriting, was stamped with the initials 'C.C.', and bore a Parisian postal stamp. In pages she noted invitations and arrangements that you will certainly remember well. She clarified necessities, also dismissals of guilt and remissions of responsibility; this judgment was shared by our guest, who, smiling, shook his head, interrogated us, cutting through the air as he waved his hands, at the same time recommending prudence to us when we began to express opinions, or to draw rapid conclusions, or to bestow benevolences or also rancorous hostility.

Thus were broken down those certainties that had been entrusted to our discretion, to our generosity and above all to our sensibility, as, with the disappearance of Gustave, we had been constrained to act without having guarantees or perspectives. The Hôtel de la Croix d'Or remained for us the ultimate reference point, since precisely in that spot Gustave had abandoned us, as protagonists, in his unfinished story. Full stop.

Having thus been dismissed at the Croix d'Or, for us every event, every memory, every suggestion could become possible, or uncertain, or partial. Perhaps because of this Madame invited me to undertake a journey, and to act as vigilant guardian of the uneasy insolence of that Bedouin, while to you, my friend, she reserved the delicate and arduous duty of frequenting that which had been our romanticized reality. And following the indications left by Gustave. To frequent, that is, the Croix d'Or, to take care that the web of adventures and episodes which Gustave himself had assigned to us by chance should never be forgotten or cancelled, in a story to be made through very explicit and suggestive notes, in a succession of determinate events which would have led us back to an auspicious serenity in once more becoming diligent and conscientious copyists, as we were before.

Otherwise, far away from Chavignolles, in places and

adventures not contemplated by a work left unfinished, we would have been lost in the unreasonableness of doubt or in a reasoning which did not belong to us, which was not yet written and thus counted for nothing. I had thus to initiate a journey for necessary investigations and remain steadily in contact with you, my friend and companion. And also to involve myself in writing letters to send you, to eliminate any possible confusion since reality and fantasy become blurred and often change roles.

In essence, Madame Caroline's letter seemed to us to recite a prayer, a supplication, an oration, albeit among dabs of face-powder, flourishes of calligraphy, prolonged pauses due without doubt to sighs of love since Madame is very subject to repeated fallings in love and amorous wanderings. Words written in haste come after maxims inscribed with an upright, imperious and authoritarian calligraphy. At times corrections concealed obscure thoughts, misguided stammering, and suggested conventional phrases, composed meditations, because it was always clear that the writer was a bearer of material and spiritual pledges which imposed careful reflections in such a way that we knew well how to evaluate the various parts of the manuscript, constructed with sentences, punctuation, messages, injustices, extortions, permissible feelings, moral homicides, unpunished ethics.

Do you remember, my friend? We were perfectly sure to be able to obtain incontrovertible evidence at the end of the investigations and thus offer to Madame unequivocal details and concrete particularity.

Harel Bey, in those moments, sighed complacently. Had he perhaps a wisdom of which we were deprived?

We read the manuscript many times, with diligence and attention. We had few qualms. A few annoyances, it's true: because of tones, accents, furious hostilities which escaped us on the first reading. We didn't think it worthwhile to take account of verbal vendettas and scurrilous apostrophes. It wasn't our business to judge. I had the burden of taking action. Cautiously, indeed, if I wanted to do my best.

In truth, I had to mix the cards, with the wisdom acquired in the years of apprenticeship in the sphere of human knowledge and the love of erudition, so that false virtues were not expected or desired. Even in the desolation of my presumed stupidity.

I didn't understand, in fact, if it was the aforesaid effect of chronic stupidity or for some other reason that I took on the burden of involving myself in investigations that were the affair of whoever had created them, in the pages of an unfinished piece of writing. Or if it were Madame Caroline who invited me, albeit with a threat against a character – as I am on account of an unfinished piece of writing – to investigate the author of this same piece of writing and the characters and events that figure in the books that have been published and of an apparently fictitious manuscript. Or else if it were Harel Bey who wished – it was clear to the two of us, my dear Pécuchet – that an apparently fictitious manuscript should be given to be published, a manuscript which one of the two protagonists of another written work, never finished, had to investigate.

I had little opportunity and time to meet you alone, my friend, to exchange with you understandings and advice on what was to be done. Harel Bey imposed himself from the beginning as my guide, advisor on moods, instigator of tasks and undertakings. But, knowing you well, it was to be supposed that you understood that the moral subjugation which was imposed on me hid, in reality, the fact that I was well aware of being the tyrant of time and of the desires of our guest. Or was that only a purpose and intention?

I was constrained then, through modesty towards the equivocal games and subterfuges that were being unrolled before my eyes, to inform you and the Bedouin of my desire to depart for uncertain adventures, unprecedented discoveries and thorough investigations at dawn on the 30th of that month, and that our guest would be accompanying me.

No one had a word to say in comment, almost as if the date, the departure and the farewells had been established by time and circumstances. The Bedouin seemed very contented.

I thus submitted myself to the unknown and to doubt, scarcely knowing what roads to follow, and whether or not they would be windswept or baked by intense heat. I had to take risks, to tolerate the unaccustomed, in order to adapt myself, with all my will and strength, to human and literary investigations in the midst of unexpected, indeed ambiguous, encounters. I advanced this as a rationale and without wishing to offend Madame Caroline, Gustave's irresponsible niece.

Harel Bey is now content to be my guide and companion in adventure.

From time to time he laughs contemptuously and nods his head with an impalpable and ambiguous meaning. He cultivates the art of writing in imitation of Gustave. In the shadow, in the silence, in blindness, alone, he amuses himself with a travel notebook in braille, bound in thick cloth in the Oriental manner. Perhaps he is compiling notes for his own pleasure and disparagement of others, using a stylus tailored to his own needs and manner.

We are travelling with indolence and ill-will in a hired calèche, driven by a slothful coachman. We are taking the Trouville road, towards the sea of memory, where began Gustave's ambiguous education, amidst reality and fantasy, fiction and truth, artifice and ingenuity, and where it was absolutely necessary to go, as it was the first inevitable, stopping-place.

A bientôt,

B.

Waiting-room of the Deauville railway station,

5 June

Dear friend,

Here is *a simple soul*[73] – our own, Pécuchet.

Yes, a simple soul that father Gustave is beginning to write about, abandoning us momentarily to the mercy of a time which seems marked by unfortunate events. Madame Caroline was whining with desperation because of her inept husband, until Gustave was forced to sell the beautiful farm in Deauville which had belonged to his mother's family. How much love for Caroline and,

---

73   *A Simple Soul* was written by Gustave Flaubert in 1876 with the intention of recovering, by the figure of a simple and candid servant, the years of a youth spent in the fascination and enchantment all consuming memories.

regrettably, a certain reluctant neglect in relation to us, astray in a limbo of pages merely sketched out, without conveying or giving a conviction of the true scents of life, even though it might be mere fantasy. Thus Gustave, occupied and preoccupied in confronting in the best possible way the debts and feckless investments of Ernest Commanville, is divesting himself of his patrimony and, urged by the lazy indolence of the moment and the inertia of thought, prefers *"to write tales in order to see"* – he says – *"if I was still capable of putting together even a sentence*[74]*"*. A simple soul now: that of Gustave. So I find myself forced to travel through pages soaked in dull autobiographical purpose and, what's more, even an obsessive search for sanctity. Cults, too, undoubtedly. Of the Holy Spirit perhaps, since *the Holy Spirit, which the Father will send in his Name, will teach us everything, and will set down all that* (he has) *said*[75] Perhaps there is also the spirit of Saint Felicity of Carthage, since also to her was conceded in martyrdom a unique grace, when she listened to the Lord; and He confided that, in her last days, he would infuse her spirit with enlightenment on all things and she would have the gift of prophecy. And Felicity taught herself to conduct her life with modesty, remembering these words, and, submitting herself, she had the understanding and knowledge to be able truly to aspire to an intimate and unique felicity.

A simple soul, indeed!

The Bedouin, meanwhile, moved about in the shadows with his clouded soul, wounded by hindrances and by an oblique will. We have arrived at this point with prudent awareness and macabre joyousness, aware of having to avoid crimes, of having to encounter manuscripts, of having to track down men and women, of having to discover and verify identities. For me, also fears as Chavignolles preserves and protects all my certainties, confirmations now lost in Gustave's bold fantasies, since the presence of Harel Bey is a nefarious sign to aim for a general and banal salvation.

Thus I fear cases, men, happenings, abominations. I am also afraid of the lack of success of a journey lost among words,

---

74   Gustave Flaubert, *Letters.*
75   John 14:26.

individuals, characters and places which sometimes evade comprehension and my indulgence. And indeed there are also occurrences – events and occasions, above all – of which it is extremely difficult to determine the nature and temporal opportuneness: when an annoying intruder, like our Bedouin, hides within the folds of real or imagined undertakings, in the shadow of other persons, also characters in the secret rooms of the semblances of fantasy: those of Gustave, I mean.

And so I have explored the reasons that will determine events. I have explored paths which might reveal the sense of investigations of antique places, amongst persons who have disappeared in time and in the pages of an impenetrable text. Using the signs of a story I have arrived at this point in the company of an inconvenient, insolent and half-blind companion, to skim through events, to verify actions, occurrences.

I initiated the investigation knowing that it was necessary to find an inn called Bellevue. And that in front of this inn, there must be a beach stretching out as far as the eye could see, defined by an ancient little hill town, surrounded inland by swampy land defining a hippodrome, as Gustave used to describe.

Harel Bey has constantly and mockingly smiled at my loving desperation and at my constant desire to follow to the letter Gustave's signs, instructions and traces. He scoffed at my journey because I undertook to follow pages written and forgotten in haste and the identity of which, he murmured caustically, is a relative option. Certainly he had in mind his own identity. At least that's what I believe.

Thus I looked for an inn, as I mentioned to you, which I knew must be called the Bellevue, even though Gustave, in *A Simple Soul*, called it the Golden Lamb. It was there, in fact, where he had made, in that story of his, Madame Aubain, her children Paul and Virginia of seven and four years and the faithful domestic Félicité spend their summer holidays – leaving behind Pont-l'Évêque and their slate-grey house, set between an alley and a street which led to the river. A story laden with memories, revisiting the past, the ghosts of past time, lives suspended in silence, or even in banality and moralizing, pain and renunciation, in the midst of life and death. Thus Gustave. At least this is what I wanted to remember or what someone wanted me to remember.

You recall Gustave's precepts and proposals when he began to spread the word that he wished to draw out from his memory-laden imagination a fable of feelings and regrets, a fable of somnolent commotion. But instead he pulled out an apologia which interpreted the truth diffused in Ecclesiastes: that knowledge and human things are only vanities.

In the event, he drew out a story about a certain Félicité, simple-hearted and with a silent and obliging character, indeed really a very awkward attitude, as she revealed herself as one who nourished simple ideals and worthy sentiments, so that there were many people who took advantage of her generosity. At the end of the tale and that is, of the earthly voyage of Félicité, she was constrained, in order to confront a painful solitude, to share her expressions of affection with a stuffed parrot, since *the future for her held no more dreams, and the distant days began to waver gently in a luminous haze. Certain animated figures began to detach themselves from the background, dear phantasms which held out their arms to her*[76].

The love for a parrot then, a love begun with a healthy affection, then consumed amongst caresses and affectations, as well as in a dialogue consisting of phrases, in nervous games carried out by bony fingers and articulated claws, in cajolery, in playing with a shawl so that one could climb disdainfully up its weft. A love which was in fact eternal, since an unexpected death had drawn the parrot into the darkness of perpetual silence, sanctified – if indeed only in the mind of Félicité – now that the stuffed bird seemed to have an affinity with the Holy Spirit. Deaths became at that point the patrons of a narrative sealed up in times and actions: the death of Virginia, the death of Madame Aubin, the death of Monsieur Guyot, of Monsieur Lebard, of Madame Lechaptois, of Monsieur Gobelin, of Uncle Gremanville: all personages brought to life in *A Simple Soul*, and finally the

---

76   Gustave Flaubert, *Letters*.

death of Félicité. Every word, every sentence, every sign was chronologically uncorrupted in memory, in the knowing crime of a writing that was shattered and lost in a truly simple soul.

Do you agree, my friend?

In this hotel dear to Gustave, at the Bellevue I mean, the atmosphere at midday, when we arrived there, was laden with rays of sunlight and heat to the point of burning eyes and faces admiring the intense green of the ocean. The weather then slowly became lost in the disturbing hymeneal song of light and shadow so that the sun towards evening began to extinguish itself, and the moon began to shine, and in the sky the stars were lost in the memory of time. *Yesterday there was God, today there is love, tomorrow there will be art*: this is what Gustave must have thought as he wrote to his friend Ernest Chevalier in September 1841. At the Bellevue, they passed the time looking for shells. *The outgoing tide often revealed sea-urchins, starfish and jellyfish. The children ran to catch flakes of foam blown by the wind*[77].

Gustave was always judiciously pleased with himself and with his adolescence: marked by such spotless virtues now that, at a more advanced age, he had fully realized that existence was no longer bearable if not spent in a literary delirium made up of recollections and obsessive attention to syllables, words, verbs, phrases, pages. The crass and egotistical world no longer conceded itself to mystery, to the marvellous or the supernatural so that authentic faith, that which had no need of shoddy learning, was in truth the exclusive prerogative of simple and superstitious beings, of people like Félicité.

It was during the search for the Hôtel Bellevue, my dear Pécuchet, when we discovered, after having briefly followed a precipitous shore with boats drawn up on the sand, the village and the Jetée Promenade of Trouville where at low tide the steamboat arrives from Le Havre, the one which does the journey in a little over forty-five minutes, at the price of one and a half francs.

Then the beach and its cabins with coloured curtains: yellows and greens in vertical stripes, and the flag blown by the wind,

---

77   Gustave Flaubert, *A Simple Soul.*

fraught on its high pole. The waves lapped the shore with delicate eddies and whirlpools, brushing up against youthful bodies buried in warm and gentle sandbanks. There were also modest groups of bathers and loud calls tempered by calm sneers. They stood side by side grouped together to test the warmth of the water which drenched airy costumes that seemed to clutch at limbs restrained in now sea-soaked fabrics.

At one corner of the beach was the overflowing mouth of the Touques, arriving there after abandoning the Seine which instead took to flowing in wide curves as far as Croisset and Rouen.

Trouville was the place chosen for the domestic intimacy of Gustave and his family, far from Rouen and well before le docteur Achille-Cléophas, Gustave's father, acquired the country house at Croisset. It was, in fact, arriving at Trouville that Gustave discovered that *the main amusement was the return of the boats, which, having barely crossed the line of the buoys, began to dock. The sails were lowered to one-third of the mast, and with the foresail swollen like a balloon, they proceeded amidst the murmur of the waves as far as the port, where they anchored. The boat drew up to the jetty so that the sailors could deposit the catch. Then women in cotton caps took up the chests of fish and embraced their husbands*[77].

This is Trouville. Magical, bewitched, inimitable. Thus baptized by Charles Mozin who extolled its merits and splendours when he took to painting the enchanted light of the Seine estuary, because this part of the Normandy coast is drenched in smouldering sunlight, hot enough to arouse stupors, offering itself to the transience of wandering phantasms. So many and for all. Even women. Above all women. And for Gustave first of all. So at least I remember, from readings and characters in Gustave's books. Or am I mistaken, my friend?

This lout of a Bedouin never yielded, either in acts or desires, to the tenderness of memory and took to shadowing me closely, without showing the least affection or benevolent piety for Gustave's memories and writings. Our man knows only to recall, and with aberrant continuity and despicable goading, his origin in a province ablaze with oblique spirits and with Levantine artifices and the foolishness of Gustave the writer who abandoned him in the midst of a project, in the midst of incomplete pages, in his indolence as a lazy and meticulous scribbler, and without offering him anything other than an ignoble nibble at life apparently conducted among the notes of those Goncourt brothers.

In short, the Bedouin is burning my neck with his unpleasant breath and angrily muttering his counterfeit memories of things and events that could never have been truly experienced since, according to what he says, even so much as a past was denied to him, and he was born abruptly and without proper documentation in a simple page of mementos.

My companion hastened to attest, in my persisting in reminding him of the touching events in *A Simple Soul,* that certain innate virtues are appropriate to a mawkish narrator like Gustave. The Bedouin was not and is not prepared to take in the dazzling beauty of these places since, troublesomely and morally, he was and is ruthless towards Félicité and her simple soul, towards that cloying affliction which irritatingly characterizes Gustave's story.

Harel Bey also had many comments to make on certain of my arguments. He asserted, with stubborn and self-satisfied sharpness, that recollections are deceptive lies and, in the greater number of cases, counterfeited and adulterated by whoever has the audacity to revisit them with memory.

I then reminded him of prohibited feelings and letters thick with omissions and admissions, of scabrous annotations, and equivocations too, like those written by Madame Caroline. I reminded him of those events and I re-evoked them with punctilious obstinacy as I was scurrying about, seated next to my senseless companion, in a carriage of 3 francs 5 cents per journey, with two robust horses drawing it, since, with scruples and according to principle, I chose to travel on a *Petite Messagerie,* settled into the rear seat, since the front one was occupied by the driver and the luggage compartment was full of our baggage.

I discovered then abruptly, amidst chatter and foolish considerations, the Hôtel Bellevue in a side-street, next to the quay.

It seemed to me for a moment that it might belong to a particular reality that existed only in collusion with the imagination, so that I could savour pleasing and surprising amazement. By my side, Harel Bey rendered himself mockingly participant in this exciting discovery of mine, constructed on the ambiguity of my memory and that of Gustave – at least, so it seemed to me. He contained his scorn for such inopportune sentimentality and, with arrogant diligence, comforted me, lightly touching my arm with enigmatic caresses.

I stopped the calèche beside rue de la Plage and I let the coachman go, arguing about the fare which he pretended was greater than what we had agreed on. Harel Bey intervened brusquely showing his stick and putting an end to all diatribe with severe words. The driver took off crestfallen muttering words of excuse.

Quickened steps then as I guided Harel Bey by an arm. The sea gently murmured as it retreated. A hurried pace, and we were facing the entrance hall of the Hôtel. The entrance is ample, with a white ceiling, the walls however cluttered with pastel colours, speckled with red dots. Braiding in yellow and deep red bordered the white veils of two glass doors which opened onto a flower garden, a courtyard of sun and colours.

I then asked a rather stiff and formal porter where I might be able to find Madame the proprietress (or perhaps I asked explicitly for Madame Ozeraie?) even though Harel Bey had insistently tried to dissuade me from contacting people who had not been characters in Gustave's books. He was evidently afraid of a change of roles, perhaps altered conditions in confronting a reality which was constantly more confounded with fiction. Harel Bey feared also, I am certain, intrusions extraneous to the incidents and observations that Madame Caroline solicited.

A great flight of steps turned towards the upper floors: imposing and massive. A twisted neoclassical curlicue in imitation of the unique style of the architect Balthasar Neumann. Thick brown wood, covered with a narrow woollen runner set on the stairs: with crimson rhomboids framed by two lateral strips in maroon and grey. Higher up, halfway up the staircase, a fat woman with a haughty face exchanged gestures with an ill-matched couple: she tall and imposing, he small, his face with a moustache. The corpulent woman wore a tunic and on the bodice fluttered a vermilion scarf trimmed with black lace and a ribbon of yellow taffeta. Without doubt the proprietress of the hotel since the porter approached her and murmured and gestured, indicating us with a smile.

Madame bade goodbye to the guests and came back to us with a hurried step and with suspicious perplexity. Certainly muttered complaints for our bothersome intrusion. And then a blind Arab, twirling his walking-stick in the air. Irritating indeed! And also certainly presumptuous! And not only that, ill-bred!

A pragmatic good-day followed, to initiate our acquaintance and eliminate ribaldry. I bent my head courteously when Madame approached and whispered submissively that we had come there to look for traces of Gustave Flaubert, the writer, that we were delegated to preserving his memory, his familial patrimony, and also his books, writings, and confessions, even if sometimes unpleasing and ignominious.

The lady observed us for a few minutes. Moments passed without her uttering a word. She was reflecting on the words she wanted and might be able to offer us as a gift without disclosing her reservations and discretions. A smile too, and a few carefully spaced coughs to fill up time. She observed us for a few seconds longer, to murmur finally, in an affected voice, that also a certain Madame Louise Colet – she too a writer, for so she had presented herself – had asked years ago if there were indelible traces of Gustave in this hotel. An obsessive and petulant woman, the hotel-manageress remembered, who seemed to cultivate an iron will to investigate memories which were none of her business, who was on the track of events that took place in Trouville round about 1836. And also mere fantasies and recollections.

In this place, in this spot dear to Gustave, gestures and motives were unchanged and imperishable – added Madame the innkeeper – since the only reality which retained a certain importance was the reality described in a few pages of a book and some sketches by Charles-Louis Mozin, by Paul Huret, by Louis Jadin and other painters. And also in a childhood education which preserved the silence of unappeased desires. Certainly, the innkeeper added with a touch of nostalgic complaint, a youth from Rouen – Gustave, indeed – had hardened himself in the delusions of hopes, so that he often took lodgings in the Hôtel Bellevue to recover, if only in memories, a certain Élise, the woman of his first lustful sin.

Harel Bey laughed unrestrainedly. He moved his arms about like a windmill, wounding silence and compassion. He then declaimed, in stentorian tones, a hackneyed tale about a woman who bewitched the heart of a lad, who had tormented him, who had left him prey to uncontrollable impulses, distressing sentiments, which a certain manuscript had recounted.

Madame the innkeeper replied with appropriate words, which were also revelatory. She spoke to us of that certain Madame Louise Colet who had arrived at the Bellevue to obtain proofs of the veracity of past events and yearned to understand why, even today, she was prey to a desolating melancholy, or perhaps to an amorous distress, or else an excessive affection, or to profound and intimate nostalgia.

Madame Louise had also been prompt to offer 100 francs or more only to obtain some sign or indication that might speak of Gustave's childhood at Trouville. And also a daguerreotype which portrayed him, or even senseless jottings, or notes put down in solitude, or scribbles made in childhood and objects that had belonged to Gustave and which had been negligently forgotten.

Harel Bey, who was next to Madame, concentrated and intent on understanding what was going on, touched her lightly with gestures of his hand, stroking her face, her breasts, even her hips, and raised his nose, with obscene pleasure, to smell the odours that circulated in the air. And then he murmured that an unforeseen frenzy was consuming him because of Madame's voice, and because it was so inviting and sensual and because of that body of hers which was so welcoming to the touch and to the sense of smell.

Madame smiled carelessly. Was she thinking of other things? She shook her head instinctively, and instinctively invited us with a gesture to follow her in exploring routes followed by Gustave. Was she deceiving us or was she leading us to reliable clues? We had crossed the vestibule as I clutched Harel Bey's arm to guide him. A difficult man who, from time to time, shook his head in disgust. Why? Perhaps he had in mind some obscene impulses and projects.

Our steps were modest following the Bedouin's stick, which marked time with cadenced and obsessive rhythms. At the foot of the great staircase I directed my glance upwards: towards hidden floors and rooms. We had meanwhile arrived beyond a supporting column decorated at the base with evident marks of ill-used and uncivil chisels. We had reached the threshold of a door covered by a thick green fabric, marked and faded by the summer sun. We thus arrived abruptly in a sanctuary of silence and memory. The Bedouin was shiftily attentive to footfalls and odours.

Madame went ahead of us. 'Please, please', she murmured. Nothing else. Was she trying to intuit my thoughts? My friend, I was exhausted by emotion. Gustave had frequented these places. Only that? I was waiting for something else. Also surprising revelations.

The room was empty apart from a bed drawn up to a window bathed with a faint light which filtered through purplish-red frosted glass. *In front of the window an oval opening looked out on the courtyard. On a table were a pitcher, two combs and a cube of bluish soap in a chipped plate*[77]. Do you remember these details, my friend? I discovered them among Gustave's pages – or else were they perhaps remembered by some Madame in a gossipy vein?

The wooden parquet planks were insecure, warped, scratched from lack of care and from times of neglect. The furnishings had lost any past splendour, even the original cobalt blue colour. Also soiled by past existence, by the anxiety of years, by occasional frequentations, by never celebrated anniversaries.

Madame the innkeeper had begun to circle the bed, then she placed herself upon it with languid carelessness. She spread out her legs and brought her knees up to her breast, nearly touching it, squeezing it certainly with the naturalness of a trade learnt in squalid houses of ill-fame. I then became aware of her face, marked by unnatural blushes, with dirty smears, and heavy and pretentious lipstick. I noticed eyebrows defined by the black marks of burnt matches, dangling earrings, a necklace made of golden coins squandered in the folds of a fat-laden neck and the flaccid cavity between her breasts.

Madame reclined her head once more and looked at us surreptitiously. She stroked the sheets stained from surreptitious nights, she bent her head for a moment over a flounce of bedding. She seemed to want to inhale old smells, to repossess old memories, years and rashness gone astray in the folds of life, unforeseen encounters. Madame stretched out an arm and fished out from under the bed a ream of paper marked with an uncertain, childish handwriting. How many memories! Childish verses? Was Gustave already practising writing at that time? But in what time were we fishing about?

Madame breathed in noisily, poking up her nose. An unpleasant sound. Then she cleared her throat. She moistened her lips with her tongue and muttered in a harsh voice that those papers perhaps concealed an Arabian phoenix, and that Madame Louise had expressed desires and indeed a will to possess it.

In speaking with conviction of facts that had perhaps taken place and in referring to her own sensations, Madame the innkeeper revealed herself to be serious and preoccupied. She very much resembled a *Madame galante*.

Harel Bey tugged at me sharply. Free from the vice-like grip of my hand he looked for a sure support, which he desired. But off he went, sniffing the air. And murmuring, too. Madame was within his reach. She knew it well. The sense of smell had not deceived him. Abruptly he took the chance of rounding on Madame. Almost an invasion; he was an ill-bred man, without inhibitions, like a wolf. I then had an impulse of good will, a wave of courteous feeling, a surge of shame and remorse. At the same instant, however, I realized that our Bedouin was not intent on meddling with Madame's body, but was ransacking the air with his hands, palpating the arms of the lady, subduing some quality akin to the worst kind of entreaty and passion.

He laughed and, scorning us, asked if that packet was the proof of the moral infidelity of Félicité, of that woman who was the protagonist of that dishonest tale called *A Simple Soul.*

Madame smiled with ancient malice and removing from the hands of Harel Bey his ill-gotten gains, suggested that among those papers was enclosed, with purple ties, a scroll of letters which someone had written on behalf of Félicité, Madame Aubain's domestic servant, who, as Gustave recalled, had come to pass a summer at Trouville, by this time only a memory and dulled by melancholy, the time in which Gustave was seized by love for a certain Élise Schlesinger.

At that time Trouville was resplendent with barely perceptible feelings and Félicité, the servant with a simple soul, kept and preserved many of them. Ancient passions of her own that were important in her dreams and sentiments because they belonged also to Gustave. One went to Trouville in that period to treat breathlessness. One went to Trouville to cure the illness of neurasthenia, which had affected little Virginia, the daughter of Madame Aubin, just as, in the preceding years, it had struck Gustave. One went to Trouville to make sacrifices in the hope that idleness might be therapeutic since one spent the time there sewing, plaiting rushes, weeding the lavender. Nothing else except waiting, and waiting.

Death perhaps or the sacrifice of purity to the point of death, as Gustave implied in telling with carefully chosen words a fable which referred perhaps to Saint Felicity, who consummated her loving virtues together with Saint Perpetua; and together they died in the glory of the Lord – as the apologist Tertullian reported.

The Bedouin then began to recount other facts and other gossip with morbid curiosity, which were to do precisely with Félicité, to draw forth accounts which seemed to contain scabrous, unforeseen, licentious secrets, or perhaps, he pronounced with sly emphases, they were only memories of apocryphal minutiae, of reckless games, of illicit unmaskings, of subtle ambiguities.

Madame galante felt herself, without reason or purpose, to be owed opportune inquiries and promptly interrogated Harel Bey, subjecting him to explicit requests: whether by chance or for her own purpose Félicité might have kept up a correspondence with certain women whom she might have been able to receive in the room which she had occupied in that summer, at the time of the holidays in Trouville.

Harel Bey became instantly serious, his face marked by serious attention, by a disturbed conscience. He spoke with unexpected honesty and, shaking his head, pronounced bitter rebukes in relation to Gustave. He invoked as testimony the disconcerting writings and notes of this same Gustave, who had veiled, with improper words, very explicit sequences of certain events and actions. *In primis* a very resonant name, chosen with ambiguous timeliness. Félicité, to be precise. And it was to Saint Felicity the martyr that Gustave had had recourse in choosing the name for his story, a name undeniably obtained elsewhere, perhaps from reading Chateaubriand's *Martyrs*. Saint Felicity, indeed. Saint Felicity who fell pierced by the horn of a bull to defend her Christian faith. In the same way Félicité in *A Simple Soul*, passing through the meadows with Madame Aubain and her children and encountering a bull with smoking nostrils, pawing the ground and wanting to disembowel the woman, had dared to defy the beast, putting forward the ardour of her own impulse as an ordinary but pure woman.

Was Gustave nostalgic? I find it difficult to believe. Am I becoming insensible to feelings, my friend?

Better: ephemeral morality and hypocritical behaviour? Possibly, since Gustave had made allusions, and without subterfuges: thus pronounced the Bedouin, with no beating around the bush. It was a paradigm of a sexual confrontation, he continued. An attempt at violence, repeated and futile, as Félicité remembered with bitterness *a field of oats* (in which someone) *attacked her brutally. Terrified, she began to scream*[77]. From such an allusive beginning, Harel Bey began to pontificate, he proposed that the task Gustave had set himself was to preach the goodness of a humble and unprepossessing creature, to describe a path toward knowledge of sanctity based on wisdom, tradition and tranquil felicity, as well as by opportune silence about one's past, and also of a shy reluctance in relation to one's solitude and impalpable suffering. For the love of a parrot called Loulou.

Madame galante, in a sudden outburst, retorted abruptly to the Bedouin's words, since according to her they were now to do with other matters, a different story, a story taken from a tale of Gustave's, while Félicité, the Félicité to whom she had referred, was a lady who had lived well beyond the range of a fictional narrative. A thin line, added Madame, separated assumed truth and narrative fiction, which, with the capacity to be either veracious or false, could lend itself easily to multiple and differing interpretations. Could one distinguish and reason with sensible remarks?

The Bedouin smiled with sly good will, pronounced words with a robust voice, affirming that if anyone had never looked among the folds of lines never written by Gustave, Madame Louise would have had little reason and many scruples in writing a manuscript intent on narrating facts and events to do with Gustave's life and the chronicles that he had taken to recounting.

Madame galante began then to walk about the room, with unexpected gracefulness. A few steps, it's true, only a few steps. Suddenly she granted us the courtesy of a bow, and drew near to us with a cautious discretion. She gathered us into a tight embrace and whispered to us that she had allowed Madame Louise to search between the bed-sheets. She laughed as she offered us, with effrontery, examples of the intemperance of Louise, who had given herself over to obeying her own instincts, to smell the bed-sheets almost as if she could in this way gather up the odours of Gustave's love-affairs, of the women he had seduced, of the passions he had experienced.

Louise had obtained, or so it seemed, a story to tell, stuffed with fantasies and bitterness, with which to confront Gustave with invented happenings, narrated with acrimony, now that fiction and reality could be easily confused, exchanged, and arbitrarily turned upside down.

Gustave would thus have had, so *Madame galante* suggested to us, to pay a stiff sum if the reality found by Madame Louise were to become an account accepted as truth, even in equivocal jest, even in words written and non-written, in pronouncements barely accepted, in pages both authentic and apocryphal.

Madame galante moved close to the bed again and sniffed at the sheets. She glanced at us with ironic suggestiveness and asked whether we knew Madame Louise personally and if we had ever thought or imagined or presumed that she personally might be a new Madame Louise, she who was accompanying us on this journey into memory.

Then, suddenly and brusquely, the Bedouin silenced Madame with an oppressive clasp of her trunk within his tightly crisscrossed arms so that the lady could no longer breathe. Harel Bey moved arching his body so that Madame fell helplessly across the bed, while the Bedouin covered her with his body. Harel Bey then took to sniffing her with frenzy.

He sought the opening between her thighs, her genitalia so that he could smell whether or not they belonged – he murmured to me in hurried words – to a character of a tale never told. He possessed the ancient gift of recognizing the effluvia of the most intimate secrets of a woman and to distinguish age, virtue and rectitude. He was grasping Madame, enjoying her in an unseemly way to the point that it suddenly seemed to me that the lady had stopped breathing, that she was losing consciousness.

Thus rapidly, without further thought or reflection, I hit the Bedouin with the penetrating touch of the point of his stick. I hurt him deliberately and brought him back to his senses. Then I dragged him by an arm, holding on to him with unnatural force.

We left the Bellevue very quietly and troubled. We followed the Vallé going along the Port d'Echomage since the station was a kilometre away, on the other side of the canal towards Deauville. We are there now. I am writing while we sit and wait for the train. Harel Bey is reading his notebook in braille and, from time to time, writes annotations with his stylus.

Until very soon, my friend. Soon, with news of the journey.

B.

On the train to Paris

8 June

My dear friend,

Here are the *Memoirs of a Madman*[78].

Unusual and singular principles are the protagonists of these pages that I am on the point of writing to you. An unexpected encounter, an unforeseen acquaintanceship has fed doubts, fomented intrigues, taken control of things to the point of giving new and different emphases to past events and old stories. Gustave, above all Gustave, and that intemperate series of events of which he speaks, in lengthy extracts, in the manuscript which Madame Caroline, his niece, sent us. Indications which have arrived opportunely for me, as investigator of the lives of others and irreverent stirrer-up of consciences.

I would say confessions. Similar to those that prompted Gustave to look closely at the past, to express judgments and diverse and irreconcilable summings-up, to put together, after irrelevant mental exercises, considered philosophical reasonings, historical dramas and re-evocations, a memoir of remembrances and confessions. Gustave was young then, and paid the price of his youth with agile mental gymnastics which drew upon illustrious past events. It's true that he had read and meditated on the *Confessions* by Jean-Jacques Rousseau, and had opportunely taken to extracting from them admissions and revelations on his own childhood and youth.

Undoubtedly an act of courage. In recounting also scabrous episodes, in the laments for wasted and misspent days and youth, he exalted himself recalling the intense odour of the latrines of Rouen's Collège Royal where he had been sent for his studies and where, in the midst of immense puddles of urine in which one could have drowned a horse, *they smoked Maryland cigarettes and masturbated poetically with frozen fingers*[79]. But was it really appropriate that I should have been so scrupulously curious in investigating the recent and remote past of Gustave, who was our father?

---

78   '*Memoirs of a Madman*'. The story was written by Gustave Flaubert in 1838 as the sketch for a more complete autobiography.

79   Gustave Flaubert, *Letters*.

I had my doubts, and I expressed my perplexity to my travel-companion. In reply the Bedouin began to smile unpleasantly, began to press me to inspect, with little apprehension and few scruples, the life of Gustave, and to seriously investigate his wicked crimes and his good actions – if indeed there were any, since Gustave's dreams were puffed up and rhetorical, given his eccentricity. So that he imagined and fantasized dramatic love-affairs amidst gondolas, masks, and great ladies fainting in coaches lost in barren and inaccessible places. And furthermore to be so capable of absolving one's immoral distractions! - if indeed they existed and if they were opportunely venial, because Gustave had never *loved a regular life, according to a fixed schedule, an existence marked by a precision watch*[80].

The Bedouin appeared to me, when he was inconsiderately eager to engage in dialogues based on improper knowledge, more and more an intriguer and the worst possible assistant, almost an *agent provocateur*, who recklessly meddled in the lives of others, disturbed them with his bizarre manias, put forward obscure threats only to restore his own accommodating truth. Is that what you believe as well, my friend?

Often I ask myself if and how much our Bedouin is dangerous with his unexpected and inconsiderate idleness, with his way of leading an existence improperly detached but pregnant with hidden rancour and unconfessed acrimonies. He seemed so at times, recounting his *terrifying visions, to want to send me mad with terror*[80].

A few hours ago, in the train where, settled well and comfortably, I am trying to write this letter, I had an unexpected encounter which I mentioned at the beginning of my letter. And also the opportunity to exchange words and thoughts with an individual who was sitting facing me in a state of disconcerting immobility. At first he scrutinized me and the Bedouin with insistence, then instinctively and abruptly, with an indelicate frenzy, agitated his hands in front of the damaged eyes of my companion: I would say with insolent indelicacy and a displeasing demeanour.

---

80   *'Memoirs of a Madman'.*

This individual abruptly laughed, pressing his mouth within his two cupped hands, blew into them making an indecent noise, since vulgar, sputtering gusts of breath broke the silence unpleasantly. Thereupon he squatted in his seat while the Bedouin began to move near him, sniffing the air which this man had traversed, settling himself back in his seat to observe and scrutinize us, leaving a heavy stench in the air which even I noticed.

This individual resembled someone I had certainly encountered in other places, in different circumstances, in times past. It's possible that he was a character created by Gustave, or an actor in his book, or a figure who had escaped from invented dramas or stories which had remained incomplete or half-told to fellow writers. His face was marked with deep wrinkles, his hair was thick and curly, his neck bull-like. Examining one by one each of his features I found nothing familiar, and yet the whole revealed physiognomies lost in memory or in some déjà vu.

Settled into his corner he began to leaf though a newspaper (it seems to me it was the *Gazette* or perhaps the *Petit Journal* or perhaps, more probably, *La Défense*) with inattention, to make an impression and to sustain his indifference. He didn't linger on any single page or article. He ran over the titles, barely moving his lips and shaking his head. He noted certain words haphazardly, totally ignoring my companion, who was seated next to him. And then he got up with ostentatious indifference and positioned himself between me and Harel Bey, proffering to the Bedouin his massive body, clothed in brown garments, his dusty broadly striped trousers, polished shoes adorned with spats, a tail-coat and a waistcoat tightly fitting his body. A bow-tie closed a carelessly folded collar.

Harel Bey blew his nose noisily, drawing out viscous drops of it with disgust, as if his sense of smell had been offended by insolent and oppressive impurities.

My travel companion stood up brusquely. He felt the wooden seat on which he had been seated, garnished as it was with a thick leather headrest. He sought my hands for understanding and comfort. He squeezed my fingers. He caressed them while, with habitual slowness, he moved away a few steps. A few metres, more or less. Just enough to permit him to listen to and comment with his conscience the low murmur with which the traveller thought fit to communicate, at least with me.

This man, this stranger, then hastened to smile at me. He rubbed his hands and raised his chin at a slant to indicate the Bedouin. He then came out with a tangle of words in a low voice, with a hesitant preoccupation. I listened to him grumble, in peevish and cautious murmurs, that he felt disgust towards mutilations. It was for this reason that he took care to avoid them, to take pleasure in safeguarding himself from those subdued and recurring nightmares, which also seemed to be premonitory signs, almost sinful vices, the revelations of death. Therefore, he reserved to himself the right to be a ruthless and brazen assassin on inevitable and singular occasions.

I felt an indefinable unease, almost an oppressive anguish, which I can scarcely describe to you. I thought of Gustave when he was writing: *how can I succeed in rendering in words things for which there is no language that can possibly express them ... expressions and mysteries of the soul unknown even to the soul itself*[80]? I remained impotent faced with such ignominy.

Then it seemed as if the man wished to remain quiet. He stretched out his arms with a common gesture, murmuring a few last comments and apprehensions to restore his body, to fully recuperate an equilibrium shaken by the presence of an unforeseen mutilation.

Following which, he settled himself next to me and began to torment my ears with words and sighs. I then became aware that his breath had an acrid tang, almost as if continual stenches pervaded him, engulfed him, wrapped him round, in witness to a tension mixed with a recent anguish, with perennial unhappiness, with unknown but probable ill wills which afflicted his thoughts.

What to say to him then? That *he was born by an act of fate when one day his father returned from merry-making excited by wine and by gluttonous festivity, and his mother profited from it using all her feminine arts, spurred also by carnal passion*[80].

Abruptly then, perhaps mellowed in body and spirit, the man recounted to me unexpected and abnormal confidences. First he confided in me that there were *days in which* (he felt) *a profound weariness and an indescribable sluggishness which* (enveloped him) *like a shroud wherever he went: its folds* (suffocated him) *and oppressed* (him)*, and life weighed* (on him) *like remorse*[80]. Then he murmured to me about the licentious reasons that induced him to remain in Deauville for days, in a furnished room at the Souverbille in avenue de l'Hippodrome, at the cost of 10 francs per night, and where, at the railway station, he had hurriedly got onto a train without a reservation or ticket.

He was wickedly addicted to racecourses, hippodromes, betting, the debts of which he didn't know how to free himself, because they were beneficent panaceas to enable him to forget a spell in jail which for years had robbed him of his time. Acts and gestures which overwhelmed him with treacherous and inconstant thoughts of lascivious intents.

He began to live at Deauville, at the Souverbille, after having encountered, suddenly and by surprise, tastes only imagined and, as *a poor madman without clear ideas, without opinions ...* he had begun to look *at the water flowing between the underbrush of trees that bent their boughs to let fall their blossoms,* he began to contemplate ... *the moon on the bluish background of the sky which illumined the room and drew strange forms on the walls*[80].

Then more convenient thoughts on his inveterate and inopportune habits or manias had spurred him to look for refuge along a *plage fleurie,* on the left bank of the basins of Bassin à Flot and Retenue. A failing then, a deficiency in truth, all in all a mutilation. Even if a mutilation of memory, a delusion which brought out the habit of a common sort of existence. Never should one avoid the practice of folly since it is the single, original condition for keeping oneself far from commonplace bestiality, to which belong the everydayness of things and a commonplace existence.

He wanted to protect and preserve his dreams. And *among all the dreams and memories and reminiscences of childhood* of which he had *conserved a small number* (and) *with which* he amused himself *in moments of boredom. So that in evoking a name all the characters* which had animated his youth *returned to life, with their customs and their way of speech*[80]. And for this reason too he had settled in Deauville.

He laughed with irritation and embarrassment, then he confided to me that he had always lived amidst stories that didn't belong to him, perhaps in dreams, or even in events that had happened to others, or in happenings suspended between atrocities and penal judgments, often written down in fictional notebooks as often occurs when encountering by chance ambiguous writings by ambiguous authors. I didn't understand whether, in this case, he wanted to refer particularly to Gustave. Certainly it was the equivocality of his words and the concession of wayward significance to whomever tried to interpret them.

I was then alerted to this way of his of interpreting reality and signs of reality, so that I lent myself to the conviction of making him a participant, albeit with vague references, in my investigative activity concerning a memoir about Gustave and the memories that regarded him and the characters who accompanied his life and his works.

Therefore, I asked him for judgments, I asked him if he had ever engaged in this type of investigation that now occupied me beyond the licit and the imaginary and that required, in some way from me, an explanation of the provenance and attribution of a certain text.

The man raised his head. He looked with aversion at the profile of Harel Bey who, a few paces away, seemed now only a step distant from us. The man drew near to my face, breathing his stench upon me without moderation or regret, with, even, impudence. I had an impulse of revulsion, but I smiled at him courteously and graciously, although ready to retreat as soon as he dragged me into indecipherable dramas, in tales that failed to satisfy my interest and my mission and what I had in some way to verify.

He murmured to me – now that he had moved somewhat apart from me, with his mouth negligently turned upwards into the air – that he was very learned and experienced in manuscripts and that he had, through experience and necessity, examined a great many of them. And not all of them were worth anything, however much they weighed in pages or reams. Some were interesting, indeed. Histories and lives accomplished unsparingly and unreflectively. At times banal, at times agitated, without arriving at the point of engraving themselves in the passage of time or history. One should never avoid the ideals transmitted by one's ancestors, he suggested, in a seductive and peremptory tone, designed only to enslave rites and customs – and he added; *carriages, horses, armies, uniforms, beating drums, turmoil, dust and cannons dragged over the paving-stones of the towns*[80].

This last judgment involved him directly, since he was resolute in recognizing that it was not possible or realistic to foresee what, at the very end, might be hidden within a manuscript in its drama and its characters. Many were the spells, the intrigues, the concoctions and the contorted compilations which mixed up intentions and distracted one on purpose. Thus surprises and delusions. And also illusions since, incautious in expressing judgments, the readers were unaware of the trivial desires of vainglory of those intent on writing spurred by suspect passions. Was he speaking of Gustave? It seemed to me that he was speaking of facts and events regarding our father, also because his citations seemed very similar to those written by Gustave in those memoirs. And the madman? That was a story to verify uncompromisingly. Hence I lent myself voluntarily to what he had perhaps in mind to tell me.

The man was standing up and swayed back and forth in front of me. He put his clothes in order, running his hands up and down, smoothing the materials, following the contours, the wide and narrow folds. Then he bent over and picked up the newspaper that he had dropped in the ardour of being courteous and in talking at full spate.

He turned it round and grabbed it rapidly without a glance with affected, unseemly, irritable movements. Without forethought or full awareness, he offered the newspaper to Harel Bey, putting the pages close to his face, touching it lightly. My companion pushed away this studied and deliberate insult with an aggressive and rebellious movement, flinging away the pages and snorting with indignation.

Our fellow traveller then let the newspaper fall to the ground and kicked it away with impudence and anger. He drew near me and confessed with excessive emphasis that, through no will of his own, he had been ordered to compile dictations and summaries of manuscripts for the Tribunal of Paris, and that he had abandoned these functions and responsibilities when he had been subject to an investigation under the accusation of uxoricide.

A charge, to tell the truth, that he had scornfully rejected, arguing that the guilt attributed to him might even be true if the accusations were assumed to be false. This, in fact, was written down, in turbid and intriguing letters, in the notebooks which he had in his care. Reading or studying these pages it was easy to conjecture how precarious was the distinction between truth and falsehood. Also the hypotheses of possessing certainties when one was not in possession of a manuscript which, among underhandedly false pages, revealed how chancy it was to accuse or exonerate with fantastical hypotheses or concrete conveniences.

Notebooks are always useful for saving a reputation, this man then suggested to me, because they are ambiguously interpretable, just as is any sign of consideration or judgment.

The man began once again to walk up and down the carriage, moving as if weighed down by thought, disturbed by words pronounced, phrases sketched, uneasy opinions. With fear, he glanced at the Bedouin from a distance, grimaced in his direction, and cut the air with his right hand, opened out like a fan in front of his face. He thus gave himself the illusion of liberating himself from contact with the other's breath.

Harel Bey, scornfully and frighteningly, began to shout ferocious words, almost a dark litany, a prayer saved in memory. He instantly silenced words and thoughts. Also attentions as well as an opportune respect, since the traveller drew close to me confused and took a place next to my seat.

Then he whispered conventional phrases to me, conventional phrases governed by the precariousness of an unforeseen outpouring of speech. He recognized, admitting to it openly, that he feared more than anything else for his esteem and the truth, since one and the other honour were much frequented affectations of merit, as reported in chronicles and politics by domesticated newspapers and presses used for flattery.

These were the words of that traveller, my dear Pécuchet, when the train abruptly stopped, screeching on the tracks with a brusque noise amidst clouds of bitter and nebulous smoke. I looked around, beyond the windows obscured by fog. Thus I discovered a deserted station, sunk and lost in an obscure countryside, forgotten by men, immersed in the first shadows of a warm summer evening, suffused with melancholy and preoccupations. I looked searchingly into the face of the traveller sitting next to me. The man smiled at me, shaking his head. A little apart from us, Harel Bey sniffed the air with complacent unconcern.

The Bedouin turned his glance towards us. He agitated his hands to gain attention and murmured to himself that it was now time that light be shed on unpunished crimes. He stretched out his arm and, pointing his index finger, searched for the traveller with his infamous history as an uxoricide – thus he specified.

The man had fears and shivers of fear. He moved near me and with a mere thread of voice asked me if this Bedouin was a professional agitator, since he was busy setting verbal traps and all sorts of rubbish to arouse suspicions when, at the moment, the accusation in relation to him was only that of instigation. His wife had disappeared, that was indeed true, but nothing more. Perhaps it had been a suicide, the man added, but to tell the truth the circumstances didn't release him from importunities and suspicions. There was, in the midst of it all, a rat-poison that he had bought in the hardware store a few days before the disappearance of his wife. It was perhaps also his phobic aversion to disabilities, as indeed he had revealed, without malice or any other purpose, that his consort was afflicted with a moral mutilation since she had a facile propensity to amorous enjoyment with other men. Thus the man confessed to me without digressions or anguish.

I searched his eyes to understand if he was lying deliberately or simply from habit. I perceived unease and trouble, also the desire to narrate in his own manner the circumstances and events of his life. I understood that he longed to recall and evoke once more the devious life led by his wife, so lucid with oblique shadows. I understood finally that he had in mind, as an auspice, to be able to evoke again everything that had happened to him to an unknown person like me, who was able to lend him an ear, without necessarily wanting to understand or intuit the actions and the decisions undertaken and embraced without apparent reasons.

He then began to speak about the work he had done in the Tribunal, where from morning to evening he had to transcribe the rolls of the trials, of every trial, whether notable or obscure, even the one, now celebrated, that had involved a man of letters named Gustave and a certain lady called Emma, afflicted – she too – with moral disability.

He then lingered, with equivocal accents, on the Public Prosecutor of the trial, the imperial advocate Ernest Pinard, who had made charges of moral corruption, rather than asking the jury to convict the accused – who in his opinion was manifestly and incorrigibly an immoral writer – of a crime committed without pity, decency or repentance. The woman, the aforesaid Emma, had suffered a horrible death, an obscene agony, amidst a certain homicide and an uncertain suicide, achieved only in the work and in the imagination of this writer of infamous notoriety. And then the man began to speak of the *idea of something without end ... which turns one pale ...* to speak of *the dead in their coffins, of long centuries which they spend under the earth, full of noise, sounds and cries,* while they are *calm in their rotten boards, in a sad silence interrupted only by the fall of a hair or a worm slithering on the flesh*[80].

I heard these words with a vague sense of discomfort and distaste. I alerted my mind because I noticed that the man was following paths already travelled, certainly in some memoirs of a madman. I looked instinctively at Harel Bey. He was keeping silent in his nook. He was, however, vigilant, and kept an ear cocked for certain phrases and remarks. From time to time he urged me on, moving his fist in the air, so that I might draw closer to this unknown traveller, so that I might listen to him even more intensely, question him to still greater depth, without pity or remittance.

With the pretext of a discourse that the man had begun,

and indeed to satisfy the indiscrete petulance of the Bedouin, I asked for news of his wife, of her untimely death, of obscure circumstances, underhand events, perverse breaths and expenditures on inappropriate defences.

The man shook his head almost as if he were speaking to himself, as if he were confessing displeasing events, thirsting to lighten a conscience overburdened with misdeeds. Then he moved, with a heavy step, towards Harel Bey. Confronting him, he let loose a stream of offensive words, of mocking and wilful provocation; he stretched out his arms to push him lightly, but deliberately and dangerously.

The Bedouin tried to regain equilibrium, cutting the air with approximate, uncertain and clownish gestures, while at the same time, with a mere thread of voice, he murmured that the odour of death purified the air, now that the virtues of homicide were exposed in public and words pronounced thus far were clothed in doubt. Yes *doubt* (which) *is death for souls, the leprosy that consumes corrupt individuals, the illness that derives from knowledge and leads to madness, since madness is the doubting of reason. Rather reason itself*[80].

I suddenly noticed that the man was now, unexpectedly, prey to an uncontrollable fear and was rapidly retracing his steps, stumbling and with trembling legs. He pressed against me and began to recount to me, with a voice lacerated by emotion, other events of his life and the memories of others.

Thus I received diverse confidences, laden with ambiguity, marked by personal fictions, burdened with shameful equivocations. The man rambled on an on, uttering words and more words, so many, one on top of the other – a torrent of words. He told how one day someone, perhaps a foreigner, possibly a policeman, had revealed to him that his wife was dead, and had died amidst atrocious tortures, secret pains, extraordinary agonies, and had accused him of having caused the disappearance of her body. It was indeed a false accusation, so this man assured me, even though, just at this same time and without any reason, he had horrible intentions which drove him crazy and made him insecure, frightened of his own movements.

Often, in fact, he had had fantasies of doing away with his wife. He had dreamt of leading her to the banks of the river, now that the countryside *was green and decked with flowers, and of throwing her into the water with the brutality of desperation. The water was swirling in fact. The concentric circles raised by the fallen body seemed to extend to infinity. This was what he imagined. And then he saw the current resume its placid course. The silence was then broken only by the murmur of the water which flowed between the bulrushes and caused the reeds to bend*[80]. Instead, his wife had certainly departed on a long journey, this the man told me for comfort and self-defence, since he remembered clearly having seen her *put on a light dress of white muslin through which one could glimpse the soft contour of her arm*[80]. In truth, clothing suitable for a journey already planned since he himself had purchased the ticket for the trip and had escorted her to a train on a certain morning, well before appearing in the Tribunal to perform his usual duties. Egypt, Cairo, the Nile, as far as Esneh, this was the itinerary, he remembered it well.

The itinerary mentioned by the man was in truth, my dear Pécuchet, the same outlined, with irritating vehemence and bitter irritation, in the manuscript which we received from Madame Caroline. A coincidence? Or perhaps this obscure traveller was, he too, a character in some book, story or idea of Gustave? Harel Bey has taught us things, to mistrust above all equivocal signs, words said in the ardour of often false narrations, not untrue by their nature but by how they are included in narratives.

I began then to follow with attention the words of this traveller, his telling of happenings and undertakings which followed the disappearance of his wife, of which in truth he had very quickly – this he assured me – had information only by indirect and sometimes humiliating occasions. In defamatory, often anonymous, letters, which accused the lady of being an adulteress, of nurturing insolent feelings, and him of having perpetrated, with impunity but with a sadistic awareness, ignoble actions: to the point of murder. They were letters marked by an obscure handwriting, added the man, stamped with legible postmarks. Luxor, Egypt, they said. They were then *bitterly cruel memories, which returned, which wounded. Thus, hours of suffering, full of weeping without hope, with sobs which covered the breaths*[80].

The man proclaimed himself innocent. Innocent of every act and gesture made, of every sentiment expressed, of every intention entertained. He confirmed this with enigmatic gestures and an awkward smile since, as proven by witnesses, he could state that he had spent all his time, hours, days and weeks, in tribunals and racecourses transcribing acts and marking on race-cards the names and numbers of capricious, arrogant, losing horses. The man told me this with a malevolent smile; he threw out challenging curses, above all towards the Bedouin when the latter, by instinct and knavish convenience, asked whether his wife responded to the name of Élise, if she had shared her bed first with a certain Emile-Jacques Judée, then with Maurice Schlésinger, if she had ever known a certain Gustave of Rouen – who had given signs of madness when, as a young man, he became lost in fascination in the rooms of that gloomy castle of Marny.

The man remembered having heard things about this woman, and also having learned of episodes and skulduggery from manuscripts and publications which he usually read to learn about life and its performers. Indeed Élise, of whom, while contemplated *from a distance while she was in the water, one was envious of the gentle, peaceful waves which splashed against her sides and covered her panting breast with foam*[80].

The man had turned white at the Bedouin's words. He moved near him with incautious irreverence, even heedlessness, because he hadn't well understood how much or how this Bedouin could have been able to intuit his movements, react promptly, proceed actively, be cruel.

I don't know the actions nor do I have any certainties, dear Pécuchet, because I was swallowed up unexpectedly, and for some minutes, in the obscurity of a tunnel. I intuited, however, sequelae and gestures which succeeded each other in the darkness, beyond having heard a stirring of arms and bodies, a suffocated cry which froze the spirits, mine first of all.

I am only certain that the man, this unknown narrator of

ambiguous happenings, disappeared in the shadows leaving neither a trace nor a note. A sudden ailment or a death by the hand of an enemy?

The only sign of his presence on this train, from which I am writing, is the newspaper he had with him. An equivocal paper, full of obscure news, articles, events, but which displayed in full sight a space in bold type which recited: *If any one of the characters created by Monsieur Gustave Flaubert of Rouen has the desire and enterprise to harass with wild molestations the man who arrived from the Orient, whom we know to be interested in his own benefits to the disadvantage of the other actors, let him take the train for Paris from the Deauville station. To set the intrigue in motion, you must bustle and create a stir around the man who is leading by the hand and for unforeseen itineraries that blind Bedouin.*

Must I then remain on the alert, my friend? Fear friends and enemies of Gustave's, as the manuscript of Madame Caroline says? And if this narrative is deceiving us about truth and lies, where can we find opportune and legitimate reasons? To whom then should we concede allegiance? To Harel Bey? To Madame Caroline? To the hostess of the inn at Trouville?

Portez-vous, bien[81]!

B.

The tavern Chaîne-d'Or, Les Andelys,

12 June

Dear Pécuchet,

Here is *November*[82], the season of the soul. And also of colour, it's true!

It's appropriate to remember November even now: in late Spring, with summer at the door, in days of stifling heat and cruel sweats, when, in the ambiguous noting down of certain memories – Gustave, *seated in the carriage, in silence, his face exposed to the wind* (allowed himself to be rocked) *by the movement of the gallop and watched the road disappearing beneath him ...* Then (Gustave thought) *of all the journeys he had made to reach Les Andelys and*

---

81   Keep well!

82   *Novembre*. Autobiographical novella written by Flaubert in 1842.

(allowed himself to travel freely and lose himself) *in memories*[83].

Monsieur the Bedouin, meanwhile, has directed and intensified every one of my literary and informative investigations into Gustave's writings with fruitless wilfulness, paying homage to the most banal of daily events as if he could thus discredit the merits and substance of a writer like Gustave. Then he condemned me to a prolonged pause of silence and, scarcely disembarked from a carriage coming from Rouen after a payment of 2 francs 50 cent, began to mutter about how and when we should exert ourselves in our investigation.

With laborious promptness and perfidious sagacity, I was then chained, constrained to the point of having to listen to senseless accounts of our exploration and our journey, almost as if we had been protagonists, at the moment and without perceiving its legitimacy (and this is a perfidious opinion of my perverse companion), of a tale of Gustave's of whose existence we were unaware. My dear friend: is this what we are, in fact? Then should we not have made that trip in November to look into the concreteness and veracity of such a supposed state of affairs? I am confused, and I confess that I find myself in a condition of extreme unease and profound disturbance, now that I am unable to identify the times and places of the events through which I am living. I wish you were here to comfort me and at the same time to consider such troubling possibilities, having recourse, as is our wont when we are entangled in existential doubts, to Théodore Simon Jouffroy and Jean Philibert Damiron[84], who initiated us, with equilibrium and order, into modern philosophy.

Meanwhile, Harel Bey, excited and troubled in following these routes and amidst meek emphases and insinuations, upon arrival at Les Andelys, at Petit-Andely – having travelled beyond the ample loop of the Seine and La Roque and La Vacherie – began to sniff the air with exploratory relish, to indicate to me directions and steps to be taken, finally to impose on me a prolonged stay in the shade of a parish church next to a tavern.

---

83 Gustave Flaubert, *Letters*.
84 Philosophers cited in *Bouvard et Pécuchet* and considered in it particularly prolix and tedious.

To refresh us, he explained with great authority and firmness.

A pleasure, all in all, to share in the silence of a palate exposed to the merit of a sumptuous snack, based on stale bread, lardoons of lean pork and two skewered chicken thighs (*a la* Germaine or *a la* Marianne, Madame Bordin's cook[85]?). Thighs in truth very well preserved and full of flavour, thanks to having been smoked on an oak wood fire, which gives to meat an intense, characteristic and bitter savour.

A snack pulled out of a dirty haversack, swollen with secrets, appetizing secrets. I'm sure of it! And then a few drops of wine, consumed at the tavern a few steps away. Sips of a full-bodied wine from Gaillard, certainly vines from the hills that enclose us, from a fruitful territory which has always been abundant in good wines, as the alcohol and intense sugars blend with grapes fermented according to ancient and precious recipes. I mixed the wine with tasteless spring water. The Bedouin instead sniffed it and drew from it instant, immoderate inebriation, and he yielded to the ecstasy of the surroundings, which reminded me of November, where *a brook ran over the stones, green lizards and insects with gilded wings climbed slowly along the embankments of the road ...* (and) *the sun bestowed a handful of coloured pearls, of fiery stripes*[86].

Harel Bey then took to reciting false and inopportune memories, to skimming over intricate itineraries fudged from his mind so that he could obtain narratives appropriate to the difficulties of the investigation, adapted to confound the truth and lies of the manuscript that Madame Caroline remitted to us.

Harel Bey also gave way to recriminations, as he usually does. Complaints, in truth, which have the taste of secret vendettas. He immediately made me aware of the inopportunity of granting Gustave easy absolution, at least from us who are his creations without definite features, as he underlined with malignant emphasis. I believe that this definition is completely inappropriate so far as it concerned him, because he never obtained a real baptism

---

85   Characters in the book *Bouvard et Pécuchet*.

86   *November*.

from Gustave. Ill-will, therefore, unyielding and unremitting.

He then involved me in petty and senseless complaints about the necessity of being, through circumstances and our own interests, ready, indeed to be solicitous, to rewrite concepts, lines or pages of this manuscript which appear to us contradictory and ill-adapted to our most hidden necessities, to our desire to belong to a concrete reality, even if always in a narrative of a certain writer named Gustave Flaubert.

He then discoursed on the opportunities, if they exist, to introduce corrections and variations into the conduct and lives of other characters, above all those who might be abandoned, like ourselves – he affirmed shamelessly – in a limbo of indolence, or even dead through sheer forgetfulness. And then there are other characters that Gustave discarded recklessly or with ill-will – continued our Bedouin – to truth, fictionalized even if believable, or he created them and then abandoned them to themselves: perhaps through neglectful incuriosity or careless resolution. All in all, something for which Gustave ought, in a certain manner, to be legitimately responsible.

So far as such accusations are concerned, I believe that one must grant a certain credit to our Bedouin. My dear Pécuchet, I should like to remind you, in all good faith, of writings and readings that we undertook, simply out of deception and carelessness, going on to ransack, search thoroughly and scrutinize the writings of our father.

Do you remember, in fact, the outline of *A Night of Don Juan*[87]? Insatiable love. Our father imagined that he was giving himself up to humane and philosophical speculations. Recount a carnal love by means of a mystical love and narrate at the same time ascetic mediations through sensual passions. Don Juan and Anne Marie, the nun! To yearn for love. To desire the Madonna on the one hand, and to have Jesus in one's body on the other. A libertine and a nun: a fine sort of people! The ambiguity of spurious artifices, so that one could have and desire an epitome between sex and the sacred, and thus slide into a perversion of the senses, from

---

87   Gustave Flaubert, *Letters*.

mystical ecstasy to the lustful carnality of a body.

But first came his presumed story about Anubis with his jackal's head, who presided over the funeral rites in the fantastic Carthage created by the fervid mind of our father Gustave. Do you remember, my friend? It all began, as far as I know, on a fine day in November – it was in 1860, when Gustave arrived suddenly at the house of the Goncourt brothers to lament about the inhuman labours of trying to render truthful a Carthage swallowed up in its own mysteries, joyous in its amusements, obscure in its mythological cults.

And then there's the story of the sons of the dervish[88]. Another likely fable directed by Father Gustave, as he set himself to summarize for his friend Alfred Le Poittevin in a letter of May 1845. Father Gustave had in mind to recount wise precepts of Oriental life, from when certain sons of the dervish began to hunt their fortune in various ways and with various outcomes. At the end of the story, nothing had been achieved except by the one who had gone in search of love, who confirmed that the only love which could be attained was unhappy love.

Thus many and various characters, all astray in an ephemeral memory and in the unwilling game of mystification, justifiable only because to conceive them there was a very scatter-brained and passionately impudent writer. Father Gustave, that is. In the face of such insolent heedlessness could I and should I have taken upon myself the care of defending Gustave? I didn't do it! Should I have done so, my dear Pécuchet?

Harel Bey suddenly stopped reciting inopportune memories, as he found himself prey to excessive whims and excitements since, with persistent continuity and subtle pleasure, he had continued to inhale spirits from the mugs of Gaillard, to invoke taverns diligent in not allowing the alcohol stored in musty rooms and behind the counter of a tavern to evaporate.

I called him to order when, now a slave to moody disturbances, to repetitive stammering, to disordered movements and irritating

---

88   Gustave Flaubert, *Letters*.

frenzies, the Bedouin began to swear and curse and make rude, ill-bred noises with his nose, sniffing disgustingly at everyone and everything: the counter, the glasses, the smoky air, our clothes, and even the hostess, who, according to him, was full of feral effluvia that were wild and penetrating, almost an exciting odour of menstrual secretions, of sex, unclean sex, which reminded him, with grievous excitement, of a particular story by our father when, barely a youth, he was discovering carnal love in womanly arms and, with brutal intuition, abandoned himself to pantheistic ecstasy, to the unwholesome pleasures of lasciviousness. When the love had been consummated the woman *returned to the bed. She slipped between the sheets overwhelmed by pleasure. She trembled and cuddled up under the blankets ... Then she fell asleep abandoning herself90* in the debilitation of just experienced gratification.

I called him to order suggesting that he have a peaceful, silent, solitary rest, if only for a few seconds. He then began to toss about, to grumble, to condemn me for cowardly moral squalor and bourgeois vices. He rose up uncertainly on wobbly legs. Shakily he moved a few steps agitating his arms, breathing heavily, sniffing the air with greed and contempt. He muttered a few words to the hostess with self-satisfied irreverence while he moved away with tentative steps, in his uncertain obscurity, between the tables and customers.

Thus, with wavering steps and disequilibrium, he tried to discharge his anger and fear. He then became lost in the air of a blazing midday, scarcely beyond the threshold of the tavern that we had taken to frequenting when the Bedouin had confessed to me that he wanted to share close at hand the olfactory pleasures of wine.

Moments later I found him again, on the ground, squatting on the grass of the field in a garden that opened on a courtyard, squeezed between sheds and imposing trees, just beside the path that led to the tavern. It appeared to me at once that he had, perhaps in contempt, something of the attitude and character of Gustave, almost as if he were putting into practice his philosophy of carelessness and scorn, *yawning, doubting, messing around, and fantasizing*[89]. Opposite him, in the shadows of the nearby hills could be seen Petit-Andely and Grand-Andely, with houses piled up precipitously, distant among themselves, divided by a railroad which wound around the dark profile of a station. On one side the Church of Notre-Dame with its two towers imprisoning the façade, in another corner the ruinous profile of Castle Gaillard, the Norman castle in Saracen garb fortified at the beginning of the 13th century, which had been erected in this place, with its stone dungeons and a quadrilateral ground-plan, enclosed within parapets topped with crenellations.

Harel Bey heard steps coming closer and he suddenly leapt up. He calmed down immediately when he recognized me by the sound, by the odour of my body afflicted with moist secretions, wrapped up as it was in woollen clothes to protect me from the damp winds from the hillsides. Harel Bey smiled at me and began to speak of ancient legends, of fables, of recollections and tales true and imagined. He also mentioned that, after our arrival in the tavern, he had heard from a table next to ours (as he was alone while I was away informing myself of business, customs and opportunities of the place) oaths, prayers, orations celebrating a certain Henry the Norman who had granted title, fame and certainties to that territory.

The Bedouin then asked for more certain memories, or appropriate stories, or even invented ploys that carried knowledge about that Henry.

Thus I recited commodious compendia, founded on the nostalgia of the studies which I conducted with you, kind friend, when, with diligence and fervour, we undertook, in order to please Gustave – since that is what he imposed on us in the story which pertained to us and in some way still pertains to us – to practise the science that concerned the Norman troubadours. Thus we discovered *Henry le trouvère*[90], do you remember? Only

---

89   Henry le Trouvère, French poet of the 13th C. An illustrious cleric, he wrote the allegorical poem *La bataille des sept arts*, in which, speaking ironically about the ways in which art was understood, he announced in advance the playful and realistic liberty of his most famous works: *Le lai d'Aristote* and *Le débat des vins*.

90   Frères de Goncourt, *Journal*.

rhymes it is true, and in 'langue d'oïl', as the music was lost over time, with the ballads, refrains, virelais, rotruenges. I spoke thus of Henry to our Bedouin.

Then, in the silence of midday, with mild breezes when bodies and clothes seemed to shiver because of cold gusts of wind or warm up abruptly because of a sudden swelter, Harel Bey asked me, with a persuasive voice, if I thought that I had rendered appropriate memory and merits to Les Andelys and to that troubadour with my prattling as a modest moralizer and very boring literary educator.

At first I failed to understand the meaning of this harsh rebuke. I understood, however, its intriguing alcoholic arrogance. He approached me and began to utter nonsense verses in the manner of the *fabliaux*, almost laments or stories or verses or anecdotes among lies and fictions. It would certainly have been opportune to pass hours waiting and listening in some square, or inn, or bordello, or gaming-house. But instead we were squatting in a garden of a tavern which faced Les Andelys.

Harel Bey then began to tell tales learnt only minutes before in the tavern. It was indeed true that I had left him alone only for a few moments, but the Bedouin knew events and tales of which he should not have had any notion. He started to boast of his knowledge of *The Battle of the Seven Arts* of Henri d'Andely. Perhaps he was only telling tall tales, perhaps he was speaking the truth, trotting out, in any case, obsessive accusations towards Gustave. He accused him of practising his art, he meant by this his writing, in a capricious manner, in so much as, by nature, he had a great propensity to tell stories with oratory.

It was in fact November, proffered Harel Bey. A Parisian November, indeed! he concluded, cunningly. He said not another word. He awaited my questions. Clarifications were what he desired. He rubbed his hands, he snuffled, he felt my face.

Oratory, everything arises from oratory and not from the Calvary of writing!, murmured Harel Bey suddenly. He then laughed and came out with a subtle play of words and memories with Gustave as guest that day: it was 1 November in 1863, in the house of the Goncourts, where he was living at that time and thus witnessed the events and words spoken, even though in a strange book that was the account of a future story.

Throughout the entire day, without a moment of relief, with a shrill voice, almost as if he were performing a theatre in the boulevards, (Gustave) *declaimed his novel ... The subject was the loss of a young man's virginity with an ideal whore*[91].

Thus was born *November*, explained Harel Bey, a story which is a mingling of dreams, aspirations, melancholy and misanthropy.

Harel Bey suddenly fell silent satisfied and scornful. Then he moved with mellow cheerfulness, oblivious of the alcoholic effervescences which gave him the odours and pleasures of drunkenness, and also difficulty in walking.

He drew near me furtively holding out his arms. He murmured to me that we had tasks to accomplish, also missions, perhaps vengeance as well for which it was legitimate and opportune that we should decide to visit the church of St. Sauveur, as we had decided some time ago. When had we decided this? Truthfully, I didn't remember this particular, my dear Pécuchet, or indeed if it had been discussed between the Bedouin and me. I thus suspected a dirty trick put in action by our friend, also because I had revealed my desire to visit St. Sauveur only to you. Do you remember?

The Church of St. Sauveur welcomed us a few hours later, in an afternoon still drenched with sunlight, with its cruciform ground-plan and with the splendid Gothic of its nave.

I led Harel Bey by an arm, and described to him the pathways and places that we visited. I told him about architectural memorials and colours on canvas or lights filtered through large windows and shadows. I thus made him a party to the beauty of the façade of the church, of the choir with columns and triforate windows, of the baroque Ingoult organ, of the beautiful 13th century statue of *Christ Blessing*, of the 17th century altar, of the *Adoration of the Shepherds*: a painting which reproduced, I murmured to him, the stained glass window by Philippe de Champaigne that the

---

91   An old maid.

Cathedral of Rouen exhibits in the cross of the main altar.

We proceeded in full respect of the place, with the Bedouin unrestrained in whispering about the events and causes that awaited us. Or his wishes that the prelate we were to encounter had the ability and desire to narrate events, or to provide proof or disproof of words and facts to be verified. He hoped above all that there would be clarity concerning that enigmatic phrase of the official of the Khédive of Cairo with which he noted that Gustave was to be considered *une vieille femme*[92]. Hence it was now our business to discover when Gustave had become so, and if it was since childhood, since the ignominies resulting from the faintness he suffered in the winter of 1844.

Father Tabarant, the prelate of St. Sauveur, was kneeling in prayer on the marble pavement of the church. He was to one side, near a minor altar dedicated to the Virgin. Intent in prayers recited in a low voice, he moistened his lips tirelessly in a subdued and rapid murmur which the memory of long custom assisted, and accompanied in the pauses of fatigue, of salivation, of swallowing.

He became aware of our scuffling footsteps, those of the Arab – uncertain since he was afraid of the irregularity of the flooring: the marble slabs and the sharp mortar connecting strips. The prelate surprised us with a sidelong glance, with the summary and surveying look and movements of an old janissary. He pronounced words of polite welcome, intoning them like a litany, intermingling sharp phonemes with the prayers he had just uttered.

He looked stupefied at Harel Bey, his blindness, his loose and idle way of walking, his unbeliever's clothes of vivid colours and bizarre forms, which recalled countries clinging to doctrines which he feared through evil reputation, through vexatious orthodoxy, through the narrow-minded hagiography practised with conviction in our country.

I scrutinized him while he scrutinized us, all the while continuing to psalmodize, and to move with studied slowness

---

92   Master and confessor.

in our direction. I then squeezed Harel Bey's arm as a sign of agreement, despite my not having with the Bedouin familiarity or observances in common, and distrusting every possible alliance or pact which might signify, at least for him, mutual confidence and a sharing of ideas and thoughts.

Father Tabarant reached us, dragging his cassock with nonchalant charm. He was happy and satisfied, it was written on his face, that his habit was black, to signify the mourning and suffering of his church, that it was of this smoky colour to note and sum up the candles lit in praise and for our God, his Saints and the Virgin Mary, mother of all mothers, that it was fragrant of vapours from the incense burners waved to cast spells to combat demonic presences.

He then looked at us with spite and close scrutiny. In a sharp voice and with a harsh tone he asked me if it was my custom to fail to make the sign of the cross in traversing the threshold of the house of our Lord.

The Bedouin consigned himself to courtesy and moderation, drawing the attention of the priest and saving me from the embarrassment of having to provide an adequate response to Father Tabarant. He smiled, murmuring unexpected words of beneficent praise, which Father Tabarant welcomed with relish and satisfaction. But the Bedouin was an unprincipled falsifier in his behaviour and gestures so that, if only to make use of propitious occasions, he began to utter appropriate words and among these, in a voice scarcely audible, he expressed to the priest the spirit which had led us to him and indeed the necessity of obtaining from him reliable information about Gustave, about a manuscript, about a story entitled *November* and about *une vieille femme*.

Father Tabarant stirred and with a movement of his hand invited us to follow him, albeit walking very slowly, almost as in a procession of rituals and observances, into the sacristy, into the room of mutations, of liturgies enclosed in sacred texts, read scarcely audible in a low murmur, often forgotten through boredom and indifference.

The priest took off his cassock and dressed himself in vivid apparel: a stole, laces and ample soutane, also embroidered with Flanders lace. While he was carrying out these operations he was contrite, he made evident the particularity of being *magister et confessor*[93]. So that, several times, looking at us with haughty indifference, he murmured for us the word *placet* while he directed his eyes upwards.

I drew near him and I admonished him with memories. I reminded him that the Abbé Jeufroy, a person very highly esteemed at Chavignolles and his brother in faith, had gone to some trouble to inform him of our interest and of our needs, of our desire to learn things and events to do with Gustave. Yes, our Abbé Jeufroy had been there, do you remember, Pécuchet? One of the main founders of the party of order after the revolution of 1848 and who commanded fear with his subtle and intriguing power, but towards whom we felt attracted when, unexpectedly, changes of disposition, fallings-out among us, shattered nerves and unmotivated anguish threw us into a state of unhappiness, apathy, to the point of a devious desire to put an end to our days by committing suicide.

But then there came for us the redemption of scattered thoughts and neglected actions, as we became compromised (by chance, fortune or a secret desire?) by the ceremony of an Easter mass, celebrated by the Abbé Jeufroy, august and radiant in his lace-trimmed chasuble. From then on, my friend, and for a certain time we began to read books which recounted the Gospel, intent as we were to reach a certain perfection between virtues to be acquired and humility to be practised.

We then frequented, for certain periods and purposes, the Abbé Jeufroy. We were assiduously faithful, practising an impetuous devotion and you, my friend, squandered a lot of your time reading the *Manual for Seminarists* (a work in two volumes), in quenching your thirst with the *Water of Health*, in declaiming short prayers, in aspiring to enter into the Third Order of the Franciscans, in wanting to carry out a pilgrimage in order to

---

93   Master and confessor.

reach the Sanctuary of the Holy Virgin at Délivrande: a statue of the Virgin which escaped the sack of the Normans in the 9th century, then that of the Protestants in 1562 and finally the fury of the Revolutionaries of 1793.

And the books that you read to indoctrinate yourself? The *Examination of Christianity* by Hervieu, *The Catholicism of Perseverance* by Gaume, and then the writings of the mystics: of St. Teresa, of Louis of Granada, of Simpoli and of Monsignor Chaillot. We were very appreciated by the Abbé Jeufroy, above all thanks to you. I recognize that, my friend, since you had the impudence to ask the Abbé Jeufroy, as you well know, if he could express such esteem by means of a letter of presentation for Father Tabarant and thus to have knowledge of all the requisite truths.

Father Tabarant indeed who, once he had finished the devotional *placet*, began to shake his head as if he were subject to perplexity and doubts. For several seconds he scrutinized me and Harel Bey without seeing us, then he motioned with his chin at the Arab asking for explanations: if he shared, for example, the deeds and feelings of Gustave, if he too were part of the history to be checked, of the history that we are indeed investigating, as the Abbé Jeufroy had told him in his letter, for that Madame Caroline Commanville, niece of Gustave.

Father Tabarant then crossed himself and genuflected in front of a wooden crucifix, fastened to a wall between bookcases full of cloths and objects of sacred benediction. He began to speak, to evoke, to invoke long past summers and times. He remembered, for our knowledge and instruction, that Gustave was often in these places, had also lived in the house of his friend Ernest Chevalier, so that he had had the opportunity of knowing him, of visiting him, of receiving confidences.

The Bedouin was pleased to have these enlightenments from *Monsieur le prête* and burst out with praise for him. He then drew near me quietly and sought my shoulder with his outstretched hand. He hugged me, pulling me closely to himself, and in my ear, with a high-pitched voice so that this priest could hear, he asked me why Gustave, the *vieille femme hysterique*[94], in a carriage at night at Pont-l'Évêque, had been overwhelmed by fear and unreason, and had never again been the same, as he himself had described in the third part of the manuscript of Madame Caroline.

Father Tabarant then spoke of imprudence, of truths that were unknown, of careless expressions, of a will ceded to intolerance, because on the events of Pont-l'Évêque too much had already been said, betraying the will of God and giving free range to false beliefs.

Harel Bey began abruptly to drag his feet with rapid, uncertain movements, moving them to the rhythm of his blind man's stick. He moved wilfully in the direction of Father Tabarant, since the priest's voice had indicated the direction to him. He accosted him head on, his face almost touching that of the priest. He said that Madame Caroline was looking for a truth that was henceforth also his own, now that this manuscript had infected him too with curiosity. He added, with an altered voice and his hand stretched out in the warm air of the rectory, that as to the incident of Pont-l'Évêque he recognized as the sole truth that which could be drawn from the remarks in the manuscript.

Father Tabarant then spoke with fragile emotionality. Also with momentary hysteria. Of a possible sacred illness. Of a shudder of fear or of an indefinable form of panic. From obscure causes, hidden in the folds of a childhood marked by unexpected expectations, also by indecent vices since absinthe, tobacco and the frequenting of brothels had accompanied Gustave too often in the first twenty-two years of his *life, which was so active, passionate, and stirred by emotion, full of contradictory impulses and a multiplicity of sensations*[95].

Then, to recover his breath and more opportune words, Father Tabarant closed his hands tightly in prayer, opened his mouth and smiled condescendingly, reciting *Levo oculos unde veniet auxilium mihi. Amen, amen*[96].

---

94   Gustave Flaubert, *Letters*.
95
96   I raise my eyes towards he who gives me help.

The Bedouin, always close by him, brandishing his blind man's stick, suddenly seized his shoulders and shook him, mishandled him, pushing him to left and right with his staff, with short, continuous and rapid blows. No words, only unreasonable indignation which made him froth at the mouth with shortened breath, in apprehension of maintaining his stability and controlling his fears.

Father Tabarant released himself rapidly from the pressure, pushing the Bedouin away. He came beside me and began to whimper that this Arab was *la vraie vieille femme hysterique*[97] if he were seeking, with such means and efforts, the reasons for the hysteria of Monsieur Gustave. He knew little of the reasons and occurrences since the young Ernest Chevalier had never spoken openly about what had happened at Pont-l'Évêque. But instead, as priest and confessor he had been able to learn unexpected details, under the obligation however of the secrecy of his profession. It was certain, and this he was able to affirm and enunciate, that damaging and treacherous circumstances had cast a pall over that boy called Gustave, the work of devious figures – that is women – of perverse and morbidly dangerous females who responded to the names of Eulalie, Élise and Louise, finally also Emma, and that he had never understood if they were real creatures or had been created simply from Gustave's imagination.

The Bedouin then turned up his nose in a sign of agitation. He pointed his head and face upwards. He squatted down on all fours and began to drag his stick along, which he beat on the ground with an obsessive cadence.

Harel Bey sniffed the air in front of him, searched for a trace which would lead him to the corner in which Father Tabarant had quickly barricaded himself. Unexpectedly, Harel Bey stopped suddenly to face me, tracing my smell, lost in a trail of indistinguishable odours. He became aware of my particular smell and shouted to me so that I would understand his motives, which were aimed at knowing why two women were interested in the

---

97   The true hysterical old woman.

incident at Pont-l'Évêque. Why Madame Caroline's manuscript gave no indication of it. Why did this priest defend Gustave, perhaps to redeem him from events, inconveniences, unexpected circumstances?

I pronounced a few words, my friend, to free him from rancour. I moved a few steps so that my hand could comfort him, give him support above all in his indignation, so that the priest, in a changed situation, might have the courage and dispatch to tell us what he had to say. Without shame or reproaches or justificatory deceptions.

Father Tabarant whispered in a singsong some devotional words to free the Bedouin from spite: *Levo oculos unde veniet auxilium mihi. Amen, amen ... Levo oculos unde veniet auxilium mihi. Amen, amen,* he repeated. Then he murmured some words, first with a mournful intonation, then in a tone adorned with new energy.

A very strange event, it's true, since, according to the words and guarantees of the priest and according to gossip and what has been related, on that night in that particular place, at Pont-l'Évêque to be clear, there were two carriages proceeding in opposite directions. And in these carriages there were perhaps, or certainly, Madame Eulalie and Madame Élise, the ladies who were Gustave's first loves.

The road was narrow, and the horses, excited by a storm streaking the sky, were running out of control through an air laden with an intense odour of damp and muddy earth. A collision was inevitable, disastrous. It was then that Gustave lost himself in the fog of unconsciousness, gripped also by uncontrolled hysteria to the point of losing his reason, and, without anyone knowing how he had arrived in that place, whether or not he had travelled on one of the carriages, and whether, at that moment, he had been snatched from the arms of one of the women, and, indeed, if these particular women were truly on that road and in that place, if they were real and not the fruit of a literary fantasy.

My friend, thus every testimony of what happened on that night is true and false at the same time. This also includes the words of the reverend father, reporting words known in the confidence of the confessional, perhaps from Ernest Chevalier. Words which at times refer to the fact that, beyond the official account according to which Gustave was in the company of his brother Achille, our man was accompanied by the carnal Eulalie, who had granted him sensual love, or else that he was with the angelic Élise who had bewitched him with romantic love, or otherwise that he was alone since Eulalie and Élise were together in a carriage.

Nothing else, then. There was no aggressive wickedness, purposeful insolence, or outrage of intimacy. There was perhaps the awkwardness of a boorish nickname: *vieille femme hysterique* as someone baptized Gustave, since *a day didn't pass without him seeing every now and then passing before his eyes a great number of horses or fireworks*[98].

The Bedouin then pronounced in a stentorian voice that of such conjectures there were no traces in the manuscript, that Father Tabarant had devious interests, all aimed at hiding the proven truth, that the supposed truths expressed by the Father were of no use for the benefit of the niece called Caroline, for the conscience of an Arab like himself forgotten in pages of notes, for the scruples of a wretched rural intermediary like me abandoned in a miserable village called Chavignolles, that it was now time to come to terms with the sluggards, with the counterfeiters of truth, with the mentors of deliberate falsities, and also with a homicide.

Father Tabarant became alarmed. He looked at the Bedouin with suspicion and preoccupation, and murmured with a mere thread of voice his devotional prayer: *Levo oculos unde veniet auxilium mihi. Amen, amen ... Levo oculos unde veniet auxilium mihi. Amen, amen.* And then he added with words barely murmured that Gustave had asserted that *there was nothing better for him than a beautiful, well-heated room, with the books that* (he loved) *and with all the free time that he wished. As to health ... healing* (was) *so slow in these miserable nervous illnesses that* (it was) *very difficult to notice any improvement*[99].

Harel Bey barely smiled at him, his face swallowed up in

---

98   Gustave Flaubert, *Letters.*

99   Gustave Flaubert, *Letters.*

indifference, a look without expression or emotions, blind in ideas and words. He moved closer to me with an uncertain step, the stick for a guide. He asked me in an undertone if I too supposed that this priest, who was so fearful between prayers and reckless words, could possibly be the young protagonist of *November?* He was convinced in fact that that hero did not die from sadness, consumption or a melancholy lack of will-power after having spent his life in sloth, in the way that Gustave had written.

Harel Bey was persuaded now that the young man had settled down in the church since it was true that one day *he had had the desire to be a priest to pronounce the orations over the body of the dead, to wear a hair shirt, to prostrate himself in the love of God*[99].

Father Tabarant heard this speech and wrapped himself closely in his lace-trimmed soutane. He then raised his arms to recite once again: *Levo oculos unde veniet auxilium mihi. Amen, amen ... Levo oculos unde veniet auxilium mihi. Amen, amen,* to protect himself from unwelcome, menacing, cutting words. He took a few steps to draw near me. He moved close by my side and whispered to me excessive, immoderate, apprehensive words, because he was frightened by the shameful boldness of this Bedouin who appeared to him to be enraged to the point of craziness, madness indeed, still more, a maniac.

I left him prey to tremors and incautious memories, while, with Harel Bey, who was urging me to go back to being his peripatetic mentor, I regained the entrance to the church. Steps taken wearily through tensions and preoccupations, but also through fear of hindrances, of obstacles that might have been overlooked while our minds were elsewhere.

Then suddenly, with frenzy, with energetic tugs, Harel Bey turned away from my side, murmuring hasty excuses now that, unexpectedly, he had become aware of having some words to settle with that priest who had been very intent on defending characters and friends of Gustave without in the very least caring about that manuscript we were investigating.

The Bedouin turned back, clutching his stick with zeal and vigour. I saw him moving away with determination and I remained waiting, in obvious distress, with reluctantly having various thoughts. I know nothing about either the words or the deeds exchanged in the church. I heard only the stick beating upon the floor. I heard footsteps come and go with ready self-confidence, with prompt diligence, with a lively accent, with unsuspected vigour.

I heard nothing else.

We returned to the inn after an hour of hard walking. Tomorrow, save for unexpected events or injunctions or different orders, we will be on our way, and leaving at dawn.

I hope to see you soon my dear friend, soon.

B.

Café du Port-de-Fer

14, Boulevard Poissonnière, Paris,

18 June

Dear friend,

Here is *The Legend of Saint Julian the Hospitaller*[100]. And it would be appropriate to remember on this occasion the cult of Our Lady of La Salette, now that, from what we can observe, our own land, from the time in which our father had the impulse to compose *Saint Julian*, was pervaded by ancient furores of religious devotion, of high and robust lineage.

Here is the cult of Our Lady of La Salette and that of Saint Julian the Hospitaller which had great glory, since, for long periods and in distant lands of intense heat, the litany of *Bénédictions et malédictions, prophéties de la révélation privé*[101] was uninterrupted. Saint Julian was able then, with good reason and with worthy devotion towards his mother and towards his consort, to become the archetype of the Marian cult.

My dear Pécuchet, at the moment I feel reconquered and fascinated by past ardours now that we are dedicating ourselves, with courteous respect and with meditated devotion, to sacred purposes. Do you remember? Do you remember that midnight mass when the incense rose up towards the ceiling of the church

---

100   Gustave Flaubert wrote *The Legend of Saint Julian the Hospitaller* in 1877.

101   Benedictions and maledictions, prophecies of intimate revelation.

and a great garland of lights adorned it while enormous candles illumined both sides of the tabernacle? We had then, my dear friend, moving flashes of faith since we took to assiduously studying the Gospels – in particular, passages of Ecclesiastes, of Isaiah, and of Jeremiah – the *Imitation* of Thomas à Kempis and the *Manual for Seminarists*. We also contemplated – to experience astonishment and to be overcome by ecstasy – a good pilgrimage to some sanctuary dedicated to the Virgin Mary, so that we could recite with other pilgrims the faithful hymn of praise: "*Mother most pure, Mother most chaste, Mother most amiable, Mother most venerable, powerful Virgin, merciful Virgin*[102]!"

Were we true believers or astute simulators, trying only to please our father Gustave?

Now the Bedouin and I must attend to matters concerning St. Julian the Hospitaller and, perhaps as well, the cult of Our Lady of La Salette, since Gustave sometimes went around repeating that he would have been *pleased to be a mystic* (because it would have been) *agreeable to believe in Paradise and to drown in a sea of incense*[103].

Here we are then confronted with the Legend of St. Julian the Hospitaller, now that a certain entreaty has resulted in the recounting of this story, hitherto lost in time among the writings of our father. The initiative and the affront for this paradoxical violence are the work of a woman – perhaps a virgin disguised as a woman to tempt our redemption? – whom we have met here in Paris, glimpsed for the first time in a corner of the baroque salon of a restaurant, marked by blushes of alcoholic viciousness, the slave of several bottles of wine and a crystal goblet.

But there was something profoundly mystical in this apparition, as it seemed to us that we had been summoned to a mission accompanying a beautiful Lady who seemed to want to invite us to have no fear in the face of a squalid and completely unedifying story, because she was there before us to reveal lost wishes.

She was a lady consumed in the solitude of a lament, in the midst of lights sketched by the semi-darkness and the silence of

---

102 Gustave Flaubert, *Bouvard e Pécuchet*.

103 Gustave Flaubert, *Intimate Thoughts* – published posthumously.

bated breaths, and who was intoning, with a voice thickened by alcohol and by betrayed memories, the poem of places and legends, of a host who had become holy, of epic episodes recounted by preachers and by storytellers, because in that poem she wished to live, to be greeted as a pilgrim, and above all as a wanderer who had lost her way and who, on *holy days, when the great bells of the cathedral spread joy in the people's hearts* (she would have seen) *the inhabitants leave their houses, the dances in the squares, the barrels of beer at the crossroads ... and, when evening had fallen, the sobs* (would have overcome her)[104].

The lady struggled thus in the torment of melancholy, in the bewilderment of a path never found, of libations indulged in with frequency, and which belonged often to the customs of wayfarers, of poets, of assassins by profession or simply for pleasure. She struggled also because each plea for salvation went unanswered. Because no one believed any longer that *the Son of Man* (would come) *in such an hour as ye think not*[105].

Harel Bey and I, industrious and tireless travellers among Gustave's books and stories, took in without curiosity the rhythms of that long, rambling account, the frenetic flow of a narrative, set out with surges of drunkenness, the melody of an incautious bewilderment that often ended in a sneer of febrile excitation. We marked in our memory, amidst words repeated in a whisper with the intention of sealing such touching nostalgias and remembrances, the words of that lullaby, the dictates of a prose, the airs of a song for a lost love, a song of desperation and anguish.

We listened to it with compunction and embarrassment in the expectation that events and chance might be able to clear up our perplexities and doubts. We waited fearfully for the end of the account, hoping that that woman might have had an occasion, a way or an opportunity to arrive at our table and give us a plausible account of her confusion, of her determined will to offer refuge to the story of St. Julian: a story from which she believed she had been exiled with impunity or unjustly ostracized, in enigmatic

---

104   Gustave Flaubert, *The Legend of Saint Julian the Hospitaller.*
105   Matthew 24, 44.

148

circumstances, by the storyteller who had transcribed it.

Gustave had granted diverse and oblique hospitalities in his story: *an old man dressed in sackcloth, a rosary at his side, a knapsack on his shoulders; ... a gypsy with a braided beard, silver bracelets on both arms, and flaming eyes; ... an old, learned monk* (who taught) *the Gospel, the Arabic numerals, the Latin letters, ...* and then *master apothecaries ... equerries who amused themselves with javelins ... a band of adventurers ... a girl with large black eyes like two sweet lights*[105].

Personages, true or fictitious, who had first swarmed in the mind of our father Gustave, and who then were granted space among the lines of a narrative without arrogantly asking anything but expecting to be well designed and treated. At least for the time being. And *Madame la Chanteuse?* We had to look into her intentions, diversions and requests.

Harel Bey and I had arrived recently in Paris, in late afternoon, after a journey spent in the silence of reflections and expectations, also admiring a landscape that had kept us company for timeless hours. A coach, which had no other passenger, carried us along very indirect cobbled roads. After leaving Les Andelys, we travelled towards Gaillon, where we were welcomed by what had once been a splendidly turreted castle decorated with arabesques, and which now was a horrible jail with prisoners indiscriminately locked up and forced to labour from seven in the morning to eight in the evening – so our coachman informed us with a horrid sneer. The chatter of my companion relieved my melancholy thoughts. The Bedouin asked promptly for the names of the places that we passed, which he then repeated several times, like a litany, so that his memory could guide him on other occasions or at need. Thus we passed, while grinding cobbles with thick wheels of wood and iron, Neaufles, Dongu, St. Clair-sur-Epte, Ecos, Gasny, as far as Vernon, where we stopped for a rest, just beside the mill next to the old wooden bridge restored after the infamy suffered during the War of 1870.

We resumed our journey without entering Mantes, which I wished to avoid – after payment of a toll of 50 soldi and despite the acid remonstrations of the Bedouin since the coach had to follow treacherous, unpaved secondary roads. All this to avoid the spot where the fatal encounters of our father with a certain lady called Louise had taken place. We took an oblique direction towards Poissy after leaving behind Les Mureaux, Medan and Villennes. The portentous silhouette of the Church of Our Lady of the Assumption welcomed us, to restore our spirits, with its two Romanesque bell-towers, its portico with two tympanums, adorned with a suggestive and fantastic bestiary, with putti riding on sea-monsters and with a symbolic representation of the Annunciation exalting the virginity of Mary. Churches dedicated to Mary seemed to be everywhere, so that I began to reflect upon what awaited us now that we had to deal with St. Julian the Hospitaller.

Paris welcomed us, once we had passed the villages of Maisons-Laffitte, Houilles-Carrières-sur-Seine and Asnières on roads adjoining the railway station, and there we had the dismal fortune to encounter the members of a German choir. *The men in tail-coats, the outfit of a workman dressed up in his Sunday best, they seemed to me to be returning from the Montparnasse Cemetery after burying Giacomo Meyerbeer* the composer and with him his celebrated works *'Robert le Diable', 'Les Huguenots', 'Le Prophète', 'L'Africaine'. All of which seemed a tavern-production, an academy of rabble. I seemed to have returned to a celebration of '48 ... There was something that frightened me about these choristers*[106].

However, we were able to while away the time of waiting, as Madame expected us at Bonvalet for an evening of rehearsals with songs and drinks. This had been promised us by Monsieur Lafosse, Abbot of Saint Julien le Riche, to whom I had applied through letters, recommendations and as a guide, considering him a scholar particularly devoted to the legend of Saint Julian. This Abbot, a holy man, had meditated on and written anecdotes and histories of Saint Julian of Cennonia (an enlightened man of extraordinary virtues since he had resuscitated three corpses), of Saint Julian of Alveria (a man profoundly overcome by the desire for martyrdom, who offered himself with sincerity and a sure

---

106 Frères de Goncourt, *Journal.*

instinct to the persecutors of the faith), of Saint Julian the Monk (who had had a very arduous life and who died pierced by the weapons of a knight), and above all of Saint Julian the Hospitaller, who mistook – through prophecy and considerations, as the profaner of wise and astute families – his mother for his wife and his father for his wife's lover, so that, driven by uncontrollable anger and wounded honour, he killed his parents and, because of those deaths, took to expiating and repressing his voluptuous passion for blood.

The Abbé Lafosse had narrated this to me in a letter, adding, as a summation of information and doctrine, that a certain woman, reciter of the legend of Saint Julian the Hospitaller in Paris, in a good restaurant in the boulevard du Temple, mixed up languages and words narrating her sad experience as a refugee since, in a night of infamous drinking and heretical temptations, she had consumed mixed and fermented alcoholic drinks beyond measure. She had thus lost her ability to reason and her sense of place, as well as the will to continue her existence, in a tale in which, she asserted, a writer had made her the protagonist of events, among holy processions, moral sacrifices, devout marriage ceremonies, rash sexual abstinences and holy rituals offered to the Creator.

The ritual of the Offertory had become, in brief, a necessary habit, first weekly, then daily; it was transformed into a need, an obsession, disordered to the point of ignoring all moderation. In a night of revelry and gluttony, in order to forget her condition and misfortunes, this woman had taken to consuming the vilest, most adulterated kind of alcohol – perhaps absinthe – so that, in the disorder of drunkenness, she had lost for moments her own identity and found herself no longer able to take part in a tale in which she had thought she must and would be able to live forever.

She had recognized herself to be, from then on, a pilgrim without a past or future, wandering in a Purgatory of waiting, hoping that the tale would once again take her in, be her home and hospitable refuge. In her heart, she wanted to be able to belong forever to the story of Saint Julian the Hospitaller, written by that Monsieur Gustave Flaubert of Rouen, and in those pages she yearned to regain hospitality and respect, as well as appropriate lodging and function.

Paris welcomed us, after we had slipped away as best we could from the irreverent rashness of the choristers and wanderers who seemed to be lodging near the station, and the city beguiled us with a day of splendid colours, of intense perfumes, so that the Bedouin was intoxicated in the bewilderment and the consternation of his sense of smell, following trails of fragrances, odours of newly-opened flowers, of warm bodies, of rich sweats, of pools of sunlight, of dried-up dung, of oily scrap-iron, of flatulent viscera, of rotten teeth, of trees in leaf, of open sewers, of prostitutes' genitals, of pigeon excrement, of priests' cassocks, of newly-cut grass, of *toilettes de nécessité*[107], extremely convenient at 5 to 10 cents, of a city which presented itself, scantily dressed and neglected, to mockery, to gossip, to being *the terminus for all the fortunes made in the provinces*[108].

Paris welcomed us when a modest but pretentious coach abandoned us in the square of Château d'Eau, where the boulevard Sanit-Martin occupies the space of an ancient bastion of city walls, suppressed under Louis XIV. The price of the journey was 50 cents, even though the coachman was not wearing a *chapeau blanc*[109], nor were the wheels of the carriage lined with rubber, nor was the collar of the nag garnished with a tinkling bell. These are signs, as you well know, which in the capital distinguishes, to sight and hearing, service and quality.

Harel Bey clung anxiously to my arm, bewildered by a sensation of vertigo caused by the whirlwind of the carriage, by the fragrance and stenches which, rapidly following one upon the other in intensity, had crushed him, constraining him to rub himself and massage his nose, wounded in its sense of smell.

He struck the point of his stick several times on the ground in fretfulness and anxiety. He muttered words faint with emotion and sought refuge in an accommodating alleyway, in rue Beranger,

---

107 Public toilets.
108 Frères de Goncourt, *Journal*.
109 White hat.

at the Café du Jardin du Theatre. He then began to ask me, with anxious concern, names of streets and squares, also of boulevards and stations since, in the confused disorientation of the carriage's frenetic wanderings, he had perceived near and far, by sniffing the air and hearing noises, the residence of Messieurs Huot de Goncourt, at 43 rue St. Georges, a little beyond the Church of Notre-Dame de Lorette, behind the Chaussée d'Antin: a home in which he had lived when abandoned by Gustave and which he had left to become messenger of documents and writings on Gustave himself. Indeed, also to escape from the deafening noises of the workshop for the manufacture of wind instruments of Adolphe Sax, which was across the street.

I reassured him, informing him that Monsieur Edmond de Goncourt now lived alone – since his brother Jules had died – at 53 boulevard Montmorency, in a home which, purchased for 83,000 francs, was a *great tasteful plaything... two drawing-rooms, the sunshine among the branches... a small wood silhouetted against the sky, ... a corner of the earth and the flight of birds passing overhead*[110] and at the back his beautiful garden counterpointed by a solid grove of trees, a delightful plaything being transformed into a true *Maison d'un Artiste.*

I then began to remind Harel Bey of the chief reasons for our visit to Paris, the wish to keep an appointment with a certain Madame who was the subtle preacher of a misguided legend, and we wanted to have clear judgments on the story of St. Julian: the umpteenth work of Monsieur Gustave.

Having put his interests and his troubled spirit in some sort of order as best I could, I began to sip *un boisson de citron pressé*[111] as the Bedouin began to murmur into my ear perfidious, indecent and false words.

He spoke of blood, and death through asphyxiation, since this was an act and gesture carried out without noise, fingerprints or revealing stains. He spoke of murder, albeit casually, half smiling, obscurely threatening. I understood very little of his passion, I

---

110 Frères de Goncourt, *Journal.*
111 A lemonade.

understood that he would have, with determined desire and pleasure, disarmed the boldness of that woman of whom the Abbé Lafosse had spoken to us and who, on our behalf, he had contacted, so that we might meet her a few hours hence.

Harel Bey was afraid of an idle defence by this woman towards Monsieur Gustave and his niece the heiress, since, so far as he had understood, this writer of legends and shady chronicles was hoping to acquire a role as protagonist, even if only secondary, in the story of Saint Julian, and to remain there in harmony with herself and her conscience marked by an obscure past.

All this the Bedouin said sneeringly, revealing to me a new and unaccustomed aspect, indeed an evil and hellish one. All this murmured the Bedouin in a tiny voice that appeared to negate the words just pronounced. This said the Bedouin and at once began to speak of mischievous deeds, a facetious spirit, cantankerous fantasies. This said the Bedouin and he immediately let his head hang loose in an unfeigned doze, awaiting events and an appointment with an intriguing interlocutress.

Next to our table a rabble of *National Guardsmen, half-drunk and with their shakos hanging behind their heads, bellies sticking out, pipe in mouth ... Amidst sips of beer, to say nothing of full glasses, emerged all the foulness and squalor of the low-life of Paris... Outrageous indecencies to make the tarts laugh, and all intermingled with uncivil hatred towards the church, sneers against the saints, Paradise, the Virgin... This is a squalid and ignoble France*[112]. I remained listening, appalled, while the Bedouin was crumpled up in an abandoned half-doze, his head in his intertwined arms. I am sure, in fact, that he was attentive to the words and jokes that had been exchanged.

Some hours later we abandoned the Café du Jardin du Théatre to ascend once more the rue de Vendome. Harel Bey beat his stick on the ground to test the way ahead, having little pity for the passers-by as he tapped them abruptly and impudently, though not hard. We thus regained the passage behind the theatre of Madame Virginie Déjazet to later emerge in boulevard du Temple just as

---

112 Frères de Goncourt, *Journal*.

evening was falling, insinuating itself with ill-will between the silhouettes of majestic palaces pointing to the sky, adorned with stuccoes and iron-work balconies wrought by master blacksmiths.

I advised Harel Bey at that point to adopt behaviour appropriate to the inquest, to our status of being advisors to Madame Caroline, procurers of truth and rightful business. In reply he drew into an alleyway and began to write, with a firm and rapid hand, on his braille notebook, which he drew from a pocket of his caftan.

Concise signs as a nervous movement of the hand scratched a waxed cloth with zeal and vehemence. Succinct notes, certainly. A memorandum for eventualities and extortions, perhaps to recall ideas for criminal plans, or sordid fantasies for summary judgments. Finally, he smiled at me, as is his custom when he entertains strange ideas, plans intrigues, proposes possible illusions to himself. He grabbed my arm with a strong grip. He remained in silent thought and, as a shrewd blind man, began to show, with discretion, the walking stick that accompanies him as a civil sign of his disability.

We wandered about for several minutes, with intentional pauses and easy steps, until we reached 29 boulevard du Temple, as far as the Restaurant Bonvalet.

We found a large and singular locale. Thus it appeared to me. Bronzes, silver, and majolica of irregular craftsmanship were the bases for oil-lamps and rocaille *abat-jour* vases. Heavy wooden tables set with tablecloths of Flanders linen, Solingen cutlery, Sevres porcelain. So it seemed to me. Solicitous shadows since the faint light of the candles was lost in the amaranth and gold of the wallpaper. Two low, wide windows produced a natural light and a muffled, funereal atmosphere.

On one side, half-hidden in brocade hangings, an inlaid wooden stage offered poetry readings or song recitals for the attention of customers, usually inured to the food and carefully selected wines.

I imagined all this because on that day the restaurant was closed for rehearsals and for the weekly repose of the personnel.

Open only to our vices thanks to the recommendations of the Abbé Lafosse who had done us this favour.

With my companion clutching my arm, his stick gathered up in an inoffensive fist, I crossed the dining-room heading for a table in the corner next to a window looking out on the street and buildings, as well as with a good view of the artists' stage.

At that moment, a woman on the stage was showing off her voice, reciting bastardized words, all mixed together in drunken cadences, with inevitable slips, given that alcohol was in control of both sound and memory. From time to time the woman gave herself a boost, amidst the trembling of her accents and movements. With neither modesty nor remorse, she readily gulped down wine from a labelled bottle which encumbered her feet. She then fell silent for a few moments to experience the warmth that bathed her body, pacified her limbs, granted her a few appeased breaths, recovered memories, unexpected self-assurance.

Once more the woman threw herself back into logorrhoea, into rigmarole with an infinity of mysterious words, bizarre little verses, homilies in lame rhymes. It was always about St. Julian the Hospitaller, and about what that writer Gustave might have offered her in the way of comfort and welcome: a consoling literary refuge for a feckless guest. The woman spoke without pausing for breath, and told stories in extreme cadences, with long-drawn-out sips, rivulets wetting her lips and chin, eyes flaming in a scabrous manner, with deliberate provocations, with desolating distress. Finally, with forced words, with an occasional but necessary toast, scrabbling among her memories, she concluded with these words: "This was the story of a certain Gustave, a writer, just as you could find in some apocryphal manuscript, and it's also the story of abandoned melancholy and of hopes now looked for in some other place, a place without borders or customs, it's whispered that the evil-intentioned will use their astuteness just as he who wrote of St. Julian is evil-intentioned. *Bénédictions et maléditions, prophéties de la révélation privée* of Madame Caroline Hamard, niece of that Gustave Flaubert, writer".

We listened to the woman, her performance, her way of telling stories as a mixture of fantasy and reality, her flashy exit from the scene, almost as a character of ambiguous appearance. Then in the silence of a darkened stage, of a curtain closed in haste, I began to take a look through the window next to me.

I spoke to my blind companion in a low voice, murmuring to him feelings and solaces. The building facing us was in fact number 42. Gustave had lived in that building during one of his Parisian sojourns. I spoke a few words to reassure the Bedouin that in fact we seemed to be under a spell of improbable coincidences: it seemed that the Abbé Lafosse had been a prophet of providence and opportune surprises.

Harel Bey bent his head and manifested obsequious reverence, anxious to demonstrate gratitude and proof of devotion and forgiveness. He uttered words which were indistinguishable from each other but marked by a tone of pardon, prayer and ecclesiastical cadences. Abruptly he turned his head around and strained his eyes into the darkness. A pair of hands, his hands, which at times spoke, began to flutter in the air, then closed into a funnel in front of his mouth. Once more he inclined his head towards me and expressed himself clearly in words, maintaining that he would have had great enjoyment and delight if he had been able, after the informal and public ritual of approach, to speak alone to that Madame la chanteuse. He wished to know things that had to do with himself. An act of abandonment as well. Indeed, a negligence of affection. And also sentences to do with the dubious morality of certain writers. The tone of his voice was inclined to the tragic even if it concealed various intentions, treacherous plans of which one should be cautious.

Suddenly, without clear reasons or a sudden change of mood, he began to sniff the air, to utter assessments and opinions on the food, based on discourses and harangues he had heard in the salon of the Goncourt brothers. Then he spoke of restaurants, cafes, brasseries and patisseries where various writers (Alfred de Vigny, Alphonse Daudet, Théophile Gautier, Charles-Augustin Sainte-Beuve, Hippolyte-Adolphe Taine and George Sand, the Bedouin recalled) often dropped in and ended up having a meal and telling each other amusing anecdotes that were then collected and reported in a newspaper. A L'Havre, rue St. Lazare. Au Véfour, rue des Petits Champs. Au Paillard, rue de la Chausée d'Antin. Au Maire, boulevard St. Denis. Au Brébant, boulevard Poissonière. Places of encounter and ribaldry for dinners or snacks worthy of sumptuous stories. Above all at number 7 rue Mazet, at the restaurant Magny where, one day, Gustave had begun to tell how *as a young man he was so vain that, when he went to the brothel with friends, he chose the ugliest girl of all and wanted to fuck her in front of everyone, with his cigar in his mouth. He didn't enjoy himself at all, but it was for the sake of the audience... In spite of his frank nature, Gustave was never perfectly sincere in speaking of his feelings or about his sufferings or his loves*[113].

Harel Bey remembered these episodes, fixing his eyes on the void and gesturing with his hand to gain attention, particularly the notice of a waiter, for the opportunity and pleasure of ordering, in memory of the Goncourt salon, a Berçu steak with mushrooms from Carrière-sous-Bois. He got little attention for his desires and tastes, as the waiter to whom he signalled shrugged his shoulders and murmured that he had orders, for our menu, to serve us only bottles of Château-la-Tour, since Madame la chanteuse had taken on the role of being our hostess to confirm promises and vows and to recount her existence, which was in truth singular and strange.

The waiter murmured these words with a bizarre intonation, and immediately took his leave. He was an ageless man, or a man of many ages, young and old at the same time, both attentive and inconsiderate, with a body marked by neglect of his health, wearing a modest frock-coat with large grease-stains. Abruptly, Madame appeared from the dark, with caution and the step of an artiste, wrapped in a dense and nauseating cloud of alcohol. She sat down at our table, demonstrating, now that she had begun to speak to us in a lisping and febrile sing-song, an interest and a certain seductiveness in regard to the blindness of Harel Bey.

She was a woman licentious in words and dress, her broken

---

113   Frères de Goncourt, *Journal.*

and improper speech full of trivial errors, accompanying an ill-kept body. Her breasts, marked with wrinkles and creases, were loosely accommodated in the cavities of a black corset, cut generously low. Her outer garment was in brown wool, and in the pleats of her skirt and corset two rows of buttons with dark ribbons made a bold display. Some jewellery – an amber bracelet, a cameo, a pin with an ivory portrait.

Suddenly it seemed to me that I knew this woman, her clothes, her way of moving about carelessly, with risky, extravagant manners. Above all it seemed to me that she was pronouncing words that I had already heard, words that were punishing to a civilized ear. It is certain that she was luring Harel Bey with crude obscenities, and she kept repeating, in the midst of her speech, furtive movements and glances, which meant clearly that a dining-room was not sufficient to satisfy all the needs of the flesh.

Suddenly I regained the memories that had initially escaped me. Another woman, the same clothes and speech. Do you remember, my friend? I am speaking of the manuscript that the Bedouin gave and of a certain Madame Louise, one of Gustave's women. The chanteuse dressed and expressed herself in the same manner: so it seemed to me. Just as it appeared to me that she was Louise. Or had Louise been described and recounted in that piece of writing, disdainfully it is true, copying a certain Madame la chanteuse who asked Gustave to accommodate her within his story of Saint Julian the Hospitaller?

I noted then that Harel Bey was writing in his little notebook, that he was also smiling, that he withdrew himself with ironic negligence from the insidiousness of Madame. This lady warbled on, accommodated herself uneasily, glanced with gloomy cupidity at the empty glasses. A signal, then, agreed upon in advance perhaps, as a hand moved through the air and a tiny waiter, bald and severe, succoured us with three bottles of Château-la-Tour. He uncorked them with ritual obsequiousness and filled three glasses. Madame engorged the liquid in her glass in one breath so that the man, with rapid movements, refilled it, and then abandoned us with cadenced steps, moving with difficulty.

159

I thus took advantage of distractions and digressions to press the woman with speeches and questions, to listen to her above all on presumed truths, on possible gossip, on certain and uncertain happenings. I spoke to her about facts, happenings and circumstances, about Gustave, about Paris, about the undesirable companions and unwholesome moods of the writer. Madame listened to me, swallowing the wine in generous draughts, looking around her with a bemused air, glancing from time to time beyond the window to glimpse the building opposite. Then she bent her head and uttered uncertain words, muddled up by a tongue swollen by alcohol and rich in memories.

She confessed her feelings, her passions, her abandonment of modesty when Gustave settled in the hotel opposite, number 42, as a guest. She had asked him for help and at least a line in his works so that she might have the opportunity to trust herself to a written page, a dwelling-place which could accommodate her as a true personage.

Gustave distanced himself from affections and entreaties, as an astute but singular guest he had ensured that his *maman* could take a room in the same building, on the floor below his. *Yes, his mother, resembling a Moslem princess. His mother who imposed on him a thousand unimaginable tyrannies. His mother who continually had need of him*, as manuscripts and apocryphal memories recorded, Madame told us, continuing to swallow wine, mangling nouns and verbs in alcoholic confusion.

Harel Bey then began to pepper her with pressing questions and in peremptory accents, to give her little chance of escape, to rein her in with impudent insistence, even as the lady begged for some sort of refuge. He embarrassed her with such crude words that Madame la chanteuse, in a moment of perverse lucidity, put forward excuses and murmured that other women had also asked, albeit with conflicting reasons, for hospitality from Monsieur Gustave.

A certain Louise and a certain Emma, in truth, who had flirted with Gustave, in the virtues of exasperated passion, to obtain refuge either in a dense correspondence or in a scandalous book.

The one boasting of past amorous devotions and shameless love-makings, the other vaunting indecent romantic intrigues and trials for obscenity.

At that moment, for singular gossipy attention, I asked Madame if she might have known these women personally now that she was expressing pungent judgments, with a complete lack of diffidence. Madame began to drink with obstinate impudence, to think while playing with her glass, glancing at me with a look lost in space, smiling with alcoholic charm at the Bedouin. Suddenly, brusquely in fact, in an outburst of words and spasms of gurgling, she admitted to having read a great deal about these women and that, in conclusion, she could well say that those two women were very little suited to Gustave, now that, precisely because of their harmful presence, *Madame la mère*[114] had begun to complain of imaginary but lacerating illnesses. Consequently Gustave, overcome by such lugubrious circumstances and tormenting exasperation, had freed himself from the two women with ill grace and with agonizing farewells.

To placate words, insalubrious thoughts, and anguish, Madame gulped down three glasses of alcohol, albeit with the insecurity of a hand afflicted with uncontrolled trembling and a mouth twisted by a compulsive tic and a foamy dribble. She observed us with studied slowness, even winked at us and murmured words which concealed unappeased rancour and intoxicated confusions. Finally, she added that she was inclined to give us help, since Gustave, or whoever else in his place, whether we ourselves or Madame Caroline, had granted her, if indeed only tardily, an assured haven, had offered her, that is, a story in which she could obtain refuge, or indeed we had bestowed upon her a free promise of a future conformable to her desires.

Madame's voice was broken by uncertainty. She began to sip wine with a pacified slowness, almost as if she had lost consciousness and awareness. She turned round confused, shook her head, looked at us, searching out our eyes. The Bedouin

---

114 Madame the mother of Gustave.

abruptly stretched out his hand and touched her face. He began to caress her with voluptuous languor. His mouth brushed across the mouth of the woman. His breath was corrupted by the pungent and bitter breath of Madame.

Harel Bey asked the lady, with haughty and decisive grace, if she, with sincere goodwill, had really thought that she could be a character in Gustave's works because, in truth, he couldn't imagine her appearance as a woman of such shrewd fascination linked to circumstances or volumes which had to do with Gustave, and in particular Saint Julian the Hospitaller, who was now so venerated and respected as to validate the saying that *those who have not said their paternoster to St. Julian many times, even though they have good beds, will be ill-lodged*[115].

The lady smiled with complacent derision. She replied that, even though shameless and on occasion wanton, she could have asked, with obstinate determination, for hospitality from Gustave, since clearly in the past she had been another woman. So that, in the story in question, she could have been able to act the part of the lady and wife of Julian the Hospitaller. And that, at the first meeting, he *had been dazzled with love, all the more since Julian had until then led a very chaste life... She was truly gracious and shapely, with her slender waist... An enchanting smile parted her lips. The curls of her long hair were caught in precious stones... and the youthfulness of her body could be discerned under the transparency of her tunic*[116]. Thus in her mind, when she was young, and long before she had taken to alcohol, she would certainly have been able to resemble the wife of Julian so closely as to be able to play her part. Thus she would have merited acceptance and love, and also a conjugal life which might contemplate *a castle of white marble... a grove of orange-trees... the shores of a bay where pink shells cracked beneath the feet... fountains in the rooms, mosaics in the courtyards... kennels, stables, an oven for the bread, an olive-mill and granaries. Also a pergola for relaxing outdoors and a lawn for pall-mall*[116].

Thus Gustave should have been able to offer her hospitality in

---

115 Boccaccio, *Decameron*.
116 Gustave Flaubert, *The Legend of Saint Julian the Hospitaller*.

his *Saint Julian* without second thoughts or hesitations. Now that Gustave was gone, her proposals and suggestions – she confided to us with a spirit of revenge and inflexibility – remained valid, so that she could finally put an end to this life of hers consumed in reciting and singing, with ill-will, the legend of St. Julian amidst bottles of Château-Latour in the Restaurant Bonvalet in boulevard du Temple.

Madame Caroline, now the unique and legitimate heir of Gustave's stories, was indebted to her in the matter of failed rights and claims and was obliged to welcome her among the actors of that short story, to grant her a space so that she might recover an existential reality missing thus far: that is to be real above and beyond a presumed idea which remained that and nothing more, amidst the imaginings of a writer uncle.

Suddenly Harel Bey began to sniff the air, to sniff the surroundings with insistence and distaste. He bent over to one side to sniff Madame more closely, to perceive her odour because, I imagined, he believed that the fragrance and the stench might offer him disclosures, resolve dilemmas, free up solutions. With an agile hand opened out for touching, for manifest intrigues, he violated hidden intimacies: the buttocks, the breasts. He stopped abruptly because of difficulties of position and equilibrium. Then he got up, pulling his chair behind him with strident screeches. He took a few uncertain, insecure steps and his hands moved about in the air, looking for the solidity of a body which he supposed would be revealed by the odours of clandestine secretions.

Then he embraced Madame from behind. He clasped her roughly, he squeezed her tightly without pause, love or respect. He began to explore with impertinence the folds of her body and then carefully brought his fingers to his nose, taking a deep breath so that the stench could inebriate him with signs and revelations – this he murmured with mockery and irreverence.

Abruptly then, with a rapid movement, he bent over Madame's neck and murmured into her ear a lood of words so that she would understand him, surrender
to him, surrender her will and authority to his seduction. He embraced the woman, pulling her to him, forcing her to lean

163

against his body, to remain standing, to entangle arms, to mingle breaths, so that he could violate the intimate cleft of her sex and then sniff his fingers which had plunged into her groin.

In this instant of forced intimacy, the Bedouin, turning towards me, winked and uttered words that were succinct but clear, so that I would understand that this woman was in reality – Harel Bey was certain of it – a character from some story. Possibly she had issued from some story of Gustave's; however, it was not certain that it was the one in which he narrated the story of Saint Julian. The Bedouin was convinced of that, insofar as the sex of Madame was odourless, no humours were secreted from it, it did not disclose the languors or emotions of a person.

I then tried to forestall Harel Bey's recklessness, uttering words without sense or inclination, questioning him with imploring looks. I acted with excessive discretion and took little care to draw out impediments and excuses since, without offering me a hearing, the Bedouin and the lady suddenly disappeared in the shadows of the place, as far as the entrance, where they were swallowed up in a darkness which did not allow their traces to be followed.

I heard only hasty steps, a few sighs and devious noises as if they had wanted to have sex, albeit in the impotence of characters in some story or book lost in the fantasies of a writer. They reappeared moments later beyond the reflections of the window.

Profiles cut out in the night, distinguishable only in the uncertainty of footsteps and movements. They stopped – I saw it clearly – next to number 42 of the boulevard and, after seconds, entered the doorway, becoming lost amidst the shadows, silences and crimes to be carried out.

I am now waiting, with no peace and with comprehensible anguish, for Harel Bey to rejoin me here at the Café du Port-de-Fer, to respect an appointment. Chance and caution induce me to harbour anxieties and contrary thoughts, because I don't know the intentions and habits of the Bedouin, so that it is possible that he has already indulged in irreparable gestures. He was determined in his actions and thoughts when he discovered that Madame la chanteuse sought to practise for years his very same vice and asked forgiveness so as to find a book or a story willing to concede her shelter. Harel Bey understood then that this woman was a dangerous and untrustworthy adversary, following the same path as he followed himself.

I have with me the Bedouin's notebook. He lost it through haste and forgetfulness in the restaurant. I took trouble to read words and thoughts in it. I learned only that Harel Bey is very diligent, indeed even with the impairment with which he is burdened, noting down points in a clear, incisive and rigorous manner. I amused myself with these tactile symbols to pass the time and alleviate the anxiety and stress of waiting.

Is this the true story of Saint Julian the Hospitaller as one can admire it in a stained glass window in the church of Rouen, in the native city of our father Gustave? I have my doubts, but I comfort myself in thinking so.

Au revoir, mon ami. A bientôt[117].

B.

Hôtel de Normandie

9 rue de Bec, Rouen

21 June

Dear friend,

Here is *Herodias*[118], now that we have hastily retraced our steps and without interposing considered thoughts or devious desires on decisions. A reluctant journey, at least as far as Gillon, then like a shot here we are at Rouen, the city of our father Gustave, having travelled alongside the Seine, touching at Pont de l'Arche, Feret, Orival and Oissel. A unique necessity, which could not be postponed, justifying the breathlessness of this deliberate journey. You will see, my dear Pécuchet, you will see!

Here then is Herodias. Herodias indeed, almost as if to celebrate the painting by Gustave Moreau, which is part of the exhibition at the International Salon and which represents, with supreme skill, a lascivious Salomé: wrapped in seven veils riddled with embroidered arabesques and adorned with a magnificent

---

117 Goodbye, my friend. See you soon
118 'Herodias', a work written by Flaubert in 1877.

diadem, she is conceding her body to a nymph's dance which was the prelude to an unseemly and tragic sensuality and to a heart-rending panegyric to death. Come Lord, come and *libera nos a malo. Amen*, says Matthew and so said I. Come Lord, come – wrote Mark the Evangelist – and he was constrained to add: *But when Herod's birthday was kept, the daughter of Herodias danced before them, and pleased Herod. Whereupon he promised with an oath to give her whatsoever she would ask*[119]. Come Lord, come. Amen, amen, I concluded, certain to please some pious soul.

The Bedouin seemed fascinated with these devotional rigmaroles of mine, even in the case of mere cautious prayers murmured under my breath, even if complaints aimed at avoiding emotional interferences. My companion shook his head and urged me to conscientiously speak to him there and then of Rouen, Gustave's birthplace, so majestically treacherous since, in his view, it must have hidden improper secrets about the strange existence of our father.

Amen! – I muttered to cut short thoughts that would have necessarily arisen from the great quantity of reading in which we engaged, my friend, when we were lacerated by solemn thoughts, indeed even from the mere ideas of God and eternity. Do you remember, Pécuchet? Do you remember the *Catechism* of the Abbé Gaume? Do you remember the *Examination of Christianity* by Louis Hervieu? And further, the mystical authors that we had the opportunity and the desire to study and consult: Saint Teresa, Saint John of the Cross, Louis of Granada and Monsieur Chaillot? Do you remember, my friend, do you remember?

Now I have the obligation to spend my time speaking of Rouen. Yes, indeed of Rouen, where the scoundrels wander about *with pinched elbows, nose to the wind, stick in hand and grey hat on head* ... and turn *the corner of the rue Ganterie*[120]. Rouen where it is possible to let oneself be rocked, not having any debts to settle or credit with anyone, a father in particular, in a boat moored in the waters of the Seine, thus admiring a splendid Normandy sky

---

119 Matthew 14:6–7.
120 Gustave Flaubert, *Letters*.

above one's head. Rouen is fundamentally also a *stupid homeland*[120]. Yes, indeed, Rouen.

The sun was high above Rouen when we arrived. It illuminated the square with brilliance, slanting among the steeples and pinnacles of St. Patrice, reverberating on

the silhouette of the Tour de Jeanne d'Arc. At that moment, in that warm, abundant light of early afternoon, I began to recount to Harel Bey the stories carved beyond the pediment. They were sculptures of excellent workmanship, set out with ecclesiastical meaning and taste to recall, in their sequence and groupings, the stages of the divine Passion. Appropriate figures in truth, with vivacious gestures, expressive features. From afar, they appeared to be the figures of an animated crèche which did not at all mock the cruelty and stupidity of vice.

Harel Bey, immobile, listened to me with distaste and ill-concealed boredom. His face, clearly revealed in the haze of the sun, had clenched jaws and eyelids, and a wrinkled forehead. I spoke to the Bedouin, among hyperbole and recollections of readings and studies carried out by Gustave, of our summary investigations of places and routes visited in our father's books to preserve truthful recollections of them and to understand why he made huge sacrifices to complete certain of these works and abandon others completely or leave them unfinished.

Thus I closely followed the Bedouin and in one ear I whispered considerations and comments so that from my words he might be able to perceive what we had seen with our eyes and our feelings. Thus I began to narrate, impulsively and emphatically, the story of Herodias, the ignoble obsequiousness of a tetrarch, Herod Antipas of Machaerus, who had abandoned dignity and prestige for a woman who was the wife of his step-brother, a woman who, pursuing her own self-interest and desire for prestige, had seduced him. She granted him, in full honour and free enjoyment, now that she herself no longer aroused in him desire and pleasure, the body of her daughter Salomé, who *moved her feet to the rhythm of a flute and a pair of crotales. Her shapely arms seemed to beckon someone who was fleeing from her... Her gestures seemed to emit sighs and her whole body expressed such a languor that it was not clear... if she was feeling faint in his embrace. With half-closed eyes she gyrated her waist, moved her stomach with undulating movements, caused her breasts to rise and fall*[121].

Without notice or forewarning signs, Harel Bey abruptly began to beat his stick on the cobblestones, to give clear signs of restlessness, to sniff the air with his nose to sample fragrances and stenches, to distinguish breaths and accents. He calmed down for a few seconds, only to then importune me and murmur in my ear that he had remonstrations to make in connection with those rash travellers who, in setting down itineraries and diaries of exploration, had arrogated to themselves the rights to narrate a world that they knew not at all.

These characters had even begun to make pronouncements on the Orient, to write things about those lands, habits and persons, dipping the pen in their own crude memory as Occidental hacks. He did not in fact single out anyone in particular, neither specific persons nor events, it's true, but Harel Bey smiled with ill-will and intention. He formulated criticisms and accusations only about circumstances that related to him, since, as he suggested to me with words scarcely murmured, even though he was a Bedouin, Arab and Oriental he had been imagined, created and finally abandoned by a writer who was of European blood and extraction, French no less, who had even gone so far as to narrate unworthy Oriental adventures which he had had, almost as a sinister purveyor of images and feelings of others.

Not few were his emphatic words, laden with unwholesome spite and deliberate ill-will. And furthermore they had been already recounted and boasted of in letters to relations and friends. It was on Gustave above all that the Bedouin meant with such words to pour out his spite, as it was indeed our father who had not hesitated to transcribe outrageous phrases: *These shaven cunts make a strange impression. However, these women have a flesh as solid as bronze, and mine had a stupendous backside... We had a fuck in*

---

121   Gustave Flaubert, *'Herodias'*

a hut that was so low that one had to crawl to enter it. We screwed on a piece of reed matting amidst four mud walls... We organized a morning with some girls. I screwed three women and I had four fucks: three before lunch and one after dessert... At Esneh in one day I had myself 5 fucks and 3 blowjobs: I say this frankly and without paraphrasing[122].

To cut short discourses and summary judgments, I reminded him of our commitment, the journey, the desires to investigate, with self-abnegation and objectivity, Gustave's travels to the Orient, a prostitute, stories of immoral loves and perverse sensualities, since a promise and a vow had been offered to Madame Caroline, the niece. By time and chance readings, we now had to deal with this brief story which had taken as its pretext the situations and poses depicted in a painting by a certain artist.

The Bedouin squeezed my arm and asked me, with sudden frenzy, if it was indeed true, as he imagined, that that body displayed in that story spoke of cruel passions, of erotic confusions, of unlikely seductions for which that figure, especially in the iconographic version of the Holy Roman Church where this impure dancer was mentioned in the Gospels only through her maternal descent, had been conquered by a fear of deadly expectations, of voracious anxieties, which did not in fact belong, according to her, to the kingdom of Judea which was represented there. *Come, Lord, come and libera nos a malo. Amen. Come, Lord, come* – I repeated in a low voice.

The Bedouin felt presages of fear in my words, which recounted obscure passions, but also in the limpid air of this square, dedicated to penitence and to the condemnation of criminality and the worst errors of time. Presages which in truth concealed a troubling hypocrisy towards unfettered sex and the frank couplings of ancient and Oriental peoples, even though the Bible itself is an accredited testament to incest and unscrupulous sexual practices.

The Bedouin referred his thoughts to me without hesitation, after having sniffed the air several times, exercising his sense

---

122 Gustave Flaubert, *Letters.*

of smell in every direction in search of anxious moods, almost as if diverse and hidden fears could bridle men and women and agitation could become a usual sentiment like perplexity: now a common practice for whomever, fearing just about everyone, trips over his own shadow.

Harel Bey began to laugh and with an insolent roar even began to tease me. He baited my interest with a continual sniffing and a murmur of excited words which suggested to me that there were mortal perils to the right and left of us, obscene annoyances, indecent impudences, given that, for example – and he could smell it in the air – stray dogs and cats were coupling freely in the parvis of the cathedral.

I recalled him to order with an iron grip on his arm, supporting his insecure gait with my leg, and pressing against his side with the weight of my body. Then I pulled him aside in an angle of rue de la Grosse Horloge, in that clot of trellised brick houses which cling together voraciously so as to create fascinating alleyways: a sober tower crowned by an 18th century cupola and a Renaissance arch surmounted by a wooden arbour hosting the polychrome quadrant of a clock.

I clutched the Bedouin by his arm and asked him for an explanation of his desire for the madness of thoughts and irritations. Harel Bey lent his head on my shoulder and murmured to me that he had other recriminations to set in motion towards this Occidental world which, from the beginning, had offered vile hypocrisies in talking with vulgar relish about the Orient, uttering false beliefs about its corrupt customs, its luxurious and barbarously uncivilized practices.

I turned spitefully and rebuked him with an angry voice, saying that he could well be right about these slanders, but, as in the old saying, a dog burnt by hot water also fears cold water. The Christian man of the Occidental world, who is so afraid of the torments of Hell represented in ecclesiastical tales as horrible sufferings, is obliged to live in fear so that when in public he admonishes practices that offend the common morality while in the privacy of the bedroom, of brothels and of citadels of sin he is happy to frequent and practise disbelief, immodesty, filthy habits and immoral vices since, in such circumstances, opportunities and places, he is cleansed of the disposition to fear.

I then harangued Harel Bey with curses and cries to remind him that it was about time that we began to engage once again in our investigations, to give priority to our dignity as collectors of observations and investigations. I reminded him of his official functions and roles, his dependence on predetermined and rigorous orders according to which he had to be in this moment, in this city, in this adventure, wrapped up in business and events in this story of Gustave's which gossiped about Herodias. And Gustave gossiped by his own license while he was still living at Croisset: and it was at the end of 1876, obsessed by his mother who had now been dead for four years. It was almost an idolatrous fetish, given that he walked round and round the house inspecting wardrobes and chests and trunks to recover clothes worn by *maman*, and touching them and feeling them and sniffing them so that he could sense yet again her presence or dream of reliving days spent in her company.

I then drew up concise conclusions, reminding Harel Bey that it was our obligation and our first act of obsequiousness to consider the details of a manuscript and the desire of a niece. Then to travel through every period and on every street, to know and frequent the places, like Rouen for example, to take up quarters in each of them, as for example at number 9 rue del Bec, at the Hôtel de Normandie, 30 rooms at 2 francs per bed, 10 and 20 with lunch, or 20 including lunch and dinner at 2.50 francs, or full pension at 8 francs.

Harel Bey abruptly raised his nose and began to walk with hurried steps, beating the ground with his invalid's stick with hollow and disturbing sounds, murmuring words and maxims and pulling me by an arm so that I had very little time to scold him for his gestures and motives. Hastily and impulsively we crossed rue de la Grosse Horloge, then place Vieux Marché and rue Crosue without pause, breathlessly and with urgent and reckless gait.

We avoided passers-by and carriages. From time to time the

crack of a whip surprised and frightened us as it sliced through the air with a furious hiss that mingled with the hollow trot of cab-horses.

Suddenly, without any apparent obstacle or danger, Harel Bey stopped fearfully, turned his head to look for guidance, for some offer of a tacit explanation. He then began to feel the rustications of a building, at the beginning of rue de Lecat, a little beyond rue de Crosne. He was seeking some comfort with his hands, refuge from unexpected pain and disturbance. I read in his white face a secret fear that was troubling him, as a light trembling afflicted his body and his right hand lost its grip on the stick.

Concerned, I supported him with my arm under his armpit and I became aware that his limbs were limp, lost in his bewilderment, lost in an instantaneous indisposition which had possessed his body and whitened his face. His chest moved with weak breaths, with studied movements, according to an Oriental custom: practised occasionally by a person who wanted to overcome moments of extreme suffering, as he had explained to me with a wealth of particulars and arcane words during the trip to Trouville in a carriage, on a day of sea-fog.

I asked him the reason for his unexpected faintness; if he would like, given the circumstances, to have the help of a doctor or the aid of a specialist experienced in blood-letting. Or if he would like a carriage that could take him back to the Hôtel de Normandie. Or if, finally, he preferred to regain his breath and continue the journey and the investigation.

He squeezed my hand as a sign of friendship and comfort, seduced me with an instinctive embrace, leaning his head on my shoulder and offering himself pallid and weakened. Instinctively he began to tell me that he had breathing difficulties, since an oppressive stench was obstructing his nostrils and his throat, preventing him from taking in clean air, from sensing gradations of smells, from perceiving aromas and fragrances, almost as if they were acting as substitute senses for the sense of sight which he was no longer able to enjoy.

As I bent over him, while his breath mingled with mine, I

noticed an unpleasant stink in the air, a smell of putrefaction, of decomposition, an ugly stench heavy with death. I sensed that Harel Bey, in the moments before, with his olfactory capacity and perception, had breathed in the odour of death, experiencing an instant panic, disconcerted and bewildered, because, so it seemed to me, he had never until then breathed in the characteristic miasma of putrefaction.

I offered him the support of a sustaining arm pulled him along beyond the corner of rue de Crosne so that he might escape, at least for some moments, those lugubrious effluvia, and reacquire control of his sense of smell and the strength of his limbs, still limp with a terror which had abruptly undermined all self-assurance and sense of security.

The street before us, heading towards rue de Lecat, also imprisoned by a torrid and overcast midday, ran along a grey stone wall marked by ample niches and brick pilasters. Heavy iron gates marked the entrances of a gloomy edifice, from which excruciating effluvia were emitted in gusts by a wind made turbid by a sultry heat; an odour which betrayed lugubrious rituals, indeed death itself in the form of corpses in a morgue.

A brick pavilion with large windows, surrounded by borders of plants and surmounted by a tiled roof, hosted dissected corpses on marble slabs on the ground floor. Death, then, the face of a horrible and rotting death, seemed to dominate time and to symbolize the deterioration of men and things, but not that of Harel Bey burdened by his bewilderment in the presence of a smell which, signifying death, must then have appeared to the Bedouin, as a character in a story, completely unknown.

Harel Bey leaned back his head and smiled at me. At once he began to joke with spirit and initiative. He was completely recovered from the abuse of his sense of smell so that he wished to hearten me and to confide in me, with mischievous and irascible witticisms, that reality is always gloomier than the imagination, since that place, putrid with evil stenches, was pregnant with an odour of which he could not distinguish the origin or genesis.

Harel Bey had, however, the ambition to know and learn

that that edifice, that pavilion of the Hôtel Dieu, circled by a grey stone wall, consumed by time and by the filth of evil odours, was the place where Gustave was born and had spent his boyhood, amongst a row of great windows, almost horrid ashen mouths, and under a slate roof outlined against the grey sky tainted in places by a blue altered by light rain.

All this Harel Bey remembered, taking up again and repeating Gustave's words and memories when, by instinct or effort, the writer had evoked again the places of his childhood, sometimes in speech, sometimes within the lines of a letter or of a piece of writing. Also moments of rage and deception as were those of the time of the cholera epidemic of 1832 when one heard, beyond the walls which closed off the habitations of the hospital, the rancorous death-rattles of the dying, who were expiring in the furies of an incurable and flagellating disease.

We began once more to walk hurriedly since our efforts were leading us to the Hôtel Dieu, to a room with a patient in pain, suffering from age and ill health. Halfway along rue de Lecat, we traversed a gateway, while a clock struck the hours and a bell-tower resounded with rings to mark the times of meetings and visits.

Harel Bey pressed himself closely to my flank and listened to my accounts of persons that we encountered. From time to time he smiled at me, beat his stick on the ground, squeezed my arm with his hand.

We crossed an ample space paved with cobbles, and alleyways thronged with invalids, with men and women scarcely able to utter a word, with nurses who walked away rapidly and busily, with sisters of charity who, wearing white cowls and walking with slow and discreet steps, were fingering the beads of their rosaries as they murmured prayers in a low voice.

We arrived at a low cottage, beyond the western limits of the hospital, backing onto the surrounding walls towards rue de Girardin, marked with thick trees bending beneath the weight of years and of heavily-laden, curving boughs. A flight of stairs in ferrous stone, with an ample curve, wound up to a door burnished by varnish, time and use, which opened onto a corridor weighed down with the dank fog of silence and darkness.

A small room that welcomed us was enveloped in darkness. Harel Bey sniffed the air with unmannerly ostentation. He suddenly become pale, since, as he whispered to me, he sensed the odour of presences marked by abandon, by the renunciation of existence. The silence of illnesses and old age frightened him. He began to move around carelessly, stumbling here and there in the unevenness of a green granite pavement, chipped with use, gnawed away by neglect and civil duplicities.

For me, only for me, crepuscular glimmers of light began to reveal presences and absences, to identify a face which might be friendly towards me. I busied myself with what there was to be seen through shutters left partly open, since they were not all kept locked and offered narrow interstices of air and dust through which flashed filigreed streaks of light.

In that hospital room, in that reserve of lost souls, in that ward *pour femmes vieilles et malades*[123], we hoped to be able to glean some words, remarks and recollections of Mademoiselle Julie, called la Tata, who had been in Gustave's house since 1825. Madame Caroline had assured us this, as she had acted, with fascination and impudence, upon some of her Normandy relations so that we could obtain encounters, confidences and recollections regarding la Tata. Because of the many years Mademoiselle Julie had spent in the service of various demands and claims, because of the age she had unexpectedly attained, because of the discomfort of a cruel failure of memory, because of a lethal myopia, she was now constrained to living in the Hôtel Dieu while waiting to be removed from the hospice by some charitable relation and transferred to some hovel in Fleury-sur-Andelle where she was born, a little beyond the forest of Longboël, just before the Seine reaches Andelle itself.

Harel Bey began once again, with impudence and effrontery, to sniff the air. He moved into an alleyway and flicked through his blind-man's abacus. He read hastily with his fingers, he even

---

123   For old and ill women.

wrote with his sharpened stylus and he then turned his head in every direction to say, with distinct and articulated words, that we had the obligation to speak with Mademoiselle Julie de Fleury about effects, affairs and happenings that were to do with the writer Gustave. He sought to recover his breath, murmuring words charged with anxiety, running through a series of manual signals which, slicing through the air, hectically sought attention.

The bed of Mademoiselle Julie was in a corner, against a wall, concealed in shadows because the window, which was at one side, permitted only a slanting light to enter. At times the gloom was pierced with gleams of light which clung to the wall high up and to the ceiling, generating skewed geometric figures, almost hexagons sliced cleanly from misshapen rhombi.

I then uttered a few words and began to relate aloud that I had told my travel companion an ancient story, that I had noticed a heavy odour of death at the presence of this tale, of having on this account suffered with a sense of mysterious warnings, fears and reproaches and of being caught up in very painful feelings to do with bloody rituals and events in the lives of Herod Antipas, Herodias and the beautiful Salomé: *For John had said unto Herod, It is not lawful for thee to have thy brother's wife. Therefore Herodias had a quarrel against him, and would have killed him; but she could not: For Herod feared John*[124] so that Herodias was compelled to resort to the magic arts of seduction of Salomé the beautiful: her daughter and the granddaughter of Herod the Great.

While I was relating all this to Mademoiselle Julie, I had quietly and circumspectly drawn near to her bed. Meanwhile, the Bedouin began to laugh scornfully with ill-concealed amusement, to crack his fingers and to murmur, with irony and jubilation, that now the time had come for us to carry out a blood-ritual, to offer to death a certain Mademoiselle, and that we should have a taste for revenge, since that writer of Rouen, indeed that Gustave, had abandoned us to an ignoble fate.

---

124   Mark 6, 18-20.

I had taken, in this hubbub of gestures and words, a few aimless and inattentive steps, when I noticed two skeletal hands passing lightly over me, almost caressing me, searching for me with insistence and determination.

Then a hoarse voice, consumed by silence and thoughts, confided to me that Salomé – only Salomé – was beautiful and seductive, that *under the blue-tinted veil that hid her breasts and her head, the outline of her eyes, the chalcedony of her ears and the whiteness of her chest could be distinguished. A shimmering silk scarf covered her shoulders and was tied to her hips with a belt worked in gold. Her black trousers were studded with mandragoras, and she, with impertinence, beat her feet shod in slippers made of hummingbird feathers*[125].

Salomé, continued this hoarse voice – yes, Salomé had lent her body to Mademoiselle Eulalie Faucaud, who revealed her nudity to a seventeen-year old Gustave in a room of the Hôtel Richelieu, in rue de la Darse, Marseilles. Eulalie, like Salomé, was a young woman with a melancholy look, who gave herself up to desire and sensuality. Eulalie, yes, Eulalie majestic and magnificent in her splendid thirty-five years. Eulalie with her seductive exoticism. Eulalie who moved about languidly in a patio adorned with the jet of a fountain and exotic flowers. Eulalie who gave to Gustave *one of those kisses in which one puts one's entire soul ... and* (then) *she began to suck* (his cock). *Then there was an orgy of delights, then tears, then letters and then nothing more*[126]. Only memory remained, only the sweet memory of Eulalie who from Lima had disembarked at Marseilles to deal in 15th century ebony furniture set with mother-of-pearl, which everyone marvelled at.

This was what was murmured by a lady whom I found within the white sheets and piled-up pillows, supporting as best they could a skeletal head – indeed diaphanous, defleshed and dematerialized by old-age. Here was Mademoiselle Julie, here was the woman whom we had to meet, so that she could tell us about Gustave, of the stench of corpses which had scarred his boyhood, of the death that had governed sentiments and passions.

125 Gustave Flaubert, *'Herodias'*.
126 Frères de Goncourt, *Journal*.

Harel Bey furtively came close to the bed, dragging his feet, seeking textures in the air, fingering a bed head, folds of blankets and bedclothes left haphazardly. He began to take deep breaths and to analyse the surroundings by smell, mumbling that he was aware of a penetrating odour of creolin, that his sense of smell was offended by stenches of decomposition, that he was stupefied by not knowing why on earth they had to be amidst such filth.

I spoke some rigmarole about phantasms of the past and about Gustave, who loved to recall – this was made explicit, in respect to him, in the confidences of a manuscript that Madame Caroline had sent to us – a happy and loving childhood, spent in the autopsy room in a *Hospice de l'Humanité*.

The light touch of a hand brushed the arm of the Bedouin. Surprised and frightened, Harel Bey moved aside instinctively as if to avoid insidious contacts, mixing of humours, epidemic contagions. Then he promptly began to ask questions: whether Eulalie, like Salomé, concealed in the intimacies of her body the odour of death, if she had violated the virginity of Gustave to infect him with obscene and harmful proposals, if she had conceded herself to him to obtain a pledge of love, perhaps even the head of some character that Gustave would have created in memory of this tactile and olfactory experience, probably the head of an Oriental, even a Bedouin, certainly of a misbeliever abandoned in a Journal of some Occidental writer.

Mademoiselle la Tata turned her head towards the half-closed window. She raised an arm with fatigue, almost as if she wanted to seize the air, to capture a modest ray which was warming a cone of light and dust. Then slowly she searched for my hands, my face. She appeared alarmed and flushed by diverse and disturbing feelings. She seemed to hold within herself a troubled fear and whispered to me with a trickle of voice that she required reasons and judgments on why this man accompanied me, since from the stench of his body she perceived improper remarks, unexpected impetuousness, homicidal desires. Above all, in his face, opinions, characteristics and smells that did not belong to him.

Alerted and warned by Mademoiselle's sentiments, I began to

look and to judge, in this semi-dark hospital ward, my companion who, immobile, was sniffing the air with resolution, like a proud boor attending to raids and booty. And I began to feel vexation and embarrassment because of Harel Bey's presence; he seemed an extraneous interference, a shadow which appeared under false pretences. His stealthy gait, his unusual blindness, his way of proceeding with practices that were in fact ordinary, yet which in his case nourished troublesome uneasiness, the same which can be seen in the game of hide and seek, of enticing and deceiving, of living and dying.

Nevertheless, I assured his good qualities if only to reassure Mademoiselle Julie, and thus I told her some consoling lies and I also sang praises of my shady companion. I spoke of Harel Bey as a man intent on healing wounds, on investigating illusory appearances, both on his own account and that of others, on associating with indiscreet occupations simply to verify, for example, truths and lies on the life and works of that Gustave of Rouen whom she herself had served with so much love and for so many years, until she reached the point of surviving him.

I murmured this to her for consolation, while in truth I kept watch on the Bedouin who was finagling with his senses and at one time smiled maliciously at my words, sniffed the air, and palpated the fabrics of the bed to the point of touching the skeletal body of Mademoiselle through them.

Unexpectedly and rudely Harel Bey began to grumble with verbose agitation, to pile question upon question, to interrogate, demanding instant replies: whether it was true that Gustave's youth was marked with perilous encounters, with unusual customs, with amorous precocity, with the penetrating odour of death and sex, as in Herodias where Salomé, throwing herself upon her hands, with her heels raised up, seemed to move like a gigantic beetle.

At once then the Bedouin drew close to the bedside dragging his feet, by touch he searched the pillow for Mademoiselle's head. He pressed his ear against the mouth of the lady and awaited words and laments.

Mademoiselle jerked herself away, displeased, even afraid. She released some irritated utterances into the air to distance this man from her, to be able to breathe. She became more tranquil in her thoughts when the Bedouin stood up and, in the breathlessness of effort and tensions, offered to our eyes a face marked by signs of aggressiveness.

La Tata Julie smiled maliciously and began to tell stories of a childhood in which one paid the price of unexpected worries. And thus it was for Gustave, distancing himself from the welcoming arms of Eulalie, laden with disgust and bitterness, and without being able to feel any other sensations except that of a profound and disconcerting sense of prostration, of infinite bewilderment, of death, of the odour of fear.

The lady was beautiful, it's true. She was a magnificent and sensual woman of thirty-five years who had seduced a boy with a look, a smile, a transparent silk dress, a sinuous and maternal body.

Gustave was Iaokanann and not Herod Antipas, Eulalie was Herodias and not Salomé. She was a little whore who wanted to corrupt an ingenuous and sensitive boy, nourish herself with the vigour of puberty. Eulalie also resembled a depraved and meretricious Nubian, an obscene bacchante of Lydia. Thus Gustave wrote his tale on Herodias referring back to these tragic and dark personal experiences, reliving a sudden rape, the loss of the senses, the bitter stench of sex, its humours, its secretions, the agonizing odour of fear because of a sin which had to be expiated with a supremely Christian repentance.

Mademoiselle Julie then calmed down, exhausted by words and recollections. She half-closed her eyes and abandoned herself to an acquiescent and restorative silence.

I then looked intensely at her face and thought of that acute odour of death that certainly must have accompanied acts, events, sentiments in the childhood of Gustave even to the point that the phantasms of the past, the ineradicable visions of a childhood spent next to an autopsy room at the *Hospice de lHumanité* had not been tattooed on the flesh of his soul as the manuscript of Madame Caroline seemed to want to relate and give to be understood.

Meanwhile, Harel Bey had once more begun to sniff the air, to palpate the headpiece of the bed, to wring his hands with an unusual frenzy. He bent over the lady's body again to listen to the beatings of her heart. He sought her face with his fingers and pressed his ear to her mouth to draw from it words, trickles of final breaths, memories remembered almost at the point of surrendering life.

The Bedouin smiled with shameless malice, with joyous obscenity, with visible perversity while with an arm stretched out he clasped the legs of the lady so that there would be no starting away or rebellion – this at least is how it seemed to me.

Meanwhile dusk was falling beyond the closed window and Mademoiselle's body seemed to become defleshed, to become the protagonist of a strange and ambiguous story constructed of fear and of death, of sex and of smell, of ambiguity and of sin. I closed my eyes and began to sniff the surroundings, looking for ancient miasmas, the imprint perhaps of that stench in which Gustave had lost his youth and sentiments.

A hand then touched me with a light gesture, caressed my face, looked for the creases of my features.

Harel Bey was next to me, oblivious of his negligence and his indecent fixations, and the face of Mademoiselle Julie, la Tata, seemed to me to show once again its natural pallor.

This is the true story of Herodias which has as its protagonists Madame Eulalie Faucaud and Monsieur Gustave the writer: the odour of death and the fear of sin – at least I believe so.

Regards from Rouen.

A bientôt,

B.

Auberge de Roumare,

Croisset

22 June

My dear Pécuchet,

Here is *The Temptation of St. Anthony*[127].

---

127 *The Temptation of Saint Anthony* was written initially by Gustave Flaubert between May 1846 and September 1849. Rewritten in 1868. Revised finally and published in 1874.

Here is the temptation of St. Anthony by the hand of a certain writer in the grip of seductions, enticements and desires among lands of hermitages and lost myths in the Thebaid, in that Egypt that Monsieur Gustave frequented with singular impudence in his youth, as a piece of writing by Madame Louise has recorded. Thus to identify himself with the wish for solitude, but also to deliver himself from the anguish that tormented him, Gustave took to engaging with determination in the ancient resource of a pilgrimage to a suitable place, along a river on which boats were moving rapidly right, left and centre along the luxuriant banks.

Gustave carried out his own hermitage in a house infested with phantasms, if a manuscript provides even today confirmation of such suppositions, and recalls that it was the residence of Abbé Prevost who carried out there all sorts of eccentric and imprudent duties and affairs amidst colours and sounds, lights and shadows of impeccable splendour.

The location of that voluntary isolation was, as you well know my dear Pécuchet, at Croisset, in a *lovely house, with a façade in Louis XVI style, situated at the foot of a hill on the banks of the Seine, which in truth looks like one end of a lake, where the waves give one a sense of the sea*[128]. In this dwelling there is a study enclosed by a massive oak bookcase with spiral columns, a fireplace, a few watercolours and an etching by Callot representing the Temptation of Saint Anthony, not of outstanding execution but which pleased Gustave very much. Indeed, it reminded him of the marionette theatre of Père Legrain, which he sometimes had the opportunity to watch when he was a boy at the fair of Saint-Romain, recalling the ancient legend of the dragon Gargouille who had the wings and body of a reptile and who lived in a cavern near the lower Seine, in the wide bend where the Romans erected Rotomagus. And this legend was a dirge of *fabliaux* since this ferocious Gargouille was satisfied only with offerings and annual sacrifices until there arrived in that place a priest called *Romanus* who freed the countryside of the dragon, obtaining in

---

128 Frères de Goncourt, *Journal*.

exchange the conversion of all the inhabitants and the edification of a church with the exclusive rights to the payment of tolls. *Libera nos a malo. Libera nos... Verily, verily, I say unto you, Whatsoever ye ask the Father in my name, he will give it to you*[129]. Thus said Father Romanus and subdued the monster, and dragged him out of the town tied to a leash. *Death! To death*! cried someone. *Libera nos a malo. Libera nos... Verily, verily, I say unto you, Whatsoever ye ask the Father in my name, he will give it to you...*, even death, if that is what you want. And they wanted death. Gargouille the dragon who demanded an offering every year was thus put to death. *Libera nos a malo. Libera nos.* But inexplicably the neck and the head of the dragon would not burn. Perhaps a miracle? *Verily, verily, I say unto you, Whatsoever ye ask the Father in my name, he will give it to you.* And they asked then that the neck and the head should be placed on the walls of the city in the form
of stone gargoyles to ornament the cornices, and to be like paladins combating infamy and demoniacal temptations. To celebrate their deliverance from suspicious and sinister events they created for themselves a *fĕria*, with revelry and carousing in the streets, gambling and acts of mock daring, or watching the marionettes of that strange character Père Legrain, who enriched with his inflammable presence the pandaemonic miscellany of shouting, sweating and arms expended to seduce other arms offered in the confidence and solitude of a fictitious pleasure. *Libera nos a malo. Libera nos... Verily, verily, I say unto you, Whatsoever ye ask the Father in my name, he will give it to you.* Perhaps a *libido sciendi* or, in truth, the desire for knowledge?, asked father Gustave on that occasion.

All this was told to us immediately, at the very beginning of our first encounter – in a very ambiguous manner and tone of voice, and with difficulty in expressing himself – by Monsieur Auguste Léger, the gravedigger of Croisset. He welcomed us as a host resolved to provided everything, even information after compensation and a promise of very costly and abundant wines and liquors.

---

129   John 16:23.

He welcomed me and Harel Bey in a vile hovel, squeezed up against a bare stone wall, riddled with holes caused by neglect and by filthy rodents that fearlessly frequented this rat hole, running along, fat and fleshy, seeking meat or anything else edible, even morsels bitten off bodies foul and stinking from abandonment.

It was, to sum up, a treacherous hovel, marked by three wooden walls with uprights bolted together by bands and wedges of tin, forced into unsuitable use, given that they were visibly precarious. The other wall, the fourth, the one wall that was built of real stone, belonged to the cemetery which adjoined it, so that the niches were a necessary support to the wall itself, and still more so since they were crammed to bursting with the excavated coffins of the rich; the poor were destined to rapid corruption from earth and water since they were buried in the naked earth. That cemetery could also seem like *the tomb of a pharaoh... where the darkness is thickened by the distant haze of aromatics...* and one could hear from time to time *a doleful voice calling out* or one could see *suddenly coming to life repugnant objects painted on the walls...* or one could feel oneself *brushed by soft wings, and by terrifying demons who screaming in one's ears hurled themselves on the ground*[130].

Harel Bey listened to words and explanations without comment or expressions of interest, adding solely that he didn't give a damn about tormented spirits or extinct revellers, or even about tormented voices or repugnant objects, still less about horrifying demons, because he had never gone to *Canopus*[131] *to sleep upon the temple of Serapis in order to have dreams*[132]. He was silent for a few instants and then seduced Monsieur Léger with a gift, as a sign of friendship and hospitality – so he murmured treacherously. A gift that he had acquired in a tavern of the lowest class and cleanliness, after having put up a very apt argument about the price and the contents. It was a flask full of a liquid of uncertain colour and with a distasteful smell: a sort of alcoholic elixir in which it was as well to place little faith. Having handed

---

130   Gustave Flaubert, *The Temptation of Saint Anthony*.

131   A city in Egypt on the peninsula of Abuqir, on the largest branch of the Nile.

132   Gustave Flaubert, *The Temptation of Saint Anthony*.

over this gift, and with barely a sign, the Bedouin took to writing vigorously, tracing signs scratched in his notebook, pressing on the stylus with nervous, but ample and correct, frenzy. From time to time he sighed, sniffed the corrupt air of the hovel, made a grimace with his mouth and hastened to breathe out uneasily.

Not a comment or lament for the logorrhoea of the gravedigger, who seemed a succubus full of evil mutterings, afflicted at the same time with shameful anxieties, evidently subject to verbal difficulties, agitated by stressful recollections, mortified also by words pronounced in haste which seemed to flee from his mouth.

Harel Bey listened and noted down points of interest while seated in a corner, on a dirty and soil-streaked squared-off stone.

Monsieur Léger then mentioned to us that he passed the time, amid the silences of morning, in this remote, ephemeral place. He confided, and very much in order to be accredited a good table, in the unexpected announcement of a sudden and unforeseen death so that he would be called upon to carry out his trade, which he had only recently learnt and from which he now sought opportunities and means to satisfy himself in the evening in the taverns of the place. Especially to greet the morning carousing with red wines of good and substantial alcoholic content.

Monsieur also confided to us, if only in the uncertainty of a lisping speech and of an impoverished process of reasoning, that he was henceforth and irremediably governed by the obsession with sin and temptation, and that he claimed the right to drown sadness, torments and desires in alcohol, and to not have to listen to voices *as if the air were speaking* and, in temptation, said: *do you desire women? … or great riches? … or a shining sword?*[133].

The gravedigger then began to tell stories about the recent past, sufferings as well, bantering with words painfully drawn out of his memory. He chattered on about contemptuous abuses of power and about the crude punishment of prison in which he had undergone agonies for having committed errors and vices, without ever having obtained decency or discretion. It had

---

133   Gustave Flaubert, *The Temptation of Saint Anthony.*

befallen him in fact to have to submit to the shame of shackles, as the gendarmes, warned in advance of the occasion, had thrown themselves upon him to reduce him to the yoke of irons in *une maison de passe a 40 fr.*[134]in place Maubert in Paris, which he had been accustomed to frequent carrying with him a daguerreotype camera with mercury-coated plates, of which he was an assiduous and capable user.

In the presence of the elegant prostitutes of the *maison*, he had taken to fussing about, on a day of melancholy and worries, with the certainty of impunity and the desire of oblique tastes, around the body of a young girl who was suffering with a serious illness. He had stripped her and laid her supine with open legs, and her breasts in full sight on a divan in rococo style, and draped with a cloth of vermilion damask, and had taken to inspecting her and gazing upon her with immodest and indecent interest.

He had remained for a number of minutes and with disgraceful interest around these white limbs that seemed very near to death, to eternal sleep, to silence. To study her with lustful interest, to spread out as fully as possible her thighs, crossed so that in a narrow opening of withered limbs one could glimpse the pubis and the curly hair which embellished it. He had finally taken to touching it, then to tasting it, finally to palpating it continually, with insane frenzy and sinister desires. He had believed that this body spoke to him and repeated to him endlessly: do you desire *perhaps a body as cold as the skin of serpents, or perhaps large black eyes darker than the mystic caverns? Look at my eyes... I am not a woman, I am a world. From the moment that my clothes fall away, you will discover on my body endless mysteries*[135].

He had felt – he confessed it to us without restraint or modesty – ungovernable impulses, licentious instincts, an obscene will, to the point of conceiving the desire to violate this body exactly as it was, the body of a woman dead or dying. Nothing else did Monsieur Léger the gravedigger recall of those tragic hours, of those acts, except confused practices and experiences around those

---

134   A low-class hotel used by prostitutes.
135   Gustave Flaubert, *The Temptation of St. Anthony*.

cold, waxen limbs, unnatural proposals and desires, instinctive excitations when his erect penis, swollen and aching, had placated itself, abandoning itself to involuntary spasms that had soiled his own belly with viscous sperm.

For his evil intent he had served sixty days in prison among constrictions and ignoble abuses. He emerged from it tempered and instructed in the ways of penitence and the fear of sin because, in this place of suffering, he had got to know a priest who was also a prisoner, at first immoral and afterwards repentant, solely through the grace of the precepts of prayers which he recited continually and which he in fact understood because they were in the language of ecclesiastical use. *Deus meus, ex toto corde poenitet me omnium meorum pecatorum, eaque detestor, quia peccando, non solem poenas a Te iuste statutas promeritus sum, sed praesertim quia offendi Te. Amen... Ex toto corde poenitet me omnium meorum peccatorum. Amen... Poenitet me meorum peccatorum. Amen... Meorum peccatorum... Amen*[136].

That priest had striven with all his soul, in truth with shrewdness and cleverness, so that the gravedigger would acquire the principal value and the substantial weight of knowing how to recite prayers in an unknown language. And only so that his mind could be distracted from temptations, still further as his body was subjugated by a penis rigidly and painfully turgid in unceasing remembrance of those limbs of a dead woman which had been intensely desired and which now, in memory, were desired more than ever to compensate for the regret of a failed coitus. To exorcise such sinful temptations Monsieur Léger had imposed upon himself the duty of remembering, upon the occurrence and presence of unmanageable desires, that *souls are capable, even more than bodies, of achieving ecstasy. So that, to keep Eustolia with impunity, the bishop Leontius castrated himself, putting love before virility*[137]. And the gravedigger wanted then to learn the Magnificat. And from then on he took to declaiming the Magnificat. And from then on

---

136 My God, I repent and am sorry with all my heart for my sins, because in sinning I have merited your punishments, and far more, because I have offended You. Amen. I am sorry with all my heart for all my sins ... I am sorry for my sins... For my sins. Amen.

137 Gustave Flaubert, *The Temptation of St. Anthony.*

those words filled the emptiness of a conscience which sometimes strayed. And thus it seemed to him that he had been reborn. And it seemed to him that he was following a path strewn with rose petals. And it seemed to him also that nothing else could be more beneficent than murmuring in a low voice the holy words *Magnificat anima mea Dominum / et exultavit spiritus meus / in Deo salutari meo / quia respexit humilitatem ancillae suae. / Ecce enim ex hoc beatam me dicent omnes generationes / quia fecit mihi magna, qui potens est, / et sanctum nomen eius / et misericordia eius in progenies et progenies timentibus eum*[138].

Thus having discounted sin amidst the cries of unfulfilled desires and having caressed a sort of sanctity through a forced abstinence and a hymn of reparation, Monsieur Léger, almost to cure himself of the last blameworthy temptations, as indeed of frequent and compulsive masturbation which was a faithful companion of his solitary way of life, had begun to indulge in alcohol.

He had even gone so far as to abandon Paris and the apprenticeship as a portrait-artist in daguerreotypes at the *"Maison A. Bertrand" – 34 rue Dauphine, – daguerreotypes, in black and white or in colours, on paper or on silver plates, in relief or in stereoscope –* or so at least he maintained with magniloquence and effrontery which perhaps suggested that it would be wise to grant little faith to this discourse. He had thus made his return to Croisset, to the town which had granted him birth, to offer himself as a skilled daguerreotypist, as a consummate portraitist, as a provider of particular, indeed scabrous and improper, services and desires, jockeying as best as he could with a daguerreotype with a double-element lens and rail of 400 francs and with silver emulsion plates of 4 francs each.

Harel Bey abruptly beat the ground with his stick, making hollow sounds and the echo of a hovel which trembled precariously. He asked for solidarity and attention so that we

---

138 My soul proclaims the greatness of the Lord / my spirit rejoices in God my Saviour / for he has looked with favour on his lowly servant. / From this day all generations will call me blessed: / the Almighty has done great things in me / and holy is his Name. / He has mercy on those who fear him in every generation.

might hastily glean information about those stories of Monsieur the gravedigger, which had the value of revealing the dark sense of the odour of sin. Thus we would have been able, suggested the Bedouin with ambiguous and oblique words, to be ready and diligent to investigate this writing of Gustave's, which seems to be calling us into temptation, to investigate it through and through, and uncover embarrassing intentions and ambiguous desires.

Harel Bey was silent for a few moments moving his arms around like a windmill. He was looking for a face or a body with whom he could have an intimate talk, ready for the exchange of confidences.

The air was saturated with unpleasant, suggestive, almost irritating odours. I was aware of this, noting besides, in my innermost feelings, that the Bedouin had never made the least lament about such an abundant display of crude smells, nor had he taken to sniffing about as was his custom, even indeed with an annoying insistence, so that he could identify places and persons, become aware of instincts and hidden desires, since the sense of smell was for him revelation and knowledge. And indeed Monsieur Léger had an indelible mark of stench, a stink peculiar to a man very averse to washing himself, certainly in love with his strongly reeking underclothes.

Harel Bey winked with cautious amusement and discrete derision, he seemed to be obeying a pact which enjoined upon him the repression of curiosity and notations which could have disturbed our interlocutor. I imagined that the Bedouin did not wish to annoy the gravedigger because he was amused by his oblique way of talking, greatly diminished by the laboriousness of language and by a memory much decreased by alcohol.

Meanwhile Monsieur the gravedigger continued to chatter and give us information including exact reasons for his having been a participant, even though only of second rank and as a daguerreotypist, in the life of Gustave the writer. He had, in fact, obtained occasions and fortune, as a certifying witness with camera and magnesium flash, to participate in spiritual rituals when the solitary writer of Croisset must have been influenced by the odour of sin of sanctity of a certain Anthony of Coma. By underhand means, through acquaintances formed in taverns frequented by heavy drinkers, the gravedigger had managed to obtain the job of executing for Gustave some daguerreotypes in remembrance of outlandish figures while the writer was busy, spending days and months in the study of his hermitage facing the Seine, on the temptations and the life of that Saint Anthony who, at twenty years of age, had turned himself into a recluse because he wanted to attain perfection, so that he *sold everything that he possessed and gave it to the poor*[139]. From then on the Saint had begun to battle with Satan who, thousands upon thousands of times, had tempted him so that, raising his stick to protect himself from the insidious perversities and evils of the devil, he repeated forcefully: *Auditui meo dabis gaudium et laetitiam exultabunt ossa humiliata ... Cor mundum crea in me Deus ... Redde mihi laetitiam salutaris tui*[140]. Thus repeated and repeated Anthony the hermit, swallowed up in a hostile desert where the horizon was lost in a disquieting and desperate infinity, while Gustave the writer, comfortably settled in his study, took pleasure in writing of all this.

Monsieur Léger abruptly began to move with his unsteady steps, to inveigh against his lost earnings because Gustave had died well before he was able to settle his account with him, even though, he confessed with a light heart, it had not been he who had entrusted to him orders and commissions for daguerreotypes and other things. A murky task after all, added the gravedigger, and committed to him by an obscure, faceless voice, encountered by chance and fortune in the tavern of Père Guillon, on the banks of the Seine, in a night of a waning moon and of glasses of Calvados emptied hastily, for a bet, with games and jokes by suicidal drunks, since they had nothing else to do but to swallow alcohol to the point of losing dignity and consciousness.

Monsieur Léger remembered, so he told us, only the hands of that individual with an intriguing appearance, who had brought

---

139 Matthew 19:21.
140 Let me hear your joy and gladness, and my humble bones will rejoice ... Create in me a pure heart, oh, God ... Retturn your gladness and salvation to me.

him the francs in clinking coins, playing with them in his fingers, conjuring with the reckless desire to deceive sight so that he might accept the task of making impressions on metal plates. Or was that individual not, by fate or by chance, or also through alcoholic forgetfulness or through a subtle and unknown play of ambiguity, some rash, heedless drinking companion: *peut-être Paul Helleu le pêcher, peut-être aussi Charles Fournier le menuisier de bières, peut-être aussi encore Jules Maquet le bruleur de cidre*[141]? In truth the gravedigger did not think to add anything else, since he didn't remember anything else: mainly since he no longer remembered the faces of his drinking companions because they were all lost in the opaque halos of petrol lamps and in dazzling sparks of alcohol which, in time and with time and after glasses sent down the gullet in a rush, were in a complete muddle, all mixed up in appearances and delirious dazzlements of mind and hallucinations of will.

Thus, after this encounter of chance and illusion in the tavern of Père Guillon, the gravedigger had begun to busy himself with magnesium, to follow the traces of the hermit Gustave, to make flashes here and there with a new spirit, very much involved in the adventure of a rediscovered work that seemed to offer him unusual and thievish opportunities. Also an onerous and troublesome mission, as he had learnt from public gossip in taverns, but also from fishermen on the river or amidst the stalls of the market, that that writer was obsessed by speaking too much and writing of temptations, so that he had begun to weave stories on demoniacal intrigues and holy saints, to free himself from undesirable afflictions, from an unwholesome odour of sin which disturbed him *surtout dans les affaires de sa vie sentimentalle*[142].

Harel Bey then coughed, as a sign of annoyance, as if he wanted to put in a word, impose himself in the conversation and intrigues that henceforth seemed to be taking the direction of indecent indiscretions and obscene chatter. He raised his nose to

---

141 Perhaps Paul Helleu the fisherman, perhaps also Charles Fournier the casket-maker, perhaps also Jules Maquet the distiller of cider?

142 Above all in his sentimental affairs.

breathe in this unwholesome air. He agitated his arms according to habit and conscience. He beat the ground with the point of his blind man's stick so that that touch, in a spurt of dust, was a recall to order, to an attention that he wanted to impose without any other sign or invocation. He was silent for a few seconds, and for those seconds, with his hints of intimidation and message, he prevented us from chattering, moving, breathing.

The Bedouin then began to talk about cemeteries, about the silent dead, about Gustave's sudden illness since little was known about the circumstances and facts that had led to his death, if it was necessary or not to listen to Georges Pouchet, *professeur d'anatomie et ami de Gustave*[143], who had asserted that the death of Gustave Flaubert, writer, was to be attributed to a bout of epilepsy accompanied by apoplexy, and that it was opportune to remember that *l'écrivain et l'ermite de Croisset*[144] had certainly wished to be buried in the cemetery of his hermitage and definitely not in the monumental cemetery of Rouen, beneath a fierce sun, lost in the fragrance of hawthorns, and positioned there to dominate a city lost in a great slate-coloured shade while all around *his corpse nothing but machinations and human documents out of which* during his life he would have *been able to carve out a fine novel of provincial life*[145].

Thus murmured Harel Bey with a point of malice and subtle satisfaction for obscure handlings of thoughts and memories, of words pronounced to bewitch and confuse others, since he put very little faith in his words, in his manner of speaking which was impudent and inconclusive. He was finally appeased in the fulfilment of an obscene mockery, and pulled himself up with deep breaths and puffs of air. He wrote down some brief notes in his braille notebook. He read them with his fingers and caressed the knob of his stick with scurrilous sensuality. Thereupon he began to babble about the value of a gesture, of a word, of a role.

Monsieur Léger alertly sought the hand of Harel Bey. He

---

143 Professor of anatomy and friend of Gustave.

144 The writer and hermit of Croisset.

145 Fréres de Goncourt, *Journal.*

caressed it with satisfaction and ill-bred pleasure. Then he came alongside the Bedouin and began to murmur a flood of words in his ear, impassioned too, even stammering, babbling, because of some memory which imposed on him unaccustomed pauses, which required sips of poor Calvados to be continuous, fertile, rich in subjects and gossipy interjections. Thus, with relish, and also by necessity, he uncorked a flask certainly obtained as a gift from some miserable being to whom he had offered himself as assistant in his desperation. He gulped down swallows and swallows without spare or conscience.

The gravedigger's steps had become uncertain, even up to a metal box tied up with laces and twine a short distance from Harel Bey. His speech was certainly not confused now that his tongue had been loosened and he preached with no let-up about the odour of sin which had afflicted Gustave from the time in 1845 when he had admired, in the city of Genoa, at Palazzo Balbi, a painting by Pieter Breughel with a Saint Anthony besieged by temptations and seductions. Gustave had recognized in it the penitential practices of privation and of a hermit's life which he must have kept well in mind since he had wished, in truth and one day, to expiate every unhealthy principle which might ever torment him and which certainly had already in some way tormented him. Anthony the Saint, then. Anthony. Anthony depicted while blessing by the Master of Saint Veronica, represented with the book of Holy Scripture in his hand by Hieronymus Bosch, painted praying by Diego Velasquez, pictured while suffering bestial tortures by Matthias Grunewald. Anthony. Anthony the Hermit, Anthony the Abbot, Anthony the Great, Anthony of Egypt, Anthony of the Fire, Anthony of the Desert, Anthony the Anchorite. Anthony.

Oh glorious victor over the Devil / armed in a multitude of manners against You / Saint Anthony the Abbot / continue your victorious works against the Inferno / conjured up for our damnation. / Save our souls from those fatal blows / fortifying them in spiritual battles / To our bodies bestow constant health / Drive away from the herds and from the fields any evil influence / And the present life, your tranquil mercy for us, / let us be wise and ready for the perfect peace of eternal life

– some good Christian would have supplicated in invoking the protection and magnanimity of the Saint.

Oh, Anthony, Anthony Thaumaturge! Amen. And Gustave perhaps remembered all this, or thought that he would have perhaps remembered it in some memory searched for with servile will. Anthony. Anthony the Hermit. Anthony the Abbot, Anthony the Great, Anthony of Egypt, Anthony of the Fire, Anthony of the Desert, Anthony the Anchorite. Anthony.

Harel Bey suddenly sniffed the air, with little oaths and casual curses to distract his thoughts. Thereupon he uttered some words, firm and agitated, censuring Gustave's regrets, since that writer had never given any sign of repentance for cruel and inhuman actions, for sad forgetfulness, for having kept him at the mercy of the Goncourt brothers, who were fussy, fastidious, squeamish individuals and shrewd gossipers in truth, and seduced only by authoritative and powerful friendships. Gustave, with no scruples whatsoever or repentance for guilt, had begun, precisely in the salon *d'une maison d'artiste* of those two brothers adorned with silk tapestries of Beauvais or of Gobelins, to speak of his plans and his desire to write a book on the Orient, which would have had as a protagonist a certain Bedouin to whom he would have given the name Harel Bey.

Then, victim of his passion for inducing unreasonable reasons and seeking justified vengeances, the Bedouin began to write in his notebook with vigorous marks, to stammer words, to ask in the end, and peremptorily, that the gravedigger tell him about the images that he had impressed with magnesium, even though he was unsure about who had wanted them or if they had been imposed on him, with subtle deception and cruel scheming, so that Gustave would not succumb to the odour of sin.

I glanced at Monsieur Lèger while, crouching with a wild, frantic look, he spilled out his secrets, opened a chest full of effects and affections, of memories also, of distractions even, of knowledge both useful and superfluous. The chest rapidly became a gutted belly, all its contents ripped out and scattered, revealing itself as having granted a capacious welcome to miscellaneous knickknacks, transparent ampoules for salts, strips and sheets of gelatine with silver bromide. Also empty bottles of Calvados, empty flasks of wine with labels adorned with floral decorations and Norman letters. And then piles of daguerreotypes pulled out by the handful, without measure or order, almost clues and lost testaments to an ambiguous past, amidst the sweet and bitter flavours *des maisons de tollérance*[146].

Immobile for a few instants, Monsieur Léger meditated while he gathered from the bottom of the chest daguerreotypes on paper and on plates, held together by a thin burnished thread, perhaps wool, perhaps cotton discoloured by time. The gravedigger unravelled it slowly and handed the bundle to me, fanning it out like cards for *le lansquenet.*

Obscure shadows with grey borders, faded, striped with filigree. Figures then, images scarcely delineated with contours lost in other figures, in profiles of objects and tufts of vegetation. Seven in number were the images that he offered me. Like the deadly sins, *les fleurs du mal*, Monsieur the gravedigger suggested in a low voice, barely murmuring.

Harel Bey laughed with anger and asked Monsieur Léger if he had enjoyed his work as a daguerreotypist now that, he was certain, that of gravedigger was for him only a scandalous passion. Then he struck the wooden panelling of a wall with a hail of blows, using his stick as a club and swinging it about without pause or precision. The Bedouin had hidden frenzies, and also anguishes – so it seemed to me – from the moment that Monsieur Léger announced, in alcoholic tones and cadences, that he would show me, to satisfy my indecent curiosity, the daguerreotypes that revealed a secret side of Gustave.

Was Harel Bey afraid of something? It is difficult to imagine it, my dear Pécuchet. He was restless and frenzied, this much is certain!

Here is Croisset, the gravedigger observed suddenly, and he selected a faded daguerreotype with his right hand. It was clear

---

146 Bordellos.

which of the deadly sins was represented. Envy marked this image, as it was certainly known that Gustave felt rancour towards St. Anthony the Hermit because of the lowly hut of his penitence and his miraculous acts, even though the hut was made of mud and reeds, adorned with mats, supplied only with a knife, a bowl and black bread. Croisset could also have been a den of seclusion and contrition had it not had that long curving alee, exposed to the midday light, a true avenue and entrance to the house of a literary man – I suggested with a pinch of malevolence.

Anthony had contemplated *with a single glance the Southern Cross and the Great Bear, also the Constellation of the Lynx, of the Centaur and of the Dorado, the six stars of the constellation of Orion, and Jupiter and its four satellites, and the triple ring of horrendous Saturn. All the stars, all the planets, that men would discover only later on*[147]! – recited Harel Bey. He was not at all pleased and began to beat the floor with precise touches of his stick to indicate that he had opinions to express on the sagas recorded by means of magnesium.

Monsieur Léger took a sip, then another, then another still. Unstable, he looked for something to support his precarious equilibrium. He came across my shoulder, offered for that purpose while, clutching in his hand another daguerreotype, he said that he possessed the proof of another of Gustave's sins.

The daguerreotype I was now protecting from the tactile curiosity of the Bedouin illustrated pride, that same vice that Anthony had practised passing among the fathers of the Council of Nicaea, who *crowd together, beg him to intercede, kiss his hands ... he enjoys beyond all measure their humiliation*[147].

I began then to utter frank words so that the Bedouin could understand the sense and meanings. I mentioned then Gustave's guilt. I spoke of his pride, as Monsieur Léger had exerted himself to concede to the writer, who it seems had requested of him precisely the snapshot of his sin. Thus I listed, in a loud, clear voice, the figures recorded by the magnesium, albeit in the shadows of the nitrates.

---

147   Gustave Flaubert, *The Temptation of Saint Anthony.*

An open compartment, a precious safe full of intimate secrets of a wardrobe, since underwear is personal when it is not proudly displayed. Few then were the shirts either for daytime or night, few the skull caps, the frock coats, the vests, the trousers, the shoes, the ties, the flannels, the belts. Instead there were thirty-four pairs of gaiters of every kind, colour and workmanship, because they were the garments that could be displayed for one's pride and glory. Indeed, he had intuited that they offered themselves as a secret indemnity for esteem, for authority and credit in one's own eyes even if one didn't dare to display them in public.

Harel Bey began to recite, with words uttered sparingly as if the murmur was a lament, a reading carried out attentively. Of Saint Anthony, in fact, from a passage that Gustave had attributed to the Saint not at all forgetting himself: *Enjoying his inactivity, he stretched his limbs out upon a mat*[148].

I understood immediately that the Bedouin was trying to trap me in an obscure and malevolent game, and that he was perhaps in cahoots with that Monsieur Léger. He had not, at least so far, given to understand that he wanted to penalize, with words of sarcasm and ridicule, the odious foul smell of the gravedigger which was very evident and repellent. And precisely he who was the doctor of smells and magician of stenches.

Thus I imagined that there was between them an original understanding, indeed an acquaintance and, from the outset, an audacity, in no way belligerent, which filled me with fear and insecurity. I murmured suitable words and spoke about another daguerreotype which I had in my hands, also this one appropriate for pointing out the capital vice of which the Bedouin had spoken, reciting the words of Saint Anthony.

Sloth now, since Monsieur Léger the daguerreotypist had had the intuition of depicting the canal beyond the window of Gustave's studio. There was not, in fact, any exercise of virtue in that scene off boredom, suffering from phlegm, smoothed by stillness so that it was obvious to think and mention sloth.

With a hollow sound the gravedigger moved a bottle taken from a metal container, placed among rags and inane bits of rubbish, for the most part waste paper, rusty remnants, odds and ends of rubber. He then began to swallow in big gulps and to recite rigmaroles in the irritated tones of raunchy drunkenness. His breath fouled the air, penetrated, was displeasing to the point that I quickly turned away to avoid its offensive, sickening whiffs.

The tablecloth was of linen... upon it pieces of red meat, enormous fish, birds cooked in their plumage... fruits of a thousand unknown colours... purple crystal flagons sparkling like flames[148], declaimed the gravedigger, winding up his discourse with a passage from Gustave's *Saint Anthony.*

Harel Bey suddenly asked what evidence in terms of images and truths I might have at hand to incriminate the writer of Croisset of this other vice since, as the Italian poets Dante and Petrarch recited, for the pernicious sin of gluttony one is wounded by a lashing of lurid rain or because of it one loses all virtue and honesty.

I shuffled through the bundle of daguerreotypes with a rapid, impulsive gesture. I looked within and finally drew out the one which for me represented a feast of the sin of gluttony. There was some excessive shadow, it's true, borders corroded by acids and the focus not sharp due to haste, almost as if the daguerreotype had been taken surreptitiously in the interval of a meal or of guests waiting to feast in good spirits.

The table was in thick walnut and decked with a finely embroidered tablecloth. Only one place was laid and next to it, on a silver and crystal serving plate, an immense turbot garnished with a voluptuous cream sauce, rich in seasonings and succulent juices. On one side a *soyer*[149] with strawberry and apricot ice-cream and a bottle of Saint Estèphe, with the label in full sight.

I then described to the Bedouin the image that Monsieur Léger had taken with a flash of magnesium so that he could note down and register in his notebook the annoyances and intrigues of that entertainer of private matters and of irreverent glances who was our daguerreotypist and gravedigger of Croisset.

Abruptly, then, Monsieur Léger began to protest with words

---

148 Gustave Flaubert, *The Temptation of Saint Anthony.*
149 A glass of ice-cold champagne.

confused by alcohol. He proclaimed an obvious innocence since he had simply lent himself to serve a particular desire and will, only because someone, a writer perhaps, called Gustave perhaps, felt excited by the odour of sins, and especially capital ones.

Harel Bey suddenly beat the ground with his stick and asked if we had decided to travel to the very bottom of this road of investigations and analyses now that there were only three daguerreotypes lacking to finish off the entire matter and understand with good reasons the obscure motives for which Monsieur Gustave had written the *The Temptation*. Thus he invited me to think about a fifth daguerreotype, on greed in truth, as there had been granted to him merits and virtues since he well remembered, at the moment, that Gustave had spoken of great poverty, of a threadbare, tattered cloak, of a lack of sandals and bowl, even though Anthony, hermit and saint, had been very tempted when he came across a silver cup which had hidden in the bottom golden coins for which *nothing now was impossible for him! All suffering was finished!...* (and his) *heart leapt! It was delightful*[150]!

Jalousie windows open in the background and a clutch of thick shadows which swallowed up the form and appearance of an ample armchair in the foreground, with a bearskin spread out on the floor. In a corner, abandoned on the ground, a strange toy, almost a doll made of rags which held tightly in its embrace a horse lacking its head, and with its tail cut off. I described this troubling image in a piercing voice so that Harel Bey could understand. As a comment then, I added that it was to be interpreted as the ambiguous presence of Madame Caroline who, when she was a young child and orphan, through the chances of life and her own misfortune, had lived with her uncle, the hermit of Croisset, and was raised there with attention, affection and the odours of sins in which Gustave loved to indulge and recklessly hide.

Harel Bey laughed complacently while the gravedigger sniggered insolently, stewed as he was with beverages swallowed without restraint or fear, bemused with the insidiousness of no

---

150   Gustave Flaubert, The Temptation of Saint Anthony.

longer remembering where he had drunk other bottles of wine or Calvados or whatever it might have been. In the squawking of the angry, uproarious walking and wandering about of Monsieur Léger, the Bedouin said aloud that as far as he was concerned that image of the daguerreotype was also very pathetic because it evoked again a period when greed had not yet corrupted Gustave. That toy of Caroline's, so tender, so infantile, so perfidious in its singular eccentricity, was the prelude, it was clear, to an insidiousness of which Gustave should have been aware. Also to avoid the effects of a bankruptcy undertaken with negligence and light-heartedness by Madame *la nièce avec son epoux*[151], Monsieur Ernest Commanville, whose letters of credit Gustave had honoured to avoid a bankruptcy which was about to befall them. From then on, after that time it's true, Gustave had taken to frequenting the gluttonous hunger of possessing and conserving as best he could in the panic-like fear that he would have nothing else for an impending old-age.

I remained without breath or words listening to the Bedouin rise up to defend Gustave from whom he had been divided and with whom he had rude disagreements about a paternity that had never been recognized. Thus I expressed with sarcastic words my surprise, that fascination of being wrong through hasty and false judgments.

Harel Bey laughed scornfully and began to gesticulate effectively. He put out his finger, as only he knew how to do, to signal that he had a request, also a piece of information, and still more a piece of news. In truth, he did not forget ill deeds already carried out, but as an honest and decent man, which he insisted he was, the Bedouin wished to avenge the summary justice which, with twisted and equivocal words, condemned, with crude aphorisms and metaphors, a niece even more than an uncle, but regarding this same uncle it was justified to see whether he had lent himself to the intriguing wishes of his niece Caroline.

Monsieur Léger immediately stopped short when he heard these words. He shook his head and sought a sentence, a saying,

---

151 The niece, with her husband.

a locution to request clear explanations. He renounced this with conviction when he caught sight of the Bedouin's face which, impenetrable in its blindness and in an unforeseen silence, rejected attacks of words, of sayings, of discourses. The gravedigger once again took the path of chronic drunkenness, taking deep gulps drawn recklessly from a flask of the worst possible aspect, filthy, scarred by scratches and blows. He then crouched down in a corner on the ground and began making signs and marks in the dirt. He turned his head towards me and asked, in a lisping and tangled loquacity, what image I would now show to represent lust, that carnal intemperance which for Gustave had been very close to fatal.

I drew out from the pack the penultimate card. A poor daguerreotype, inept and clumsy in inspiration. Tall majestic linden trees which, with their dense verdure of boughs and leaves, framed the profile of an elegant house. Also ornamental shrubs growing closely together to conceal access roads, little alleyways, slanting paths. Croisset displayed, among faded contrasts and nitrates arranged with an alcoholic will, a heart-rending sweetness and touching melancholy of colours, lights and shadows, just as that manuscript that Madame Caroline had recited.

Monsieur Léger did not ask for explanations, busy as he was in sniffing bottles and uncorked flasks. In tasting various alcoholic beverages. In rinsing his mouth in irritating, assiduous, scurrilous swallows. I glanced at Harel Bey who, immobile, seemed to be asleep or was waiting for words from me that would clarify acts and silences of Gustave in confronting fear, the intense odour of that sin of lust.

It seemed to me then, my dear Pécuchet, that I was enveloped by a penetrating stench of hastily consumed coitus, by the scent of a woman of *longue orgie* who was walking in a state of untidy dress in that garden, who was claiming a right acquired through experiences and apprenticeship, who was demanding to be introduced into this grand house and also to engage there, in happy occasions and opportunities, in sex and in love-affairs, even indeed in the room next to the one in which there rested *une vieille mère*[152], an adored mother.

Harel Bey suddenly sneered, sought me with an outstretched arm and began to murmur ambiguous phrases. I understood, however, that he wanted to play dirty tricks on the gravedigger who by now was betrayed by his sin, by low-quality and dangerous alcohol, by the pleasure of losing his reason in a reckless drunkenness, without anything else to which to dedicate his will.

Harel Bey sneered again, now with sonorous accents and towards Monsieur Léger. The latter responded with resounding blurts, with vomit stinking of wine, with a froth of regurgitated saliva. He moved his head without understanding words or wishes. He nodded and sneered with reckless, uncertain, involuntary words. Then suddenly he collapsed, his body bent double in an unnatural manner. A hoarse cry, a shudder, and a flow of vomit which covered his chest and thigh with regurgitated alcohol, of a bitter fermentation, of foul odours. Then, precisely then, Harel Bey began to shout loudly in a screeching voice. To curse, also. To murmur with accusatory tones that he was aware of a foul stink, the loathsome stench of a filthy body, an odour of vulgar coarseness, of mortal sin.

A furore, indeed a wrath took possession of the Bedouin, enslaved him to malevolence and hatred towards that Monsieur lying on the ground in the humour of his viscera. It was a rash nature with obscure thoughts, because of a crime perhaps, that made the one and the other, the Bedouin and the gravedigger, accomplices in nefarious intentions and causes – at least, so it seemed to me.

I was confused, my friend, now that Harel Bey inveighed and offended with an immoderate anger and with vindictive accents against that miserable man who had never hurt him before, even though he'd had ample reason to do so. To quiet down the spirit of the Bedouin I reclaimed his attention. Speaking breathlessly, I reminded him that we were at the end of this intricate journey, sown with sins, which was concerned with the temptation of St. Anthony. To distract him from his ire, I spoke to him of

---

152   An elderly mother.

another ire, that which was described in the book which we were investigating. Instinctively then I glanced over the daguerreotypes which I had in my hands. I bent the corner of the last one with a rapid movement to separate it from the other six.

The grains of nitrate, concentrated or diluted in ample or minute images, offered a confused image with profiles, faces, mouths and noses superimposed, while in the background there appeared unmistakably the silhouette of the house of the writer of Croisset. Looking with attention I discovered that there was only one face depicted on it, which was multiplied because of reflected lights so that, even though appearing disguised among other faces which seemed indistinguishable, it showed, in full evidence, features and irregularities which were unmistakably Levantine.

I reflected for some seconds amidst embarrassment and perplexity now that I was sure that the image showed Harel Bey and I was well persuaded that, at the time of the daguerreotype, our Bedouin sojourned in perpetuity, in intentions and care, in the home of Messieurs Edmond and Jules Huot de Goncourt. Thus Monsieur Léger must have practised his trade in other times if the model had been Harel Bey the Bedouin.

Strange alchemies those that come from mixing time, places and persons, but also truths and fictions, where actions and presuppositions are intertwined in an equivocal manner, and without conceding the possibility of discernment.

Suddenly I pulled Harel Bey by an arm so that I could murmur to him with firm accents, despite his protests and caprices, that it was time we removed ourselves from that mess, from that rash odour of sins, and that we should once more begin to follow our own path and explore perhaps whether it was the case to examine another story of Monsieur Gustave.

We left Croisset and the refuge of Monsieur Léger the gravedigger with caution and sagacity. However, we abandoned a man on the ground, without any concern and without offering him assistance or mercy. So the Bedouin insisted in decisive tones. The gravedigger lay motionless in the filth of vomit and drunkenness, in an unconsciousness that perhaps disguised a violent death by crime or suicide probably.

My friend, I am disturbed and preoccupied by such incidents and unforeseen happenings. Nevertheless, I keep faith in a promise and an undertaking. I will write to you certainly from Sens, from the Yonne, to tell you more about our investigations and encounters, to narrate to you the most recent events of our wanderings.

Au revoir.

B.

Buffet Les Deux Fleuves, Sens.

25 June

Cher ami,

Voilà Salammbô, voilà[153].

Salammbô. *Her hair, sprinkled with violet powder and gathered up on her head in the form of a tower after the fashion of Canaanite maidens, made Salammbô appear taller. Pendants of pearls hung from her temples as far as her mouth, which was as red as an open pomegranate. On her breast thousands and thousands of brilliant and variegated stones resembled the scales of a moray. Her arms adorned with diamonds emerged naked from her sleeveless tunic, which was starred with red flowers... a large purple mantle, made of some unknown material, trailed behind her, making a wave that seemed to escort her every step*[154].

Salammbô splendid. Salammbô attentively enshrined. Salammbô described in a book about which that imbecile writer who goes by the name of Charles Baudelaire wrote[155] *"that it was a great success. Two thousand copies sold in scarcely two days. An incontestable fact, whether you like it or not. A fine book full of defects which, however, would have driven many critics mad, in particular one like Hippolyte Babou ... What Flaubert had done could have been done only by him. Too much trash in the midst of so many marvellous things, expressed in an epic, historical, political form ... In truth something stupefying in the choral gesturing of so many human beings"*. Perhaps

---

153   *Salammbô* is a work that Gustave Flaubert began to write in 1857.

154   Gustave Flaubert, *Salammbô*.

155   Charles Baudelaire, letter to Poulet-Malassis.

also a piece of writing with a subtle point of sadistic imagination: so dear to Gustave – so said Charles Augustin de Sainte-Beuve.

Salammbô was also printed in a volume for which had been devised *an authentic Carthaginian binding made of a brownish Japanese leather resembling a human skin just emerged from the Breton tannery of Meudon, and with the flaps made of a barbaric silk depicting owls embroidered in gold on a blood-coloured background*[156].

Salammbô. Salammbô splendid. Salammbô similar to a meteor that flashes suddenly and unexpectedly. Gustave, as you know well, my friend, mourned in some way the atrocities of barbarities. He also mourned an age in which force, boastfulness and simplicity governed. Gustave *mourned a primitive and depraved age, the bloody age of battles, of heroic undertakings, of intrepid and savage times, marked by crude colours but sumptuous with various gewgaws*[157]. Salammbô, then!

I believed, after the obsessive practices and verbose ambiguities of the temptation, that the Bedouin and I could have investigated among the words, acts and contingencies which concerned *Salammbô*. Which concerned this story of Gustave's, so that we might be able to analyse circumstances and to verify encounters following new, and, in fact sober, itineraries. At times indeed the writer of Croisset had the unseemliness to abandon himself to *sentences which profoundly disgusted the conventionally well-thinking... to horrors upon horrors... to twenty thousand men so starved that they were forced to devour each other... Bestiality and homicidal madnes*[158], as Jérôme repeated in the saga *Justine, or the Misfortunes of Virtue* by Donatien Alphonse François, Marquis de Sade, whom Gustave loved to keep in mind and to whom *he returned as to a mystery which attracted him*[159], because, in his opinion, he was the last word in Catholicism ... and because there was in fact in de Sade the spirit of the Inquisition, the spirit of the medieval church, the horror of nature. In de Sade there was never either a tree or an animal.

---

156   Edmond de Goncourt, *An Artist's House.*
157   Frères de Goncourt, *Journal*
158   Gustave Flaubert, *Lettres*
159   Frères de Goncourt, *Journal*

Essentially, the Bedouin and I had to opportunely conduct only true and legitimate interrogations in order to verify, for example – well beyond the facts and personages mentioned in Madame Caroline's manuscript – if it were indeed true what was said in literary circles and among the few friends, among certain admirers and the many denigrators and sarcastic spirits, about Gustave, that that story had been inspired by a certain Koutchouk-Hanem, an *almée* whom Gustave had met in Egypt, and that there was a secret version of this story, a first draft written for youthful entertainment or amiable pleasure.

Those indiscretions could have been gleaned from what Gustave himself had written to his friend Louis Bouilhet in November 1850, and that was that he had had in mind a very beautiful subject for a new novel: an Oriental woman who wished *to be fucked by a God... and to have as background the ancient, immutable and tenacious Arab rabble*[160]. That is, it would have pleased him very much *to make something purple. As to the rest, the characters and the plot, that would be a matter of mere details*[161]. Indeed, Gustave was completely indifferent to the events to be narrated. That is, what really interested him most was to create and offer to the reader a modulation of colours.

And was such a story or initial draft, even if only in outline or manuscript, ever given by Gustave to a friend or interested buyer? There was gossip about this, and it was much speculated in the literary salons, after the dispute which Gustave had with the editor Michel Lévy who wanted to give him only 10,000 francs for the work on *Salammbô* while Gustave, even though highly esteemed by everyone as a man of profound scruples and extremely generous in living for art and without compromises, asked for 30,000.

Or perhaps that manuscript or draft was sold by thoughtless heirs: Madame Commanville, I mean? Sold in fact to a lover of immoral writings to finally end up in the hands, through various commercial manipulations and exchanges of money, of a skilful dealer and crafty collector of antique and licentious books, even

---

160 Gustave Flaubert, *Letters*.
161 Frères de Goncourt, *Journal*.

though he was also a zealous lover of operatic melodramas (in particular, for example, of the *Aida* of maestro Verdi from Roncole di Busseto), but also an attentive and expert procurer, used to dealing in beautiful Oriental women at very convenient prices.

This man was indeed the proprietor and custodian at Sens, in the Yonne, of a very good and extremely well-frequented antiquarian bookshop – 16th century Bodonian and Aldine editions of the works of Pietro Aretino and above all the splendid 1556 edition of *La Corona dei cazzi, sonetti lussuriosi* (16mo, 114 leaves, with an obscene print on the frontispiece), but also, among the few good licentious things, those of Giorgio Baffo (a work in 4 vols., 8vo, 1771) and of Nobile Socio (in one volume, quarto, 1533) and of others still (Pierre-Corneille Blessebois, Francesco Baldovini, Franz von Bayros, to mention only a few), all chosen to gratify the obscene whims of readers competent and unrestrained in these matters. *Most of the books were bound in a Jansenist binding – whores dressed up as nuns… and opening them one found the meander with a phallic motif, decorations in the form of a hairy pussy, ornaments in the form of female buttocks*[162].

This man, whose name is Léon Grappin, is a native of Laval, in the Mayenne, where his father runs a luxurious bordello, animated by young girls between twelve and fourteen years of age, in rue Crossardière, where a fuck costs just 2 francs and with supreme gratification for the clients because the young girls are all of rare beauty and type, sold by their parents for a fistful of francs and held in virginal segregation until the first violation to which they are subjected by a thuggish father – this was related to us, in malicious confidence and in a spirit of aleatory and jolly gossip, by some chatty women who had travelled along with us, first in the carriage and then in a cart and who, to my mind, had something in common with these intrigues of trafficking or, to say the least and with spite, might have been rabid devourers of *The Devil in the Flesh* by Chevalier Andréa de Nerciat.

With a father as owner and manager of a profitable brothel,

---

162 Frères de Goncourt, *Journal*.

Léon Grappin obtained, through paternal generosity, an income consistent with satisfying the most ardent pleasures and to thus reserve for himself an existence without anxieties or upsets, and totally dedicated to the acquisition of obscene images, licentious stories, both published and unpublished manuscripts on the condition that they were indecent and amusing, with shameless illustrations.

Of such plausible and improbable events, at one time one could obtain the most appropriate information and very suitable tales by frequenting the literary salons in Auxerre, the capital of the Yonne – as I was assured by a certain poet encountered at a staging-post, among involuntary confidences and deliberate diffidence. In each meeting of frivolous vagabonds or rascally scribblers, in fact, it was quite usual – the Bedouin confirmed, with remarks and murmurs, based on his past compulsory sojourn in the salon of the Goncourt brothers – to make, as a slothful pastime and expected perfidy, with words governed by the desire to show off and in the memory of diaries or loose leaves, scabrous comments on the love-affairs of certain gentlemen, on their practices with *filles de noce*[163], even though such gossip, in various disputable cases, can be corrupted and alarmed by an ineluctable falsity.

Thus ambiguous words, uncontrolled voices and eccentric allusions are often rash and careless accounts, turbulent reports, barbarous twaddle with which to divert oneself, gossip, chatter away, above all during a journey: the reality of which, in truth, I am not familiar with, not having ever, as you well know my dear Pécuchet, frequented brothels, not even *the boulevard des Italiens between the Maison d'Or, the Opéra, the Libraire Nouvelle, the Café Anglais and Tortoni,* called *the clitoris of Paris*[164]. Faced with the boorish indelicacies and coarse fantasies concerning this Léon Grappin whom we wished to meet in Sens, I recruited our Bedouin, who knows things, and even more than one can imagine.

Harel Bey turned out to be a convincing narrator, citing pages, lines and notes of that Journal of those Goncourt brothers who

---

163   Ladies of pleasure.
164   Frères de Goncourt, *Journal.*

at times offered appropriate accounts with no equivocal terms. *District of high-class prostitutes: 120 avenue des Champs-Élysées* (or was it at Palais-Royal? Or at Saint-Denis? Or at the boulevard de Sébastople? Or at place Maubert? One is as good as another). *First floor. The shutters allow a little light to filter in... A majestic white staircase, carpeted... bedroom: a large padded box, full of frippery of red satin edged with purple... Louis XVI bed... There are no courtesans there, only whores. They offer neither more nor less of the same things that the women of the brothel offer... they are simply, precisely, whores*[165]. In those places an immoral and caressing odour at once induces one to follow desires and instincts. It is difficult to understand if the whore has a good odour or not, certainly she doesn't have a bad, harmful or unpleasant one. But like all genital odours, it is a strongly equivocal smell, pungent, amoral.

I listened with attention, with good reason and an appropriate conscience – it was obligatory when Harel Bey was narrating and this happened during our stay at Melun while we were waiting for Monsieur Grappin, the music-loving and pornographic bookseller, son of the owner of a famous brothel, who was making haste to return to Sens from personal excursions to European auctions so that he could have interviews and ordinary exegeses on the oblique truth concerning a first printing of a book by Monsieur Gustave and other things.

For two days, in the delay in arriving at Sens and its Cathedral of Saint-Étienne, behind which rose up the tour de plomb and the *tour de pierre*, we conversed with pleasure and good-will about our new adventures in the complex and substantial pages of *Salammbô*. I was, in such predicaments, the hard-working companion of the Bedouin in exhausting walks from the Hôtel du Grand-Monarque in rue Miroir (40 rooms at 2 to 3 fr.), where we were staying, as far as the Gruber beer-house, or to the Church of St. Aspais, or to the Cathedral of Saint-Étienne.

I often encountered in Harel Bey an exasperating mutism, a poorly concealed animosity, irritated murmurings. In one circumstance I had to confront a critical, hostile and obscure

---

165 Frères de Goncourt, *Journal.*

interference on his part.

We were walking in avenue Thiers pressed closely together, with my arm guiding him and with his stick beating time to our steps, when the Bedouin stopped abruptly, a little before we passed beyond the old town, to let me know that he had great difficulty in understanding the reasons for my moral distaste and my ferocious ethical boastfulness in regard to the literary enterprises of that Monsieur Grappin

My words, the Bedouin stated with firmness and surliness, were the worthy daughters of a pitiless and persecuting inquisitorial will, and they conveyed judgments governed solely by a partiality that they did not merit. Hence he had qualms, he asked if we might ever be able to move forward with our investigations now that I had become paladin of so much sluggishness and moral stuffiness, and just when we had only a few steps left to cover before drawing conclusions and sending messages of certainties or doubts or oddities, according to the cases and circumstances, to Madame Caroline, Gustave's niece.

Harel Bey began to chatter about diverse pieces of knowledge, dissimilar moralities, divergent ethics. He reminded me that we were now busy following traces, stories and plots created for *Salammbô*. At the right moment then, we would have had to dissolve preconceived impediments to arrive at the city of Sens and to speak there, without acquired prejudices, with Monsieur Grappin in order to obtain from him news about a certain Koutchouk-Hanem who, an *almée* in Egypt, had been, to listen to that writer Louise Colet, the divine inspiration of every writing of Gustave's on the Orient and who now, in French territory according to rumour, was engaged in a very dishonourable trade.

We had in any case the sentimental and bibliographical obligation to verify whether or not the rumours about a first, secret draft of that novel entitled *Salammbô* had any truth. For these two principal and noble reasons we should not then have wandered off into senseless actions or blind alleys. We should not have wavered from our responsibilities with pleasing speeches and provocative entanglements, from which his diligent reproach about a practice that I defined, on account of my disgraceful moderation, pornography and about some sellers of books and libertine images, whom I had called pornographers.

In his opinion I was wasting time about an improper way of speaking which could have delayed investigations, thrown us off the track, dissolved understandings which were necessary and urgent. In fact, from this adventurous and peripatetic excursion he hoped to be able to cut out for himself at the very least a place in a story and to have a certain domicile, in the present and in the future, in some written work of Monsieur Gustave's.

I asked him then to be clear, to explain his intentions to me, to exclude however from his purposes any immoral actions, and, if he wished, to make me a participant in his doubtful perplexities, in his preoccupations, in his dilemmas.

Harel Bey squeezed my arm with a dolorous grip almost as if he meant to propose to me an alliance of understandings and he began to smile at me with conciliatory sarcasm. He then let go of my arm and, in a corner of the street, drew from a secret pocket of his caftan his notebook in braille. He leafed through pages feeling, in an orderly way and with intensity, the upper corner.

From time to time he suddenly stopped reading, letting his fingertips run over the pages with points marked in relief. He turned over words and phrases with his lips moving in an imperceptible murmur. Once more he quickly took up his examination, running through the pages alertly, stopping for a few seconds now on this, now on that page. Suddenly he closed the diary and put it back in its secret place. He seemed satisfied to me. He smiled at me and drew near with a persuasive air and movements.

Without warning, license or permission, Harel Bey began to tell strange stories, to pose troubling questions to me, to solicit appropriate responses that would clear up at least some of his unresolved dilemmas.

He began to sniff the air and to discourse on the meagre functions of the other senses compared with that of smell. To note whether from images, for example, it was possible to perceive an intimate smell, the first signs of what was to appear; the visceral essence of everything was, in reality, perceptible only by means of smell. Indeed, the sense of smell was governed by effluvia and stenches which integrated the scanty geniality and dubious ductility of the other senses, since for him the sense of smell was the primary one, the testament to each particular, strong perceptive impulse. Hence he did not understand that unfair fuss made about the sense of sight, for example, which granted only a reality in one dimension, with no relief, without the emotional intensity of knowing how to fully perceive intimacy.

These remarks of his, explicit and careful in expression, were intended to change the nature of all my disapproval and vituperation towards the pornography collected by Monsieur Grappin, since it was as a particular and unique mark of perception.

The Bedouin smiled and lifted up his nose, breaking the silence of my thoughts, now gathered together in sapid reliefs and in ambiguous realities. Thus I followed the train of his reasoning, both in decided pronouncements and relevant suppositions, in order to ask him, without rhetoric or irritating whimsicality, if there were not for him certain appearances and forms which, even without being in themselves filthy, were prone to induce excitation, to cause a turgid awakening of the penis abandoned for a time to the tranquillity of abstinence, to stimulate lascivious immodesty and shameful lust. If that word 'pornography' were not indeed a sign so preponderant and magical as to eclipse the seductive wake of an odour of mounting, oestrus, of coitus.

Harel Bey drew near to me and began to palpate my trunk, my arms, my shoulders, to finally press my face between his hands, to draw it to his own, to caress it. He then murmured appropriate, indeed seductive, words, which recalled to the mind ancestral fragrances, the secret taste of carousing carried out by bodies marked by beads of sweat, of the languid humours of sex, of the bitter stench of filthy buttocks.

In the play and the occasion of odours exchanged, mingled, sniffed, in the ardour of the sense of smell, one had to nurture

– the Bedouin recalled to me with appropriate vindictiveness –
a discretion in admiring a body, recognizing it in the signs and
aspects of silhouettes and forms, when only the sense of smell
knows how to guide so accurately the impulse.

It was a fascinating affirmation, my friend, so that to free
myself from the blasphemous keenness of the Bedouin and his
intrepid loquacity I drew away brusquely and, with an abrupt
movement, I admonished him, because dusk had now fallen, in
the midst of sighs and murmurings of unseemly ideas, and we
were still very far from our lodgings in rue Miroir. It was time
for us to take a rest since the next day we had to take a train very
early in the morning.

The trip from Melun to Sens was comfortable and silent.
Settled into a bench on one side by a window and closely
pressed beside the dozing body of the Bedouin, I spent the time
remembering the words exchanged the evening before with Harel
Bey. In the tranquillity of the journey and in the frenzy of turbid
accents and words uttered by the Arab, I began to count over past
love-affairs and to see if they had at least a sign or a spasm marked
by the sense of smell.

I was able to recover only visual memories, only tactile
memories in the midst of recollections of senses and seductive
limbs which hid, of this I was certain, in their appearance and
in their perfume of lavender and talcum powders, every secret
and bitter intimacy of smell. I recalled then the turbid love of
Salammbô, her losing herself in voluptuous, inebriating sexual
intercourse, *as she was invaded by a languor which made her lose*
consciousness. It was something exclusive and supernatural. A divine
order which obliged her to yield herself. Clouds uplifted her and, fainting,
she fell back on the bed amidst the lion-skins... The zaimph fell and
covered her. She saw Matho's face bending over her breast... the soldier's
kisses, more voracious than flames, made her shudder. She seemed to be
swept away by a hurricane, taken by the might of the sun[166].

At times, amidst thoughts and memories, I had the sensation

---

166 Gustave Flaubert, *Salammbô*.

that Gustave was inducing me to believe in what he himself believed, indeed that it was wise to defend oneself from deleterious sensuality, putting before it a coarse indolence. In that case then, it was possible to govern, with such wary feelings and with a controlled emotional force, all those terrible women who exhaust love through oppressive attacks, ferocious rages, intoxications that are brutal and spiritual at the same time.

Sens welcomed us suddenly, as an unexpectedly beneficent city, thus interrupting reflections and thoughts. I quickly convinced Harel Bey to recover from his somnolent torpor so that he could follow me briskly and be ready to listen to my accounts of the city and its men, now that we were back in the breach, about to investigate this further story of Gustave's. And also to look into the possibility that he might have prepared a very improper and unsuitable draft of this story. And also indeed to investigate a certain *almée* called Koutchouk-Hanem in Egypt, but who had now begun to traffic in France under the name of Zoraide Turc.

Monsieur Leon Grappin's shop was hidden away in a basement, facing the station. On the street it displayed a velvet and satin window, just next to an iron gate which closed a courtyard abandoned to disuse and with a labyrinthine hedge of pimpernels and turgid yellow dandelion flowers. In the window and finely displayed was a splendid edition of the *The Crown of Cocks, or Lust Sonnets* by Pietro Aretino, *in a folio edition feuillets en parchemin et non chiffe, sans lieu ni date, titre en lettre italique et sur le title un portrait de l'Aretin, avec une bordure en arabesque, 24 dessins obscenes de Monsieur Jules Romain*[167]. Thus was recited in Gothic letters on a notice on a board covered with Armenian cloth placed next to the volume. Next to the notice a stupendous phonograph with wax cylinders and an aluminium horn turned towards the rooms below, diffusing distorted sounds which we had difficulty in distinguishing.

It wasn't easy to gain access to the premises of the bookshop

---

167   With 144 unnumbered parchment pages, with neither a date nor place of publication, title in italic letters and on the title-page a portrait of Aretino, with a border in arabesques, 24 obscene drawings by Monsieur Jules Romain.

since one had to go down a short, steep stairway, with precarious wooden steps carefully spaced in an ancient manner. On the right, bolted to the wall and closed in by thick, filthy windows, were quite imposing showcases with detached book covers. They were beautiful to look at, as some were certainly of Morocco leather with ornaments, or framed with double borders, or in relief, or *à la dentelle*[168], with fine decorative arabesques or with Venetian binding, or with filigrees or fine borders with palmettes, or in other precious materials and workmanship. However all of them, as noted on an accompanying card, functioned as discreet covers for those volumes of Aretino or Baffo or Socio, which were of suspect and discreditable literary value.

Abruptly, almost a lament reached our ears from a singing voice. Delightful, indeed, as it trilled away with seductive skill. Words interspersed with pauses, and pauses framed by words. Then sobs which died out in a muted echo: *"Heavenly Aida, divine form, / mystic garland of light and flowers, / you are the queen of my thought"*, modulated the voice, and then, then we heard something else which seemed to fade away:... *"That I might bring you once more / the blue skies, the soft breezes of your native land, / a royal crown to deck your brow, / a royal throne for you, in the sun!"*

I then began to guide Harel Bey with an insane anxiety while the song faded behind our shoulders. A difficult journey, and the Bedouin insisted, meanwhile, on being informed about the place, the things that were to be seen, the decorations and the furnishings. He sniffed the air with neither the caution nor care of a connoisseur; then he admonished me with censorious emphasis and with malicious arrogance given that he was aware with his sense of smell of a penetrating odour that was indeed damp and stagnant, but also with something perversely seductive about it.

Suddenly we were startled by the sound of a female voice which reached us once again as it inflected: *"Return victorious! My lips have spoken / the traitorous words! Victorious / over my father, who takes up arms / for me, to give me again / a country, a kingdom*

---

168 With dentelles.

and a great name"...

The Bedouin seized my hand, which was guiding him by the arm, and asked whether by chance I recognized, in contrast to the sweetness of this song, some manifest obscenity, since he was now aware of the stench of scandalous and

immodest works and acts almost as if the books and writings scattered in that place were manifesting themselves with olfactory impressions and signals.

I deftly avoided his confused verbal pretexts because I understood that he was about to follow chance occasions which might set off verbal brawls, if only to call attention to himself. I shook him brusquely and paid no attention to his grumbling. Only firm and determined touches. In silence then, and with the danger of stumbling, we arrived at the basement, where there were books piled up everywhere.

A man who welcomed us, with a knowing smile and restless eyes, at the foot of the staircase, singing an aria: *O gods, efface! / Send back this child / to her father's heart. / Destroy the legions / of our oppressors! / Wretched girl, what have I said? And my love? / Can I, then, forget / this burning love, which, as a wretched slave, / I welcome in rapture like a ray of the sun?*

Monsieur Léon Grappin was a small man, unpleasant, obsequious, dressed in a very personal and eccentric way, at least so it seemed to me. Wrapped in a large white flannel blouse, he clutched with obsessive and restless tics a starched and shiny piqué collar, decorated with a gold filigree pattern. Around the man were thick dungeon-like walls, a hidden and occult prison from which, with determination and ingenuity, one could get out by way of diverse exits, different from the entrance we had used.

Three doors, skilfully crafted with iron and wood slats, were placed in this ample room at short distances from each other to ensure security against unexpected incursions. The free walls were covered with tapestries and provided with solid inlaid wood shelves which curved to follow the protrusions and hollows of the walls, even the irregularities of stones and masses, or iron hooks and chains, wrought and tempered in improvised forges.

With flashes of words, I told Harel Bey what I was observing, even with details, with pure sensations, with unease and even shudders. The Bedouin now took to sniffing instinctively in every corner turning his body this way and that, sticking out his chest, rotating his ankles. He sniffed with deliberate contempt, given that the air sucked into his nostrils resulted in noises which were very disapproving, fastidious and searching.

Abruptly and instinctively he began to speak of the penetrating odours, of impure perceptions, of exciting emotions, now that Monsieur Grappin, a man of commerce and intrigues, stationed himself motionlessly in front of us, sullying the air with effluvia from his groin, which were very unclean, sullied also by odours of sperm, by filthy intimacies, by the cheapest sort of floral fragrances.

Monsieur Grappin laughed with discretion and with discretion slunk away, singing the aria "... *the mighty invader? / Like mist, they faded away / at the first breath of our champion. / Come, victorious warrior, / come take the prize of glory; / victory has smiled upon you, / on you love too shall smile"...* until he disappeared in the crevices. Crouched down as best he could between the bookcases, he busied himself in turning off the phonograph.

Retracing his steps, he drew near us again. He began to question us about our interest, our taste and our hidden passion – if indeed we had such. He asked whether we were interested in negotiations to purchase or sell since he was, he murmured with visible pride and mercantile arrogance, a businessman for every season, deal and money, ready to negotiate whatever cylinder might bear a recording of *Aida*, or printed volumes or manuscripts to do with licentious matters which were worthy at least of commerce and interest.

I then tightly gripped the Bedouin's arm: I wanted him to understand what I was going to say and do and, with time and opportunity, I revealed to Monsieur Grappin that it was our urgent need and requirement to obtain reliable information about a possible first edition of a particular work entitled *Salammbô*, written by a certain Gustave from Rouen, when he was dominated by indecent erotic sentiments in relation to an *almée* of upper Egypt, who answered to the name of Koutchouk-Hanem and now, according to what we had learned from unseemly gossip, exercised an inexpedient and scandalous trade in the region of Sens, under the name of Zoraide Turc.

Monsieur Grappin moved even closer, holding in his hands a notebook, threaded with geometric and ornamental motifs and with bronze clasps, which he had taken moments before, with a precise purpose and intent, from a bureau veneered in burr walnut.

Monsieur Grappin swallowed nervously. He lightly brushed the collar of his white blouse with delicate, caressing touches. He smiled at us, and with a coaxing and mellifluous thread of voice, began to read. A few words to begin with, devoted to praising himself for the acuity and skill of his trade, especially now that he was able to inform us that he was in possession of an *Index Impudicorum Librorum*[169] and that he could obtain from it the relevant information. He then read to us, mumbling words and hiccups, and without lingering shook his head in denial. He then questioned us to get reliable information about that particular book we had in mind.

Harel Bey laughed coarsely, moved his hands about in the air to search out the man's face. He moistened it with the sweat of his hands and squeezed it in a painful, malignant grip. The Bedouin was excited now that he had begun to speak of a woman who had been daughter of Hamilcar and priestess of Tanit, goddess of fertility, love and pleasure and moon-goddess, wife of the sun-god Baal, a woman who responded to the name of Salammbô. This particular woman, very beautiful and seductive – Harel Bey continued – had bewitched and seduced, in a night of love and with the complicity of magic rites, the mercenary Matho, who had stolen the sacred veil of Tanit, tutelary patron of the city. To his own ruin and passion, Matho had then been executed amidst punishments and tortures, and Salammbô had given her own life in the light of that torment of death and fleeting love.

---

169 List of Licentious Books.

All this the Bedouin narrated with one breath, my friend, referring, although indeed in his own manner and with the skilful art of the fabulist, to the story by Gustave. He explained, with suggestive and ambiguous periphrases, the reasons for our trip to Sens and this visit to the bookshop, with its obscene writings and shameless drawings. Our interests were rigorous, unequivocal, aimed at searching for the first draft of a novel entitled Salammbô.

In truth, we also wished to know – added Harel Bey – through blasphemous desire and curiosity, the affairs, sentiments and sensations consummated in that night of love and seduction between Salammbô, the proud priestess, and Matho, the Lybian mercenary warrior. We also wanted to verify if, by chance or pure grace, such acts were or were not the transcription of events that Monsieur Gustave had experienced in person, in warm Egyptian nights in the tender embrace of a fascinating and very beautiful woman called Koutchouk-Hanem, whom Gustave himself, with licentious frankness, had described, in passages and hints, in a certain manuscript of which we were in possession.

Monsieur Grappin abruptly moved beside me, muttered some indistinguishable words, almost a prayer, perhaps the concluding song of a majestic opera *O Earth, farewell – farewell, vale of tears, / dream of joy which vanished into sorrow. / Heaven opens to us, our wandering souls / fly fast towards the light of eternal day.* He then mumbled words more distinctly to make me understand that I should save him from the clutches and words of this lunatic blind man. He said 'lunatic' with resentment and fear. I heard him distinctly, just as did Harel Bey.

The Bedouin began to laugh coarsely, almost to sneer, to move nearer, to seek the face of Monsieur Grappin whirling round his hands.

I uttered some words which might have distracted him. I spoke in a worried tone to give him to understand that they were serious and significant words. Harel Bey, now angry, began to sniff the air, to wander about, to explore books and bindings in marbled calf, in Morocco, in black or Bordeaux leather, in tortoiseshell calf, in decorated boards.

Monsieur Grappin, clutching my arm through fear and other reasons, asked me, with a thread of voice, of which manuscript I was speaking, of which woman, and if it was a question, as he had at first understood, of that Zoraide Turc he could, in all conscience, from his knowledge and through friendly goodwill, offer me appropriate information.

I thus learnt, now that the attention of the Bedouin was also turned to the words the bookseller was uttering: that a certain foreign lady, very beautiful and regal, had once – and not very long ago to tell the truth – obtained from him, from Monsieur Grappin, sanctuary and assistance. She had been offered hospitality in a *une maison de passe*[170] which he managed in rue de la Petite Ville, frequented by dignitaries and gentlemen.

Abruptly then, without giving any warning or useful information or reasons, the lady had recklessly abandoned this hospitable sanctuary, certainly lost in the solitude of melancholy and in an improbable flight, even taking with her a valise with three silk blouses (value 250 francs), six pairs of garters (200 fr.), three dressing-gowns (180 fr.), two flacons of the *Fragrance* perfume (150 fr.), four *savonnettes marées*[171], a very sought-after lotion which gave the body a primitive, acrid smell, of inguinal secretions (value 600 fr.) and finally 250 francs in small change.

Perhaps unexpected information and profane worries had encouraged that Zoraide Turc to take such extreme measures. Or perhaps the desire to flee from a certain scoundrel camouflaged as an investigator, indiscreet in the face of her work and personal matters, who was, it was murmured, an agent of the Khédive of Cairo. Or perhaps she fled enraptured by nostalgia, by an ancient love which she sometimes remembered in her dreams and in her laments, and which led her on the trail of a writer who lived in Croisset or Rouen, certainly in Normandy!

Harel Bey, very attentive to the words and ideas expressed by Monsieur Grappin, suddenly dodged shelves and books and bindings to draw near the man, to capture him with a hand

---

170   Brothel
171   Four bars of fragranced soap.

stretched out into the air, scarcely moving so that his fingertips could obtain a sure and reassuring contact. The Bedouin lingered for a long time, and with a quiet and obscure intention, on the flannel worn by the man – he stroked its folds as far as the collar, the neck so as to have the certainty of being able to offend Monsieur Grappin's breath with his own, to speak to him directly, without intermediaries, if not the air or an ambiguous distance between them.

Then rapid words, barely murmured which had the aim of learning the reasons and value of that soap which had a stimulating pungency and of a sense of smell which had, for that choice of habits and customs, much greater importance than vision of nude or scarcely veiled bodies, those that were flaunted and on bold display in every brothel.

Monsieur Grappin detached himself energetically from Harel Bey. Scarcely a few steps to disorient the Bedouin, while he moved forwards in a zigzag to confound him further. Finally, he leant against a shelf with books marked by gold decoration and began to recount, with set phrases, that that woman, Zoraide Turc, had, to beguile and impassion men, above all the sense of hearing, the sense of vibrations, but never the sense of smell.

Zoraide Turc confided and talked so that the men listened to her and became excited. So that, with ordinary naturalness, she drew forth and practised an infamous and scurrilous jargon, very little suitable even to the dignity of a maison de passe.

Monsieur Grappin, in recalling Zoraide Turc, Koutchouk-Hanem, Gustave's *almée*, and perhaps also a primitive Salammbô, began to recite phrases in a sing-song voice, drawn forth from a vulgar memory, among details lost in the frenzy of speaking and listening, listening and speaking in alcoves arranged for mercenary customs and practices. *Two tongues mingle together with clingy lickings... A bed perfumed by bodies which satiated themselves with all the joys of the flesh... To relish firm and solid flesh, stupendous backsides and a woman who undresses in order to let herself by fucked... Bodies united crushing the bed beneath their fiery impact... The hollow of the pubis gilded with the sweat of a vibrant, tensed, immodest body*[172]. Thus declaimed Monsieur Grappin in a sing-song voice, without embarrassment or the fear of humiliating our spirit or flesh, almost as if he was reading from a book taken from one of the shelves of his extraordinary bookshop.

At these words I grasped the Bedouin, I importuned him with a vice-like iron grip on his arm so that he could understand from my touch what I wanted him to well understand, that Monsieur Grappin was reciting only sentences and sayings drawn from that manuscript of Madame Caroline, if not citations and words taken from a possible first draft of *Salammbô*. In this regard Monsieur Grappin had also taken to providing information appropriate to our request to have good and reliable news about the initial manuscript of *Salammbô*.

So many voices, also gossip to believe or not to believe, murmured Monsieur Grappin. What had been said about the *almée* Koutchouk-Hanem, now Zoraide Turc, was probably credible, i.e. that she had stolen the manuscript, with impunity and recklessness, from Madame Caroline Commanville, to draw from it a tidy sum and substance. Or perhaps Madame Caroline had given it, on the spur of the moment and with reason, to the *almée* to assure her silence concerning the credible and scabrous relations that Koutchouk-Hanem had had with Gustave her uncle. Or perhaps, and even more plausibly, that the manuscript had never existed and that Madame Caroline Commanville had conscientiously decided to divulge such a fanciful lie to add greater value to Gustave's writings and to augment their sales since she enjoyed, as his heir, all the rights and revenues.

In reply, Harel Bey reached my ear, by touching and intuiting with his hands, to suggest to me with malice and sourness that that man Monsieur Grappin, in truth and certainty of facts such as these, must have been very interested in Monsieur Gustave's stories, perhaps because he too was a character in a certain tale, even if only imagined and never written, perhaps of the first draft of *Salammbô*.

---

172   Gustave Flaubert, *Lettres.*

The Bedouin, disturbed and agitated, albeit with the weariness of blindness and bewilderment, dragged me with him into the chaos of excitement. We had reached Monsieur Grappin with difficulty, knocking ourselves against bookcases and piles of books, to intimidate him with our presence, reclaiming suspended rights.

We desired proper explanations, murmured the Bedouin in inflexible tones, which would explain at least the origin and nature of those phrases uttered just now, of why Zoraide Turc disappeared and why there were such difficulties in obtaining correct information about the presumed first draft of *Salammbô*. Thus pronounced Harel Bey in an outburst, and then, through added intuition and with bewitching accents and seductive lies, he asked Monsieur Grappin if he might accompany him to a toilet because he had to satisfy an urgent physiological need.

I have nothing more to tell you, my dear Pécuchet. Nothing more on *Salammbô*, on Zoraide Turc or on Monsieur Grappin. I was never given another opportunity to encounter him, in fact. I don't know whether, through an improper choice or proper necessity or to flee the ill-bred intrigues of the Bedouin, he locked himself in the lavatory or in another private place, or indeed whether he might have fled through some secondary exit, ready and waiting for a convenient escape.

Indeed, after about half an hour had gone by, the Bedouin appeared alone from behind a door hidden by a bookcase. Not a word about Monsieur Grappin, only an invitation, in a few words, to be his escort and protector since it was convenient to leave this place in a suitable time and manner, without raising suspicions through hurried steps or distressed faces.

The Bedouin was tranquil, almost as if he had benefited from appropriate clarifications and discreet confidences. I didn't look into it further, perhaps through laziness, also through fear.

I ask your forgiveness then, my friend, for these last lines which are so meagre and confused. These last events concerned happenings and situations out of the ordinary, certainly far from my eyes and ears. Only intuition has been my aid in understanding and conjecturing. I am convinced therefore that you too might use your intuition and draw from it the right conclusions concerning such obscure and intricate facts.

A bientôt, mon ami. A bientôt, j'éspère[173].

B.

Bureau de Postes et Télégraphes rue Thiers - Mantes la Jolie

27 June

Cher ami,

Voilà L'éducation sentimentale[174], indeed a sentimental education and thus to offer a bunch of flowers to a whore *just as a lover does to his betrothed. But the warmth, the fear of the unknown, a sort of remorse and the pleasure indeed of seeing around one so many women at one's disposition procures such an emotion as to make one turn pale, and remain astonished, without moving, without saying a word. The girls* of the brothel *laugh, entertained by so much embarrassment*[175].

Here then is *Sentimental Education*, even after unexpected perils, inopportune acts and precipitous flights. Here I am, dear Pécuchet, ready to draw up accounts with myself, and today more than ever as, in these hours, I have surprised myself in being extremely fearful of Harel Bey, this eccentric who is my companion in adventures and investigations. It's true, my friend, I have had fears, even well-founded ones.

The hasty departure from Sens stirred in me vexation and regret at having passively escorted the Bedouin, at having accompanied him, offering him my arm as a substantial support, far from the shop of that Monsieur Grappin. At having then gone on, in his company, having wandered through treacherous alleyways and streets furiously besieged by rash, even dark, presences, so that it was very necessary to rapidly reach a station.

Then, in the turmoil of uneasy anxieties, I let myself be flung about by trains covering only short distances which have brought me here, in the den of a new adventure, in the re-reading and consideration of a small novel which recalls indeed a sentimental

---

173 I hope to see you soon, my friend.

174 *Sentimental Education* is the novel that Gustave Flaubert wrote between 1863 and 1869, following a first draft carried out between 1843 and 1845, to recount the moral and sentimental history of the men of his generation.

175 Gustave Flaubert, *Sentimental Education*.

education, as well as the words of Koheleth, son of David, king of Jerusalem, when he loved to talk about vanity. Vanity of vanities, said Koheleth, *vanity of vanities, all is vanity. What profit hath a man of all his labour which he taketh under the sun? One generation passeth away, and another generation cometh: but the earth abideth for ever*[176].

Also a very tiring journey in truth, as having arrived in Paris by train we crossed it fleeing northward on a patched-up, dusty road paved with cobblestones in rented carriages (rickety carts often driven by coachmen stupefied by absinthe and by alcoholic melancholy) only to free ourselves of gloomy way-stations, and avoid the peripheral hubs on the outskirts when it was necessary to stay put for some time before being able to take advantage of an opportune and suitable connection.

Thus we crossed Colombes with its Merovingian cemetery beneath the old church. Then Bezons huddled around its 17th century castle. And so also Maison-Laffitte on the left bank of the Seine near the forest of St. Germain. And then Poissy with the beautiful church of Notre-Dame, which boasts about having given birth to Louis IX, called Saint Louis. And then Epône with the church of Saint-Béat with its octagonal clock tower. A succession of towns which showed off reliable beauties, while unreliable events seemed to accompany us after the regrettable and distasteful episode at Sens. Thus we took the trouble to change carriages or carts frequently, if only to defend ourselves from the exhaustion of senile nags and the fiery driving of drunk coachmen. And there was as well a succession of devious warnings since unwholesome and dubious card-players and conjurors persecuted me from Bezons to Epône, inviting me to put myself into competition with some sleight-of-hand game. An infamous attempt aimed at robbing me of money and savings – although my blind companion urged me to accept the challenge, claiming that his help would have been opportune and profitable. I abstained, with good reason, from the incitements of my companion, certain that he would have enjoyed the inevitable defeat that I would

---

176 Ecclesiastes 1:2-4.

have suffered in putting myself into competition with one of those skilful conjurors.

All in all, disagreeable and inopportune bad spirits afflicted me, displeased and disturbed me, even within the welcoming pleasure of summer, in its luminous evenings full of a golden fragrance and of a dazzling light which I had the occasion to admire, astonished, as I travelled along streets paved with treacherous gravel.

The Bedouin, for his part, was never governed by good sense, and he reasoned with an ostentatious flow of words about facts and events that were totally extraneous as far as I was concerned, about long-past occasions and events which had nothing to do with me but on which he had an unbridled intention to proffer judgments and emit sentences. Above all concerning the Goncourt brothers and a literary salon in which gossip and irritating chatter were twittered. *The style of Julie Barbey d'Aurevilly makes one think of those children who make themselves moustaches of burnt cork... Louis Bouilhet is a poet who stinks of garlic like an omnibus... We sink further and further into the Late Roman Empire. We're falling. From the kingdom of the dressmaker to the kingdom of the great chefs... The feminine character of Sainte-Beuve has this above all: when he feels he is in the wrong, he gets angry... Compared with the spirituality of a pipe, love is a vulgar form of materiality... Victor Hugo is a force, a very great force, lashing, over-excited, the force of a man who is always walking in the wind... Dumas fils turns to prayers for redeemed whores with his Madeleines repenties... Octave Feuillet resembles his own talent: physically he sums up the distinct in the banal... The sculptor Auguste Clésinger to Madame George Sand: I will make a sculpture of your ass so that everyone will recognize it"... Théophile Gautier regrets the house that he has decorated: the artistic angulus ridens of his old age... Madame George Sand wears a pink dress, put on, it is supposed, with the intention of violating Gustave Flaubert... The madness of Charles Baudelaire serves to make his works over-valued after his death just as the guillotine raises the value of the writing of guillotined persons in the catalogues of autographs... A man and a woman must have very little modesty to fuck without being drunk... In reading the prospectus of the works which Balzac intended to write he merited 10 years more of life, just as Hugo merited 10 years less... Alfred de Musset has died, one of the least authentic originalities, the talent most influenced by Shakespeare, Byron and Joachim du Bellay, of whom he did not disdain to plagiarize an entire work in verse... Flaubert puts a ridiculous solemnity into his production. In truth one doesn't know which is greater, his vanity or his pride[177]!*

At an imperious sign from me, Harel Bey put an end to this massacre of grotesque recollections and malevolent gossip. He began to trot out witchcraft and habitual aphorisms as a distraction. Then he began to speak to me about what had happened at Sens: about the disappearance of that character Monsieur Grappin and about his bewildered excitement in relation to a flight which had been put into motion and desired only to take up again the hunt for the unseemly performances of Gustave, since it was very opportune to begin once again to play at being investigators now that we had taken on obligations and duties.

I had fears in the midst of certainties and certainties in the midst of fears, so that I put a stop to the Arab's reflections without leaving him any respite and solitary comforts in which to indulge himself and with which to construct illicit stratagems. I begged him then, and with extravagant excuses, to be my mentor, allied in confidences and in friendship, as I was prisoner of a banal fear as we drew near the time in which I would have to draw up, with a serene spirit, a summation for Madame Caroline.

I asked him abruptly, indeed at Poissy, when we were little more than 20 km from Mantes, to enable me to keep a secure watch on him and have him within my view also at night, to be a faithful friend to me and to divide with me *le lit à deux places a l'auberge des Deux Tourelles de Madame Dubut, 4 fr. avec petit dejeuner*[178]. Then within the silence and shadow of night while Harel Bey was overcome with the sleep of the unjust – so at least I believed with a dash of ill-will – I was ruined by his indiscreet snoring while I turned over in my mind the facts and feelings which were afflicting me, and also the anxieties and perplexities,

---

177   Frères de Goncourt, *Journal.*
178   The double bed at the "Due Torrette", hotel de Madame Dubut, 4 fr. Including breakfast.

precisely on the perverse actions of the Bedouin, on the stories that he told, on his way of proceeding through rage and bold decisions: often taken, it was evident, to reconcile himself with his being the spurious son of that writer of Rouen, Gustave Flaubert – let us be clear.

In such anxieties and preoccupied reasoning, I reflected on the suspicions and disturbances that the outline of Harel Bey instilled in me, also on a profile which knew how to conceal disturbing shadows even though it was marked now by bantering smiles, now by verbose ramblings, or even by the accelerated and obsessive drumming of a blind man's stick, which knew how to distract attention from considerations and prudence, even without motive or artful appearances.

From these huddled thoughts I was often diverted and infected by a stench that accompanied the Bedouin's body. I didn't know how to immediately distinguish reasons and meanings, nor stenches and negligences that were mixed together and from which was generated a repellent and evil essence. I noticed only the ambiguous symptoms and unpleasant incapabilities, and thus I let myself wallow, without any certain opinion or alternative option, in an unaccustomed and pungent cloying odour: almost like pittosporum flowers, burnt by the ardour of a summer sun.

Slowly then, unconsciously, I faded, and without realizing it, into an ambiguous drowsiness, a half-sleep, a tedious weariness. A few hours earlier I had sipped a tisane of Egyptian herbs, a malignant gift from the Bedouin which perhaps contained narcotic mixtures. Thus I lost my tenacity and lucidity as a guardian, so that I am no longer a reliable witness concerning Harel Bey's conduct, at least for that night.

I awoke at dawn of the following day – of this I'm certain – overwhelmed by the painful and tenacious stench of the Bedouin. I had however the sense and the whim to inflict my nose with fragrances hidden in a handkerchief throughout the entire journey that brought us to Mantes. Here, in the nerveless languor of a respite in the journey and in tidying-up from the sweat of the train-trip, the Bedouin promptly informed me that he was aware of having an indelible stench, gathered on the roads, perhaps at Sens, perhaps on the train or in carriages, perhaps emitted because of tension and fatigue, perhaps from corrosive difficulties on the journey, and which responded to an empyreumatic graduation, almost the principal odour of burnt sugar, but also of spilled blood, congealed after some crime committed without care or precautions.

For some moments I thought of Monsieur Grappin, of his disappearance beyond a wall of shelves of obscene books, but also of a night at Poissy of which I could not give any account or testimony but of which I had the sense that something had occurred while I was enjoying a half-sleep which wearied my mind.

I hadn't dared speak to Harel Bey about my turmoils, nor did I put forward further or more explicit details concerning his conduct. I only sniffed instinctively at his body. Instinctively and irreverently I had the temptation to take his jacket off, to search among the folds of his flesh, among the crushed and wrinkled creases of his caftan, in recesses and accesses that I would never have thought of wanting to violate.

To justify and attenuate my nervous gestures, I sought a tolerable reason since I seemed to see, and this I mentioned to him in an alarmed voice, a treacherous insect disappearing among his skin, his garments and his costume, almost as if it wanted to scrape his skin.

The Bedouin then allowed me to search him with my hands without respite or decency. He revealed a resigned complacency and courteous respect when, palpating him, I removed his sweat with the hem of his clothing to avoid the instinctive revulsion one feels in grazing a skin illegitimately moist with secretions and the moisture of *perspiratio sensibilis*.

In ransacking the recesses and hiding-places of flesh and fabrics, I suddenly and unexpectedly touched the sack of his secrets. I palpated it along the surfaces and folds. I began feeling with my fingers the unmistakable profile of his notebook. I asked Harel Bey's forgiveness for this audacious effrontery and, appealing to his indiscretion, I asked him if he would grant me the opportunity of examining this notebook to spare him the disagreeable discomfort of stings or bites of harmful insects which could easily hide there.

In rummaging through notes and intact pages, amidst lines impressed in relief or inset, amidst string bindings and decorated covers, I found between pages 52 and 53 a stain with an intense, disgusting odour which became more acute as I fanned out the pages. It was a bloody fingerprint, as I saw in inspecting it closely, the smell of which, as I sensed it carefully, was of a sugary and burning aroma.

In addition, as I gazed at it with investigative ardour, it appeared to be of a deliberate form, as precise as if it was meant to design a word, even if only in the points and orthography of the blind. I gathered together the Bedouin's fingers in my fist and guided them onto these signs, this message drawn up so that only he, or another blind person, could give a true interpretation of them and be their prophet. Harel Bey knew these marks, there was no doubt of it, since he reacted abruptly, withdrawing his hand almost as if the contact disturbed him, wounded him in his recollections, made him guilty of some accomplished fraud.

He murmured a word of explanation and said: 'Ouali', rapidly adding, in interpretation and for my benefit, reciting obsequies to the victims of prostitution and without pronouncing names or conditions or any other particulars, that this word signified protector to whom one paid tributes in order to carry out the trade of prostitution.

Harel Bay then clutched the notebook to himself to hide from my sight and sense of smell this offensive object, this emblem of guilt and crime now that it seemed certain that a homicide had been committed. He then began to murmur, with malevolence and embarrassment, that his body had acquired, perhaps in touching that obscure and troubling stain, an unbearable stench of serum and blood. Since he now had the duty of cleaning himself as best he could to honour, without provoking ill-will and protests, appointments and investigations that we had to fulfil at Mantes, at the Hôtel du Grand-Cerf above all, where Gustave the writer and Louise the poetess had bound their destinies and their bodies together according to the manual of good taste in use and in fashion among intellectuals. *"Farewell, my poor beloved, a thousand sweet kisses. What joy it would be to remain alone, alone in a room well closed, with the curtains drawn, with the door chained, with a fine fire burning in the fireplace. To be in bed, one next to the other, one closely joined to the other. To embrace, to feel each other. Thighs linked inseparably together. Arms embracing waists, mouth linked to mouth, chest against chest"*, as Gustave had written to Louise on 13 October 1846.

Fatal truths: mentioned also in the manuscript of Madame Caroline, in the exhaustive and affected correspondence exchanged between two lovers who were protagonists in a story of sordid intellectual origins. But an accurate investigation, here in this hotel, was for us an obligation and necessity, and in any case nothing else remained for us apart from the appropriateness of carrying out our obligations in satisfying this task.

Harel Bey abandoned me suddenly, leaving me in the solitude of a squalid buffet and, without help or support, began to beat the ground with his stick, seeking passages and trying to avoid obstacles. With his notebook tightly pressed under his left arm, he stopped many times without the suggestion of uncertainty or imbalance – I saw him, with a sideways glance, near my table. He chatted with the air or with guests whom he captivated instinctively with the melancholy tone of his voice. He then showed his stick and begged – I'm certain of it – for pity and charity for his disability and for that stench that rendered him disagreeable.

At the end of pilgrimages and prayers so that he might be acquitted and listened to through charity, perhaps through compassion or indeed through morbid curiosity, a middle-aged man, white-haired and hunchbacked, took him aside, though holding his nose, and offered himself as a trustworthy guide beyond the entrance to the station.

I saw the Bedouin turn aside to the right and I began to wait for him in silence, nibbling at a plate of *rillettes*[179] and sipping

---

179   Minced pork cooked in fat.

cidre doux[180]. I was not afraid of intrigues or scheming on his part as I had caught him distressed and wounded by that stench that sullied his body, that didn't grant him a sense of ease or comfort in confronting gracefully the last adventures which we had to experience.

I waited for periods that elapsed slowly amidst drinking-glasses, which were a sign of my unease, the agony of my tolerance.

When an hour had elapsed, when, troubled, I turned my head in every direction, I saw him appear in the midst of the railway-tracks, beating his stick with arrogance and firmness, asking directions in a lamenting and insistent sing-song. From a distance he shouted my name and from a distance he sought a reply so that he could rejoin me. He moved with self-assurance and ease to such a point that I nurtured the suspicion, if only for moments, that he had reacquired his sight and that he was feigning, in jest, his blindness.

He was happy, very well-dressed and rid of any stench, at least to judge by appearance and at a distance. Also severe in his manners and thoughts. When we met, while our hands sought for and pressed each other, he asked me spontaneously about my impatience in waiting, making fun even of my slothfulness, the time spent in nibbling and tippling in peace, beset with worries and uneasiness.

He paid no attention to my answers and justifications, because he had begun to talk about himself, of this bath which he had frequented, of disgusting odours, of casual encounters. Of one in particular, a little beyond the threshold *du bain chaud* (*50 cent. plus 20 cent. pour la ligne*)[181]when he had groped his way towards the Turkish baths (*4 fr. tout compris*)[182]. He was at this point in the changing-room and, carelessly, had piled up his clothes and notebook in a corner of the bench crammed with other clothes so that, in setting to rights this carelessness, he had exchanged excuses and a bit of casual conversation, to then get carried away

---

180 Sweet cider.
181 Of the hot baths (50 cent. plus 20 cent. for the wood).
182 4 fr. all included.

in a flood of chatter, anxious to alleviate the solitude and boredom of *une salle de la transpiration*[183]. He had thus discovered that *son camerade en loquacite*[184]was interested, like himself, in the Hôtel du Grand-Cerf of this little city for his own reasons. In fact, the man, who was *chauffeur de corbillard et assistant d'un croquemort*[185], had the duty, at appropriate times and according to necessity, to collect a corpse and transport it to another place and department.

Monsieur le chauffeur had then begun to narrate to Harel Bey a story of indecent states of mind for what he had come to know and to evaluate, since he maintained, with stubborn logic, that truth and lies were simply aspects extremely difficult to distinguish in the nobility of words, thoughts and acts.

It was certain, the chauffeur put forward with a trace of squalid perplexity, that in that hotel there was to be found a corpse which was the result of a homicide. And that that corpse was at the centre of an intricate story of love and of death which involved characters of certain novels, a mysterious individual who had appeared and disappeared in the space of one night: perhaps indeed in the night of the presumed murder, and the writer was one who had usurped rights which had been conceded to other characters created by him and then recklessly forgotten.

Harel Bey had then allowed himself to be seized by the words of this man for his own ends and suggestions. He had seconded him in thoughts and affectations of approval in order to obtain a permit for words and questions for le Croquemort, who in the Hôtel du Grand-Cerf was, at the time and for coherent timeliness, the despot and the archon.

To corrupt him in his sentiments and affections, Harel Bey had given to Monsieur le chauffeur, this he referred to me amid leers and winks, his notebook so that it might be of comfort to his brother who was blind from birth and without financial means, as well as knowledge of the language of Braille.

Was this gift really the truth or only an equivocal deception

---

183 A steam-room.
184 His companion in loquacity.
185 Driver of the funeral carriage and assistant to the undertaker.

in respect to me?

It is true, I said to myself, that the unexpected disappearance of this notebook invalidated any proofs of possible crimes. For moments, my friend, I was the defenceless prisoner of surprise and indignation due to my conscious ignorance of the true facts. I thus lent myself to the equivocal game of the Bedouin now that we had to follow, together and solely, two other itineraries.

Suddenly, reasoning with disappointment and reticence, Harel Bey clutched my arm and, with vigorous gestures, exhorted me to follow him so that we could resume our travels and investigations. He was anxious to proceed hastily to bring to an end this chapter on *L'éducation sentimentale*. He spoke to me rudely and hastily while he scanned our way ahead with the touch of his stick, now that we were walking among horse-drawn carriages and the questioning looks of curious bystanders towards the fountain of Nicolas Delabrosse and the Tour Saint-Maclou.

He stopped at a crossroads near rue National. He searched my face with his hands. He caressed it with his fingertips and drew me nearer, almost suffocating me, soiling my breathing with his bad breath.

Then he began to speak of blood and crime, to indicate directions and streets to follow, to affirm that we were very close to drawing conclusions, about *l'Éducation* he meant. So that, turning my head to the right, I saw the square and the hotel we were seeking.

I led the Bedouin cautiously by the hand, beyond the widening of the street, into a shadowy corner. I spoke to him resignedly to describe to him places and sensations. Now a sordid and squalid façade. Now crumbling walls and a sign which trembled in the gusts of wind and which showed Grand-Cerf. Now silence and solitude. Now an unforeseen anguish which brought back phrases lost somewhere, perhaps in letters left to careless heirs. Certainly from Gustave the writer and from Louise the poetess. Above all from the woman who knew how to tell stories about the amorous encounters at Mantes, at the Hôtel du Grand-Cerf, when she lay down *on the bed, hair spread out on the pillow, eyes turned to the sky, pallid, with her hands joined together, she dared to pronounce words of madness ... and in my arms* she was *of a warm sweetness which was at once melting and inebriating*[186].

With cautious steps we crossed a deserted hall. The Bedouin brought me closer to himself, pressing my arm, putting to me impertinent queries, asking me if there were traces of coagulated blood anywhere, or traces of a crime which had been committed, or signs of a troubled and violent death. Harel Bey seemed to draw continually closer, with apprehension and torments, so that his stick, wandering and rebellious, kept getting in my way, forcing me to keep a watch on it to avoid it striking me.

I was caught up in bizarre attentions, what with spoken remarks and customary answers, so that, without realizing it and involuntarily, we suddenly arrived *in a great salon with high windows and a monumental fireplace, surmounted by a pendulum clock in the form of a sphere and two horrible porcelain vases which held, like golden bushes, two clusters of candle-holders. On the walls there were a few paintings in the manner of Lo Spagnoletto. Heavy tapestries swept down majestically. Then there were armchairs, and shelves, and tables all in Empire style, and all of an imposing appearance*[187].

A man, who seemed to be waiting for us, was seated in an armchair close to the fireplace. He rubbed his hands and smiled with subtle malice. He was small, bald, dressed in black clothes shiny from wear and hard use. He attracted my attention with a wave of his hand. He stood and came up to us, offering himself to our curiosity.

Harel Bey began, from instinct, to sniff the air, to seek with his arm outstretched the man who was in front of him. Then he began to ramble on, talking about death, about a sweetish fragrance which polluted the air and which evoked the odour of blood. He began to ask about the cadaver, the inquest, the points of the case. Finally, he spoke about the friendship which linked him to a certain man whom he had got to know in a Turkish bath

186 Gustave Flaubert, *Letters.*
187 Gustave Flaubert, *Sentimental Education.*

and who had said that he was a *chauffeur de corbillard*[188], although he had detailed and private information of things to do with Monsieur Frédéric Moreau, the protagonist of an *éducation*, for whom we had come to Mantes.

At the mean insinuations of the Bedouin the man walked away, instinctively and hastily, from our gabble. It was obvious that he wanted to escape the gestures and words of Harel Bey. He hid himself away near the fireplace and, protected by distance, began to fuss about, disturbing the air with ill-bred gestures to get my attention; he murmured distinctly that I should pay attention to him, drawing myself away from the company and intentions I shared with Harel Bey.

I then spoke to the Bedouin and persuaded him as to the necessity of my listening to this man in private. Indeed, it was in our interest to know the facts and elements that this individual might be able to convey to us with his words and gestures. We would gain merit and clarity on that intricate event of the crime which was so intimately relevant to a sentimental education and to Monsieur Frédéric Moreau, protagonist of one of Gustave's stories. And we would then be able to close the doors on uncertainties, the abuses and nit-pickings that were now so annoying in our investigations.

I reassured the Bedouin about my acts and propositions. I left him stock-still, supported by his stick and intent on scrutinizing, with feigned interest, the murmurs and smells of the room.

I rejoined the man and I seduced him with smiles and attention so that he, in the secrecy of a conversation carried out in privacy and apart, would offer me the honour of his full confidence. He presented himself to me as *le Croquemort* of Nogent-sur-Seine, and he told me that he was from Mantes and was present in this hotel to reclaim, now that he was dead by an assassin's hand – at least that is what he supposed with unequivocal conviction – the body of Frédéric Moreau, native of Nogent and protagonist of *L'Éducation sentimentale* by a certain Gustave Flaubert, writer of Rouen.

---

188   Driver of the funeral carriage.

He began to improvise stories on the outrages and violence of that act, on the disgrace of a hand or of several hands which had, with a notebook heavy with leaves, crushed the skull of Monsieur Moreau, without conscience or remorse. He made gratuitous accusations, insolent insinuations, grave reproaches, so that it seemed to me that he was an agent of some office dedicated to the investigation of novels and stories, a dealer in ambiguous tales, in short a spy adept at seizing and passing judgment on men and things because of urgent and very personal concerns, almost as if he was, on principal, opposed to passive heroes irremediably lost amidst hopes and memories.

And still, to think about it more deeply and still more appropriately, it appeared to me that he wasn't whatever he declared himself to be and that, with exceptional effort, he wished me to believe that he was. He threw out accusations and charges almost to conceal something else, he continually glanced sideways at the Bedouin to ask for support even though he pointed at him with scorn and inveighed against him, calling him the fake hero of a fake novel. And, besides, with a shifty and ambiguous way of speaking and facial expression which insinuated monitions and understandings of agreements stipulated to discountenance the truth.

Instinctively he moved still nearer to me, constraining me to watch his face, which was agitated, apoplectic, tumid and swollen. He breathed with difficulty in the congestion that was consuming him, which filled him with unwholesome and laborious breaths. To arrive at a position of safety and slip away from broken breathing, he stretched out a hand to look for something to lean on, a concrete and trustworthy support for his unexpected fit of faintness. I denied him my side and my arm, leaving him at the mercy of his moodiness.

He then pulled up his nose several times and breathed with short, noisy gulps, after which he regained, for a brief period, a moderate pinkness, succeeded by an ashy pallor streaked by tears of sweat.

Abruptly he raised the tone of his voice in an uncontrolled crescendo, almost a howl without control or purpose. He began to speak of events marked by time, by perversions, by homicides, by inescapable necessities. He posed urgent questions and asked me if I could ever, without hesitation or recrimination, accuse Harel Bey the Bedouin of having escaped my jurisdiction, silently and in ill faith, and, in the darkness of a night that was kind to the blind, of having committed a possible homicide at Mantes, of having encountered Monsieur Frédéric Moreau, of having quarrelled bitterly with him because of his boorish behaviour, for having made fun of other characters created by Gustave. Indeed, Monsieur Moreau had offended, with iniquitous and bogus love-making, Madame Arnoux, Madame Rosanette, Madame Dambreuse and Madame Roque who were to be real protagonists of a story, of fictionalized destinies and of whatever else could and should be relevant to the true essence of whatever Gustave had in mind to narrate about a sentimental education.

Le Croquemort continued to tell tales for an indefinite time, to involve himself in a confusion of remarks and comments that only he could understand, to mutter away about intrigues concocted in a very clumsy manner, and by a mind intent on considering a certain manuscript which, in truth, was capable of concealing unreliable truths and reliable lies in order to discredit above all characters who, created in a flash of an idea or of a jest, found no trace of their existence even in the very life of he who had put them into the world, even of that scribbler of Rouen.

Shouting loudly, le Croquemort drew near me to gaze into my eyes and state, with accusatory emphases, that the Bedouin would have been able to accredit his proposition because he knew the motive of that crime and had been the owner of the weapon with which it had been committed. Le Croquemort was now completely absorbed by the passion and delirium of an investigating official who, exasperated by an unconfessed indignation and by the intractability and contentiousness of the onlookers, began to throw out silly remarks, to dismay and alarm with coarse gestures and oblique intimations.

The Bedouin, who was commanding the centre of the room, smiled at the man's protests, soothed him with appropriate courtesies, dismayed him unexpectedly referring to a notebook which he had offered as a gift to a certain driver and to an education lost in a crime.

Harel Bey then calmed down and began to sniff the air with brief, continuous, tight breaths. Finally, he began to use the stick to guide himself and sought to reach me begging for a word with me.

He asked me, though from a distance and with heavy breathing, if by any chance I had it in mind to suggest to Le Croquemort that he throw off his mask and admit to the fact that he was one of the protagonists of *Serment des amis*[189]: a work that never saw the light of day and remained unpublished, but which had left traces in the events and themes in *L'Éducation*.

For these reasons, perhaps Le Croquemort had had good reasons and pretexts for carrying out the deception and assassination, if only to obtain that position of actor that Frédéric Moreau, perhaps and with impunity, had taken away from him and thus had to repay an acquired debt.

Le Croquemort replied brusquely, with anxiety and irreverence so accentuated and false that I perceived, in the words and verses of that din, a studied performance, since I was a spectator and witness to a well-constructed swindle and fraudulence. I understood then that the events, the meetings, the occasions of quarrels and outrageous behaviour were acts and remarks which had been carefully devised.

It seemed to me at that point that, in cahoots, in a treacherous partnership, those two, Harel Bey and Le Croquemort, had deliberately killed Frédéric Moreau to share an eventual succession since it would have been Madame Caroline who would have pronounced on and defined deliberations, approved publications, indicated accounts, stories and protagonists of them to be offered for publication and reading.

Instinctively I left them to their intrigues and homicidal bragging, without offering explanations or evidence of my ill will. I informed the Bedouin that I would wait for him *au bureau*

---

189 Title of a work planned by Flaubert

de Poste et Télégraphes[190] to proceed with our journey towards Yonville-l'Abbaye, since we had an account to settle with Madame Caroline.

I am now waiting for Harel Bey to arrive, since dusk has already fallen some time ago.

We are very near the last act but, *mon cher ami* Pécuchet, I am unable to greet you joyfully after such events of extreme discomfiture and cruel intrigue.

L'Éducation sentimentale, besides being – at least in Gustave's intentions – the story of a love-romance between an eighteen-year old and a beautiful married woman, is even more – in my opinion – an unwholesome exercise in recklessly and obscenely committing a crime, with the satisfaction of Monsieur Gustave the writer, but certainly with the gratitude of a niece.

Au revoir then, and *a bientôt.*

B.

Lion d'Or

Yonville-l'Abbaye

29 June

Cher ami,

Voilà Madame Bovary. Me voilà ici[191] drawing up conclusions, settling the accounts of an itinerary marked by the works and words of Gustave's writings, of his novels, of his stories, offered up to the reading of relations and friends. Here is Madame Bovary, heir of desires and reflections, permeated by fatality, and even, according to people gossiping without at all considering discretion and moderation, daughter of a lack of shrewdness, of absent-minded fastidiousness, of negligent obstinacy, since Gustave clumsily wasted his time in unbearable re-readings and maniacal clarifications, and he consigned to some editors – first to the *Revue de Paris* with some alterations, then to *Michel Lévy*, and finally to *Charpentier e Cie* – a work that was incorrect in one part. Two genitives, in fact, placed in succession, escaped the

---

190 At the Post and Telegraph Office.

191 Dear friend, here is Madame Bovary. Here I am. Gustave Flaubert wrote *Madame Bovary* between 1851 and 1854 with the meaningful subtitle: *A Tale of Provincial Life*.

scrupulous attention of our writer, procuring for him unseemly annoyances and honest desperation. Two genitives in fact! Indeed, two genitives, my dear Pécuchet, since the phrase *"une bouquet de fleurs d'orange"* is not at all worthy of the linguistic and lexical perfection of Monsieur Gustave Flaubert. Nevertheless, here is *Madame Bovary* recognized as *a masterpiece for all those who have been confessors in the provinces*[192].

But let us return to our abrasive itinerary marked by Gustave's writings and cadenced by findings and verifications at times very little comprehensible and substantial.

A journey conducted among timely, eccentric and irresolute findings, small and great homicides. A difficult journey, since the pilgrimage became, soon and often, an essential foundation for burdensome surveillances. And still more so if one thinks of the remarks and intentions put forward by our Bedouin, a blind Arab who was my companion in adventure and who went along keeping me under careful surveillance, like a good hunting-dog, among pages written and motions elaborated by Gustave, so as to invalidate propositions and pronouncements which didn't please him and to try to rewrite, with suitable locutions adapted to his own habits and his own ambiguous interests, considerations and meanings defined exclusively by his own egotistical and vulgar proficiency.

In truth, Harel Bey was a dangerous and inauspicious companion, who caused misfortunes, acquired discredit, and offered inopportune fits of melancholy, playing on his own disabilities without conceding credit to anyone else, even to his own companion in adventure. Finally he got himself mixed up, with pernicious desire, in unseemly and brutal crimes.

As soon as we arrived at Yonville, well knowing that we were at the end of the route we had planned, we were under the necessity and compulsion to reach plausible and binding conclusions, particularly after having encountered Madame Bovary and her retinue. After having obtained from Madame explanations of

---

192 Frères de Goncourt, *Journal.*

why, for example, she had found in adultery all the banality of marriage, why she became irritated by a poorly served dish, by a half-open door, and lamented over the velvet she didn't possess, the happiness she lacked, her too exalted dreams, her too narrow home, why did she confound the sensual pleasures of luxury with the joys of the heart, why was she as incapable of understanding whatever she did not experience as of believing in anything which did not present itself in conventional forms.

Having just arrived at Yonville, Harel Bey disappeared, eluding my surveillance, my painful care and attention. He abandoned me when, all of a sudden, he had the opportunity to see this bastard land, whose language is devoid of accent just as the countryside is lacking in character. Here, where they make the worst Neufchâtel cheeses of the entire district, where, besides, farming is extremely costly because so much manure is needed for this friable soil rich in sand and stones.

Harel Bey vanished when we had almost reached Yonville-l'Abbaye (called thusly because of an ancient Capuchin abbey of which not even the ruins remain), *which is, my friend, a desolate and squalid town eight leagues from Rouen, between the road to Abbeville and that for Beauvais... One can make it out in the distance, having passed beyond the oaks of the forest of Argueil, spread out along the St. Jean hills... between Normandy, Picardy and the Île-de-France*[193], lost in antique memories. It is very difficult, therefore, to find it in up-to-date maps, or in some *Baedeker* for professional travellers, or in appendices to manuals for scholars.

Often, in the pauses of spitefulness and scowling glances, when I still engaged in oppressive supervision of the Bedouin, I had suggested to my companion the hypothesis, crack-brained in any case, that this village, which we were about to visit because it was the dwelling-place of the Bovarys, was only a part of Gustave's fervid imagination.

Unexpectedly Harel Bey began to lay down his own rules and to alter, as he saw fit, the itineraries we had already agreed upon,

---

193 Gustave Flaubert, Madame Bovary.

so as to confront in the best possible way this last stretch of our travels, our final exploration. So that, when Yonville welcomed us at its gates, just beside the curve of the Rieule, a small river that empties into the Andelle just beyond the three mills, the Bedouin informed me that he wanted to explore a route different from mine.

He began to put forward excuses, now with weary and muddled words, now with clumsy and mysterious arguments, now with a hoarse and piercing voice. He arrogated to himself the opportunity to submit to the guidance of his own nose, and also of his other senses, as a just compensation for having had to put up with remaining continuously beside me and letting himself be led like a miserable half-wit. To make me participate in his pains, he began, abruptly and in a sinister manner, to fling himself about in a reckless frenzy, to bend over backwards with wild and reckless abuse, to agitate his belly in the rhythms and abandon of a Bedouin dance, so that his caftan seemed like a multi-coloured sheet inhabited by elves who whirled and stirred themselves up, down and around to the tune of bizarre impulses, a hair's breadth from convulsions.

Stealthily then, in my ear, for enterprising confidences, Harel Bey confessed to me that a prolonged olfactory abstinence from the feminine sex subdued him to capricious insolence, to vexatious boredom, to unworthy annoyances. He was tempted to the point of using violence on women of all ages and kinds (he meant Madame Lefrançois, or Félicité the servant, or Madame Homais, or the aged Catherine-Nicaise-Élisabeth Leroux) whom he would have been able to meet in this squalid place, and this to calm an impulse that enfeebled his intellectual abilities, confined him to downheartedness, languid to the point of embracing evil impulses and unwholesome thoughts, induced him to free himself, and as soon as possible, from uncontrollable and impulsive cravings.

Hence the Arab was vexed and agitated, since he had to placate the annoyance and frenzy with enormous effort and with unnatural actions now that – he murmured to me in a peremptory tone – although amidst palpitations and perturbations, he aimed at a peculiar compensation, an erotic amusement, by smell certainly to the point of defying death, rather deaths – murders to be exact.

Harel Bey intended, more than ever, through masculine vanity and his own needs – he said – to visit some Madames and their girls *with a tanned face – a charlatan's complexion – a red waistcoat, with white braiding, a great number of silver buttons, a beret with coloured plumes, black gloves, silver bracelets and earrings*[194]. And the Bedouin spoke with authoritative and formal accents, well knowing that he couldn't deceive me with his humbug and chattering, however probable it sounded. Rapid and persuasive, he then slipped away with a simple wave of his hand, while with the other he agitated his blind man's stick as if it were a brazen bulldozer which, striking and re-striking the pavement with raps and blows, was enough to intimidate any passerby.

He promptly disappeared, sniffing the air with frenetic self-assurance, following a trail of humoral traces, of domestic intimacies, of warm bodies, of female groins, of fragrances of sex – all this he shouted at me from a distance, lying.

He hoped that I would understand only what he wanted me to understand, and nothing else. In reality I presumed, and with knowledge on my side, that he was lying shamelessly. He had, in fact, as his chief and binding reason and interest the desire to encounter Madame Bovary on his own. To argue with her, now that this so and so of a woman had let it be known, through the interpretations of the shrewdest critics in literary games and in various matters to do with the writer of Rouen, that she was now tired and fed up with having to interpret, and in perpetuity, roles, destinies and adventures attested by a story of Monsieur Gustave, and that she would have liked, in reality, to redeem herself from this infamous piece of writing and participate fully in a reality which was her own, unique and unrepeatable, since Gustave had given her life, even if only as the protagonist of a novel which at times seemed anachronistic, since she had to die not indeed for love but because of improvidence.

---

194   Frères de Goncourt, *Journal.*

An impalpable fear then overwhelmed my spirit, my dear Pécuchet, unnerved my body, weakened my muscles, as, unexpectedly, I felt a tyrannical panic to the point that I was no longer able to give meaning to the line of reasoning I was sketching out. I understood then, just in these circumstances, the contorted will and the austere tenacity of Harel Bey. The Arab longed to tie me up in impediments and wrangles. He aimed fundamentally at being able to act undisturbed for his own ends and with his own will, to abandon me in embarrassing predicaments – just at the moment in which our travels had reached an end and we should have been able to draw our conclusions.

I began then to look over my shoulder, to evaluate roads taken and ambiguous desires. I saw innumerable corpses, true and imagined, which encumbered the route we had followed. I understood the reasons and spirit of the appearance of Harel Bey as bearer of a presumed letter from Madame Caroline, of his impudently moving in with us at Chavignolles, of his desire to become a diligent companion in travels, explorations and investigations.

I understood then that our Bedouin had organized retaliations and retributions against us. Exactly that, my friend: retaliations and retributions against us, who are Gustave's legitimate sons and who to Gustave owe our existence as real personages well beyond a mere thought, since the pages written with desire and determination assigned a role to us, and a function beyond the will and the ideas of a writer.

After such cruel reflections on the Bedouin, on myself, on the two of us and on Gustave, inventor of stories and characters, I had the feeling that frenzy and fear were now abandoning me, to give place to a mania for salvation, to a fundamental will to survive, to follow one's own necessities and opportunities.

For moments, therefore, I was possessed by the impulse to rent a carriage, a calèche, without regard to expenses, to coachmen, to kilometres, to discomforts, to itineraries, in order to return to Chavignolles and to ask for comfort and support from you, my kind friend. Later, however, I had second thoughts, reflecting with calm and care. I believed that it was legitimate, opportune and humane to grant duties and support to Madame Bovary, to protect her also from rancorous excesses, from Harel Bey let it be understood, from that Bedouin who was leaving Yonville brandishing a stick with immodest and malevolent arrogance.

I chose, therefore, to reach a military garrison and ask for protection and aid, telling about presumed or possible offences on the part of a vindictive Bedouin. Then I walked with rapid steps among houses surrounded by hedges, with courtyards cluttered with scattered constructions, with olive-presses, with sheds for carts and for distilleries... amidst thatched roofs... plaster walls... little gates on the ground floor ... windows with convex glasses, with chickens rambling and scratching about... a blacksmith's forge... a white house surrounded by a tiny patch of grass adorned with a Cupid... a church... a small cemetery... the market with its tiled roof... the town hall in the style of a Greek temple.

I walked through Yonville-l'Abbaye, that shabby village arranged along a single straight road, along the *Grand'rue* with its barely noticeable shops, dwellings pressed one against the other, a café lit by a weak, oblique light. A small town dying at the foot of the hill of St. Jean.

A mi chemin[195], in a singular loop, there where the road widens and twists upon itself, there where the dust is thickest, where the talking and the din are irritating and bothersome, indeed just at that point of the main street I came across two natives of authority and rural cleverness. Indeed, personages very used to recounting poisonous gossip, to dispensing masterly advice, to suggesting appropriate behaviours.

At that time and place I got to know Monsieur Homais, proprietor of the pharmacy, and Madame Lefrançois, proprietress of the Lion d'Or inn with its row of orderly windows facing the street in the shade of prominent dormers, and where by chance I am lodging in these hours.

From Monsieur Homais and from Madame Lefrançois I

---

195 Halfway along.

learned the usefulness of gossip. I listened to perplexities and urgencies regarding behaviours and morals. I got to know which usages and customs should be avoided or condemned. I understood the necessity of practising indifference. I discovered in the end, after gossip and commonplaces, that in this unusual district there was no military garrison and that I would need to resolve by myself the troubles and dramas to do with a certain Madame Bovary and that treacherous Bedouin named Harel Bey.

Seized by impalpable fears and obscure frenzies, I hastily departed that loop of earth, that pharmacist, stock-still on the doorstep of his shop overseen by a great shop-sign with gilt letters, and that inn-hostess careful to govern her slangy and babbling idiom. With rapid and agitated steps, I set upon that road suddenly open to the dust and the northerly wind that arrived muffled since the hill of Argueil rose up as a calming barrier.

Skilfully then I dodged hollowed-out stretches of ground, which herds of cattle must have crossed so crowded together as to have left indelible signs in depressions full of drainage and irrigation water. I also avoided as best possible shopkeepers, innkeepers, Master Lheureux, clothing merchants, and the parish-priest Bournisien, all certainly made aware of my arrival and of that of the Bedouin and busy contemplating what was going on and distracted, for a time, from their fervid daily preoccupations which were to do with solemnly stuffing their mouths, the desire to exhibit themselves as fervent bigots and card players.

Perhaps fifty steps away there unexpectedly appeared in front of me a house, very well cared for at least in its external appearance, with its handsome entrance from the roadway, its flower-filled garden, espaliered fruit-trees and a pergola which discreetly extended towards the rear of the house at the edge of the river to protect against curious eyes. A warm ray of sunlight accompanied me as far as the entrance to this dwelling, to the home of Madame Bovary.

I forcefully pushed open the gate protecting the garden and went up the steps leading to the entrance. I knocked at the broad wooden door with vigorous raps of my knuckles. A dull sound accompanied my gesture, breaking an unreal silence, a tranquillity appeased by my tensions, by my fears. Unexpectedly, unobtrusively indeed, the door opened and there appeared, in a chink of light and space, the figure of an officer of the gendarmerie. Certainly that of Buchy, I thought immediately, since there was no such post at Yonville.

We gazed into each other's eyes trying to guess what right, duty or charge each of us might have. If one or other of us might have been delegated officially to this place, this predicament, this chance. If there might be hidden opportunities or rules to attend to. If there might be some bother arising from this meeting which was so unnatural, an unexpected inconvenience, at least for me.

I was the first to violate the suspicion by speaking. Thus I took courage and offered myself to the manifest curiosity of this gendarme, commending myself as a citizen of Chavignolles, also a friend of a certain Gustave Flaubert the writer, finally as a gentleman who wished to meet, for his own reasons and for moral mandates, Madame Emma Bovary, wife and spouse of Doctor Charles Bovary.

In the meantime, I began to scrutinize with indiscretion and interest this tall, thin individual, with black moustaches worn in the manner of Dumas fils, which seemed false, of a bronze-like colour. An individual with a familiar face, whom I had seen before, I said to myself, in other times, perhaps in other stories. Perhaps he was a man in disguise, involved in something illegal, skilful also in camouflaging himself, assuming diverse and surly identities.

He looked at me obliquely, that was certain. Then, in his words and tone of voice, he manifested rancour and spite.

He took pains to make me aware that he had no intention whatsoever of satisfying my request since he would have had to importune Doctor Bovary, and since the latter had gone off into the garden, in the midst of the plants and climbing ferns, to think over once again a personal drama, a vexatious disaster that had struck him, an infamous crime which had been carried out in this house.

The gendarme carried on with crude and bitter words and rigmaroles, with the intention of startling me, of disconcerting me, of wounding me to the point of stupefaction. He spoke of a certain homicide perpetrated with an act so ferocious that it forced him to have recourse to measures that were anomalous and immediate, to detain me, to question me about my movements and feelings, to interrogate me unsparingly about my alibis and about a journey undertaken with a certain companion: irrational, brigand and blind.

I understood then, because of the harshness of the words bestowed upon me by this alert gendarme, that Madame Bovary had encountered a tragic death by the hand, actions and intentions of others and that I would have to put forward guarantees not for my own actions but for those of the Bedouin, for his forays, for his going about and encountering places, dramas and unknown persons, to revenge himself on the offenses of a father as little frivolous and treacherous as Gustave. Also because – I said to myself – the incident was very suspicious since, in re-reading, even if only in my mind, Gustave's story and thereby also the life of Madame Bovary, I remembered the apparition of such a blind man, who, initially quartered on the hills of Bois Guillaume, came down to Yonville and walked the streets with the shuffling of his sabots and with the sound of his stick. He was a poor devil with a mass of rags which covered his shoulders and an old, worn-out beret, flattened like a doughnut, hid his face. But when he took it off there appeared two hollow, bloody orbits. And he was singing a little song: 'Often a lovely summer sun / makes the girls fall in love'. Whoever was this poor devil?

I straightened my shoulders and granted the gendarme an unconditional surrender. The officer smiled at me without indulgence and invited me to follow him closely and with no false step,

We crossed the shadow of an ample corridor, between walls and furniture set against them, amongst furnishings in the worst possible taste which peeped out from the ruffles and wrinkles of embroidered tablecloths and the rough brocade of the hangings. Beyond the corner shelves close by a door, we entered a hall which was a long room with a low ceiling, where one could see on a fireplace a fake madrepore next to a looking-glass. An armchair was drawn up to a window. From there it was possible to look sidelong at the people walking along the street.

I brought myself once more to the attention of the gendarme. I smiled at him while he stared at me stealthily and awaited my assent and convenience to utter words, tell stories and fantasies, offer detailed and personal accounts of a homicide, of that odour of death that wafted through that house.

For a moment I turned my eyes away from the man and began to look closely at the silent and funereal surroundings. A whitish light which penetrated the windows moved with gentle undulations so that the furniture and other household furnishings seemed almost to fluctuate, to lose themselves in sooty shadows, while the fireplace, abandoned to itself, let the last flames of the embers go out, and a clock, with irritating persistence, struck the hours.

The gendarme was now beside me: nosey, oppressive, imprudent. He seized my arm and brought me next to him. His mouth brushed my ear and he began to murmur litanies, also pleasantries and indeed inquisitions, and perhaps words in verse which he had scarcely intended *'Often a lovely summer sun / makes the girls fall in love'*. He then told me about accidental and unexpected events, of unforeseen malice since he had caught *in flagrante*, indeed on the very spot of the misdeed, a character with an olive complexion who was wearing an execrable caftan, was armed with a stick and who claimed to be blind, and to be now miraculously healed, thanks to the death of Madame Emma Bovary, to her glorious end by means of a written work which, with all honour, had the possibility of an epilogue diverse from the moralistic and hypocritical intentions of its author. This individual had then confided to him that, with the death of Madame, he could, finally and with just merit, enter into and be part of the array of characters created by that Monsieur Gustave, having the intention and will to assume the semblance and the place of that blind man who passed through the streets of Yonville and that Madame Caroline would not have been able to oppose herself to his having that role and that assignment.

The gendarme told me besides that he had remained disconcerted because of the incomprehensible tones and accents of the Bedouin who denied facts and evidence, also past, present and future intentions, and furthermore offered no reasons for investigating certainties or possibilities.

I then felt justified and painful fears because it was clear that Harel Bey, now in the grip of rash and secret impulses, had yielded to imprudence and had begun to act in an equivocal manner, meddling, it was quite possible and plausible, in that house under false pretences (which ones?) to persist and move in an improper way and thus commit other (?!) execrable misdeeds and modify, at his own pleasure, the plot of one or more stories.

Suddenly the pendulum clock beat out an hour, without time or desire to provide appropriate clarifications. It found me unprepared so that I jumped at these sounds, so strident and ill-mannered in relation to the thoughts and anxieties that burdened me.

I breathed deeply to slacken these biting anxieties, to provide some remedy to the unexpected flushes on my face, to overcome sudden palpitations and shudders. I began to walk up and down nervously, to encounter and to avoid the look of the gendarme, to keep myself alert against tiresome provocations, and to oppose accusations and roguery to do with the entire series of events – at least so far as I was aware of it and perhaps also intuited it.

Thus I chose appropriate words, also banal excuses, even intriguing but futile plots. I stated then, my friend, that death is a painful event, that it is never possible to justify harm and damage to anyone, even in the case of someone accused of causing ill to others.

I then expressed my revulsion towards gratuitous killings, even if they might be a holocaust caused by endemic malevolence, by sudden blindness, by long-planned vendettas.

The gendarme at first pretended not to hear me, then he came up to me spitefully and schemed under his breath, right into my ear, to the point of compromising, in the play of crimes of intrigues and murders, Gustave and those characters who had lived or ought to have lived in his stories. He also mentioned the perfidious deception of identities to which we – the Bedouin and I, he meant – had lent ourselves, often mixing up reality and fiction, real people and actors, real events and imagined plots.

Finally, the gendarme smiled at me, with coquetry and shrewdness. In that sudden and swift smile, I seemed to perceive a flash, an intuition, a sign in his eyes that was already known, signs of a face both familiar and Levantine, with the teeth of a nomad. It also appeared to me that he wanted to bring himself to my attention, so that he would be able to liberate himself from secrecy, unveil an assumed identity since now he continued, with full knowledge and reasons, to criticize me, to talk about the itineraries of my travels, the writings of Gustave, with that Bedouin who had been the companion of my travels and researches, and who appeared to have disappeared, certainly rigged out in Western dress, that is to say, in false, deceptive, unwholesome clothes.

Immobile, we began to scrutinize each other, to understand each other's silences, to speak with our glances. The gendarme then sighed and began to pace. He reached the window and, turning his back to me, began to tell me other truths: about a certain other character, a Bedouin perhaps. To justify the moments of uneasiness and weakness of this other character, of horrible decisions that he had to take while I, as well as I possibly could and with a distracted mind, went on to draw conclusions about an itinerary carried out within writings and various laughable matters to do with that character Gustave, the writer.

To listen to this person dressed as a gendarme, I had certainly haunted the streets with satisfactory negligence concerning what might have happened if a hybrid character of a hybrid story, never begun, had delivered blows to alter the events and narrations simply in order to be, in some manner and for a brief time, a protagonist.

This gentleman gendarme also uttered some harsh words, inasmuch as, according to his words and thinking, I had worked to infect memories and recollections of those personages who had lived on the margins of the thoughts and will of Gustave the writer, since he had had, if only for moments and in confusion, the intention to create these people and make them the heroes of pages later lost in memory.

This person in uniform seemed irritated that I had roamed about in intrigues without leaving space for the companion of my adventures, that Bedouin who resolved to claim the right to an existence as a character in a story, to demonstrate, with just merit and subtle perfidy, an obscure ill-will towards those protagonists of the stories of a certain Gustave Flaubert writer who were merely bothersome dandies in mellifluous narrations.

To distract myself and take refuge from the accusations, I began to look over my interlocutor's shoulders at what lay beyond the window. I discovered, beyond the opaque glass, clouds which *were piling up rapidly to the west, in the direction of Rouen, rapidly unrolling their black columns from which issued great rays of sunlight which resembled golden arrows, while the uncluttered part of the sky was white as porcelain. Then a gust of wind bent the poplars and suddenly the rain came beating down, pattering against the leaves.*

I tried to rid myself of the temptation to consummate and interpret in my own way an unusual and unpublished version of Emma's novel, albeit without explicit guilts or plausible reasons – since no crime had ever been foreseen in Gustave's disgraceful and subversive fantasies regarding the story of Madame Bovary.

Once again I sought the now familiar face of the gendarme. I looked at him, asking him for explanations and the logic of the homicide of which he had spoken, of unforeseen events, of accusations that had been pronounced. I also asked him about Harel Bey, about his newly cured eyes, about his capacity to disguise himself, and of being perhaps an assassin.

Very few were the remarks of excuse or annotation made by the officer.

He confided to me that, and of this he was certain even if it remained to be proven, Harel Bey had definite the death of Emma to offer a plausible meaning to the mandate assigned to him by Madame Caroline Commanville, or rather to make note of illegal acts carried out at her expense. Hence even personal interests, always if there were a mandate, if a certain manuscript were authentic and if arrogance and embezzlements of every kind had been put in motion. Of undeniable truth and in reality there had been only a notebook in braille, lost in Mantes, in a Turkish bath, in the midst of obscure intentions and artfully provoked incidents.

Therefore, it was possible to presume that the crime in relation to Emma was a coherent and deliberate one – thusly did the gendarme express himself – because such a woman would never have committed suicide, using arsenic, which Gustave had imposed on her to claim merits in the fact of guilts and in adequate expiations.

This the gendarme suggested to me of his own will and expression. And he began abruptly to recite the verses: '*Often a lovely summer sun / makes the girls fall in love*', and without any explanation or farewell he gave me to understand that he wanted to remain alone. Certainly to finalize fancies and intentions long imagined and planned, to divest himself of the military appearance and clothing which did not belong to him and were not suitable to him, to cancel traces of misdeeds and obscene crimes, to destroy every trace or step which might be proof of crimes committed.

I have no proof, as you can well imagine, in confirmation of these intuitions of mine and of such shadowy thoughts.

I have one unique lament: that of not having been able to save Emma when it was possible to do so. I should have been a more vigilant guardian in relation to Harel Bey the Bedouin, while instead I abandoned him to his homicidal reasoning, being present helplessly, without recriminations or anxieties, at his disguises, at his deliria, at his whims, at his contorted will. Recriminations don't make history, nor do they serve to reveal the diverse and less brutal plots of a novel, that of Emma, which was already a narrative reality, and by now for many years.

I am leaving tomorrow, obviously alone, since the Arab is nurturing more than ever, I am certain, his passion for homicidal disguise. At least that is what is to be supposed.

A bientôt, mon ami.

A Chavignolles. The rented calèche is robust and will quickly cover the road which separates us.

B.

A Letter

Hôpital de Charenton,
  St. Maurice,
  31 December
  Monsieur Bouvard,
  I learn with sorrow and increasing displeasure that they have disturbed you, and for a certain behaviour of mine which was little consonant to the circumstances and intentions that we planned to pursue. I needed to bring to completion a personal desire which meant, in a certain way – and you will understand me – the determination to rediscover an identity never obtained. To retaliate, with tenacity, against him who had, with evident and malignant firmness, relegated me to marginal roles, to nothing more than a thought, to a conversational quip, and not to be allowed to be what I wanted to be and for which I had been invented: a character in a story by Monsieur Gustave Flaubert.

Do you remember my friend the troubles suffered because of not being a real subject of a novel or story or pamphlet written by Gustave? You will have undoubtedly shared my anguish, you will have considered, like me, the reasons for which you were abandoned when father Gustave did not bring to completion works and ideas that were to do with you.

In truth, our cases were different. You had the misfortune of an unexpected death, the death of our father Gustave. But of this I must refer to you precise accounts and scrupulous assessments. I want in any case to confide to you a consideration: that of death is, in my opinion, an attenuating factor of little plausibility insofar as Gustave had the time and possibilities to bring to completion the novel which touched upon your person. In truth he did not do this, and it's a very concrete supposition, because of that laborious and compulsive attention to detail which distinguished him – very well known to friends and to experts – for which he lost himself in mannerisms and linguistic artifices without considering that the character compromised by his lucubrations desired only to be a real personage.

Gustave was fundamentally a fabricator of books with the rhythm of one word every hour, as Edmond de Goncourt goes around saying. Gustave's desire to make me a real character was based instead on very ambiguous considerations.

*E*verything began for me on 29 March 1862 when Monsieur Gustave Flaubert began to manifest *his dreams, his plans for a novel.* He had *a great desire, which he was unable to renounce, to write a book on the Orient... a book he had just sketched out*[196], a book he would have entitled *Harel Bey.* This then is how I was imagined and, in truth, created from a diligent and scrupulous reflection by a writer usually seduced by eccentric fables, even though they were always original.

Here I am then, forged in a manner similar to how you Christians will mould a man, making use of a prodigious but tried and true formula: *And Gustave said let there be a fabulous narrative. And there was a fabulous narrative... And Gustave said: let us make Harel Bey a man in our image, after our likeness; and let him have dominion over the plots and characters of the fabulous narrative*[197]. This in synthesis is my creation. Now, and diligently, let us go over once again our meeting, our finding each other, albeit for very fortuitous reasons, as characters imagined by that writer called Gustave Flaubert.

I cheated with you, it's true, I confess it without excuses or apologies or scruples. But I never deceived you, indeed on the occasion of our last investigation, at Yonville-l'Abbaye, precisely in the city of Madame Bovary, you clearly scorned my artifice and my deception because you were well aware of the game that I was playing. However, you were incapable of preventing Emma from meeting a glorious end: glorious, I say! I well know that Madame

---

196   Frères de Goncourt, *Journal.*
197   Freely drawn from Genesis 1:3 and 26.

Bovary should have taken her own life, I well know that Gustave loved, for his malicious book, a showy, specious, baroque ending! I could not allow him to have it. I was the creditor of a sumptuous revenge against him. I had, therefore and justifiably, to disguise myself as an assassin – as I had already done on other occasions – and thus honour my duty and mission.

I am certain, or hope to be so, that you will in some way have understood the specious reasons behind my insalubrious actions, and I am grateful for it. Besides, as I have already explained to you, I had the necessity of taking on a role, of being an actor, of taking possession of a concrete space that might offer a way of making my creation meaningful.

When I arrived in Calvados, at Chavignolles, in your courtyard and that of Monsieur Juste Romain Cyrille Pécuchet, nothing was more preferable and controversial, at least in appearance, than to pass myself off as a blind man similar to the one who moved about among the hills surrounding Yonville-l'Abbaye, and thus to take part in the luxuriant banquet of oblique ideas and original hypotheses that Gustave had spread out around the figure of Emma Bovary and her husband Charles. Do you remember, my dear Bouvard, do you remember?

A blind man introduced into that story who did not have, in truth and at an attentive reading, an existential logic of his own. He rambled amidst the pages and abruptly appeared and disappeared without reasons or merit, indeed was even able to strike terror without any apparent reason. He was scorned by the inhabitants of Yonville-l'Abbaye even though there truly were no good reasons or hostile sentiments.

Who was that blind man? I don't dare suggest to you an appropriate reply. It could well be me who was wandering about like a vagabond, in disguise, in the anguished attempt to occupy places and stories. You well know that I had an intense wish to cut out a space for myself since Monsieur Gustave had denied me the concreteness of a character in his book, and ever since he had refused to acknowledge in the very same instant that he was setting about revealing that story that directly involved me.

Meanwhile voices and false rumours had injured my pride, voices and false rumours concerning your rash perplexities towards my emotions and my impulsive affections which, according to you, would have injured and, also and frequently, disconcerted you, dear Monsieur François Denys Bartholomée Bouvard. I refer to the daggers and other instruments of torture and death with which I boorishly amused myself without making you a party to my projects, so that I often acted without your knowledge and behind your back, but not at all for diversion or scorn towards you.

Thus I harmed, and for nefarious partiality, almost all the characters in Gustave's books, characters that I drew into artifices and mystifications, for whom I lost myself in the folds and wrinkles of time, in the folds of revisited memories, in the folds of willed forgetfulness. All this was made possible by the deceptive and fraudulent silence of our father Gustave who had abandoned me in the concoctions of one of his hypothetical narrative inventions.

Thus to recapitulate accounts I want to make facts and happenings clear to you, with punctiliousness but without undue pride and presumption, with the sole purpose of making you a participant in the actions that will often have seemed incoherent and ignoble.

Thus I will narrate to you, from my point of view, events that we experienced together, offering you also clarifications and solutions regarding facts that might have appeared devoid of significance and value. We travelled the routes of Gustave's novels to encounter characters and to gather opinions to provide exhaustive answers to the questions posed by a manuscript, very equivocal in both writing and intentions – and I am certain that you share such considerations of mine, since I personally brought the manuscript to your house, to Chavignolles, saying that it had been sent by Madame Caroline Commanville, Gustave's niece.

I arrived at Chavignolles as a blind man, do you remember? I sought friendships and walked the streets with an oak stick, as it was my intention to travel through the very inferno of deceptions and revenge, displaying and emphasizing my blindness, mounting treacherous traps, even committing murder. I had to remove from the stories (those of Gustave, clearly!) characters and protagonists, impoverish their plots, throw into uncertainty and misunderstanding pages and chapters of his writing. Thus with wild sallies I murdered, deceiving their good faith and their company, several protagonists of Gustave's stories. I moved within our world, Monsieur Bouvard, a very different world from that of the readers. I moved and we moved in the world of stories and dramas, in the world of characters and of the events they experience outside of any concreteness, any fictitious reality, in the world of reading, in the world of vainglories and of presumptions written by pen or printed amidst events and circumstances consigned to the immutability of a publication.

There must always be an explicit obligation and a diligent responsibility, beyond the robust will to keep faith with one's own creative imagination, on the part of whomever assumes the creative labour of imagining characters and writing stories. It doesn't always happen thusly. And in fact it didn't happen with Monsieur Flaubert.

The negligence of whoever boasts of forging characters, only to then grant them a life according to preferences and feeling is truly exhibiting despicable shamelessness. Miserable and shameful actions that deserve to be punished without recriminations or hesitation, in an exemplary way. Hence I acted out of conscience, also in the name of others. Of so many others. Also in your name, my dear Monsieur Bouvard, and in that of your friend Monsieur Pécuchet, even though, and I am certain of it, you never had any awareness of the rights due to you as characters in a story, and this because of your accommodating temperament and your resolute emotional dependence on that father who in truth offended you.

Then I came to you in order to carry out assignments and, knowing that Gustave had an obstinate will to forget, I wished to carry out vendettas and to square accounts with whomever had rashly taken my place in the mind and stories of Monsieur Flaubert.

I came to you bearing a manuscript.

I suffered in not immediately revealing to you and to your

friend Monsieur Pécuchet a painful matter that was afflicting me. A doubt, rather. A sin of ignorance in the face of which I felt impotent, and towards which I had debts to pay if I had not been able to resolve the dilemma which tormented me. The manuscript that I brought to you to read had been written because, in some manner and thanks to your help and that of your friend Pécuchet, it might resolve a dilemma which regarded an individual – a protagonist at a certain time in Gustave's life, and her continuous and tormenting presence close to Gustave as a perturbing element.

I am speaking of Madame Louise Colet.

Who, in reality, was she? I needed and wanted to know who she might have been because I had in regard to her, insofar as it is possible from reading the manuscript, precise information on her life and on her place in the literary world. I needed to learn if she was simply a character from a novel by Gustave, a novel that I didn't know but which was in fact talked about in the salon of the Goncourt brothers, or whether that Madame was indeed a person of flesh and blood, a contemporary of Gustave's. She was, in truth, a presence that disturbed me and still disturbs me, also because at the Goncourts' she was spoken of with a certain ignominy, that she was capable of selling for seven coins to the *Revue Anedoctique* a satire by De Musset against the Académie, of intoxicating herself with furious love-affairs dramatizing her emotions, sensations and upsets, of going for promenades in a fiacre in the Bois de Boulogne with a lover to get herself fucked, of claiming Canadian ancestry to demonstrate that there was true American Indian blood in her veins, that is to say, violence, harshness and brutality wisely mixed together.

Few then were the indications that seemed to be drawn from a very strange novel, almost a compendium of Gustave's fantasies, rather than of events that had really occurred. Thus I thought it necessary that a manuscript might suggest deeper investigations into Gustave who travelled about in the Orient, to obtain information and verifications that would offer me the possibility of knowing who Louise Colet was.

Even today I have difficulty in understanding the role and character of this woman. I am displeased not to have encountered her in the course of our peregrinations: if that had happened I would have been able to settle accounts which in any case – whether fictional character or real person – deserved to be paid by her.

But let's return to ourselves and to our initiatory journey, amid deceptions and suggestions created by Gustave, who perhaps imagined possibilities and obscure acts of revenge amongst the characters of novels and stories who had had, thanks to his benevolence as a writer, roles to play, opportunities for existing.

We departed from Chavignolles, from the farmhouse that you and Monsieur Pécuchet had acquired, to lead there a diverse and particular life. A life that involved thousands and thousands of adventures, and encounters with historical personages and events, amidst original interests and singular researches. A life, however, which, point blank, remained suspended in a limbo and which did not foresee a final reckoning, a conclusive logic. I knew all this, and for this reason I arrived at Chavignolles to persuade you to be my guide in peregrinations through Gustave's novels.

In truth, my dear friend, I also had the need and will to investigate you and your friend, and understand if you, who were protagonists in a novel never brought to a conclusion, had the desire to accept a fictitious invitation by that Caroline, Gustave's niece, if only to conquer her, thus deluding yourselves that, at her command, some mercenary writer had brought your adventure to its conclusion.

I must grant you my respect and esteem, because never, during all our wandering about, did you reveal a desire of this kind even though you had understood, I am certain of it, that you were the truncated character of a truncated novel.

We went first of all to Trouville in search of an inn called Bellevue. I smiled at your preoccupations in so far as the search for an identity is a relative option. And I didn't hide from you my thoughts in this regard. You sought persons without knowing whether it was or was not possible to identify them as such. Thus you lost yourself, my kind friend, amidst human matters, even to

261

the point of bringing up Ecclesiastes in order to verify behaviours, while I sought to sort myself out amidst the awarenesses of identities. I didn't want to follow you – and you well know it – in the fondness for memories to which you were so deeply attached. I wanted only to understand if there had not been exchanges of roles, so that it was possible to encounter a real character of a story by Gustave or people who had assumed the guise of a character of a story by Gustave.

Your task was to analyse sentiments, mine was to find out if there had not been some swap in the game of invention.

Having left Trouville, we made for Paris, travelling by train. Do you remember? It was then that there appeared an unknown man. He felt contempt for mutilations – he said. And I was a mutilated man. Not at all, believe me Monsieur Bouvard, on account of an opportune blindness, as much as being only a truncated person. This travel-companion also had the presumption of being an assassin. Was he? He would have been if it had been Gustave in person – as I suspected briefly. He had the characteristics and accents. Above all a murderer, certainly! A madman, too! And Gustave loved to exalt madness, affirming that it was the only depository of wisdom, and the only means of carrying out a sacrificial act and being thus able to assure one's mother an eternity of sentiments.

Gustave, complicit in incestuous affections, intimately felt the desire and will to kill all the men that surrounded him, those whom he had created or was going to create or whom he had only imagined.

We then stopped at Les Andelys where I led you with my infirm, blind man's step. Then I explicitly invited you – do you remember? – not to grant to Gustave any easy solution. I also asked you if you had reasons for wanting to rectify in any substantial way the manuscript that I had delivered to you on behalf of Madame Caroline.

In truth, I tried to influence you, to know your willingness to modify events and characters. I tried to have you as an accomplice in my criminal (?!) plan. You had rash acts of that kind, isn't that so? Why, in fact, did you not defend Gustave and his writings in such circumstances? But why, with silence, did you defend that little book entitled *November*? I know why. Gustave had begun to talk about himself, about his carnal loves, about his contemplative ecstasies, and you did not have the audacity to put an end to that massacre of egoistic banality. You imagined that you ought, and were able, to play, and as you believed for the best, with the characters of his books. I was very disappointed in your behaviour. It was then inevitable that I take refuge in another homicide. Why another one? I shall offer explanations in a few pages.

Paris and the boulevard du Temple welcomed us. Do you remember? First we went off to spend the evening, settling ourselves as best we could in the Café du Jardin du Théatre, then heading off comfortably to a very equivocal place called *Restaurant Bonvalet* where there awaited us a certain Madame la Chanteuse. Is that true, Monsieur?

There we had to verify truths, to clear up ambiguities and concerns, as, according to Abbé Laffosse, Madame la Chanteuse must have known about events and happenings to do with that certain story by Monsieur Gustave Flaubert entitled *The Legend of Saint Julian the Hospitaller.*

You had very little ability in drawing from Madame indications and information. I had little respect, since with a shameless gesture I began to sniff at the intimacy of her groin to ascertain whether this woman was truly a character created by Gustave, and in fact one of the protagonists or secondary characters in the story of St. Julian. I had the courage – do you remember, my friend? – to drag Madame la Chanteuse to number 42 boulevard du Temple where Gustave had stayed. There I constrained her, using the seductiveness of promises, to tell me the story of her being a character who had, voluntarily or not, lost a story.

She had been created, this lady told me, to be Marguerite in the story "Un parfum à sentir" which Gustave had written in 1835 when he was fourteen years old. But she rejected it. She didn't like the idea of being part of the world of jugglers and acrobats described in the story. Nor of wanting to be a woman with horrible red hair, fat and ill-formed, dressed in a brown canvas blouse, wearing coarse slippers of thick, ragged leather and wearing on her head a beret of cotton with pink ribbons and a few withered flowers, and then to die by committing suicide in the Seine after a life of anguish and deception carried out in the world of beggary, tightrope walkers and clowns.

Madame la Chanteuse thirsted for something very different. She would have liked to be the mother or wife of Julian the Hospitaller: that moralizing story of Gustave's had such a strong appeal for her! And so, or in any case so she told me, Madame la Chanteuse had had the insolence and impudence to go, to plead her case, to the Hôtel Sergent at Concarneau, in Brittany, where Gustave was staying with his friend Georges Pouchet and was intending to work on the story of St. Julian.

Years had passed, so many that it was now in 1875, my dear friend. But time, as you well know, is a very uncertain notion for one who has to live in the writings and in the minds of novelists. I don't know the outcome of that conversation in the midst of thoughts and desires, willed and betrayed, but it is certain that Madame la Chanteuse withdrew from all time and space concerning the writings of Gustave in the expectation that she would be able in the future to live again in another story by Monsieur Flaubert, as a character more in tune with her own personality.

I understood then that she could be a rival of mine now that she too was looking for space and protection. With the complicity of Madame Caroline? I don't know. Thus I acted accordingly.

We then went to Rouen, although we ought to have gone to Machaerus, *on a conical basalt hilltop*[198], where the line of Herod lived. We went to Rouen to seek reasons for certain loves and for the tenacity in narrating certain loves. We went to Rouen, a city that invites you to isolation, because Gustave had lived there for a long time and in his youth, even if it often befell him that *solitude and work was driving him crazy*, so that *he began to talk about dances of dervishes, of a brothel of birds in his bed, of incomprehensible*

---

198 Flaubert, *'Herodias'*.

things[199]. We went to Rouen, because you, my dear friend, had wanted to and proposed to find Mademoiselle Julie, so as to be able to learn about certain events and subterfuges.

I was reluctant, and showed that I was. I was pallid when we arrived at Rouen, and I whispered to you that I was disturbed by the troubling stench of illness and old age. I moved, stumbling continually, because I wanted to make it clear that it was necessary to renounce any thought of encounters and possible identifications. I was afraid that I might be recognized, in fact! I will tell you later about circumstances and occasions when I was unexpectedly revealed as an assassin. There was no attenuating factor to excuse me, as I had acted conscientiously.

In Rouen I wished to avoid the appointment with Mademoiselle Julie at any cost, and thus I began to put forward excuses of sickness and nausea. The meeting occurred in particular circumstances, in the penumbra of a chamber. Mademoiselle had neither the occasion nor the ability to identify me. Or, perhaps, she didn't want to.

We then headed towards Croisset, the den of the wolf and of deceptions. I duped you, my friend. I knew Monsieur August Léger well. Do you remember? The gravedigger of Croisset who welcomed us in his filthy hut to give us indications and information on the *Temptation*. I had already encountered Monsieur Léger. But that is another story. Certain it is that I had indoctrinated him well so that he was capable of fascinating you with that series of daguerreotypes that I had commissioned from him when I plotted to learn Gustave's secrets and initiatives, quite beyond the desire to understand in depth his essence as a writer, without keeping faith with commitments made to characters, albeit only imagined ones.

I suppose that you intuited that between the gravedigger and myself there was an evident understanding, also a casual intimacy, a sort of bold and enigmatic bond which instilled fear and insecurity. Isn't that so, my dear Bouvard?

---

199   Frères de Goncourt, *Journal.*

Finally, I mistrusted Monsieur Lèger when he began to consume alcohol unrestrainedly. I was afraid in fact that in an alcoholic delirium the gravedigger might reveal things and events that I reserved to confide in you later, once the mission had been completed. What mission, you will ask? You will come to know intentions and objectives which are not in fact those to which Madame Caroline seems to aspire.

Then we reached Malun, before visiting at Sens a pornographic gentleman who ran a bookshop. And at Malun there occurred the unexpected – I confess it to you with sentimental deference. I was seized by the will and by the desire to kill you because of that puritanical conscience of yours which clearly contrasted with that of your progenitor, of that Gustave who was, as you well know, of uncontainable triviality.

Indeed Gustave spent part of his time, and you should be aware of this, in *trying to be a pig or in pretending to be one, in order to reach the height of those true and sincere pigs who* were *his friends*: that is Emile Zola, who was *a coarse and brutal pig, whose swinishness was applied entirely to his work as a writer*; Alphonse Daudet, who was recognized as *a morbid pig with the capricci of a brain in which madness might settle one day*; and Ivan Sergeyevich Turgenev who was *a pig whose swinishness was tinged with sentimentalism*[200].

This immoral band often liked to enjoy themselves with Louis Godefroy Jadin, the painter, who had *knotted, with a beautiful ribbon and in a ringlet sealed with wax, the cunt hairs of one of his lovers, a ballerina ... so that each time that, dancing, she emitted a little cry, Jadin could exclaim satisfied 'I know what it is'*[200]. That is what Gustave and that band of his friends were like.

As I've told you, I had a compulsive desire to kill you. I didn't do it, my dear friend, because I had a debt of gratitude to settle with you: our common instability in the future since Gustave had abandoned us in a sort of limbo. Therefore, I was obliged to murder a man, Monsieur Léon Grappin, a native of Laval, even though in appearance he didn't seem to be a personage created by

---

200 Frères de Goncourt, *Journal*.

Gustave – as in fact he wasn't. It's true that he was very similar to him because of his foul language and indecency and in being very wilful, so much so that he suddenly seemed to me to be the protagonist of the first draft of *Salammbô*, in which case he would have been a terrible antagonist for us.

Then we reached Mantes, that city of love where Louise was accustomed to concede her charms to Gustave, wearing her silk and lace dress which outlined her breast[201] and *Gustave tore it off, hurting her with the ferocity of his caresses*[201], where we had an unpleasant encounter with a certain le Croquemort. What did you feel, my dear friend, when le Croquemort told us about the death of Frédéric Moreau, the boorish protagonist of *L'Éducation sentimentale*?

For my part I had the sensation that fiction had taken the upper hand over reality in the novel, and that we could finally be inscribed in the group of those who justly and immoderately longed to be protagonists in a story of Gustave's. We could have had at our disposition various solutions to manage, since there was an opening to an uncontrolled mixture between what was fictionalized reality and what was the reality sought by some characters of a fictitious novelistic reality. And le Croquemort?

He was a valid support for mystifying a fiction which could become an imperishable fictionalized reality. I owe a debt of gratitude to Monsieur le Croquemort!

At Yonville-l'Abbaye, in the town of Emma and Charles Bovary, the irreparable occurred, as I have already written some pages back. At Yonville-l'Abbaye, nothing of what Gustave had narrated had any possibility of confirmation, and everything started when our paths suddenly separated. But we soon found each other again and face to face, indeed in the house of Doctor Bovary when I had disguised myself as an investigating policeman. I thus had the opportunity and simple merit of announcing to you, without fear or remorse, that I had committed, with decision and derision in regard to Gustave, the crime to which I aspired in secret and for which I had expended efforts and intentions to carry

---

201 Gustave Flaubert, *Letters*.

out: I wanted the novel about Madame Bovary, so well devised, to be thrown into disarray and with it its characters and its lying and tedious ethics. Did I succeed? I leave these considerations and judgments to you.

And Gustave in all this? Gustave ought to have made amends for a sin of oblivion and rancour in respect to me and should have sought to make amends for a misdeed. But in fact he retired into his domain, beside the bend of a river, leaving me in a state of humiliation and silence, even though I was already a character and a man of adventure.

For this reason, I had to vindicate my honour without subjecting myself to the kind of fawning and affability so dear to Gustave. In the end I assassinated my honoured father – this is a surprise which you certainly didn't expect to hear – being present at and participating in his death with the same coldness with which he had betrayed me after having permitted me to live.

I paid a penalty: an unexpected and undeserved blindness, albeit transitory, and that saved me.

Thus I assassinated Gustave as an act of duty – undeferrable, necessary. I assassinated Monsieur Gustave Flaubert the writer because it was my duty to do so. My dutiful necessity.

In the beginning, I had placed hope in the jury which judged *Madame Bovary*. There were all the premises for my finding the satisfaction of a verdict of condemnation. An exemplary condemnation. A condemnation to death! A condemnation that our Gustave deserved for his cruel vision of life: a life with which he always diverted himself, despising whomever expected consideration and helpfulness from him.

An egotistical and unjust man who amused himself shamelessly with others, guiding their lives according to a perverse morality, opposed to any educational ethic, one which contemplated a true and full life.

Since the tribunal did not deliver an acceptable verdict, I acted at first hand, although allowing Gustave to spend Easter Sunday with his friends, with Edmond de Goncourt, with Alphonse Daudet, with Emile Zola, with Georges Charpentier and with

Guy de Maupassant, an Easter Sunday which in 1880 fell on 28 March.

In truth, that was a very pleasant reunion. Gustave received them at Croisset, in his house just beside the Seine, traversed at that point by silent boats, and with enormous trees and plants oppressed by the winds arriving from the sea. Gustave was *wearing a Calabrian hat and a heavy jacket, trousers with wide pleats to accommodate his large bottom, with a kindly and affectionate expression on his face*[202]. He exchanged friendly civilities with them, offering an extremely delightful luncheon based on turbot with cream sauce, washed down with wines of every kind and continuing pleasurably until evening amidst stories told with humour and light-heartedness, he refused to read pages of his ultimate labour: pages to do with you and your friend Monsieur Pécuchet.

I allowed Gustave another month or so, so that he might have the opportunity and desire to reflect on the abandonments desired in past years and on the lack of paternal recognition. Then, on the morning of 8 May, towards ten o'clock, I arrived at Croisset, dressed as a Turkish bath attendant.

I was disguised, but I was perfectly recognizable by the brown colour of my skin, by my features, by the Arabic accent of my French. Mademoiselle Julie – la Tata – lacked the elements necessary to identify me. No one, in fact, had ever spoken to her of a certain Harel Bey. She greeted me without posing any importunate questions and was in fact surprised that Monsieur Gustave should have the need of appropriate baths and massages, since he had had, for that day, to accommodate himself to the demands of his work, and thus to go to Paris to consult volumes at the Bibliotheque Nationale and listen to the opinions and suggestions of Monsieur Chéron, an outstanding bibliophile, on the assumptions and principles to do with the novel in which you, Monsieur Bouvard, and your friend Monsieur Pécuchet were the protagonists.

Hence I took advantage of a gullible ingenuousness and began to make use of the very same reasons for which Mademoiselle

---

202 Frères de Goncourt, *Journal.*

Julie had welcomed me to confirm the singular benefits that one could derive from a tonic massage before undertaking a journey. Yes, exactly Mademoiselle Julie, whom we then encountered in Rouen and who I feared might recognize me and point me out as an intruder and perhaps an assassin.

Not a single question was posed to me by Mademoiselle Julie: if, for example, I had official proofs of my skills and training as a masseur, if and when I had come to an agreement with Monsieur Gustave for dispatching such a role, if, even though expert in baths and in cauldrons of boiling water or hot cloths for cleaning the body, I had need of the help and support of an assistant.

Instead I was immediately offered the license to operate alone, with obstinacy and intent (as I had foreseen in my criminal project), so that I was set to satisfy the commands and necessities of the writer, that is to be the patient provider of jugs full of hot, even boiling, water, with steam issuing from them, to facilitate, without pause or second thoughts, that reckless ablution with which Gustave nurtured himself every morning – before any other undertaking, and about which so much was said in literary circles – to be accompanied this time with suitable massages.

Mine was a solemn coming and going, planned with subtle perfidy and longed-for vengeance, now that Gustave had subjected himself to my will despite being surprised by my unexpected arrival, which I justified with insolent lies to the effect that my presence was due to the will and gift of gratitude of those friends who had arrived at Croisset to pass the most recent Easter holiday with him.

Bubbling pots began to pour scorching water into a painted copper cauldron where Gustave, drowsy in and from the fumes, was lying inert, abandoned to the negligence of the senses, to laborious breathing, to abundant sweating.

His face took on a vibrant, apoplectic pink colour. The fragility of his veins was manifest, terrible, dangerously delicate and so, to hasten the lethal results, I began to hasten my services, to pour in, in the haste of convulsive steps, water that was continually hotter, smoking, unbreathable.

Suddenly, however, now that I was moving about anxiously and breathlessly amidst smoke, clouds of vapour and the viscid humours of my body, I became aware that I was losing my sight. With the passing of the minutes, the exhaustion of the labour, the weight of tension of a crime that I was committing, my sight was becoming veiled, dark shadows were fatiguing and extinguishing my eyes and enveloping them in an opaque greyness, in an oppressive blindness.

I fell into a jumble of emotion and fury. I stumbled several times in the haste of determination and intentions, and just as I was hurrying to complete the act of homicidal destruction. I surrendered abruptly to the tension and fear now that I was forced to proceed blindly, no longer in control of place or situation, and I was aware of an inevitable atonement for malice and criminality.

Even Gustave's body was ruined in the shadow of blindness. I could no longer make it out distinctly. I felt indications of a chest, traces of a face, the contours of arms. Nothing else emerged. Thus I struggled to measure out my gestures and strength. In any case I succeeded, in the conviction of a crime now completed, in grabbing hold of that nude, viscid, heavy body. I dragged it out of the water, from a storm of smoke and heat. I dragged it beyond the washroom, beyond the bedroom as far as an ottoman dominating the studio amidst horrible Oriental knick-knacks which confirmed to me that *in his artistic nature there was something barbaric*[203].

Gustave was no longer breathing, at least so it appeared to me. His face, hot and blazing, was immobile, flaccid, certainly in the grip of apoplexy.

I left in haste and went out directly into the garden, although laboriously, ducking and dodging, feeling my way, bumping into things, ornaments and furniture. In the distress and fatigue of blindness since I now seemed to be totally blind, I reached a friendly boat anchored in the shelter of the garden pavilion, on the banks of the Seine which flowed close by.

---

203 Frères de Goncourt, *Journal.*

A terrible labour, my dear Bouvard, as every step followed the disposition of my hand's touch, which ran along a wooden palisade, one which, circling the garden, had an opening and an exit just by the berth of my boat, presided over and steered by Monsieur Auguste Léger, whom you have had the fortune to meet. Monsieur Léger is a man who submits himself willingly – as you will have had occasion to verify in person – to the corruption of alcoholic beverages and conspicuous tips. After a good drinking session he has the inestimable virtue of remembering very little of labour accomplished and words spoken. He is, however, insupportable because of that acrid stench of decomposition and death that emanates from his body, as you have been able to confirm through direct experience. I had, for this reason, to subject myself to prolonged ablutions so as to free myself from this stench of insupportable gravity.

Gustave's body was discovered, a little after midday, by Mademoiselle Julie, alarmed by the silence and the lack of her employer's departure for Paris. The lady made haste to notify, with affectionate solicitude and anguish, a certain Doctor Tourneux who in that period was replacing Doctor Fortin, a family friend. Doctor Tourneux gave himself over immediately to the urgency of the case, but he could do nothing other than to make out an act of death through cerebral haemorrhage caused by an ill-considered bath, in fact by water that was far too hot, damaging to the blood circulation.

In his report, in the clinical summing-up of the causes and death of Monsieur Gustave Flaubert, writer, resident at Croisset, Doctor Tourneux specified particulars and diagnoses which confirmed my intuitions and certainties, those of a blind man, even though, because of my blindness, I was not able to ascertain, *cum oculis*[204], the feral consequences of my actions.

In truth I owe specific accounts and unusual details about the medical witticisms of Monsieur le docteur Tourneux to the pointed *souvenirs de Maxime Du Camp l'ami infidèle de Gustave*[205],

---

204 With my own eyes.
205 *"Remembrances"* of Maxime Du Camp, unfaithful friend of Gustave.

who took pains to gossip *in aeternum*[206] on the life and death of our writer father.

I confided from then in the comfort of Madame Caroline the heiress. I wrote to her then, I asked for meetings, I pressed her closely to validate my rights now that it was she who could dispose, according to her own choice and desire, of Gustave's published and unpublished writings.

I waited for news that might settle interests, earnings and juridical recognition – a little for everyone. I asked Madame Caroline for justice, as well as redemption from my condition of poor wretch of the band that unites all the characters of Monsieur Gustave's books.

Madame could and ought to have, in some manner, followed pathways other than those frequented by her uncle, as pecuniary interests were her principle, her faith, and the aim which she pursued. This interest – or profit, if you like – could have well coincided with mine as I remained trapped in limbo, without a physiognomic condition or connotation which might turn me into a character with a present and a future. My future could have been specified by a few brief but substantial lines, even at the margin of a story, even in a few memories recounted briefly, or in footnotes, or recalled in jest or in exaggerations or falsities.

I had extreme desires, and I recognize it.

And Madame Caroline could have, with the authority acquired as heir, made me a participant in a literary reality that eluded me, that ignored me, that eliminated from the writings every interpretation of mine.

From the beginning, after the death of Gustave I mean, I waited hopefully for a new course of events because, fundamentally, Madame's desires and needs very evidently coincided with my own, indeed they very often converged. Unexpectedly and quickly, Madame avoided any spurious connection. She evaded my first overtures with arrogance because she intended to draw benefit only for herself, even though the stories were marked by a

---

206 Continually.

period that did not belong to her, by the reality of novels written and certified by past years which were unknown to her.

Moreover, Madame was prey to pecuniary ravings and ecstasies, to the point that she began to draw up accounts with figures and rights, to search exhaustively for unpublished manuscripts, to solicit discoveries which might be able to accrue conspicuous financial benefits, at least in thousands of francs.

I busied myself then, albeit blind and in poor health, to offer Madame Caroline what she wanted. I dictated to a copyist, drawing upon literary gossip heard in the salon of the Goncourt brothers where I had lived thanks to Gustave's obtuse forgetfulness, a long story with events and episodes which were highly possible, at times precarious, but connected by a logical narrative so ostentatious as to evoke comfort and security.

However, the proposed assertions necessitated proofs: this I suggested and recommended to Madame. Hence I offered myself as an accompanist and guide to an able and noble investigative spirit fit to travel amidst Monsieur Flaubert's writings.

The choice fell upon you, Monsieur Bouvard, since you were and are the most capable in wisdom and ingenuity amongst the characters in Gustave's books. The rest of the story belongs to events that are very well known, at least to you and me.

I then began to carry out, even though with distaste and though handicapped by mutilation, the law of retaliation so that, what with homicides, injuries, unforeseen disappearances, we could at last put our hands on Gustave's books, following new routes and plots that had been laid aside, also with actors relegated until then to oblivion.

In any case, I remained wounded by the obstinate indifference of Madame Caroline towards every possible change of narrative regimes just at the point that, her uncle having died through my deliberate intervention and skilful operating (something of which the niece was ignorant), Madame Caroline had the opportunity to curate, at her own pleasure and according to her own desires, permissions and interests, the characters and plots of the stories and novels of Monsieur Gustave Flaubert.

Madame never had the shrewdness to alter the peculiarities of those characters and those plots, all created with a melancholy monotony. Madame had yielded to the seduction of mediocrity, to the bustle of what had already been written and edited by Gustave, because in reality she didn't like to compromise herself with daring and intriguing thoughts, because she found difficulty in fantasizing with expressions and grammar, because it was her primary purpose and interest to profit, without fatigue and risky speculations, from every product or creation that, true or false as it might be, bore the stamp of Gustave's creation.

Before setting out proposals and offers to Madame la nièce, I had done my best, even though ambiguously I confess, to link up with other characters of Gustave's writings and to be in league with them. That is, I tempted allies and sycophants, adopting as my square, crossroads and meeting-place the propitious Journal written by the Goncourt brothers.

However, this turbid proposal of mine foundered. There weren't, in fact, people willing to concord with me or lend an ear to my laments, given that for the most part I was an unknown person and there was no citation of any kind in respect to me in any book, pages, notes or memoirs. I was, all in all, a spurious actor, without any known brotherhood, without a recognized descent.

Therefore, uncertainties, hesitations and discredit buried me in negligence and neglect. There remained nothing but an obscure pilgrimage in disguise so that, with deception and determination, I might have the opportunity of redeeming myself and offering one last gift, lethal to whomever had consciously and rudely neglected me.

Thus I imagined vendettas, and deaths, and blood, and silence. Mine were the motivations of a troubled spirit and, reflecting on such a determination, I remembered that few other characters created by Gustave had such legitimate motives for envisaging challenges and condemnations. Perhaps Smahr, the hermit tested by the devil, perhaps Anubis the god who had to make love with a woman. They too were actors lost in Gustave's memory and fantasy, characters who had never appeared in the pages of a story or novel. At that time, however, I was the only one to defend a missing right, and without even the comfort or help of a page written in haste.

Thus I was living, and am living, thanks to a mere gesture, a suggestive note, a good service proffered by those Goncourt brothers who wrote le Journal, because in it they mention me as a possible writing project, indeed a novel by Gustave.

It was on 29 March 1862 when Monsieur Gustave l'ecrivain began to talk *of his dreams, about his plans for a novel. He confided in us his desire to write a novel about the modern Orient, the Orient in Western clothes. He became inflamed at the idea, thinking about all the antitheses that would be offered to his talent: scenes in Paris, in Constantinople, along the Nile. European hypocrisy, savage Oriental scenes amidst chopped-off heads*[207]. And a single true protagonist: myself, Harel Bey, with my desires, with my proposals, with my culture, with my arrogant presumption, with my belonging to Oriental nobility, with my traditionalism.

This dream reawakened hidden sentiments. I thus found myself bustling about, enacting a barely sketched-out role, clothing vague thoughts with concreteness, offering myself as protagonist amidst phantasms and spurts of a troubled imagination. Then suddenly, without reason or fault, Gustave consigned me to oblivion, and my story became a forbidden memory while the characters of other stories and other projects settled into written pages, in books, in printings and reprintings, experiencing and stirring up banal events, ordinary plots.

Thus I began to abandon discretion and to aspire to revenge and crime. I asked to be a guide, after having engaged in apocryphal writing, arranged a deception, carried out a parricide. I waited to be provided with means for criminal actions, to consume and pervert stories told by a father, to deceive a niece named Caroline who busied herself with accounts and monthly statements in francs.

---

207 Frères de Goncourt, *Journal.*

Earlier I spoke of daggers and other instruments of torture: I thought of Madame Caroline who, in spite of my prompt invitation *post mortem avunculi*[208], believed in the opportunity to put under surveillance characters, events and spurious narrations because they did not offer her anything in terms of rights and payments.

Francs – this I learn with astonished incredulity – are a prerogative of ratiocination and persuasion for one who lives a life outside of novels, stories, novelettes and various amenities.

Therefore, for the pleasure and enjoyment of Madame the niece, but also indeed for my benefit, I offered myself to her as the bearer of a rediscovered manuscript, of an apocryphal work. I was always silent about this last particular to Madame herself so that she believed, right away because it was an ideal means of obtaining a practical solvency, in the packet of leaves and texts that I gave her almost as if it were a grace and privilege for obtaining unexpected opportunities and very easy earnings.

For moments then our spirits lived together in fraternity, and intuitively found reason and common sense in the snobbism and diachronism of our two existences: one spent in the midst of a crowd of ceremonious conventions, the other in some lines of a diary and in the drawing-rooms of those Goncourt brothers.

The manuscript was a creation contrived for deception. Well-made, I believe, since my aim was to attract interest by recounting the life, works and recklessness of that writer who had had the audacity to set aside people and characters who were no longer of use to him even after having made them men of spirit and discernment.

Hence my vendetta became absolute; the necessity of recounting an equivocal falsehood so that Madame Caroline could take it as truth in the form of an autographical text by that uncle of hers, perhaps as a diary of such intimacy that it had to be consigned immediately to interested agents, as opportunities for veneration and devotion, to be conceded by barter for a

---

208　After the death of her uncle.

resounding and conspicuous quantity of francs.

Gustave meanwhile, the uncle meanwhile, the unbelieving father meanwhile, when the manuscript began to circulate, would have had a memory marked by the improvidence of fiction, an existence marred by lies closely resembling truth, a writing harmed by the incredulity of readers, his reputation, as patron saint of arts and letters, foundered by rumours.

With advance credit, I should have been able to obtain from Madame, precisely to strengthen the assertions of the manuscript and future profits, the investiture as explorer of souls, situations and events. A thievish occasion, of the theft of intentions, so that I would have been an assassin through self-interest, a fearless and silent murderer.

Thus I would have had the occasion and affectation to encounter, in appropriate circumstances, Gustave's pupils who were the pretentious hangers-on of his stories, of his novels. It would have been agreeable and seductive to settle accounts left suspended, unappeased envies, necessities that could not be postponed, and to then rewrite plots with different protagonists.

The crimes were thus conceived as works of cunning and safeguarding, also a natural occasion to make me an actor in the region of notoriety, or a shrewd choice for being the unsuspected executioner of liberty, fraternity, equality amongst the characters already active in the novels of Monsieur Gustave Flaubert.

I am certain that, in some way, you will be able to well understand what I am going to tell you, as you have obtained from me, in the inconsiderate silence of my actions, appropriate confidences on my way of proceeding with you as a curious wayfarer. Blindness helped me, made my senses more acute, granted me the appropriate sensibilities, also for homicidal purposes.

The sense of smell perceived, in fact, the imprints of death on this or that person. Touch perceived the signs of bodies which I would have to torment. Hearing recognized the haughtiness of phonemes and declamations, so that it was inevitable to ponder, *in primis*, the irreverent impudence of a writer who, with detrimental intentions and fraudulent ardour, I murdered amidst appearances and intrigues.

Monsieur Gustave Flaubert was a man of letters who was very partial in the choice of his characters even for unforeseen loves, so that never did a single one of his characters have any certainty that his presence wasn't solely an opportunity, a casual, scatter-brained invention, simply to fill up a sheet of paper, give voice to some bit of writing, realize an idea.

Memory is a treacherous plaything, a canvas exposed to the mockery of the fragility of understanding and will, so that men and things which devise plots, and games of phrase-making, and interludes of lucidity or lugubriousness, don't go astray in the winds of tangled events, in the folds of cases entangled by manoeuvres and scheming. There remains only one sure plot, a sign, a point. Nothing else.

Congestions lacerate characters so that no protagonist is ever certain of belonging forever to a novel marked by time and by readings.

I have never had the aim, and you know it well, to rewrite plots, dramas, happenings and intrigues. Gustave was a born manipulator. I wanted only to alternate the protagonists of certain stories with other characters so that these others could be the principal actors or at least participants with a few lines to speak.

Hence the crimes had a meaning, a legitimate purpose, a dignity. Madame Caroline did not decipher these signs and messages of mine. She gave her attention to a manuscript that I offered her as a gift, insofar as it was a supposed unpublished work by Gustave, and insomuch as it was a source, possible or even probable, of desirable earnings.

I often asked Madame if we might unite our energies. Perhaps we would have had a different future, without regretting a past lost in fiction or in history. I would have been able perhaps to imagine, in the silence of fantasy, a sun which *rose behind the Arabian mountains. And the fog which was rent in great airy strips. And the fields cut by canals which were like green carpets, with arabesques of gold braid. There were three colours: green in the foreground, the red-gold of the sky behind, a burnt and shimmering tone on either side*[209].

I would have been able to see my own country for the first time. Also to perceive the waiting, the complaints, the melancholy, the illusions of regret. I thus imagined scenarios in which my fathers had lived. I descended the abyss of melancholy to discover that *the sea was so blue and transparent that I saw the fish and the plants on the bottom. It was calm and swelled with gentle movements, similar to those of a sleeping person's chest. Facing me were white houses, constructed across the hillside and slipping downwards almost to the surface of the water, in the midst of the green of mulberry trees and umbrella pines*[209].

I became lost in a past that I never had. I should have liked to purify my mind of such promiscuous illusions and to know myself better, refuse to acknowledge the others, the undaunted deceivers, the characters created by Gustave who often preened and paraded themselves, vexatious and puffed up, because they were convinced of being the protagonists of a story even though they were only the frivolous conjurors of the pretence of a reality.

Thus I began, Monsieur Bouvard, to mistrust reflected images, gaudy appearances, parts marked by arrogance, by postulated aggression, by true falsities. I chose for a travel-companion an apocryphal text, a manuscript compiled with art and bewitchment by myself. I did the best I could to seem to be the seller of fictitious dramas, trafficker of disguises, merchant of ambiguous presences – mine above all.

I wanted to steal and vilify the stories codified in books, and adapt them to my needs, make them suitable for new protagonists so that I could later propose myself, expose myself, lead the dance in the midst of improvised, unusual, artificial pages. I sought Madame Caroline in order to obtain her permission and with it violate letters, adventures, writings, narrations, since henceforth Madame was the heir and cashier of the rights. Gustave's niece negated the offer without compensating me for the intuitions and words I had spent. I deceived her then with extreme actions, to

---

209   Gustave Flaubert, *Letters*.

the point of the murder of her uncle, with the homicide of Emma Bovary who was, in truth, the reincarnation of Uncle Gustave.

My acts would have had (this was my principal goal) only therapeutic effects. And Madame, whose soul was that of a speculator and ruled by greed, was not favourably impressed. Our objectives were basically the same, once the necessary and natural retouchings would have been applied to the characters of Gustave's narratives.

Then, faced with the refusals and neglect of Madame, I began to act by myself, betraying your faith as a travel-companion. I couldn't have behaved differently, and you know it well. To safeguard myself I had to offend those characters who amused themselves with banal molestations. Indeed, boredom governed plots tied to the banality of banal stories.

The rest is of little account. You already know it yourself. Or perhaps you believe that I, a man with a dark skin, relegated to a salon of those diarist brothers, deprived of a past and of a father with the conscience to recognize me, would have been able to survive without old loves, or scents of my own country, or desires to know my past?

At night I invoked the banks of the Nile, at the place where, beyond the mist of the water, a valley *seemed to be a white sea, immobile and, behind the desert, another deep violet ocean*[210]. I was afflicted by torments and anguish. Yes, I who am an Arab with a Levantine face, with the appearance of an assassin.

However, Gustave liked me, at least in the first periods of our reciprocal esteem, and well before he abandoned me without reasons, without appreciation. During the nights, I often remained in a corner of his conscience and reproved him for his silence in relation to me.

After the anguish of disappointment, I acquired wisdom, moving to the attack on these spectral narratives. I began to observe men and things, also the tenuous atmosphere of the light of first dawn, until the moment when I became aware of the

---

210   Gustave Flaubert, *Letters*.

sense that Madame, Gustave's niece, and Gustave, the uncle, had of sin, of the sense of Western sin. Do not kill is an imperative commandment, despite the fact that they allowed a man to die in the inanition of a Journal – a man, a Bedouin, a possible protagonist of adventures and risks.

I then began to beat – and hastily – the pathways of expiation and of growing vexation. Nothing was as painful as having to experience the banality of writing. Gustave did everything possible to vulgarize ideas and stories. He wasn't an Oriental. He had neither nobility of soul, nor refinement, nor the sensibility and taste of an Oriental.

For my part I had accounts to settle with means and opportunities, and not at all suitable ones. Meanwhile Madame, among differences of opinion and doubts difficult to appease, considered me a man of ill-will and scarce merit. She was afraid that the editors might have had apprehensions and doubts in affording her the rights to Gustave's works since, through my censorious intervention, some protagonists might have disappeared from them and others, completely unknown, might appear in them.

Ad extremum, quam ultima ratio et conditio[211], so as not to leave Madame afflicted by debts and inquisitorial problems, I urged her to comply with me in the matter of homicides and interests. For my own interest, in truth, I wished only to secure recognition and space, thus abandoning that modest annotation in that Journal by those Goncourt brothers.

Moreover, I suggested to the niece that she profit from the time and circumstances now that Gustave's name was at its summit and now that yours, Monsieur Bouvard, was appreciated as the diligent archivist of the sayings and writings of Gustave himself.

Instead Madame ignored my most authoritative and urgent suggestions, reserving the right to send me, *sine autoritate*[212], as assistant in your court, Monsieur, and as apostle of your activity as investigator. Thus I began, given that spurious injunction of

---

211 As a last resort, as an extreme reason and condition.
212 Without authority.

Madame's, to behave according to my own desires and will, to play Russian roulette without fearing or invoking principles. At your side, I acted like an altar-boy in ceremonies, in your journey through pages and pages of Gustave's writings to confirm truths and lies of an apocryphal manuscript.

I am certain that you well knew the precariousness of that writing. Hence, I was indebted to you for the patience and good spirit with which you accepted me, protected me and gave me free rein. I would have wished, now that I am putting an end to these lines and recollections, to offer you a gift. I had thought of that braille notebook, so full of remarks, convictions, signs and sketches, criminal plans. Unfortunately, as you well know, I gave it as a bribe, during a stop in our travels full of plots and pitfalls, to a driver and merely to be able to speak with that le Croquemort who had dominion over him, besides being an investigator of a literary crime.

And so, please have the goodness, dear Monsieur Bouvard, to consider that intention, which I would have liked to express to you but which unfortunately I am not able to make concrete, a pledge of devotion, a remembrance, and precisely now the silence of forgetfulness constrains me to frequent oblivion.

J'espère en confidence[213] to have on my side an avenger of rights, a bit scribbler, a bit bandit, a bit miserable author of apocrypha who knows how to collect desires and to narrate this adventure.

Au revoir, mon chevalier[214].

Harel Bey

P.S. I am afraid of having already heedlessly committed, as you will have had the opportunity to intuit, a few too many homicides, of having roamed in your company through the writings of Gustave and of having devastated, with impunity and with brazen ribaldry, certain thugs collected in extremely boring fictionalized existences.

My rash and thievish behaviour can be justified by the presence of an insidious malady. Amentia perhaps. Meanwhile Edmond de

---

213 I hope in all confidence.
214 Farewell, my knight.

Goncourt, now that his brother Jules is dead, no longer wants to grant me hospitality either in the Journal or in his home because he would like to obtain the full and personal pleasure and availability of the salon, which I have been occupying wrongfully for too many years. Gustave's fault.

At the moment I have taken up lodgings, in truth in an irresponsible manner since I was obliged by the force of robust and sinister gendarmes and nurses, at *la Maison de Santè de Charenton, a St. Maurice - Pavillon 4: Archives notariales du temps retrouvé. Souspavillon 2: Hommes bâtards et assassins*[215].

It is at this institute d'aliénés et de personages perdus[216] that you can let me have any news about yourself.

H. B.

---

215 Charenton Hospital, St. Maurice. Pavilion 4: Notarial archives of time regained. Sub-pavilion 2: bastards and assassins.
216 Of aliens and lost characters.